Prais
The Gentleman's Book of Vices

"In the past (and in Miles' own stories), Miles and Charlie's love story would've ended in tragedy. But instead, Everlee crafts a scorching affair between the two damnably decent men and delivers a delicious *deux ex machina* that allows them the happiness they crave and deserve. Miles, in his gruffer, introverted ways, is a delectable foil to Charlie's extroverted amiability, but their romance is a combustible one. Everlee, however, tells a touching tale of their ability to contain that explosive spark and nurture it into a well-tended fire. All it takes is a healthy degree of eroticism, a loving family, even better friends, and a desire to risk it all for the one you love."

—Entertainment Weekly

"[A] sparkling debut... Charming supporting characters and vivid period detail enhance this enchanting romance. Everlee shows real promise."

—Publishers Weekly

"What with its brilliantly blended notes of nuanced characterization, beautifully evoked Victorian setting, scorchingly sensual yet sweetly romantic love story, and slyly witty writing, readers will want to savor every word of Everlee's splendid debut, the launch of her Lucky Lovers of London series, like a fine vintage wine."

—Booklist

"Everlee creates an intriguing cast of found family for Charlie and truly thorny obstacles for the lovers to overcome. Fans of Cat Sebastian and Olivia Waite will enjoy this queer Victorian romance."

—Library Journal

"With its potent blend of queer eroticism, found family and unabashed swoon, this romance is a resonant winner."

—BookPage

"This is a joyful, spicy romance; but with an emotional upheaval of pain and trauma you feel for both of the lovers."

—BuzzFeed

**Also available from Jess Everlee
and Carina Press**

The Gentleman's Book of Vices

A RULEBOOK FOR RESTLESS ROGUES

JESS EVERLEE

If you purchased this book without a cover you should be aware
that this book is stolen property. It was reported as "unsold and
destroyed" to the publisher, and neither the author nor the
publisher has received any payment for this "stripped book."

carina
press®

Recycling programs
for this product may
not exist in your area.

ISBN-13: 978-1-335-68000-6

A Rulebook for Restless Rogues

Copyright © 2023 by Jess Everlee

All rights reserved. No part of this book may be used or reproduced in any manner whatsoever
without written permission except in the case of brief quotations embodied in critical articles and
reviews.

This is a work of fiction. Names, characters, places and incidents are either the product of the
author's imagination or are used fictitiously. Any resemblance to actual persons, living or dead,
businesses, companies, events or locales is entirely coincidental.

For questions and comments about the quality of this book, please contact us at
CustomerService@Harlequin.com.

Carina Press
22 Adelaide St. West, 41st Floor
Toronto, Ontario M5H 4E3, Canada
www.CarinaPress.com

Printed in U.S.A.

For Mary, Tegan, Bridget, Michael
and all the other friends who saw me through.

The emotional well-being of my readers is important to me. If you would like to see specific content warnings before you dive in, please visit www.jesseverlee.com/cw.

A RULEBOOK FOR RESTLESS ROGUES

Chapter One

The Deer River School for Boys, October 1870

"Upright, Mr. Forester."

David squeezed his eyes shut, blocking out his hazy view of the top of the headmaster's desk. Every bloody thing on him hurt.

"*Now*, Forester. If you can't take a beating, then don't give them to your classmates."

What David had done to that bastard Snyder was not comparable to what he had just endured at the hands of the headmaster. But he forced himself upright and straightened his clothes with trembling fingers, pretending not to notice all the stings and aches on the back side of his body. He'd not given *this* out to anyone, but he could take it well enough.

He wiped his eyes—watering, not crying—and turned around. He stared at the headmaster's shoes.

"Go clean yourself up, and then out in the yard with the rest," the headmaster said.

David glanced groggily at the headmaster's face through sweat-drenched strands of hair. "I'm not much in the mood for cricket, sir."

"Are you in the mood for more of this?" The headmaster tapped the cane against the side of David's flank, which was so bruised that the tap hurt nearly as much as the first strike had. "Are you?"

David shook his head, grimacing. "No, sir. My apologies."

"Out of my sight, then. Remember this the next time you think to start a brawl in my corridors."

Finally, he was free. Every step hurt, but he was so eager to put distance between himself and the headmaster that he clenched his teeth and kept up a torturously painful pace down the corridor. When he got around the corner, he slowed a bit. Oh, Christ, the last thing he wanted was to go run around in the yard. The headmaster certainly hadn't gone easy on him, but even if he had, there were other considerations. After all, the story had certainly gotten around by now. Everyone would know some version of what had happened. He suspected that he knew how it would be received and wasn't keen to confirm it.

At least the dormitory would be empty. As he approached it, he glanced out the window at his classmates running about on the expansive green lawn, sporting, wrestling, getting their exercise, and soaking up the thin sunlight that peeked through the clouds. Ah, yes, just what every boy needed after a caning. Goodness knew, if he missed one day of it, he'd become instantly withered, corpulent, unmanned. Christ. He tried to pick out Noah Clarke among the distant figures. He was usually more on the periphery, so perhaps it would be possible... But the boys were all too far away to tell one from another. He gave up quickly, too sore and sticky to stand there any longer.

He went into the dormitory with its two rows of beds, all made up but with some rather differing standards of impeccability. His eyes were drawn instantly to the bed at the far end of the row that faced away from the door. Noah Clarke's was always the neatest.

But he did not find the usual, perfectly smoothed blanket on the bed at the end, because Clarke was sitting on it with his back against the wall and his knees drawn up, sketching in one of his leather journals.

David froze, still clutching the door handle as Clarke's cat-like gray eyes wandered over to him. One of them had a small bruise blossoming beneath it.

"What are you doing in?" David asked, his voice sticking a bit.

"Staying out of the way. If a schoolmaster misses me, I suppose they can drag me by the ear, but for now…" He gave a sly smile and put a hushing finger to his lips.

David nodded. After all that had happened today, he wanted to say something, acknowledge it somehow. The wanting of it was desperate and almost sickening, but he couldn't think of anything. He just went to his own trunk, which was at the foot of his bed, the one next to Clarke's. He bent down to open it as best he could, trying not to wince.

Clarke set aside his drawing things. "You alright, Forester?"

A different voice might have grated David's nerves at a time like this, but Clarke's was always quiet and gentle. It still cracked occasionally but did not seem destined to settle as low as David's had. He liked it.

"They shouldn't have punished you," Clarke went on. "Or, if they were going to, they should have punished Snyder too. Though, perhaps they thought you'd handled him well enough."

David stood up and threw the clothes onto his bed. He started unbuttoning his jacket. "Was it broke?"

"Was what broke?"

"Snyder's nose."

A huge smile broke out across Clarke's face. "I reckon so."

Good. So far as David could tell, poor Noah Clarke never bothered anyone. Why on earth David had noticed this was unclear; they ran in completely different circles… Or, rather,

David had a circle to run in, while Clarke spent most of his time alone. Still, David kept little tabs on the quirky boy who slept in the bed beside him. He did his schoolwork on time and drew swirling things in his journals; he took a lot of solitary walks around the duck pond, kept his bed obsessively neat, and generally minded his own business. He got on well with the teachers, but much less so with the other boys, who acted like he'd chosen his slight build and delicate features for the sole purpose of bothering them.

David hoped that Robbie Snyder's nose healed very crooked. If he could not handle a little prettiness, then he was better off ugly.

Shirt off, he washed up at one of the stands in the corner, scrubbing dried sweat from his face and dried blood from his knuckles. He could feel Clarke watching him, and it made his heart pound madly. Why would he watch? Were the marks on his back too horrible to look away from?

But when he turned, he didn't find horror on Clarke's face. There was an unexpected sadness instead, Clarke tensing his own shoulders like he was imagining what David had gone through. "You really got it, didn't you?"

David shrugged and went to put on fresh clothes. As he changed from trousers to the jodhpurs he'd need in the yard, he tried to position himself so that Clarke wouldn't see the worst of what he'd got. It probably showed on his face, though. There didn't seem to be an inch of him left unmarred. Even linen scraped and burned.

Clarke rested his chin on his knees. "Thank you." The grateful hint of a smile on his lips proved hard to look at for long. David concentrated on the buttons of a fresh cotton shirt instead.

"It was no trouble at all," he said.

An almost cackling laugh burst out of Clarke. "No trouble?"

David shrugged. "I get worse at home."

"Do you really?" He'd meant it as a joke, but Clarke looked shocked.

Uncomfortable now, David shrugged again. It was true, but he suddenly felt defensive about it. "Don't you?"

"*No.*" Clarke looked at him with pity. "My father doesn't beat us at all."

"Not at *all*? Is that even legal?"

"We're Unitarians," said Clarke very practically, as if this word David had never heard before cleared everything up.

"Is that like Quakers?"

"Not quite, but it's probably close enough to be getting on with."

Well, that explained a lot. Whatever Clarke was, exactly, he wasn't a normal Christian. No wonder he was so…like he was.

"Anyway," Clarke went on into his silence. "I don't understand why you did it, but I appreciate it. It obviously *was* a lot of trouble, whether you'll admit it or not. I hope you'll let me know if I can ever pay you back somehow."

No, no. David waved the offer off, feeling his face go red. "I just wish I could have got him before he got you."

"Oh, this?" Clarke touched a careful finger to the bruise under his eye. "This is nothing compared to what you just got, I'm sure. Certainly nothing compared to what he would have done."

Nothing compared to what Snyder had done to Clarke already, several times now since the start of term. Worse bruises than that little one had been soundly ignored by both students and staff alike.

"I'm sorry," David blurted.

"For what?"

"For not acting sooner." David looked pleadingly at Clarke, hoping he'd understand. "I knew it was happening. For months. We all did. I wanted to do something, I swear I did, but I was a coward, up until… I just couldn't stand it anymore. I saw him going for you, and I snapped. I shouldn't have waited to snap. I should have just done it because it needed doing."

Clarke examined David with a nearly scientific curiosity, setting his heart to pounding again. David didn't know if it was the striking prominence of his eyes or the intelligence behind them, but damn, Clarke could really *look* at a person, couldn't he?

He seemed to notice that David had gotten stuck. "It was smart to be a coward," he said with cautious kindness. "It won't be good for you, you know. Siding with me."

David tore his eyes from Clarke's and glanced out the window. He couldn't see the yard from here, but he could imagine the response he was going to get from his usual friends when he arrived among them, marked much more brightly by his defense of Clarke than he was by the headmaster's cane. They were not the assailants, but they'd long ago determined whose side everyone was supposed to remain on in situations like these.

He could probably smooth it over; he was good at that sort of thing. But damn, the very thought of what he'd have to say made him sick to his stomach.

"Who cares?" he said at last, looking awkwardly at Clarke's gray eyes for as long as he could bear it before moving his gaze to the top of his trunk. "You're worth ten of those fucksters. And you know it. That's why they bother you."

"I don't think that's quite why they bother me." Clarke gave a soft, pleasant sort of laugh. "But thank you for the kind words anyway, sweet hero of mine."

Oh, David liked the sound of that. It put him in mind of Lancelot or something, Lancelot and… Well, never mind. David only wished he had something to say to it, something clever. He had nothing, just stupid silence echoing through his skull.

"I—I've got to go outside," he stammered. "Headmaster will check on me soon, I think. I'd hate for him to catch you too."

Clarke put his feet on the floor. "I'll come with you."

"You don't have to do that—"

"I'd like to," Clarke said, grabbing his shoes. "If you're there, I'd like to go."

"No one will bother you again so soon," David managed. "You won't need me."

Clarke got up and stepped in rather close to him. Was that close? Maybe it was a normal distance, actually. Yes, it was. Perfectly normal. Why did it seem like he was mere inches off?

"That's not what I mean," said Clarke. "It's just… If you can bring yourself to go out, then I suppose I should too."

"Um, alright." David watched Clarke turn and stoop to dig in his schoolbag, returning to his perfectly normal position with a bit of smuggled bread. "What's that for?"

"If I don't call attention to myself, I can usually sneak off round the pond. Some of the ducks are starting to pair off, you know. They do that this time of year."

"Oh." David wasn't sure how to respond.

Clarke went on with a knowing nod, as if David were a perfectly charming conversational companion. "Very structured things, ducks. No taste for whirlwind romances, far as I can tell. Still." He held up the bread with an almost sarcastic smile. "They'll appreciate a wedding feast as well as the next, I reckon."

David found himself staring at the bruise on Clarke's face as he talked. He had never seen the boy look quite so animated, and the mark on him was more horrible than ever in contrast. He hated it. David should have been able to prevent it. Before he knew quite what he was doing, he reached out toward it, not touching, but coming closer than he probably should have.

Clarke went very still. "I'm fine. Really."

David still felt oddly sick over it. His stomach was turning flips. Guilt of some sort. A very strong, insistent sort.

"Are you sure you're alright, Forester?"

"Can I come with you?" The words spilled out of him before he could stop them. "Around the pond?"

Clarke stared. "Why would you want to do that?"

"Because... Because my friends are arseholes," he said. "I'll take my chances with the ducks."

Clarke gave another of those mischievous little smiles. How he still had such a spark of life in him after everything the other boys had put him through was incredible. That he was sharing that spark with David seemed nothing short of miraculous.

"Alright," Clarke said. "Good idea, in any case. If we stick together, then if anyone troubles you, I can take care of them." He flashed his teeth and bit down deviously.

David's guilt-feeling suddenly got a whole lot stronger, somehow thrumming through his whole body.

He was still in an awful lot of pain, but he tried not to show it as the two of them left the dormitory together. By the time they got to the duck pond, he'd nearly forgotten about it entirely. And once they'd circled it, tossing in chunks of bread and joking about the birds' marriage prospects, he'd forgotten to care about their classmates' opinions too, as he decided he'd break ten more noses and take ten more canings for one more afternoon like this.

Chapter Two

David

Just shy of midnight on a temperate summer Saturday. With the postshow theater crowd settling in, it was the time David Forester liked best as the proprietor of The Curious Fox. Nearly everyone who would come tonight was here by now, leaving burdensome roles and rules and even names at the door to wait around like discarded coats for their owners' return to reality. David and his barkeep Warren had gotten everyone their first pour of gin or beer or whatever syrupy concoction they preferred and secured their spots on the private-room wait list. The ebb and flow of arrivals and check-ins was dealt with, and now all that was left was David's favorite thing in the entire world:

Keep the incense lit, keep the pianist playing, and keep all his people comfortable, happy, and safe until they stumbled out from his care just shy of daybreak.

Considering the habits of the fellows who'd rented them, David knew that the private rooms would be occupied for another half hour at least. With his green leather ledger under his arm, he left his usual post by the piano to make his mid-evening rounds through the brightly decorated front parlor. While he did not own The Curious Fox—that honor unfortunately belonged to Lord Henry Belleville, a hard-to-predict baron who rarely disturbed the place with his nerve-wracking presence—David took great pride in every part of the club, from the comfort of his patrons to the details of the decor. He took a little time each night not just to check that everyone was having a good time, but to adjust feathers and flowers in the vases, fluff brocaded pillows, and check the oil in pink-shaded lamps.

One of the larger freestanding ones seemed to have gone out, unnoticed by the two gentlemen beneath it who'd scandalously stacked themselves in a too-small chair, quite absorbed in one another. It was lovely to see the introduction David had facilitated earlier this evening turn out so well, though he did need to get that lamp relit so that no one tripped on the rug. David cleared his throat, but to no avail—the gents had their eyes closed, their mouths well-attached to each other's, and apparently their ears turned off for good measure. Not worth ruining the moment, he decided, rolling his eyes affectionately as he worked around them to refill the lamp as quietly as possible, only to realize he'd left his matches with Warren...

"Need a light, *amore*?"

The sudden sight of Noah Clarke standing close surprised him, but it shouldn't have. Best friends going on fifteen years, their feet always seemed to wander to wherever the other happened to be.

Tonight, Noah wandered in tightly laced heels, leaning his bustled bum against the back of the over-occupied chair. He often did drag on the weekends, and tonight, he donned a decadent frock with puffed sleeves and blue stripes that David thought flattered his face and form better than any of his others. Noah peered nosily at the kissing couple with his kohl-rimmed eyes as he dug a mother-of-pearl cigarette torch out of the excessive puffs of padding he'd put in his evening dress.

David grinned and took the smooth, warm torch gratefully. If someone had told him, during their first tentative, confusing years of friendship, that it would lead them to this precise moment, he wouldn't have even known what that someone was *talking* about. But a whole lot could happen in fifteen years. And so here they were, lighting lamps in David's molly bar to the sighing sounds of snogging gentlemen.

When the task was finished, David passed the torch back, fingers sliding on the black satin gloves that kept his friend's vices of smoking and drag aesthetically compatible.

"You're a fire hazard, Miss Penelope," he scolded, watching Noah tuck the thing back into the outrageous fluff.

"Me?" Noah said in the dramatic, high-pitched voice he put on for the character of Miss Penelope Primrose. "What about these two, eh?" He pointed his silk fan at the very busy gentlemen, then flicked it open, fanning himself demonstrably as he got off the chair and took David's arm. "You're going soft, Davy. I remember when you'd have made them take that heat to an alcove, if not a back room."

That's because he was *supposed* to make them take it to a back room, but as Lord Belleville's oversight of the place had dwindled, so had David's adherence to any rules that didn't directly impact safety or the bottom line.

"It's a business move." David shrugged as they started walking together, back toward the bar and Noah's usual card table. "Make a perfect match just as the beds are filling, tell them to go wait their turn in a highly visible location, and next thing you know, half the place is inspired to get their names down as well." He glanced back toward the pair. One of them had lost his jacket, and the other seemed to be diligently searching for it down the front of his trousers. Though accustomed to this atmosphere he'd purposely created, David still flushed a bit in spite of himself, suddenly very aware of Noah clutching his arm and the sweet, oddly familiar scent of whatever perfume he'd put on tonight. Seeing his friend done up like some society girl always did odd things to his nerves if he wasn't careful. "Those two might inspire three-quarters of the place, actually, if they keep going on like that."

"Oooh." Noah purred and nudged him. "You inspired, David?"

"I am *working*," David said definitively. "You?"

"Working also." Noah nodded primly toward his card-, coin-, and cup-covered table, where his similarly dressed companion Annabelle Archer was counting her winnings beside their dandyish friend Charlie Price. Charlie was comforting a rather surly clerk named Mr. Brighton, who was a regular patron but not part of their usual circle of friends. "And bringing in quite the wage, if I do say so myself."

Once they got to the table, Mr. Brighton looked up at David, shaking off a bemused Charlie.

"Mr. Forester," Brighton snapped. "I hope you're here to tell her she has to give me my money back."

David looked at Noah, who'd turned unconvincingly innocent eyes on him. "Miss Penelope," he said slowly, "what have you done this time?"

Charlie's attempts at neutral comfort broke with a spectacular snort of laughter, which he quickly tried to hide by sipping from his gin and tonic. "It's not funny, really," he said, more to the melting ice cubes than to Brighton. "My apologies."

"I should think not," said Brighton. "Cheating isn't humorous."

The seriousness with which he said it did Charlie in completely, his face going red as he put his forehead down on the table with giggles. Annabelle rubbed his back in soothing circles, suppressing a sly, well-rouged grin.

Noah picked his abandoned cigarette up out of the tray, bringing it to his painted lips and puffing on it before insisting on a breath of smoke: "I followed every rule to the letter."

"Of course," David said. "And which of your rules did he object to, in the end?"

Noah smiled, that bright, mischievous grin he'd been giving since day one. Whether in response to the strictures of boarding school life, the upright expectations of his intellectual family, or the rigid image requirements of his job as a Savile Row tailor, Noah always grinned like this in the moments he found a handy loophole or technicality that would let him do as he pleased.

At the Fox especially, he had a tendency to build those loopholes in himself.

"Which rule did he object to, Miss Penny?" David repeated, as scolding as he could manage under the influence of that striking smile.

"Nothing too complicated," Noah insisted with languorous certainty. "Just the one that plainly states that nothing beats *una coppia di regine.*"

He lifted the swirling cigarette toward Annabelle, his playing partner, who looked nearly as pleased with herself as Noah did. "That means nothing beats a pair of queens," Annabelle clarified in smug whisper.

Trying to keep from losing himself to laughter along with Charlie, David crossed his arms tight and turned to Brighton. "*Please* tell me you did not agree to that rule before the game started."

"He did!" Noah chirped before Brighton could answer. "He agreed to it along with the rest of the rules, and you know *it's not cheating if everyone agrees to the rules ahead of time.*"

That last bit came as a chorus as Annabelle and Charlie recited the oft-repeated phrase right along with the ringleader.

"Yes," Brighton huffed, standing up to address David quite seriously. "But I assumed she meant the cards themselves. She might have won, if she *had* a pair of queens *in her hand*. But once it was over, she insisted that since she and Miss Annabelle *were* a pair of queens *at all times*, they didn't need the cards and locked in the win before we even started!"

It was becoming more and more difficult not to succumb to laughter. While Noah was known for inventing all sorts of confusing games, this was ridiculous even by his usual standards.

"Miss Penelope," he said, voice straining with effort. "I hate to say it, but I think you might have gone a bit too far."

"What?" Noah gasped, readying himself to smack David's rump with the fan. David caught the wrist in time to slow it, but Noah managed to sneak a little tap anyway. "I disagree, Mr. Forester, I disagree heartily!"

Normally, David let this sort of thing go, but with Brighton proving to be an even worse loser than Noah was, he thought it best to smooth the situation over. In a place like this, people could go from friends to very dire enemies rather quickly. Keeping tensions low was one way he kept his patrons—and Noah most especially—safe.

He made Penelope and Annabelle hand over their winnings, which he returned to Brighton...minus a shilling.

"For the house," David explained, waiting until the chap had wandered off grumbling before dropping the coin down the front of Noah's dress. "You do deserve *something* for that one," he said. "A pair of queens. Brilliant, really."

"I deserve more than that." Noah swatted him again before sitting beside Annabelle and downing what remained of a sweet fizz. "He shouldn't have agreed if he didn't want to play the game."

"Oh, come off it," said Annabelle, letting her voice relax to a comfortable, teasing tenor. She nudged Noah's corset-compressed ribs, making the plum taffeta of her own confection rustle a bit. "He didn't want to play *card games* with you anyway. He'd have agreed to anything he thought might get him up your skirts."

Noah spared a glance at Brighton over his puffy shoulder, one of his earrings twinkling in the lamplight. So that was what Brighton had been doing at the table: trying to get Noah to the back. A spark of irritation lit in David's stomach. As if Noah would take an interest in someone like that.

"Maybe if he'd had a better sense of humor, I'd have agreed," said Noah, pleasantly confirming David's intuition about the whole thing as he peered into his empty glass. "But Miss Penny doesn't spread them for someone who can't take a little joke."

"Doesn't spread them for anyone," Annabelle muttered to Charlie, as if the rest couldn't hear. "Far as I can tell, anyway."

Noah swatted at her, and a grinning Charlie for good measure. "What's that supposed to mean?"

"Nothing, sweetheart." She passed her glass to Noah. "Go put that shilling to good use and get us some refills, would you?"

Annabelle and Charlie waited until Noah took all their empty glasses up to Warren at the bar, then they both looked at David with very disconcerting little looks on their faces.

"What?" said David.

"This is your fault, you know," Annabelle said.

"My fault?" David laughed the accusation off, though it warmed his face a bit. "How is her creative card playing my fault?"

She crossed her arms over her padded bodice, more practically sized than Noah's since Miss Penelope was something of a costume for the club while Annabelle was consistently, relentlessly Annabelle everywhere she went. On weekend nights when London's actors were out carousing the West End streets in all manner of preposterousness, she didn't even bother changing to trousers to see her safely between her home and the club.

"I'm not talking about that, David Forester," she scolded, pursed lips pulling at the rouge on her cheeks. "And you know it."

"I do not know it," he said, unsure why his face was starting to burn. "What exactly are we talking about?"

"She's chasing off all her suitors. Again," said Charlie, a little less accusingly than Annabelle, almost apologetic. "And you are encouraging her. Again."

David wasn't sure how Noah's tendency to scare off interested blokes was his fault, particularly if they were grumpy with questionable facial hair like Brighton. But it tickled the lower reaches of his belly guiltily nonetheless. "It's not my business whether Miss Penelope accepts her suitors."

They both looked at each other, dripping skepticism.

"It's none of *your* business who's flirting, seducing, or otherwise taking up with whom?" said Annabelle. She glanced rather demonstrably around the room: to where those two gents he'd set up were still all over each other in the armchair; then to another pair, whom he'd introduced to each other last year; finally to the ledger under his arm, where he kept records not just of who was taking up with whom, but their likes and dislikes should they ever require a fresh suggestion for companionship.

"You ought to send along someone suitable for her for once. She must be the only one in this place you've never tried to set up." Annabelle lowered her chin, tapping her gloved fingers together sort of suggestively. "One might start to suspect there was some reason for that."

David let that sink in. His very close friendship with Noah certainly got them the occasional look or comment from those who saw how comfortable they were with each other. But it had been years since David had nursed any feelings that should keep him from setting Noah up with someone else.

He glanced over to where Noah was headed back to the table with fresh fizzes in hand, completely ignoring a handsome university student who tried to chat him up on the way.

"I… I suppose it probably has been a while since I helped her out," David stammered, kicking himself immediately for the phrasing as Annabelle and Charlie looked at each other again. God, how could he have let them think there was something more than friendship between them? Old habits, he supposed. Ancient ones. Ones that should absolutely not be affecting his behavior to a degree that the others would notice. "You're right. I ought to set her up with someone suitable."

He felt a hand grasp his arm from behind. Noah. He could tell from the smell of that lovely new perfume he still couldn't quite place.

"Talking about me, I hope?" Noah said, sliding Annabelle's glass across the table.

"Of course," said David lightly. "You're the most interesting topic in the club, after all." David turned his head, putting his nose right in line with Noah's temple. God, what was that perfume? The question of where he'd smelled it before was almost unbearably distracting, particularly when he was trying to get Annabelle and Charlie to stop looking at him like he was some sort of lovesick little fool. He wasn't.

Not anymore, anyway.

"I'll just…" He took a step back, adjusting the ledger under his arm. It was well past time he got back to his proper duties. He locked eyes with Annabelle. "I'll keep an eye out for someone, at least."

He wished them all a lovely next game and went to the bar, stopping at the tap for half a beer to clear his head. Setting himself up at the quiet end of the bar, he flipped through the ledger pages, looking for the false name he used for Noah's records on the off chance that the owner—or the authorities—ever took interest in the books. God, were they right? Did he really never try to set Noah up with anyone? He stopped flipping before he had to face the reality of what he'd done. While half his life was spent making sure all his people stayed safe, the other half was spent ensuring they had suitable company. Though the flavor of the matches and the exchange of money for room access meant the law would dub it "procuring" if he was caught, it wasn't, really. It was more like matchmaking, and it brought everyone involved a lot of joy.

That he'd apparently let some old, fuzzy feelings keep him from bringing that joy to his best friend was frankly embarrassing.

But who would be suitable? He couldn't seem to think of anyone, casting glances around the room for inspiration that didn't come.

He got no further in solving that question, but something about it gave clarity on another: the perfume. All at once, he remembered what it was.

He turned back and looked. The sight of Noah's smile across the room confirmed it for him.

It was lilac.

Chapter Three

Noah Clarke huddled under the low-hanging branches of a lilac bush in full, fragrant bloom. Vaguely sick with anticipation and what he supposed was the fear of getting caught, he *waited*.

He really shouldn't be so nervous. They never got caught sneaking around at night. Were the monitors this oblivious in the proper public schools, the ones with prestige and good names that his father had rejected for fear it would "fan the flame of his gentlemanly vanity" at the expense of his intellect? Surely the housemasters somewhere like Eton or Harrow would take notice of boys so regularly getting lost on their way back from the privy.

It seemed to take forever, but eventually he caught the sound of near-silent crunches and whispers of grass. It was David.

"Noah?" he hissed.

"Over here!"

"Where? Fucking dark…"

"Hang on." Noah fished a candle and match out of his pocket, fumbling in a gush of excitement. It was a little unseemly, but he couldn't help it; they'd had no time to catch up like this since returning from the Easter holiday.

David followed the candlelight a quarter turn around the

pond, moved aside some of the flowery lilac branches, and sat down. Like Noah, David was in his pajamas with a green school sweater on top. In the warm-and-cool glow of flame and moonlight, it was hard to look away from the welcome sight of his grin, but Noah managed, quickly digging a hole in the mud to shove the candle into.

"Any trouble?" David asked.

"No. You?"

"Almost," he said with a wild sort of smile. He went into his pocket and pulled out a small, half-empty bottle of clear liquid. "But fortunately, I was equipped with something to get me out of it."

"David!" Noah snatched up the bottle, squinting at the label by the candle's flickers. "Where the devil did you get *gin*?"

David looked extremely pleased with himself. "A few things may have found their way into my socks when I packed up at the end of the holiday."

"How many of these things?"

"One to bribe the monitor to sleep through our departure and another for you to try."

Noah's eyes must have gone very big, because David took one look at his face and burst out laughing.

"Christ," he said affectionately, taking the bottle back and bumping Noah's shoulder. "I forgot you were temperance people."

"We're not *temperance people*!" Noah said, failing to scold rather than smile as David went on chuckling his way through uncorking the bottle. The harsh, botanical scent of it cut right through the perfumed air. "Well, my sister *has* been arguing temperance, admittedly, though my father is still convinced of the health benefits of the occasional brandy."

"Well, this isn't all that different from brandy. Probably all the same benefits."

They caught each other's eye over the flame and grinned. "You first," Noah insisted.

David shrugged like it was nothing, but there was an uncertain edge to it that made Noah feel better about his own nerves. He brought the bottle to his mouth. The wickedness of watching his throat move, eyes scrunching up as he took a surprisingly tentative little sip of this stolen, illicit poison, sent an actual shiver down Noah's spine. It might have been revulsion, but if so, why exactly was he accepting the bottle as David passed it over? Bringing it to his own lips as if he'd done it a hundred times before? Sipping at the same bolt of lightning that must have been warming David's stomach even now?

Whether the shiver had been revulsion or not didn't matter, because *actual* disgust and panic hit hard when he tasted the stuff. He spat it right back out in a dramatic spray over the grass.

Before he'd even finished with that ungraceful move, they were both laughing so hard they were falling on each other, clapping hands to their mouths and trying to hypocritically shush each other before they got caught out of bed with the sort of contraband that left one unable to sit for a week.

David snatched the bottle back before Noah could overbalance and spill it, a tear of mirth glistening at the corner of his eye. "If it's not for you," he managed to choke out as he corked it, "then I suppose I'll save it to get more favors from the monitors."

"Davy," Noah gasped. "It is *dreadful.* What on earth could they *want* with it?"

"It will get you very drunk, if you can get some down. And you can mix it with other things, if the taste is too much." He suddenly looked more serious, but just long enough to say, "Plus the health benefits."

Back at it, their cackles breathless and out of control. Oh

God, he'd missed this over the holiday. They flopped back against the grass, shoulder to shoulder, unable to support themselves anymore until their fits turned to chuckles and finally to lingering smiles.

With the moonlight bright above them and grass chilly and damp below, David felt awfully warm and solid next to him. Noah figured he ought to move over a bit, but he didn't really feel like it, and David wasn't moving, either.

"Anything interesting happen while you were home?" David asked eventually.

Noah took a moment to think about it. His Surrey home was a quiet, studious place where things a Londoner like David might find interesting were few and far between. "I did end up asking my father about transferring to one of the public schools."

"Oh." David's voice was tight. "Um. What did he say?"

"He still thinks the prestige will make me vain, but that it's not out of the question. Did you ask yours?"

"There was never a good time. He'd have said no anyway." There was a false casualness in David's voice that declared the subject closed. He turned over onto his side, head propped on his hand, looking down at Noah. "So, are you going to go, then?"

Without you? Are you mad? He didn't say that, thankfully, but it was the first silly little thought that came to mind.

There were less silly reasons, though, which he latched onto quickly. "It's probably not worth it. I can't stay as long as the nobs do anyway. Papa expects me to start studying under him next summer, to make sure I'm ready when it's time to apply at the medical colleges."

"Oh yeah," David said, perking up a bit. "Same for me, except, you know, the medical college bit. But you're right that the nobs are different. Just met some heir at the hotel over

Easter who's planning to stay in school until he's practically at majority, then Oxford after that. Doesn't have any family business to rush into, though, so I suppose it makes sense. Lucky bastards."

"You think so?" Noah chuckled, tearing up a blade of grass and neatly dividing it into two little ribbons. "I think I'd lose my mind, living like they do."

"Fair enough. You are obviously allergic to idleness after all."

"Oh, I am not."

"No?" David snatched one of the slim bits of greenery from Noah's hand, their fingers brushing. "Then explain to me why, when you're done with your schoolwork, you start asking around to see if anyone needs their uniform mended?"

"They're nicer to me when I'm useful like that, and I'm good with a needle. Simple enough." He tried to take the sliver of grass back, but it snapped in half between them. "We can't all buy our peace by smuggling gin in our socks, now can we?"

"Suppose not. You're good at it, anyway. Speaking of." He shook off what remained of the grass and bunched up the sleeve of his sweater so he could show where the cuff was starting to unravel. "I'm going to have a waistcoat pretty soon if I'm not careful."

Noah hesitated for just a second. Should he reach out and tie the loose ends off now, or ask David to take the sweater off first? Neither seemed…quite right at the moment. He shook the curious conflict off and reached out, bringing David's wrist closer to his face, still lying flat on the grass. He dug around in the yarn to find the broken threads, tying them in a careful knot to tide things over. "That's a temporary tourniquet. Don't fuss with it, and I'll get it done right tomorrow. Knits are tricky, I'll have to do it in the daylight."

With a playful smile and a scooch that removed all remaining space between them on the grass, David rested his forearm on Noah's chest, practically draped over him as he examined the knot. "Well done, Doctor. I think she'll make it."

"Just, um." Noah didn't like being called Doctor, but found he liked the rest of this joke quite a lot. He met David's eyes as best he could in the darkness and struggled to find the punch line he'd had a second ago. "Don't forget to bring her in for her follow-up."

He'd stopped talking, but David didn't seem to be moving. He just stayed where he was, the warmth and weight of him making Noah simultaneously want to roll out of the way entirely, and yet come even closer. The air was crackling like a terrible storm was about to start up, but the sky was clear and the moon was full, and before Noah knew what he was doing, he put his hand on the dewy wool covering David's back.

"I did something interesting," David said suddenly, his voice dropping to a whisper. "Over the holiday."

"What was it?" Noah whispered back, plucking blades of grass from David's sweater because there had to be a reason for his hand's presence, didn't there?

"It was that heir I mentioned." The words still came on near-silent breaths, as if something even more wicked than the gin was coming. "Sort of a funny thing. I was charming his sister, you see, at one of the hotel events."

David's position as a hotelier's son gave him access to all sorts of interesting parties and wealthy guests, including a rotation of well-dressed society girls. David liked to talk about girls, both his own interactions with them, and his opinions on the handsome blokes they ought to marry later on. Noah didn't mind the talk, rather enjoying David's enthusiasm and pestering him for details of their fascinatingly elaborate ball gowns, though he rarely had anything to contribute. Too much bluestocking influence in his own life, he supposed.

"Was she pretty?" Noah asked.

"Beautiful."

"And her dress?"

David looked very pleased and amused, like he'd been waiting for Noah to ask that question again. "Very lovely, you'd have liked it. Pink like a shell, almost, lots of lace and layers and all that. Anyway, I had it in mind to sneak her off for a kiss, but her brother caught us and sneaked me off instead."

Noah blinked a few times, his stomach flipping as the air started to crackle again. That could not possibly be where the sentence ended. That made it sound like—

"Sneaked you off for what?" Noah said in a whisper that came out as an accusatory hiss. "For what, Davy? A talking-to?"

"Well, that first." David chuckled. "Called me a cad and a rake and all that, though, of course, I wouldn't have done anything serious. But after that, well, I suppose that's when it got interesting."

Interesting. It was starting to become quite a loaded word, wasn't it? It overwhelmed Noah with a prickly curiosity that he wanted to quash, but couldn't. Not with David practically lying on top of him, suddenly looking very much like a rake in this secluded, floral nook they'd settled in. Was this how the society girls felt when he "sneaked them off"? And as for their brothers…

All at once, he had a feeling, a *sense*, that he knew what David was talking about, and at the moment it seemed like the most interesting subject imaginable.

"Interesting how?" he asked, his voice hardly more than a breath.

David gently picked some grass or maybe a firefly out of Noah's hair. Then his voice dropped even lower, hardly audible over the ripple of the pond and the breeze ruffling the grasses around them. "Well, he offered an *alternative*, you see, to risking girls' reputations. As I say, it was very interesting to me. I wondered if it might be interesting to you as well."

The world had become very small, very quiet, very warm. There certainly was no further debris in Noah's hair, yet David's fingers were touching it anyway. "Shall I tell you what—?"

"You don't have to tell me," Noah whispered quickly, captivated by what David had said already, but afraid that if he heard more specific words, he'd have no choice but to run from them. "Just show me. If you want to."

"Sh-show you?" David stammered, like he worried Noah didn't know what he was getting into. "But—"

Noah stopped picking at David's sweater and flattened his hand instead. He made his eyes wide and his voice slow when he said, with all the meaning he could muster, "I learn better that way, David. So just. You know. *Show me.*"

The span of time that passed might have been called a heartbeat, if both their hearts hadn't been racing so hard and fast that Noah wasn't entirely certain whose was whose. More like a few dozen heartbeats, then, before David brought his mouth down to Noah's and things became very interesting indeed.

Chapter Four

Noah

London's West End, June 1885

The most interesting ideas came to Noah Clarke at the most inconvenient times.

Today it was card suits, reds and blacks on white backgrounds. From his space at the long worktables that crossed the Harvey Cole & Co. workshop—militaristically straight rows besmirched by heaps of fabric, scatters of sartorial tools, and a shamefully postured contingent of tailors in various states of dishevelment—the image took shape in his mind. As he snipped his shears through a swath of black superfine that was destined to become a simple coat, he imagined changing the path until he had a stack of clubs and spades. He'd do the hearts and diamonds out of red plush, then put the lot together into a sort of motley on a white background.

He paused his shears to reach for the sketchbook that he always kept nearby. He had an enormous collection of these by now, filled with years' worth of visual musings. There were thick leather journals he'd used for doodles and notes to David at school instead of the brilliant, society-saving thoughts that Papa had expected of him. Then came the paperbound packets he bought cheaply for himself so no one knew he had them, more pages torn out during adolescent rages than left in. And, of course, the tall, official sketchpads of his Milanese apprenticeship, where his swirling, amateur lines became meticulously mathematical for a time, before softening again once his place was secured and no one looked over his shoulder any longer.

It was one of these he used on this warm Friday evening, a little smile dancing across his lips as his pencil skated along the lines of an impromptu sketch. After last weekend's *pair of queens* debacle, David and the others would get a kick out of him showing up to the club in a concoction like this. Not as Miss Penelope; a patchwork ball gown might be beyond his dressmaking skill. He could certainly do a suit, though. *A suit of suits.* Or a jacket at least. Perhaps a waistcoat…?

His excitement dwindled along with the speed of his pencil. With the London Season in full swing for the visiting gentry, every gentleman in England had swarmed the Savile Row tailor shops with a mile-long list of the basic, boring styles that were popular this year. Noah would be lucky to steal himself an hour to make a card suit *pocket square*, he was so overbooked.

With a sigh, he closed the sketchbook and picked the shears back up. He got the rest of the piece cut out and carefully removed the pattern paper, folding it up along its designated lines and returning it to the large envelope that held all the other pieces of the custom pattern. The cutter that Noah worked under—an elderly genius by the name of Ambrose Covington—was among the Cole & Co. designers who took their patterns as a matter of great pride and secrecy. That Noah was even allowed to cut pieces for him at all was testament to the esteem he'd won.

Noah closed up the precious envelope and held it to his chest as he squeezed between the tables. Every window on the Bond Street side was open, and while the workshop had been stale and sweat-smelling earlier when damn near a hundred of them had been at their work, the breeze moved pleasantly through the space now that the skyline was going orange at last and most had gone home for the night.

Noah took a moment at the full-length mirror and rack of jackets beside the door that led from the workshop. The rumpled tailors had to fix themselves up before stepping foot in the pristine, plush showroom. He straightened his necktie and slipped his own silk jacket over shirtsleeves wilted by a full day in the too-warm workshop. He shook out and smoothed his collar-length hair, making sure it looked deliberately dashing rather than just unfashionably long, then covered calloused hands with a pair of white gloves.

He strode out into the elaborate showroom with its wood-paneled walls and rows of dapperly dressed dummies. It was nearly empty of clients this late in the evening, just one nervous valet talking livery changes for some earl's household.

He found Mr. Covington in one of the velvet settees, an ankle up over his knee and his enormous white mustache buried in a record book marked *Rosenby*.

That name on the spine lit Noah up with a manic energy. Lord Archibald Rosenby. The most excessive, eccentric, and interesting client in Mr. Covington's portfolio. A client whose orders Noah had never touched.

Trying to keep his pace reasonable so as not to startle the other cutter's client, Noah crossed the showroom and held out the pattern envelope to Mr. Covington with his eyes trained on the hand-lettered name of the account in question.

"Mr. Clarke," said Covington with a friendly nod. He didn't take the envelope, but instead reached into his pocket. He tossed Noah the key to his pattern drawers. "You can go on and put that back yourself."

He looked back down at his records, making notes in the Rosenby book in a way that was certainly a dismissal. When Noah didn't move, Mr. Covington glanced up from his notes with an expression that might have been a smirk or might have been a frown; it was hard to say what precisely was going on within the twitches of such an impressive mustache.

"What's Lord Rosenby coming in for?" Noah blurted, trying and failing to blunt his eagerness. "Anything interesting?"

One of Covington's snowy eyebrows—hardly less luscious than the mustache—drifted upward. "A greatcoat." He turned the record book to show Noah where he'd done up a few sketches right overtop the printed ledger boxes, the lines slim and sweeping. "He's just back from a Mediterranean tour. He was inspired by some of what he saw down there."

Mediterranean.

"Mr. Clarke, are you quite well?"

"Mediterranean," Noah repeated. "I assume *la bel paese* caught his attention? Florence, perhaps?"

"Milan."

Perfetta.

"You know," said Noah, "I studied in Milan under Fiore Corsetti for two y—"

"Yes, Mr. Clarke." The mustache twitched again. This time, the smirk was unmistakable. "Seeing as I have known you for much longer than five minutes, I am fully aware of the time you spent *under Fiore Corsetti.*"

There was a teasing lilt to it. Noah put a hand to his chest and pretended to blush while Covington peeked over at the other cutter and client to ensure such jokes were not being overheard. It wouldn't do for the clients to realize that their tailors traded in bawdy humor while they sweated through their shirtsleeves in the workshop.

"I admit," Covington said, "I could use some expertise in the Milanese style for this one, but I was planning to give the bulk of the work to Cecil Martin. You got the last assignment. It's Martin's turn, I believe."

"B–but the *style*—"

"Rosenby's not asking for anything overly authentic. Martin is trained in the style well enough."

Noah managed to keep his mouth shut, but only by gritting his teeth. Cecil Martin. Covington's other senior workhand. All the high-level tailors had reputations, and while Noah was known as a *Corsetti-trained cutthroat*, Cecil Martin was Covington's *true savant*. They typically divided projects on an alternating basis (with Martin clearly favored when Noah wasn't there to stake his claim, though he could not prove it).

But stake it he would, this time. The Rosenby assignment had Noah's name on it. His mind raced through their standards of practice, desperate to find the technicality that would win him this prize.

And wouldn't you know it; he found one. He couldn't quite suppress a smile.

"Lord Davenport," he said.

"Pardon?"

"Don't you recall?" Noah said as casually as possible. "Last season, Mr. Martin took the Lord Davenport account from me out of turn. Not that I blame him; it's all water under the bridge now—" (it was not, actually, Noah was still quite irritated) "—but in any case, he'd certainly agree that he owes me one. He's an honest chap, Mr. Martin. He'll sleep better knowing we'd squared things off like this."

"Squared what off?"

Noah whipped around. It was Cecil Martin himself, clearly on his way out for the night with his hat on over his tight, dark curls. He paused between Noah and Covington, peering innocently at them. "What were you saying about me? Hopefully nothing to do with that seam I bungled yesterday. I've been hoping that everyone forgot all about it by now."

"No, no," said Covington, playing right into that shameless display of calculated self-depreciation. "Mr. Clarke was just saying that you wouldn't mind if I put him on Rosenby next week."

Noah tried to keep his face very neutral as he and Martin sized each other up. Martin's arms were crossed over a smart, moss green jacket. As a *true savant* and the only Black tailor on the payroll, he clearly saw no point even trying to blend in like Noah did, all-out tonight with cats printed on the silk of his tie and a strip of velvet around his hat. The way he pursed his lips showed he wasn't keen to give up such an eccentric client, either.

Finally, he cocked his head. "That's interesting. I thought—"

"It was your turn," said Noah quickly. "But if you remember the Davenport account—"

Martin held out a hand. "I was going to say: I thought you were already behind on your assignments. Are you certain you should take on another just now?"

Noah felt like he'd been stripped to some rather embarrassing underthings right in the middle of the showroom. "I am *not* behind," he insisted. A dishonest assertion, perhaps, but they didn't need to know that.

Mr. Martin didn't argue. In fact, he looked much too comfortable with the whole thing as he shrugged. "If you say so, Mr. Clarke." He adjusted the fall of his jacket. "Do let me know if you become overwhelmed, though. I'll be happy to step in and take a bit of the load off."

He smiled and headed off toward the door that led out to the Savile Row storefront, leaving Noah fuming and flushing much worse than he would have if Martin had given a proper fight.

"He has a point," said Covington, once Martin was gone. "Are you certain you can manage it?"

"Of course I can," said Noah, certain he could make it true through sheer force of will. After all, his will was clearly stronger than Martin's, who would rather sit by and hope his rival failed than play to win. Dear Lord, he would sooner die than ask that man for help. It was all he could do not to stick his tongue out at his back like a child. "Don't worry yourself, Mr. Covington. When exactly is Rosenby's first consult?"

Noah got the dates, the times, and the invitation to sit with Mr. Covington for a spell as they discussed the design details for the assignment. By the time he got the pattern put away and his station situated for Monday morning, it was past seven and he was exhausted.

Still, when the lumbering front door closed the dummies behind him for the weekend, he skipped heading home to his rooms in Piccadilly. His sister, Emily, was staying with him this summer, and with her around, there would be no relaxing at home anyway. Instead, he left the impeccable streets of Mayfair behind and went to join David among the trash, trade, and bewildering treasure to be found in the Soho district.

It was like a switch flipped once all the nice houses and private coaches gave way to tenements and crumbling cobbles. When David had first lost his fortune and started finding himself in this neighborhood, Noah thought he'd gone mad, but the area's charms had grown on him. Now he very comfortably passed sketchy theaters and seedy pubs to the boisterous multicultural market on Berwick Street, though food was secondary to another neglected craving. He ducked into an alley, removing his white gloves before reaching into his coat pocket for cigarettes and a torch.

After he lit the vogue and got his first soothing breath of smoke, he noticed two gaudily dressed women making eyes at him from farther along the shadows. He shook his head before the offer could be made, but flicked the cigarette case open and held it out. With a little hesitation, they each took one and let him light it. With his own cigarette still streaming between his lips, he went back into his pocket to trade case and torch for a pair of pearl drop earrings. He tucked back the hair that hid the holes while he was at work, fastened the jewelry to his ears, finished off the cigarette, and tipped his hat to the whores.

"Buonanotte, sorelle mie." Goodnight, my sisters. Though the girls weren't Italian, everyone around here knew a sprinkle of the language as slang. They laughed as he left the alley in search of supper. After a quick piadina and gelato acquired without a lick of English, he left Berwick Street with a swish in his step and started through a series of familiar, twisting alleys, at last stopping at the dingy gray door with the little fox's face scratched onto the metal knob that marked the entrance to David's club.

He knocked in the pattern he and David had invented in their boarding school broom cupboard days. While they'd ceased meeting up to snog amid cleaning supplies and lilac bushes years ago, still Noah held his breath until the door opened. It wasn't so different a use, after all. The knock that had once declared "not a teacher" now served to imply "not an officer."

The hinges creaked, a bell-covered curtain jangled, and then David was leaning in the doorway, the warmth on his face so classically *David* that it might have been easy to forget how much time had passed since the knock was first used, but the short, tidy beard he'd grown and the lanky height of him kept Noah firmly—if a bit wistfully—in the present.

"*You* again." David shook his head but still smiled at his own joke. "Goddamn, what's a nice girl like you always doing in a place like this, anyway?"

"Oh, you know." Noah straightened his cuffs and tried not to look too pleased. "Just following you around until the end of time."

David grinned like there was nothing he'd like better. "Well, in that case, follow me inside, would you? Doors open for real in an hour, and I'm still getting things ready."

Holding the door open with one hand, he used the other to usher Noah through the rows of belled curtains that led to his most ungentlemanly gentleman's club. Some of the knots in his shoulders started melting immediately under the warm, familiar weight of David's palm. It didn't matter that the smell of incense and sight of a fabric-draped ceiling meant that sleep was hours off yet; David had cultivated a peace in this place that worked better than a nap to restore Noah's energy.

And thankfully, as the proprietor's best friend, he got perks along with the peace, including entrance before the doors technically opened for the night, a seat on the most comfortable sofa, and his favorite gin fizz procured within minutes of arrival.

Most importantly, he had immediate access to David, who was still, after all this time, the person he wanted to share all his news with. As he settled into a solitaire game to keep his antsy hands occupied while David and Warren prepped the parlor, he explained the situation with the Rosenby account and Cecil Martin.

"Have you lost your mind?" David said, laughing as he went on cutting lemons behind the bar with a towel thrown over his shoulder. "You're behind already. Why the devil would you take on another account when it wasn't even your turn?"

Noah slapped a three of hearts down so hard the rest of the column skittered sideways. "You don't get it, Davy." He pulled the next card. It was shite, so he put it in the middle of the deck and took a fresh one from the top. Much better. "No one's place is assured at a shop like Harvey Cole's. An opportunity presented itself. It could have spelled disaster if I turned it down."

"But it wasn't presented to you," said David, his scruffy face unable to stay serious despite some obvious effort. "You stole it."

"I did nothing he didn't do first. I was settling the score."

"Coming from the person who just insisted that *nothing beats a pair of queens*, I'm afraid I have my doubts."

Noah watched David smile and shake his head as he gathered the lemons up into a bowl. Despite his words, he didn't look annoyed. In fact, his green eyes sparkled a little as he brought one of the lemon wedges over, holding it up in offering. Noah nodded and lifted his glass so David could squeeze the juice and drop in the peel before settling on the sofa beside him and drawing the next card.

A disgusted sound came from a stepladder in the center of the parlor. They both looked over at Warren Bakshi, the barkeep, who was rolling his dark eyes as he lit each candle in the enormous crystal chandelier that hung from the cloth-draped ceiling.

"Got a problem, mate?" called David.

"It's nothing," said Warren, a cynical smile belying his words as he reached for the next candle. "Just you two. All snuggled up playing cards like sentimental old biddies. Sometimes I worry I've taken a wrong turn and wound up in a quaint little teahouse."

"A terrifying prospect," said David. "Don't quaint teahouses treat you like a church treats a vampire?"

"Something like that."

Since Warren was an East Ender with Punjabi parents and a habit of seducing anything that stood still long enough, Noah figured it wasn't far from the truth.

"Sorry to break it to you, Warren," Noah said, "but a little sentiment is actually quite good for you."

"Yeah," said Warren flippantly, grinning as he got the last

candle. "So's getting some trade every once in a while, but that doesn't seem to trouble you much."

"What?" Noah prickled, taking a sip of his extra-lemony fizz to buy a little time. "You can't possibly mean that I don't... Because I *do*. Ask anyone." Noah fanned himself with his next card, pretending it was for emphasis rather than to cool his burning cheeks. "The blokes won't leave me alone, most nights. I probably get as many propositions as you do."

Warren shook out the match and laughed as he made his way down the ladder. "Yeah, but how many of them do you take?"

"Davy, tell him off."

David bit his lip with a sort of uncomfortable amusement. "I mean, he has a point, doesn't he? Annabelle and Charlie were just saying I ought to—"

"David! Are you on their side?"

"Look, Penny." Warren sauntered over, peering down at Noah with his arms crossed. "If you're wound tight enough to cause trouble at work as well as the card table, then it's well past time you put the poker chips down and *unwound*."

Noah scoffed at the accusation and the filthy gesture Warren gave to go along with it. "Oh, what do you know?"

"As much as I want to." Warren's handsome face broke into a grin. "I've got access to the ledgers."

Noah slammed his next card down. "You wouldn't."

"Pretty sure I would."

"David won't let you." When David did not speak in agreement, Noah whipped his head around to look sternly into his scruffy face. "Isn't that right, Davy?"

David grimaced, looking guiltily toward the bar. "I don't know," he said slowly. "Maybe it's worth taking a look." A bit reluctantly, he turned to Warren. "Mate," he said. "Go get the ledger."

The barkeep's smooth features went very naughty. He was

behind the bar with the green ledger in his hands before Noah could blink. Noah got up and tried to get the book from him, but Warren dodged and held it out of reach.

"Let's see." Warren traced the feathered pen down the records of private room rentals.

"This is ridiculous," Noah said with another unsuccessful grab for the ledger. "Room rentals won't tell you anything. For all you know, I'm out trolling Hyde Park every night."

"Nah," Warren said wickedly. "If you were doing that, Forester would certainly have caught you at it by now—"

David cleared his throat loudly to cut him off, turning quite red in the face. "Warren, please forgo your gossipy speculation about my habits and get back to Noah's well-recorded ones, would you?"

"In that case… April fourth," Warren declared, reading from the ledger as if it were an official parish register. "With one of the actors. They were only in there twenty minutes, probably because the previous record was…" He laughed, flipping pages. "You don't even want to know."

David bolted up, abandoning the cards to spin the ledger around on the bar, checking for himself. "Noah!"

Noah's face burned as David came over to him. He tried to flinch away, but David caught him, looking mildly horrified. "It really isn't any of your business."

"Everything that goes on at the club is my business," David said with an oddly determined look on face. His hands, large and warm, settled on Noah's shoulders, working the muscles gently. "And I've neglected it in regard to you. I'm sorry. I don't know why, I just…"

He trailed off as Warren leaned over the bar. "You going to remedy the situation, Miss Matchmaker?" Warren said.

David went quiet for a moment, going a little more firmly at the knots in Noah's shoulders and not meeting Warren's eye. "Yeah," he said a little uncertainly. "Yeah, I suppose I ought to."

"No, stop it," said Noah. "I'm not in the right mood for your matchmaking."

David shook his head, that determined look returning. "After this long, you'll be in the right mood for anything with minimal effort."

Noah took a deep breath, trying to pretend that was ridiculous. Never mind that the air he took in smelled like David's cologne, or that the firm hands rubbing his stiff muscles made him want to arch his back like a damn cat. David had always been strangely good at this sort of thing; even now, when Noah was annoyed and defensive, it was hard to resist relaxing into such a skilled touch.

"I'm just looking out for you," David said, still a bit like he was trying to prove something to himself. "You're the prettiest thing here. Blokes ask after you all the time. And not arseholes like Brighton: good blokes, who could give you a happy evening if you'll let me send them your way."

Noah closed his eyes as David took his attentions from shoulders down to one of his forearms, poking at knots that hadn't been eased in ages. "I don't know, Davy…"

"You need to relax, beautiful," scolded David. "All you do is work."

"I like it that way."

"Went for a little play on April fourth, though, did you?" Warren teased. "And with an actor, no less?"

Noah rolled his shoulders back and offered the other arm. "Well, I'm not made of stone, am I?"

"Sure about that?" David looked concerned as he reached Noah's overworked hand. "You feel like you might be, bloody hell. You're going to wreck yourself at this pace."

"Mmm, yes, that's the one." Noah grimaced as his muscles started to give in and relax that very particular cramp that came from too many hours with the shears. "Anyway, wrecked or not, this most recent opportunity has tipped me over the edge. There will be no slowing down anytime soon."

"You know what you need?" said Warren. There were footsteps from the bar, then Noah's eyes shot open as a warm hand pressed against his back and next thing he knew, he and David had gone from a step apart to pressed tight together with Warren's arms serving as the vise. "A little help from someone you don't have to impress. A friendly sort of thing. Keep it very *casual*."

The sudden closeness of David's scruffy jaw and the lovely full mouth that had been the first to ever kiss him caused Noah's brain to short-circuit something dreadful, and the hot press of their bodies didn't help one bit. Some old butter-flies he'd forgotten about took flight in his stomach, and for a wild instant, all he could think was that Warren had a very good point…and unless he'd imagined that twitch against the front of his thigh where they were smashed together, David was intrigued by the idea as well.

But maybe he had imagined it, because David unfroze the instant Noah met his eyes. He stepped to the side, calmly removing Warren's hands from both of them. Reflexively, Noah glanced down to the buttons on David's pinstriped trousers, looking for strain, but David turned to the bar and Noah came to his bloody senses before he could be certain.

"Interesting idea," David said, stammering a little as he finally closed up the ledger and tucked it securely in its place under his arm. "But I don't think—"

The patterned knock pounded out from the front entrance, making David jump so guiltily that Noah and Warren both laughed, releasing the rest of the tension as Warren went to get the door and Noah took a very deep, very focused breath.

David cleared his throat and smoothed the strand of tawny hair that always fell into his eyes. Still looking a touch flustered, he went to gather up Noah's abandoned glass and busy himself with topping it off.

"Anyway, beautiful," he said, this standard drink preparation seeming to take quite a lot of his attention. "Don't worry about him. You just get all prettied up and be your delightful, charming self. *I* will send the appropriate drinks and men your way until some combination of the two gets you good and relaxed." He pushed the now-full glass across the bar, its ice clinking and fresh bubbles popping. "Do try not to take all their money, though. When you're dressed as Penelope, it hurts their pride to lose to you."

Noah rolled his eyes and accepted his drink. He watched Warren lead a couple of regulars in and take their coats. "Fine," Noah agreed at last. "I won't let them win, but I can at least play by standard rules. I *suppose*."

David took a moment to make sure that Warren had made the gentlemen comfortable before going on. "Look. I can't tell you to put your physical needs before your need to win at everything. I'm just saying that whoever wears the pants ought to pay for the room anyway, so if I introduce you to someone, you have to leave him with *something* to give me later."

Noah sipped the refreshed drink, impressed to find it as perfectly mixed as the original had been. "You really know how to walk that line between matchmaking and procuring, don't you?"

"It's a razor's edge sometimes, but it's something to stand on."

"Just don't go to prison, please. I've followed you to a lot of dodgy places, but I'd hate to have to follow you there."

"Stop it." David turned away and started fidgeting with

the bar utensils, as if he and Warren had not already gotten them in perfect order. "You wouldn't follow me to prison."

It was Noah's turn to shrug, feeling he'd need a bit more context to determine whether or not that was true. He washed the notion down with another fizzy sip. "I suppose I'll go get dressed, then."

"Go with that striped skirt, the blue one."

"You think so?"

David nodded. "And the, er, you know. The what's-it-called. The pillow arse thing."

"For the thousandth time, it's called a bustle."

"There's only space for so much in here." He tapped his head. "No need for me to waste it on clothing terminology when I have a world-class expert like you at my beck and call."

Noah glared at the flattery and got a grin in return. "So. The Prussian damask, you say?"

"No, the blue-striped..." He paused, catching Noah's teasing look. "Yes. That one. Trust me."

Noah caught the key when David tossed it to him. A few of those butterflies were still going strong, making his voice come out a bit flirty when he said, "Will you come lace me up in a bit?"

"Of course," said David, turning a little pink. "Twenty minutes?"

"*Perfetta.*"

He blew a kiss, ensuring that David had put it securely in his pocket before heading off to let himself into the back hallway, unexpectedly energized by the whole exchange. Of course he and David wouldn't act on the little rush Warren had inspired—they were friends with an interesting little history, nothing more—but it was still sort of fun to dip into that playful old dynamic for a moment.

Noah passed through the back hall, purposely nudging more

belled curtains so they glittered out their music behind him as he passed by closed doorways. The back of the Fox boasted four bedrooms and two staircases: one that went up to the private parlor, and one that allowed for a hasty exit to the alley in the event of a raid.

He unlocked the biggest of the rooms, which was supplied with a wardrobe and vanity where David let a select few of the girls and drag artists stash clothing and cosmetics. It was technically against the owner's wishes that anyone come in early or use the rooms for free, but David had bent the rules for Noah, and once that got out, he had to allow a few others the honor as well.

Noah unlocked the wardrobe and waded through waves of lace and silk to find his Prussian damask, along with his own chemise, petticoats, and bustle. He got all his things out and heaped them on the four-poster, where the plush linens were all done up and lying around, waiting to be ruined. On top of the pile, he added what he'd brought in his pockets from home: pearls, stockings, and razor.

That was the first order of business, of course. He examined his pointed chin in the mirror above the vanity. Even nearing thirty as he was, he'd still never managed to grow anything resembling an attractive beard. It was a Clarke family curse or blessing, depending on whom you asked, his father and uncles remaining a bit scraggly and unmanned until their forties. Still, nowadays, the scratchy patches on his chin and lip were just notable enough by nightfall to require a touch-up.

He took another good pull of his drink, then got the rest of his shaving things and makeup out of the drawer, put his hands in the pink-patterned wash bowl Warren had prepared, and began the process of becoming Miss Penelope.

Once his canvas was smooth, he got the powder and a nice dark lip paint situated. He was just starting on the kohl, when the tinkling sound of brass bells from the hallway made him freeze with the stick halfway across his eyelid, staring at his ghostly unrouged reflection as he listened to the bells and footsteps.

It wasn't Warren or David, and while it didn't sound like the stomping madness of a raid, it didn't sound right, either. That was all he could figure out before the door to the bedroom flew open so hard it banged against the wall.

Noah dropped the kohl and spun around, failing to fully swallow a scream. He clutched at the edge of the vanity behind him as he stared at the figures in the open doorway.

It was David after all, but not just David. A gray-haired gentleman in an exceptionally cut coat was gripping the nape of David's neck. A third man, squat and red-faced, loomed behind them.

Noah gaped at the sight of David, who for years had roamed these rooms like he owned them, suddenly looking young, frightened, defeated. The men didn't look like officers, but who else would have reason to push David around like this?

Whatever it was, it was bad. Very bad.

The first man turned a pair of bright blue eyes on Noah. "Who the devil are you?"

"No one!" squawked Noah on a surge of terror, lowering his head and trying to wipe the lipstick off onto the back of his hand. "No one at all."

Trying to hide his face behind his long hair while still keeping an eye out, he watched the icy man give David a nasty little shake. "You know, David, when I told you to let *no one* in before opening, that's not quite what I meant." He turned back to Noah. "Get out. Now."

"Y-yes." Fumbling, trembling, heart pounding, Noah started trying to get the lids back on the cosmetic pots.

"Don't bother with that. *Get out.*"

He got his razor case and was about to put it in his pocket, when he slowed, just slightly. He looked over his shoulder at David. His mouth was like sand and there was rushing in his ears, and he wondered…

David shook his head a tiny bit. "Go."

Not wanting to make whatever this was any worse, he put the razor case in his pocket. He stepped awkwardly around the pack of them. He tried to swallow the sawdust in his throat as he locked eyes with David one more time. David's mouth twitched just enough to beg Noah to get out.

He finally did, closing the door quietly behind him. Numb and tingling, he returned through the curtains, putting pace after jingling pace between himself and whatever was happening to David in that room…

He suddenly sprinted the rest of the way up the hall and out into the parlor. Warren was back, looking surly behind the bar. The fellows he'd let in earlier were gone.

Noah threw himself into the edge of the bar, grabbing Warren by the sleeve. "Who are those men with David?"

Warren spent an eternity glowering at the back door before he finally answered. "Lord Moneyballs and his little cranberry of a crony."

"*Who?*"

"Owner of the club. I don't know his real name."

"The *owner?*"

"Yeah." Warren twisted the yellow topaz in his ear nervously. "He almost never comes here. This probably isn't good."

"Obviously, it's not good!" Noah slapped both his hands down on the bar. "Warren. Did you see them? They look like they're about to hurt him!"

Warren shook his head warily. "Lord Moneyballs don't like getting his hands dirty. Even if David had done something to deserve it, he probably wouldn't handle anything like that himself."

"*Probably wouldn't?* What do you mean he *probably wouldn't?*"

"Come on, mate. You can't really be that naive." Warren rolled his eyes and sneered in the direction of the icy aristocrat. "It's a sodding molly club. You think someone's dear old gran owns the place?"

Noah's stomach dropped clear through the floor. "What should we do?"

"Well, they told me to leave," said Warren.

"Me too." Noah narrowed his eyes. "We're not going to listen, are we?"

"Are you kidding?" Warren snorted, waving Noah around to the back of the bar and pulling him down to hide in a shadowy spot near the icebox.

Chapter Five

David

David was unfortunately familiar with the sensation of Lord Henry Belleville's hand on the back of his neck for one reason or another. Tonight, the fingers dug in with a pressure that indicated *immense displeasure*. David tolerated it unflinchingly until Noah was out of the way, then started trying to shake him off. The baron tightened his grip just enough to show he was undaunted, then let go on his own terms.

Holding his breath, David whipped around to watch his club owner's measured paces to the fireplace. He had no idea what the man was doing here, but it was obviously very bad business. The baron usually went to the effort of pretending to be cordial. At first, anyway.

Lord Belleville stood waiting for a moment. The lines of a fine suit that had probably been made by one of Noah's prestigious contemporaries flickered in the glow of the fire. At last, he accepted a cigarette from his secretary, Mr. Parker. Once it was lit, he took a deep, lingering pull on it.

"Dear God, David," he said, "will you sit down already?"

David startled and went for the sofa, but a cold glare stopped him short. Mr. Parker took the spot. Stomach sinking, David followed the line of Lord Belleville's gaze to the four-poster bed. There was a silent command in the baron's pale eyes, which were a deceptively pretty blue in the sunlight that was not so convincing filled with tonight's firelight and anger.

Though the place struck him as childish and degrading, David was in no position to argue. He perched on the edge of the bed next to the pile of Noah's drags. His pulse thrummed as he sat there, rubbing a scrap of the frock's lacy, lilac-scented trim between his fingers, mind racing with all the things he might have done to deserve this unpleasant visit.

Lord Belleville released a slow stream of smoke. "I give you complete reign of this place with the expectation that you can follow my very simplest of instructions."

"My lord—"

"Don't interrupt me." He put the cigarette in the ashtray and wiped his fingers on his handkerchief. "What in blazes were *four* men doing in *my* club before the doors open?"

"Four men?" David's head stumbled over the question. Tonight's early patrons couldn't be what he came here to discuss. "But… Warren's the barkeep. He's supposed to be here."

"Oh. Three, then. That changes everything, doesn't it?" Belleville stalked toward the wardrobe, rolling his eyes and tucking away his handkerchief. "We'll have to discuss that infraction later. I have more important things to deal with than your insolence right now. Mr. Parker, will you please…?"

Mr. Parker smirked down at David. Oh, how he wanted to smack it right off the secretary's ruddy face. While an earlier, gentler version of Lord Belleville still haunted David's mind in moments like these, he had no such positive memories of Parker, who'd always treated him like some sort of gutter rat.

"We got tipped off by our fellow at Scotland Yard," said Parker with a trace of sneer. "They're going to raid the place tomorrow."

Raid. No one spoke that word within The Curious Fox's walls unless absolutely necessary. Raids were referred to only in sideways terms so that when the stark syllable rang out, it was sharp enough to cut straight to the quick and get everyone on their feet and out the door as quickly as possible.

"Shit," David whispered, trying to keep his voice steady. "S-so we're heading home for the weekend, I take it."

"Your little barkeeps and patrons are heading home, yes," said Parker. "You, on the other hand, are to stay and clean the place up before they get here."

"What do you mean, clean it up?" Resentment combined in a froth with David's fear, making his voice louder than was wise. "This club is bloody *spotless*. Do you have any idea how much—?"

A thud cut him off as Lord Belleville kicked the wardrobe door so hard it unlatched. He pulled it the rest of the way open, revealing a collection of frocks and petticoats that really wasn't supposed to be here at all.

"Does a *spotless* gentlemen's club have this?" Belleville asked in a faux-pleasant voice. He crossed to the fireplace, where a stand held a few birch rods wrapped in spirals of satin. He picked one up and whipped it around so it sang. "Or these?" David winced, but Belleville threw the thing to the ground. "How about this?" He yanked the bedside drawer fully out of its place, bottles of oil and pots of cream all smashing and clattering to the floor and rolling off in separate directions.

He put his arms out, indicating every inch of David's careful, loving decoration. "Every time I come in here, it looks like you've set off another bomb of lace and glitter. Anyone walking in is going to know *exactly* what's been going on. They're going to bust that door down, and whether anyone is here or not, they will take these dresses and these bottles, and your little Greek statues and satyr paintings, and they will use it all to convict you on conspiracy at best." He got in David's face, cold and furious. "So you will *clean it up*. For your own good."

David's hands were shaking, so he folded them tight on his lap. One of the bottles had cracked, sending a flowery scent into the air. The peeling label claimed it was peony, but there was a harsh, cheap edge to it. He stared at the slowly expanding puddle of oil and nodded silently.

"Parker," said Belleville. "Go tell them to bring the trunks in. Use the back door."

David watched Parker's shoes until the door had closed behind him. Trunks? What would they need—?

"So sorry, David."

He looked up, shocked. Belleville's eyes had warmed up a bit. "Sorry?"

Belleville leaned against the door with his arms crossed. "For Parker. He was a bit harsh with you, I think."

David wasn't foolish enough to believe that interpretation, but he was so grateful to hear the calmer cadence in Belleville's voice that he couldn't imagine trying to argue with it.

"It's fine." He took a shuddering breath. "My lord, may I ask a question?"

Belleville sighed. "I suppose, poppet."

"Why do we need trunks?"

"Was I somehow unclear about the need to remove evidence?"

"What about next weekend? Can I put the club back together once this raid is behind us?"

He put his fingers to the bridge of his nose. "Look. This is a complex situation. I don't think there's time to get into the details just yet—"

"Forgive me, but I have a feeling you're not telling me something."

Belleville looked harsh for a moment—frightened, even?—but the expression softened before David could make sense of it. "As I said, poppet. It's complicated."

Complicated. Of course. That was the name of the game with Lord Henry Belleville, after all. Over the long, *complicated* years of their acquaintance, David had been everywhere from this man's bedchambers to his club parlors to his payroll; called everything from precious to pathetic, proprietor to *poppet.* With their prior dynamics pruned, save for owner and manager of The Curious Fox, David had hoped that things might be simpler. And they were, sort of, during the day-to-day running of the place.

But on occasions like tonight, just the two of them, David felt the desperate young man he'd once been try to break free and start begging the baron for more information. More safety. More poppets.

Complicated indeed.

"So. I'm to just…" David paused, touching the lace of Noah's dress again, rough and blue and lilac-smelling enough to keep him grounded in the present. He would ask the question, but he would keep his voice even. He would not let that frantic feeling claw its way to the surface. "I'm to pack all the decorations up in trunks."

"We'll have it all brought to your house in the morning for safekeeping."

"What if they come tonight?"

"They won't." He came closer and stroked David's hair. The touch felt like a cockroach crawling in his coat sleeve, but David tried not to let that show. "I know this seems a bit intense, but it's serious. I just don't want to see you get caught up in something you can't get out of." He ran his thumb along the hairline a few times. "Let's talk more tomorrow. Join me for luncheon. I'll tell you everything then."

David didn't like the sound of that. As proprietor, he deserved to know the details now. But Belleville's temper had finally cooled; David wouldn't push his luck just because his own temper was flaring. He had a furious feeling in the pit of his stomach that he didn't have much luck to spare.

"Now, you'd best get to work," said Belleville. "I'd hate to think of you here alone terribly late. You ought to make quick work of it, and go home to get some rest." He nudged the broken bottle with his toe. "Start with this before it ruins more of the floor, would you?"

Lord Belleville turned and left. His footsteps vanished in the direction of the back exit.

David bent down and scooped up the slippery bottle. Belleville's words and snide refusal to pick it up himself festered like fever in the pit of David's stomach. Fuming and alone, he pretended like he was going to throw it against the closed door, but he didn't actually let go. He just squeezed it too tight. It crunched in his fist until a stab of pain made him drop it.

Damn it. A nasty little sliver of amber glass had lodged itself into his palm. In a cloud of flowery fumes, he managed to get a cloth out of the other bedside drawer and leaned his elbows on the vanity. He got as much of the oil off his shaky hands as he could, but his fingers were still too slick to get hold of the splinter.

Fuck it. It wasn't bleeding much anyway. He decided to focus on the rest of the mess. His lordship was right. There'd be no saving those inches of wooden floor. Trying not to let his despair about the whole situation attach itself to the stain, he wiped up what he could and adjusted the bedside rug to cover the rest. He put the other bottles away, and when that was done, he started hanging up Noah's things. He put the strand of pearls around his neck for safekeeping and was very careful not to get any oil or blood on anything.

Once the actual mess was cleaned, he looked around at the objects of Belleville's complaint—the birches, the fine fabrics, the pretty Greek painting above the mantel. He couldn't bring himself to start on that, so he lay down on the bed. Maybe he could just lock himself in and stay here until the rozzers came and dragged him out. The club was stunning. At the moment, he felt more loath to ruin all his work than he did to be punished for it.

He threw his arm over his eyes, ignoring the throbbing in his palm. Down the hall, he could still hear knocks and bumps as someone brought trunks in the back door, likely leaving them stacked in the dark landing near the stairs, empty and waiting to eat up almost five years of his care and creativity.

Once those sounds ceased and he knew his lordship and the rest had left, he sat up, running his fingers over Noah's pretty little pearls. With the baron gone at last, David's mind relaxed enough to realize he already knew what was happening. He was no genius, but he wasn't as stupid as Mr. Parker thought he was. This wasn't the first tip-off they'd received, but it was the first time he'd had to send the decor clear out to another location in response.

Lord Belleville had no intention of reopening the doors next week. David knew that sure as he'd ever known anything.

David returned to the front parlor. At first, he thought it was empty, but after a moment, he spotted a stream of smoke rising from behind the bar.

"You can come out." He sighed. "They're gone."

Noah and Warren popped up like the world's strangest jack-in-the-box: a glittering rake who looked fully prepared to stab someone and a slim, powdery ghost with a lit cigarette between his smudgy red lips. David couldn't help but laugh.

"What's so funny?" Warren demanded. He took the vogue out of Noah's mouth and took a deep pull on it. "Bloody hell, what did they want?"

David groaned and leaned on the bar. "There's going to be a raid this weekend."

"A raid?" Warren repeated. "*Now?*"

"Yeah." Suddenly exhausted, he slipped the pearls off his neck and returned them to Noah, pooling them in his friend's paint-stained palm. "We're closing for the weekend, like we've done before, but this time, he wants me to 'clean the place up.'"

"Clean it up?"

"Pack all the questionable decor in trunks to have it sent to my house in the morning."

Noah looked a little lost. "You don't usually do that, do you?"

David shook his head. "Never. The bobbies take things sometimes, yeah, but there's nothing in here that we can't afford to lose, and certainly not much that serves as real evidence. I've already got a whole routine for this kind of thing, but there's nothing illegal about some art and velvet. Dismantling the place has never been part of the process."

"Are we shutting down for longer than a week, then?" Warren asked.

"I have no idea. He said we'll talk tomorrow."

"Why not tonight?"

"Because he can't very well talk on my turf, can he?" David snapped, bolting upright and beginning to pace. "Got to get me to his place, where there's servants everywhere, and his wife is home, and I can't make a fuss."

"Davy," said Noah gently.

"I know. I know, I'm sorry." He ran both hands through his hair. "It's just always bloody like this. Always." He sighed out a breath, trying to get hold of the roiling fear and anger that threatened to overflow. "Anyway. The two of you ought to go home. He wants me to handle it myself."

"I'll stay," Warren offered.

"No." David shook his head firmly. "Please. I'm in enough trouble as it is."

"For what?"

"Letting blokes in early. Keeping drag in the big room. *Mollying* the bloody *molly* bar up too much for his lordship's *masculine sensibilities.*" He squeezed his hand into a fist, a sharp stab reminding him too late that he still had a shard of glass stuck in it.

There was a tapping from across the parlor. The patterned knock. A few extra flourishes meant it was Charlie Price, who had long ago smiled his way to the illicit honor of early admission. Probably his lover Miles too, a quiet fellow who preferred to arrive while the crowd was sparse.

Well fuck. He supposed it was time to start this game, then, wasn't it? Turning everyone away as they arrived, watching their faces go green at the word *raid*, gritting his teeth through his inability to answer any questions about when they'd be opening again. First Charlie and Miles. Then some of the others who came in early to change. Then the pianist, of course, the doorman, the serving lads, all out their tips and maybe their wages for who knew how long...

David started for the door, but Warren steered him back to the bar. "You sit."

"I've got it," David snapped.

"Not a chance. This is Charlie Price we're talking about. That bugger talked you into free drinks for a damn year. Christ, he even talked himself into the *sapphists' place.* You think *you* of all people can turn him away, just like that? Let me handle it; I'm the only one who's immune." Warren raised an eyebrow at one of the paintings. "Unless you want to give in and turn this into a going-away party for Apollo and the rest."

It was tempting, but he resisted. "No. Go get drunk with them. Pick somewhere safe, yeah, mate? I don't know who else might be on the rozzers' list this weekend." David sat heavily, put his head on the bar, and pulled a few shillings out of his pocket. He slid them blindly down the bar toward Warren. "Let's meet back here on Sunday evening. Whatever's going to happen should have happened by then, and we can work out what comes next."

Warren put the bills in his waistcoat pocket. "Will do, guv." He kissed David on the head and rubbed his back. "Coming, Penny?"

"Like this?" Noah's laugh was laced with anxiety. "My face is unfit for polite—or even impolite—society. I'm going to clean up before I go anywhere. Give Charlie a kiss for me. Two for Miles."

David listened with his eyes closed to the sound of Warren gathering his things, taking a quick shot of whiskey for fortification, and leaving through the layers of bells.

Once he was gone, he felt a sweet hand stroke his hair. It was a small touch, familiar, friendly, and soft. The sensation tingled gently down David's spine, relaxing the edges of him as he got a good, deep breath for what felt like the first time in ages.

"Davy?" said Noah.

"Hmm?"

"We aren't going to jail, are we?"

David sat straight up, the moment of respite popping like a balloon as *jail* stabbed nearly as sharp as *raid* had earlier. "Stop saying things like that."

"I'm serious." And he looked it, in spite of the uneven eye makeup and the bloody-looking smudge of paint near his mouth. "What if—?"

"*We* aren't going anywhere." He poked at the pearls that

Noah had wound around his wrist. "*You* should get ready to join the others, though. I've got a lot to do."

Noah pulled a face. "Is he coming back tonight? Lord, um, Ownerballs, or whatever you call him?"

"I doubt it. I'm surprised he even came in the first place. He usually meets me at The Hydrangea—his proper club— or sends Mr. Parker."

"Then I'll stay and help you."

David shook his head. "No."

"Why not?"

"Because I can handle it. And, you know, just in case someone does come tonight, I'd rather... Noah, what are you doing?"

He had turned his back and gone over to the liquor, pulling things down. "Getting out what you need to make me another drink. Go put the kettle on. I want a toddy."

"Noah."

"Just one. *Per favore?*" He batted his eyelashes, looking ridiculous and too charming to be believed.

"This isn't fair," David complained. "I've already sent Warren off. I'm undefended against this sort of begging now."

Noah produced two mugs, a most tempting implication.

David sighed and got up. "Just one. And then I really do need to get to it."

He went to the kitchen and got the water heated, then came back to mix the highly particular gin toddy that had been the first instance of liquor that Noah managed to swallow, two types of gin, some sugar, and enough lemon juice to melt a hole in a reasonable human's stomach. Once he finished, he passed one steaming mug to Noah. While David had been busy with the drinks, Noah had settled himself crisscross on top of the bar and pared down comfortably to his perfectly fitted flowery waistcoat and lace-trimmed shirtsleeves.

Noah accepted the drink and lifted it. "To the health benefits."

"To the health benefits," said David, the ancient in-joke springing to both their lips automatically.

David usually preferred his own feet on the floor, but it was an exceptionally stressful evening; he hopped up on the bar too, though he did not go so far as to tuck his feet up under him. They sipped the first hot drops of their toddies in companionable silence.

"Thank you, *amore*," Noah whispered. "You're the only one who gets this just right."

David liked hearing that, though he couldn't quite say the same for the tart drink. He set his own aside, then looked sideways at Noah, who slumped a bit in that quaint posture only a sprite like him could manage.

"Are you really going to be alright?" He looked sharply at David. "You don't think the owner's in trouble do you? Trouble that might find its way to you?"

Trouble? A little twinge in the pit of his stomach told him Noah had a point...but no. While he and the baron were not as close as they used to be (and thank God for that), he'd still have been clearer if the cops were closing in. David glanced around at his beloved club, all pink and purple, gold and glimmering. Belleville was right. The trouble was David, dressing up the club and flouting its rules like he owned the place himself.

"I just need to get this place beyond reproach," he said. "That's all. It will work out if I do that. I'm sure of it."

Noah started tracing the pinstripes on David's trousers with a light fingertip. It felt very nice. "You should let me help you."

David tousled a hand through his own hair. "It's just going to be depressing."

"All the more reason to have some help." He traced another

pinstripe, pocket to knee. "What sort of friend would I be if I couldn't stick around for the depressing bits?"

An old resentment popped out of nowhere, like it had been lingering in the marrow of David's bones for the words that could set it free again. While he didn't think of it much anymore, Noah had *not* always stuck around for the depressing bits, spending some of them so far away that weeks could pass between the penning and receiving of a letter, no matter how urgent the subject.

Not that David had any business brooding over that *now*. Noah had come back when it mattered most. He was older and better too, offering to help with the club and continuing on with this pinstripe-tracing thing that was so pleasant and shivery and frankly a bit possessive in a way that...

"Anyway," David said, shifting on the bar and going for his drink with the wrong hand to disrupt the whole business before *another* outdated feeling could come back to haunt him. He grimaced through a sip of the awful toddy. He was drinking it too fast, but it was too sour to take down any other way and he needed something to help get his head back on straight. "I'm sorry that tonight went sideways like this. I had, um, a few ideas of who to set you up with." Yes. Setting him up. That had been the goal. "Looks like that wasn't in the cards, eh?"

"Oh, stop it." Noah turned adorably pink under his powder. "You've got much more important things to think about than my—"

"Poor, neglected cock?"

"David!" He shoved him with a shoulder, but sort of stayed there, leaning in.

"You're right." David put an arm around Noah, knowing that a casual touch mixed with a bawdy joke was just the thing to dispel any inconvenient feeling. "I'm sorry. I'll never concern myself with your poor, neglected cock again. Promise."

With a little huff, Noah rested his head on David's chest. "*Grazie*."

A sudden jolt of pain shot through his palm as Noah grabbed his hand and gaped at the glass still wedged into his skin. "Davy! What is this?"

David snatched his hand back warily, peering at the dried blood. "Bit of glass."

"How long's it been there?"

"Bottle of oil broke in the bedroom."

Noah looked extremely skeptical. "How, exactly?"

"Accident."

"What sort of accident?" Noah stared while he tried to figure out exactly how to explain it. When he failed, Noah slipped down off the bar, shaking his head. "I don't think I like him. The owner."

David had hoped that Noah would never need to have an opinion of Lord Belleville. "He's under a lot of stress, I think."

"Hmm." Very huffy, he snatched down a bottle of the cheapest gin in the place, something he'd normally never touch. He brought it back with a few of Warren's bar towels. "Well, let's get that thing out, then."

David sucked a sharp breath in through his teeth as Noah used his calloused, steady fingers to try to get hold of the splinter. It was lodged in deep. Shame mingled with sharp pain as Noah's overworked fingers started to redden. "Stop," David said. "You don't have to do this—*shit*!"

He grunted as Noah, with a perfectly calm countenance, gripped him tight and dug in until he got the glass between his nails.

"It's alright. Just hold still," Noah murmured as he dragged the damn thing out. Some of the tight, throbbing pain went with it.

He put the little amber dagger down on the bar and mopped the streaks of blood pooling in David's palm, applying pressure to the center. He was gentle, but so steady and straightforward that it suddenly seemed a wonder he had not followed his father into medicine. A rush of pure affection blossomed through David's chest. Noah's head was bowed, so David leaned in and kissed the top of it, his senses filled with the smell of lilacs, tobacco, and talc.

Noah looked up, a curious expression on his face. Damn, had David lingered longer than was natural in the kiss? Before he could draw breath to joke the awkwardness away, Noah handed him the cloth, indicating that he should keep up the pressure, and kissed David back sweetly on the cheek. He certainly did not linger, but the heat he left behind him did, staying warm even as Noah turned to clean himself up and pop the cork out of the bottle of swill.

"What a way to celebrate," David said, throat trying to constrict around the quip he was sure could save him from this overwrought reaction to a normal interaction. "I think I'd prefer...literally anything but that."

The acrid scent of the alcohol cut the air as Noah poured it on the clean towel. "I'm not drinking it. I'm keeping you from getting a fever. Now hold still."

He grabbed David's hand suspiciously tight, then dabbed the gin-soaked bar towel over the gash. All stress-induced amorousness vanished as the stuff burned David's skin like a beesting in the depths of hell.

David yelped and tried to pull back. "Are you mad? That's *gin*."

"Of course it's gin." Noah looked amused at the sheer horror that must have shown on David's face. "Davy, please tell me you know what I'm doing."

"I know that fucking *hurts*."

"It kills the microorganisms."

"The *what*?"

"It gets you cleaner than water. You should do this if you get cut. Especially if you cut yourself on something you found in a private room bedside drawer." Looking satisfied with his sadistic ministrations, he took David's handkerchief from his pocket, folded it up, and put it in the center of his palm. He used a comically fine little square from his own waistcoat to tie it off. "Did you not know that? About the liquor? It keeps wounds from turning."

David peered at the bottle. "Are you trying to tell me this stuff has health benefits after all?"

"I suppose I am." Noah chuckled and blushed a little. "It was well-proven in the seventies. Papa's been having Emily and I do that for ages; I can't believe you didn't know."

"Well, your father hasn't spoken to me in ages, has he?" muttered David, examining the wrapping. "Anyway, thank you. You don't have to take care of me like that, but I do appreciate it."

Noah shook his head affectionately, dabbing at a red spot that had splashed onto one of David's pinstripes. "Cold water on this. Don't forget."

"*I* will definitely forget, but my new valet is good about all that."

"That's right," Noah said with dramatic, almost Penelope-ish enthusiasm. "Forgot about your new valet. That pretty thing that walked out of one of these paintings and into your employment."

"Stop it, he was qualified."

"And how is our little Hyacinthus getting on?"

"Oh. Well enough."

Noah snorted. "You hate him, don't you?"

David rolled his eyes, giving in to the sigh of frustration he'd held back since he hired the chap. "He hardly speaks! It makes me feel like I'm one of your tailor's dummies. Pretty or not, if I'm going to wake up to the same face every morning, I'd like him to at least be able to chat about the weather."

"Sounds like you need a lover, Davy. Not a valet." He smiled up, way up, since David was on the bar and he was on the ground. Finished cleaning, his hands rested on David's wool-covered thighs. His eyes had gone mischievous. Set against the mess of half-done makeup, he looked almost elfin. "Tell me. When's the last time you had a really riveting...*conversation about the weather*? You seem awfully concerned with who's taking care of me, but who's taking care of you these days?"

David wrinkled his nose and tried to brush the question off, but Noah dug his fingers in and literally stopped blinking until David couldn't resist his intensity. "No one."

"No one?"

"No one important." It didn't come out as casual as he'd hoped. "Well, it's like Warren said, isn't it? No better place to discuss the weather than the park."

Obvious disapproval pursed Noah's lips even as he clearly tried to fight it. "Interesting choice for the man who's always warning the rest of us about the forecast of entrappers and syphilis over there. I do hope you remember to bring your umbrella."

"What would you have me do instead?"

"Hmm. Let's think." Noah came in close enough that David had to open his knees a little to make room as Noah walked his fingers nearly to David's pockets. His body was a bit languid, like he'd drunk more than he actually had. "If only someone, somewhere had poured years of his life and energy into a...

oh, I don't know, *a gentleman's club* of some sort where chaps seeking that sort of company could safely—"

David put a finger to Noah's lips, dodging a second before he got nipped but successfully cutting the idea short nonetheless. "Taking up with my patrons is too complicated and twice as likely to end badly than an occasional trip to the cottages. Trust me."

Noah lifted a skeptical brow. "Occasional?"

David felt his face burning as the tips of Noah's fingers traced the edges of his pockets. They'd known each other so terribly long, and now lived in a world where tickling flirtations like this were about as normal as a handshake. But it hit David strangely after everyone's insinuations. "Considering you function on a quarterly schedule at best," he said carefully, "I'm not quite sure how to answer that question in a way that's meaningful to both of us."

"Davy…" Noah's voice trailed off as he went on tracing the openings of David's pockets, threatening to dip his fingers inside but never quite doing it. "Davy, do you ever think about… Um. What I mean to say is that when we used to get lonely, we would, er…" He cut himself off, giggling a bit. "Sorry. I'm drunk."

Drunk? No. Tipsy, perhaps, but unless the fumes from the swill were really that pungent there was no way Noah was fully drunk on what he'd had tonight. His temperance-inclined family might have bought the act, but David had worked a bar long enough to know an excuse when he saw one.

The notion of what he might be trying to excuse sped David's heart up. Could Warren's teasing suggestion have gotten Noah's genuine attention? Noah never wanted to talk about the years they'd spent, in school and a few years after, supplementing their friendship with hurried hand jobs and snogging sessions that they'd barely understood the meaning of back then and had never found occasion to discuss once Noah left for Italy. But what he'd just said…it sounded an awful like he might be suggesting…

"We would what, Noah?" David coaxed, the words rasping in an unexpectedly husky sort of way that surprised them both.

It startled Noah out of whatever had possessed him a moment before. He stepped back, leaving a cold tingle in all the places he'd been touching, smiling so perfectly it might have been painted on.

"Why," he said quickly, almost panicked, "we…we used to plan your inevitable wedding! You always did want to get married. If you need more than the occasional company, you could always find some terribly wanton widow. You're doing better for yourself financially than you were when you swore off matrimony."

"*Married*?" David was so utterly shocked that he was laughing before he could be disappointed. "Are you mad?"

"You're inclined to women when the situation is right."

"The situation being right would include a woman being inclined to *me*." It was so completely ridiculous that David couldn't seem to stop chuckling. He'd lost his reputation, his family, every hope of a normal future a very long time ago. He was just glad that living as a sodomite suited him so well, the alternatives having been celibacy or mouths he couldn't feed. "My God, Noah. You cannot possibly think I'm husband material these days."

"Well, I don't know. Let's see." He smacked the side of David's leg, suddenly not just sober, but borderline *caffeinated*. "Stand up and let me get a good look at you."

David got down from the bar, chuckling in spite of himself as Noah put a finger to his own chin and appraised him. Though he'd never managed to get into his drags, a quick change of posture and expression did more to transform him than any number of petticoats. "Hmm. Turn around. Back again. Quite appealing, I think. Healthful." He pursed his lips shrewdly and widened his eyes. "But are you able to provide?"

"In this business?" He grinned, unable to keep from going along with the game. "I should think that my wife—and all of my lovers—will be perfectly comfortable."

"Fair enough." Noah reached out a hand, uncovered by black satin, but perfectly posed nonetheless. "Can you dance? Debutantes absolutely require that, you know."

David took Noah's fingers and twirled him under his arm before pulling him back in to put a hand on his waist. "I think the steps would come back if I got started."

For a second it seemed they might put that to the test, as Noah flashed a smile so charming and coy that one might think he'd come straight from some finishing school. But instead of dancing, he pretended to swoon, falling against David's chest as David wrapped arms around him to keep him upright. "Goodness. Well, in that case," Noah whimpered dramatically, "all that's left is your ability to produce a pack of strapping boys."

"That's part of marriage?"

"The most important part."

"Well, what do you know? They say that's my specialty."

"Splendid!" said Noah with another irresistible grin. "Call the parson, we'll wed on Sunday!"

"Sunday it is."

And then David leaned down, put a hand behind his stunning, brilliant, hilarious friend's head, and kissed him.

It was a lark. Of course it was a lark. Of course it had everything to do with the fact that a peck on the lips was nothing between them or any of their friends. A joke, a tease, and well within the rules of the game they were playing. But when David pulled back, he found shock on Noah's parted lips.

David's heart skipped a nervous beat. He stood Noah up out of the fake swoon, balanced on his own feet. "I'm sorry," he said. "I didn't—"

Noah grabbed him by the shoulders, giving a wild sort of look that was not drunk and was not joking. With no warning, he pulled David in for another kiss, harder, longer, and not a lark at all.

What the hell was happening? His mind didn't know, but his body seemed to. He pulled Noah close and slid a hand into his hair before he'd even decided to, as more years than he cared to count evaporated in an instant. Good God, who had he been kidding? No lingering feelings for Noah? Bullshit. He'd fooled no one but himself, and even that deception was so flimsy that the mere flicker of Noah's tongue against his lips reduced it to rubble.

He grasped tighter and kissed harder, fingers flexing against a silky brocade vest to prove to himself that the solid warmth of Noah's body beneath it was real. They fell without effort into a messy rhythm David had thought was still buried under the lilac bush, and that frantic, familiar caress of Noah's mouth felt so good that David's cock decided he'd become a teenager again, stiffening so fast that it would have been embarrassing if Noah weren't so obviously in the same boat.

Having spent a good deal of his adolescence trying to get his hands into Noah's trousers before anyone could catch them at it, his fingers itched with the old habit to slide across Noah's lower belly in search of his fastenings. David felt Noah draw in a sharp, enticing breath as he gave in to the impulse, groping for a button that wasn't quite where he'd expected it to be—

A knock on the door hit them like a crack of thunder. They

jumped apart, wide-eyed and frozen like they were about to get one hell of a switching.

But of course that was absurd. *Goddammit.* David scrubbed his face with his hands, which were tingling in protest of the interruption. Some patrons were here, the first of many who would need to be turned away tonight. They weren't in trouble. They weren't caught. Yet somehow, this felt worse. *Fuck*, David loved his patrons, but right now he hated these ones like he couldn't remember ever hating any of them. Oh, they all had their nights of sloppy drunkenness or drama, but *this*? Unforgivable.

"I'll be right back," he said, trying to keep the bitterness out of his voice.

Considering how certain he was that the moment was ruined, he was shocked when Noah grabbed him by the front of his coat. God, Noah's lips, parted and messy with makeup, called to David like a sweet he'd had snatched away before he was finished. Neither of them spoke for long enough that the patterned knock came again, louder and impatient.

"What do you want me to do, Noah?" David asked in a desperate whisper, fighting the temptation to drop to his knees, locate the misplaced trouser buttons, and pretend he could not hear the knocks at all.

"Just tell them to go home," Noah whispered, more rational than the fantasies racing through David's head. "Then put a note on the door, saying you're closed. Everyone else will fill the details in, and you can call on the staff tomorrow."

"Noah—" David faltered as he put a hand on Noah's where it still clutched his clothes. "When they leave, are we...? What exactly are we doing?"

Noah made his eyes wide, his voice deliberate and full of sly, secret meaning that David hadn't heard in years. "I'm helping you clean up the club, David," he said. "Why don't I go see about the trunks? They're stacked by the back door, aren't they?"

Just as David's fingers had grasped for a particular button, Noah grabbed hold of a tidy excuse, each following the rules of a game they apparently hadn't forgotten.

"They're in the stairwell," David said, playing along. "It's dark back there. So. Be careful not to, you know."

"Trip on anything," Noah said.

"Yes."

The feeling of disconnection when they finally parted was almost painful. David felt every inch of distance as he went for the front and Noah turned toward the back.

Meet me at the pond, the ducklings have hatched.

Second-floor broom cupboard, I left my sketchbook up there.

The dorm is empty, now, right now. Perfect for studying, don't you agree?

David took care of his duties in a daze. Then followed the irresistible pull back to the one match he'd never dreamed of making in this place.

Chapter Six

Noah

Noah wandered to the back with his heart going like one of those noisy Singer machines. He passed through the door, then the rows of pulled-back curtains, past all the bedrooms on either side of the dark hallway. He peeked into the big one. It reeked of that perfumed oil that was clinging to David's clothes, but there was no sign of whatever trouble had led to David's splinter. Even Noah's things had been put away. He resisted the urge to make sure David had hung things up correctly, and a second urge to wash the mess of makeup off his face. If he stopped now, to do anything, he might come most unfortunately to his senses.

He went downstairs to find trunks stacked in the tiny entranceway, half-blocking the door. Very dark down here. All shadows and a single sconce. He found a stray trunk to perch on. It had not happened like this for years and years. But it had certainly happened enough back then that Noah knew what he was supposed to do now.

Vaguely sick with anticipation and arousal, he *waited*.

Just as he was starting to worry (*Think!* Not worry, nothing to worry about) that David had changed his mind (which would be *fine*), the footsteps finally came.

"Noah?"

"Over here."

He lit his torch to light the way, then grasped the hand David offered, standing and letting himself be pulled into the cold, damp, pitch-dark space under the staircase. David wasted no time pressing him gently against the cool wall and leaned in just the same as he always used to, nuzzling into the sensitive spot just under Noah's ear.

"I see you found the trunks," he whispered, breath shivering against Noah's skin and fingers digging into his hips a little tighter and lower than he'd have dared at fifteen.

Noah closed his eyes and tipped his head back against the wall as the whispers became little kisses that trailed lightly along his jaw. Oh God, if they were really going to do this again, after all these years, they could have gone into one of the rooms. Why had he made David come down here? They didn't need to meet up in a *stairwell*. They were fully grown for goodness' sake, a fact distractingly apparent as Noah slid his hands up broader shoulders than his memory had mapped out.

"Yes, I found them," Noah whispered, trying not to completely lose his head at the feeling of David's face in the crook of his neck, soft lips and rough beard that sent shocks of ticklish sweetness straight to his groin. "Were the blokes at the door alright?"

"I think so."

Noah twined his arms around David's neck and pulled him closer. David was still taller, but not by as much, so when Noah leaned up and David stooped just a bit, they lined up perfectly from the pleasurable press of their ready cocks, up past clicking waistcoat buttons and racing hearts, to the suffocating crush of neckcloths, and finally the sweet warmth of noses and foreheads touching as their gin-tinged breath dared them to close the little gap that remained between their mouths.

"Davy."

"Shh." The gentle hush tickled Noah's lips for just a second before David tipped his head to the side and pressed him with a kiss so comforting and soft that it was like sliding into a warmed featherbed.

If Noah were a better friend, he'd resist this regression. David needed a strong drink and a hand with the cleanup, not a stairwell snogging session with his silly old schoolmate. But David didn't exactly kiss like a schoolmate anymore. A few seconds of his tongue skating expertly over Noah's lips again and he was done for, opening up and letting whatever had been building all evening wash over him at last.

These foolish kisses felt better than anything Noah could remember. They felt like coming home to find everything had been stunningly redecorated, all the things he loved most polished and properly displayed at last. David still tasted and felt like *David*—like the first person he'd ever kissed and had probably clocked the most hours with, all told—but the fumbling ferocity Noah remembered had mellowed into something deliberate and achingly sensual. He alternated shallow and teasing with deep and delicious until Noah was at once resentful that he'd missed whatever had happened in the interim, and yet painfully grateful to whatever had turned the awkward David Forester into the best kisser on the planet.

David put both hands on the sides of his face and pulled him in even tighter, tight as he could, shoving his thigh between Noah's legs and moaning into his mouth. Noah couldn't resist pushing into the hot friction David offered, suddenly feeling like he'd gone back in time in more ways than one as he shamelessly rocked against David's leg. It was so incredibly *stupid*, but Noah couldn't make himself care as the sweet rasps of pleasure built up between them more quickly than they should have. Hands roving, hips grinding, more rhythm, less control, until Noah was panting and squirming and oh God, if they kept going like this he was going to embarrass himself, and soon…

"Noah."

The amused breath in his ear made him drag his nails down David's shoulders. "Hmm?"

David swept a tongue around his earring like the pearl was a piece of candy. "Are you going to spend?"

"Oh *God*." That tongue was going to spoil the integrity of its own question.

"You are, aren't you?"

"If I do, it's your fault." He leaned his head back as David rumbled with laughter.

"My fault?" said David, half-chuckle, half-growl as he somehow crushed Noah even tighter against the cold wall of the stairwell. Far from disrupting the moment, the innocent playfulness got both of them breathing harder and clutching tighter, David pulsing his hips in a familiar, regular tempo against Noah. "I didn't ask you to go months without any trade, mate. That was…mmm, fuck—" He bit the curve under Noah's jaw. "That was your choice."

"God, please. Please, don't," Noah gasped, clawing at David's shoulders and trying desperately to remain on this side of insanity. "I don't have any other clothes here except frocks."

David just kept rubbing up against him, his eyes reflecting the dim light of the sconce with an evil sort of mischief. "So just mop yourself up a bit and—"

"David Forester, do not spoil these trousers. Do you have *any* idea of their quality?"

"Oh, alright."

Noah breathed deeply, trying to get ahold of himself as David took a step back. His body screamed in frustration, but his brain fought back. This was the sane maneuver. The right thing to do. If they'd gone on like that, he wouldn't have been—

Oh. *God.*

"Davy! What are you doing?"

"What do you think?" This time, David really did growl, a low, rough sound that Noah had never heard come out of him before. "I'm getting these quality trousers out of the way."

Before Noah could wrap his head around that, David had unbuttoned his falls and unlaced his drawers. He reached in and put a firm hand around Noah's cock, freeing it confidently from the folds of fabric like they still did this all the time. The direct contact was shockingly intense after all that unfocused rutting, David's quick, sure strokes startling his crisis a few steps out of reach and promising a higher peak than the one he'd been teetering on.

Ciao, brief sanity; it was gone for good this time. Noah attacked David's buttons, shoving his hand desperately into the pinstriped wool to grasp his eager prick, aware of nothing but need and heat and habit. David choked out a shocked groan as Noah started tugging on him, fast and hard like they used to do back when they didn't know what they were doing or how much time they had to do it in. David sped up too, and the stairwell filled with the sounds of their frantic stroking, their muffled moans, the obscene rattle of the pearls on Noah's wrist…

David gave an unexpected little twist with his hand and suddenly Noah was coming so hard that stars flashed behind his eyelids. David gasped in surprised pleasure as Noah's spend made his next strokes extra-slick, prick pulsing as he came to a crisis that shook his whole body. For a precious few seconds, everything in the whole world became wet and warm and perfect.

And then Noah kept his eyes shut and tried not to move, because when he moved, it would be over, and when it was over, he would cry. He wasn't sure why he'd cry, but he was suddenly very certain that he would.

David recovered first. He released Noah with a sweet laugh and an amused curse that chased the threat of tears away and instead lit a little light in Noah's belly.

Laughter. Yes. Laughter was a good thing. It meant this wasn't as serious as it had felt for a moment there. Nothing to worry about; just a release of tension between particularly tense friends. Like the old days. It hadn't ruined them then, and wouldn't ruin them now.

Instead of crying, Noah found himself groaning dramatically. "We're a complete disgrace, aren't we?"

"Don't fret." David's voice was a little winded, but cheerful. "My trousers are most definitely spoiled, but I saved yours from the worst of it."

Noah couldn't help it. He laughed so hard that he full-on snorted, and then they were both such a mess with a mad fit of giggles that it was a wonder they ever made it upstairs to get themselves put back together.

Once again, they were lucky that Warren had expected to be open tonight. Between the two of them, they'd managed to get up to a lot of trouble that required bar towels.

"Well, there you have it, beautiful. It's not quite the match I was planning on, but I did keep my promise to take care of you tonight." David dabbed at his own waistcoat up near the shoulder, looking impressed. "You really do need to get up to trouble more often, you know."

Noah glared at him. While his own clothes had been mostly spared, there were other casualties. "You got some in my pearls, you monster. I don't want to hear you complain."

"Let me see."

"It got between the beads here, look. I can't get it."

David took Noah's wrist and pulled the offended pearls into his mouth. He sucked on them for a moment, closing his eyes and licking his lips when he was done. "Mmm. There you go. All clean."

Noah swatted his chest, a naughty thrill running through him. "You ought to buy me a new set."

"A new set?" David laughed. "Mate, your pearls are going to have to get up to worse mischief than that if you want a whole new set."

"*David!*"

This sort of buoyant vulgarity suited David very well, and Noah couldn't keep a stupid smile off his face as he watched his friend bundle up their scandalous mess. As he brought it to the washing basket in the back, he licked another speck off the side of his hand in a casual way that Noah suspected he'd remember in his own bed one of these nights. God, when exactly had David gotten so *sensual*? A few years working a club like this had obviously had their effect on him. By the time he returned from the back (in a different pair of trousers), Noah had *reconsidered* the highlights of the evening extensively enough that he was just about ready for another go.

David, on the other hand, had deflated a little, his blushing levity replaced with the beginnings of awkwardness. He came back around the bar and poured himself a little of that gin that was really only fit for antiseptic. He shot it back straight, then faced the beautiful parlor with his jaw set like he was surveying an opponent.

Poor thing. Their distraction had been lovely, but in the end, that's all it had been: a distraction. And that was… That was *fine* with Noah, of course, but it felt very bad to know that all the same troubles would still be waiting for David when it was really and truly over.

Noah hesitated. Maybe they could extend this respite a little. For David's sake. He wrapped his arms around David's waist from behind. He rested his head on a linen-covered shoulder, overtaken by the scent of sex and sweat and melting pomade. They were both horrible; they were sticky and disastrous. Noah wouldn't have let either one of them at his card table in this state. But there were no cards tonight, anyway. No one to be presentable for.

While the prospect of dismantling the club was a grim one, there was something appealing about it. All this warmth and affection… He couldn't think of a better way to express it than to help see David through this.

"Shall we—?"

But David cut him off. "Well, beautiful, I suppose it's time to get you home."

The cozy bubble around them burst in a stab of unexpected pain. Noah flared upright. "Excuse me?"

David turned around, bewildered. "Do you want me to come along for the walk?"

"Who said I'm going home?"

"I have to get the place cleaned up."

"I'll help you."

"I don't need help." David tried to smooth a hair behind Noah's ear, but Noah jerked out of reach.

"Oh," he said, crossing his arms tightly. "So, it's going to be like this, is it?"

"Like what? It's not like anything. I just think you ought to go home and get some sleep, that's all."

"Some sleep. I see." Noah snatched his jacket off the barstool and hitched it over his shoulders. "I'll just be getting my things, then."

As he started for the back, he heard David sigh before following him. "Will you stop it, please?"

Noah pushed the door open and flicked one bell on each curtain as he passed beneath. "Stop what?"

"You know what."

But Noah was swept too far into the cloud to emerge from it now. If he stopped being angry, he might find something much worse underneath, so he stormed into the too-flowery bedroom with all the fury he could muster. He threw open the wardrobe and gathered up an armful of clothes—lace, silk, cotton, beads, and ribbons all in a heap—and tossed them onto the bed. Then some bonnets, boots, boxes of gloves, and pins. There was a discreet suitcase on the bottom for transporting things to and from the club. He grabbed that and opened it on top of the pile. The dresses wouldn't fit, but he started loading up the smaller things.

"Noah." David leaned in the doorway, that hair flopping back into his face. "Do you want to talk about—"

"What I want..." Noah faltered, his fingers clutching the bonnet in his hands so tight he had to make himself drop it onto the pile before he spoiled it. Did he want to talk? If he did, what on earth would he even say? Talk was very cheap, as he'd always been taught. It was actions that revealed the truth. "I want to help you clean up the club, David. That's what I want."

Based on the way David's brows went down, that wasn't the answer he'd hoped for. Before Noah could figure out how to fix his disappointment, he said, "Well. Um, let's start with your things, then. His lordship was very upset to find the stash."

Noah glanced over David's shoulder at the bed. It looked like half a dozen coquettes had spent themselves on it and melted all together into the counterpane, leaving their worldly dressings behind. He wanted to shove it all to the floor and topple David to the mattress, where their mouths might be put to better use than mere talking. Instead he said, "Hard to blame him for that, honestly. Much of it is going dreadfully out of fashion."

Trite as the joke was, it lessened the tension a bit. David gave just enough of a smile to settle Noah's heart down to a reasonable rate. "Should I have it sent to your place?" he asked. "Or will Emily wonder where it's come from?"

Noah sighed at the mention of his sister's continued presence in his home. "I'm not worried about that. I'm more concerned that she'll remember the joys that rational dress has robbed from her and steal every last ribbon. Not sure which would be worse."

"That would only be fair, I think. Considering."

"Whose side are you on?"

"Never mind. Would you like me to keep it for a few days? I can have it brought to my house with the rest and we can sort it out later."

"I'm at least living with a woman until my sister goes back home. You have no excuse for having all that stuff, and if things are bad with the club and the owner right now, I'd hate to think my drags might make it worse for you."

"Noah, look." David licked his lips, looking suddenly reluctant. "If my name and address are associated with this place, and whatever's happening results in someone searching *my house*...then it's far too late for me anyway."

A weight that had been flirting around the edges of Noah's mind all night finally crashed all the way through in a horrible thrill. David was in very deep. He could call himself a matchmaker and a proprietor and a gossipy good friend. Technically, he was those things, and plenty more, to all his grateful patrons.

Outside these walls, though, they had other words for a man like David Forester. Words like *procurer*, *conspirator*, and *bawdy-house keeper*.

"Noah?"

Noah grabbed David's hand, squeezing it as he stared at the covered bed. "Let's get it into one of the trunks, then, shall we?"

When they'd finished with the drags, he and David went for a bite to eat at another Berwick cart (Greek this time, David's preference and one of the few still open at the hour). Considering the circumstances, Noah assumed they would return to the club to finish the job, but that was dashed when David finally sent him home. He'd had some excuse for separating, something so trite that Noah hadn't been able to argue with it and couldn't even remember it now.

That was still stinging as he made his way along Piccadilly with his suitcase full of paint and baubles in one gloved hand. Summer had been slow to arrive after a chilly spring, so the weak warmth of the day had given way to a horrid, sticky chill. The street that flashed and bustled all day was quieting down, particularly as he left the main thoroughfare and dipped into his usual shortcut. He lived in a building of modern, private apartments for professionals, mostly bachelors and many of them bespoke tailors like himself, well-off enough for nice rooms reasonably near to Savile Row, but unable to afford closer lodgings in Mayfair proper.

The doorman let him in the front. With a brief tip of his hat for the fellow, Noah went down the hall to his own set of rooms. Still agitated and using half his energy staving off moody memories of David's kisses, he fumbled the lock twice before smacking the door frame a couple of times to let off a little steam. He got it right on the third go, the key turning smoothly and the bolt clunking open.

The door entered right into his small parlor, which was dimly lit by a single candle.

It was just enough to make out Emily in her nightdress with a heavy candlestick hoisted over her shoulder like a cricket bat.

She screamed. He screamed. She swung hard, and Noah ducked in a panic, his hat flying off his head as she whacked it murderously.

Carefully, he peeked up through mussed hair to see his sister staring at him, chest heaving as her face began to show the realization that she'd come about two inches from braining her own brother.

"Noah!" The candlestick fell to the ground with a horrible bang. She stood him up. "You're not supposed to be back for hours yet! What the devil were you pounding on the door for? I thought someone had broken in!"

Noah blinked rapidly, clinging to one of her arms. He was shaking a bit, staring at his hat where it had landed on the other side of the room. It had a terrible dent in the side. "Strange night," he said weakly. "Sorry to sh-shock you."

"Oh, my *heavens*!" She tossed his suitcase aside and ushered him onto the divan, moving a heap of sketches to the carpet to make space for him to sit. She lit a lamp and knelt on the cushion next to him. She examined the side of his head, lifting locks of hair as if to assure herself she had not, in fact, killed him.

"If you'd hit me with that thing, I think we'd know, Ems. It's just my poor hat that's been murdered."

Contented that he was unharmed, she sat heavily beside him. "My God, my heart is about to escape my chest." She clutched the front of her quilted dressing gown, her delicate features twisted with guilt.

"Have I killed *you*?" he asked. "You look like you're having an apoplexy."

"You don't even know what apoplexy is, you fop." She sighed and fell back against the pillows. The ribbon had come off the end of her wispy braid, which was unraveling over her shoulder. "What are you doing home, anyway? It's Friday, isn't it? What's the matter?"

Lying to her was useless, so he chose the truth. "My club's being closed for a bit."

She gasped. "Were you raided again?"

"No, no. Not yet. David got tipped off in time. Sent me home." He put away his coat and gloves, then gathered up his crinkled hat. He popped the side of it back into place, but it was still unpleasantly creased. "I hope none of the neighbor chaps do ever think to break in on you while I'm away."

"Don't change the subject." She gathered up her lost ribbon and shook it at him like a floppy schoolmarm's stick. "Awfully lucky, don't you think? Getting a warning, this time? Last time—"

"I don't want to talk about last time."

"Of course you don't. If you talked about it, you'd have to admit how stupid it is that you keep going to this place at all."

"I should never have told you. You have a real way of making a person regret their integrity."

"I'd have figured it out anyway. Only disreputable gentlemen's clubs would have you out so late all the time, and the rest is simple enough to surmise." She wiped a finger over his chin, where he must have missed a spot of powder. "It's lunacy, Noah. It really is."

He shook her off. "Complain all you want. It won't change anything. I can't be changed."

"I don't want you to change. You're perfect just as you are." She hesitated and Noah glared, silently demanding she stop and leave it at that. But no. This was Emily, after all; there'd be no stopping until she'd said all she had to say. "*You* don't need to change, but your actions can be changed," she blurted, like she'd die if she couldn't scold. "The places you stay until three in the morning can be changed. The *people* you surround yourself with can be changed."

"This again." Noah snatched his suitcase and went up the narrow stair toward his bedroom. He heard her slippered feet shuffling after him.

"You're in the prime of your life, with a real future ahead of you. You cannot keep risking everything because David Forester thinks he's invincible. I know he's been your friend forever, but—"

"He was your friend too."

"That doesn't have to blind me to what he's made of himself."

"He's done the best he could with a bloody rough go of it—"

"Plenty of people have a rough go without taking charge of a brothel."

Noah paused on the upstairs landing, taking a deep, barely controlled breath through his nose. "It's not a brothel; it's a club."

"Men pay him so they can bugger each other in his establishment."

"Every club has its amenities."

"He is a criminal, Noah."

Noah perched his hat back on his head and leaned against the bedroom door frame. When he crossed his arms, he made sure a few pearls escaped the bottom of his sleeve. "Right. Wouldn't want to be seen cavorting with criminals, would we?"

"Don't you dare; you know what I mean. He's a *professional criminal*."

"I don't care."

"You should." She shook her head and began worrying the end of her unraveling braid. "One of these nights, there's going to be no tip-off. There's going to be no escape. You are going to be arrested right alongside him, and while your employer has a high tolerance for eccentricities, that tolerance is not infinite."

Noah met her eyes furiously. "Sounds like my problem," he snapped.

"Come off it, Noey," said Emily softly. "It's well past time you do as we've been suggesting for years—"

"Stop it—"

"—and get yourself a nice fellow to spend your evenings with. Someone like you, with talent and ambition. People do it all the time. Did you ever read those pamphlets Papa gave you? It's a perfectly natural arrangement, and I think you could be very happy if only you'd do things properly instead of sneaking about in bawdy houses and playing right into the moralizers' hands."

He snatched Emily's fraying hair off her shoulder, combing the braid out with his fingers and starting over, unable to stand the feeling of his idle hands.

"You and Papa have spent too much time reading your *enlightened pamphlets*. When one of them explains how I'm supposed to find a 'nice fellow' without going somewhere like the club, perhaps I'll be more interested." When he reached the end of her hair, he held the braid together with pinched fingers and passed it off for her to hang on to until she could tie the ribbon. "Could I have a bit of peace now, please?"

"Alright, I'll leave you be. For now." She leaned in and kissed his cheek. "Sleep well, Noey."

He didn't quite resist the urge to slam his bedroom door, but he did not give it the full force.

She'd been living with him for a few months now. She did this, every so often; find a specialist willing to take her on, learn all there was to know about pharmacy or optometry or—this year—obstetrics, fingers crossed that it would be the thing to get her taken seriously as a physician in her own right. It was not easy, trying to practice formalized medicine as a woman. Noah knew that. And he was glad to be able to help her when she had to stay in London for her next desperate ploy.

Or, he would have been, if she were even slightly easier to live with for longer than a week at a time.

It wasn't that he did not get along with his sister. They'd been close growing up, and able to carry a lot of that old affection into adulthood. Aside from the obvious tragedy of their mother's death on the day of their birth, Noah knew he was fortunate to have the family he did. But their situation was naturally uncomfortable. After all, everyone had expected Noah join their father's medical practice; most fathers would never have accepted his abdication, nor Emily's—a daughter's—willingness to step into the vacated place.

While the outcome seemed positive, it still created a vague friction, a sense that all was not *quite* right with the Clarkes. The tension was particularly pronounced here, in the close quarters of rooms he was used to occupying alone.

He shook off his annoyance and set to emptying his suit-case, putting away gloves and hats and costume jewelry before it could tangle and crease. When that was taken care of, he fetched hot water from the kitchen, washed up, and changed into the nightclothes the maid always put out for him before she left for the day. While he was thinking about the maid, he locked the spare wardrobe and made certain there was nothing embarrassing for her to find on his clothes later.

Dr. Phillip Clarke had made sure that his son knew physics and biology better than any tailor ought to, and so Noah was not surprised to find that David's attempt to spare his trousers had not been entirely successful. With a heavy sigh, he took them to the washbowl and did what he could.

Noah laughed a little as he finished the task, heat rising to his face as he thought back on the feeling of David cleaning off the pearls with his mouth. God, he really could be filthy sometimes. Emily was right about one thing: he wasn't exactly a *nice fellow*. Yet honestly, could Noah have really spent a better evening with the sort of man his family would prefer? Some serious-minded politicker who spoke of their love in inscrutable German terms and medicalized role assignments? This was England, and in England, it did not matter if your evening was spent with a well-lettered lover who "prioritized Uranian companionship" or a friend who called himself a sodomite and sucked semen off pearls; it was all the same if you wound up in court.

Emily suggested a *nice fellow*, but Warren's suggestion had been better: a *casual companion*. Well, it didn't get much more casual than David Forester, did it? Part of him was tickled that they'd actually fooled around again after all these years, happy and at peace with the simplicity of choosing each other again instead of seeking out something complicated.

As he finished with the stain, though, and returned to his bed all alone, another part of him poked at a very sensitive spot behind his ribs. It was a part that still resented being sent home. A part that wondered if, perhaps, they'd been a little *too* casual about it. A part of him that still felt fifteen and thought that at the *very least* David should be in the bed next to him after a stairwell meeting like that...

No.

No, that part of him clearly needed to get some sleep.

Chapter Seven

David

David couldn't remember the last time he'd slept so badly, which was saying something. It took a long time to drift off, and when he finally did, he dreamed like he'd spent the evening breathing in dodgy opium rather than innocent cleaning supplies. Nightmares of lost keys and swinging bobby bats brought him kicking and screaming to his dreamland knees, but when he looked up, he found Noah smiling down at him in full regalia, coaxing David's head under layers of fragrant petticoats. The muddled scenes of pleasure and pain had him tossing and turning all night, until at last he sat bolt upright in bed, sweating, confused, and hard as a fucking rock.

He flopped back down into the lonely embrace of his pillows, pulling one over his head to block out the summer daylight that always came too early for his liking. What the devil had he been thinking, sending Noah home last night? David hated waking up alone in the best of circumstances. Yet here he was doing it of his own volition, in spite of Noah's arguments, because...why? He should have let Noah help him with the club. Should have brought him back here after to talk about what happened in the stairwell. Or to do it again, do more, do *everything*. Or at least wake up together this morning to linger and assess whether anything had actually changed.

What sort of idiot would send his best friend home under those circumstances?

The sort of idiot, he realized grimly, *who knew good and well how it would have gone, and couldn't deal with it.*

Because David did know how it would have gone. They wouldn't have talked about it, because Noah had never wanted to talk about it, even back when they were at school and doing it every chance they got. At first, that had bewildered David, who found talk of fancies and feelings to be a lovely escape, but Noah was different. The Clarkes were rational, action-oriented dissenters, obsessed with hard work and suspicious of pleasure. Noah rebelled against it as much as he dared, but to some extent, accepting his friendship, his affection, or his delicious kisses meant also accepting how he routed those messy things through excuses, loopholes, and even the character of Miss Penelope.

David had never been entirely sure what Noah felt for him, but whatever it was, it had never been strong enough to break the pattern. If Noah had spent the night, he wouldn't find *lingering and assessing* to be a good excuse to stay. In lieu of an excuse, he would leap out of bed so he could get to the workshop for a few hours on a damn Saturday like he always did. With all these old feelings so raw from their sudden re-emergence, the loneliness of watching Noah rush out the door would have been worse than this one, which David could, at least, say he'd chosen for himself.

Almost certain he couldn't fall back asleep and *very* certain that easing his morning tension with a wank would only make him feel worse, he sat up and rang for his valet. Matthew Shaw—*our little Hyacinthus*, as Noah had called him— gave him just enough time to get his head on straight before entering his room with a tray of tea.

"Thank you," David said as Shaw set the tray on the nightstand. The first sip of extra-sweet tea jolted him into existence. He blinked hard and laughed a little. "Damn. Strong, eh?"

As David had complained to Noah, Shaw was an attractive but relentlessly *mild* chap. He peered at his employer with mild blue eyes, cocked a mildly blondish head to the side, and said in a voice very much like warm milk, "Is that a problem, sir?"

"No, no," David insisted. "It's perfect. You're perfect. Thank you."

Shaw went about his duties, the scratch and clank of coals and tools very awkward in the absence of speech. As the tea began to reanimate David, he wanted to start gushing about last night's adventures while Shaw prepared the vanity with his handsome reflection parroting him in the mirror. Not the *stairwell part*, of course, but the rest of it. Any servant had to be extremely well-vetted before they could enter David's employment, so it wasn't as if the fellow didn't know where David went in the evenings. His previous valet had always been more personable, more apt to ask for coded versions of club gossip. But as for this pretty replacement, Noah was right; he'd accidentally chosen the fellow based on what he'd like to see in the morning, rather than who was best suited to his own habits.

Just as well, though; the cool contrast of Noah's ear and the pearl set into it was still too heavy on David's tongue for him to trust its ability to speak on any other subject anyway. He accepted a dressing gown and tried to let the quiet routine of getting ready for the day settle his nerves.

It worked fairly well until the very end, when Shaw held out his jade green morning coat.

"The green," David said, staring stupidly at the thing.

"Yes," said Shaw. "You're calling on Lord Belleville this afternoon, aren't you?"

Somehow, he'd managed to forget that fact so thoroughly

that he didn't even remember mentioning it to Shaw at all. *Meet me for luncheon tomorrow*, the baron had said. *I'll explain everything then.*

As he shrugged on the coat, he regretted his ungenerous thoughts about the valet's disposition; not only did he always keep David on top of his schedule, but could be trusted to remember details that David would rather forget. Like the colors and coats that Lord Belleville preferred to see him in, and David's consistent willingness to play along with things like that if it might win him some scrap of what he wanted.

Shaw tidied up the vanity. He fetched some breakfast along with the post, which David accepted in a chair before the fireplace. He was too stressed to eat much, though he managed to take a few bites of toast once they were coated in butter and honey.

He went through the first few letters distractedly, until he got to one from Noah. David blinked at the name, certain he must be imagining things. Why would Noah get up and write a letter early enough to arrive at David's by eleven? He ripped into it to find one of the shortest messages he'd ever received in his life:

My dearest Mr. Forester,
I hope you slept well.
  I am always, your most devoted,
Mr. Clarke

Though the sentiment was snarky, Noah's willingness to send it warmed something in him. Noah wasn't talking about what had happened, perhaps, but he was clearly still bothered that David had sent him home. David was so surprised that he couldn't help but wonder: what might have happened if he'd given Noah a chance last night? Allowed his friend the opportunity to talk or linger or otherwise surprise him before they both spent a lonely night in their own beds?

"Everything alright, sir?" asked Shaw.

David cleared his throat of the guilt and speculation. "Would you kindly reply to Mr. Clarke? Let him know that I send my regrets for last night's lack of hospitality, and that I'd like to see him for dinner tonight."

"Of course, sir. Shall I tell him to meet you at The Ailing Hare?"

Another detail remembered: that David nearly always went back to that grimy old haunt after visiting Lord Belleville, reminding himself of the life he'd been trying to escape when he returned to the baron to beg for better work.

"Yes, Mr. Shaw," said David. He spared a gentle smile for his silent valet. "And thank you. I'm quite fortunate to have your skills in my service."

The fellow didn't smile, but David fancied that the blandness might have softened a bit around the edges as Shaw nodded and went to handle the correspondence.

It would be good to have dinner to look forward to, to know there was something waiting for him beyond the looming threat of returning to Lord Belleville's home, pleading his case for a club that the baron considered to be little more than a thrilling and dangerous toy.

Lord Henry Belleville had outfitted David with very nice lodgings as an employee, but it was nothing compared with the nobleman's own place in Grosvenor Square. It was always strange to visit this luxurious neighborhood now. While the Foresters were a few generations removed from any titles, somewhere along the line an earl had left his favorite niece some London property that eventually became The Hotel Silva, the stunning cornerstone of the Forester family's fortune. By the time David's father inherited it—and the ability to start on its eventual ruination—it had been an important enough fixture in the lives of the *ton* to secure the family a good number of respectable invitations. Noah had been right about David's previous marriage plans; for a few optimistic years, he figured he could charm some spare daughter from a noble family and find a place over here himself.

But it wasn't to be. Drink, debt, and an explosive temperament finally got the better of David's father. His attempt to escape fate through insurance fraud left himself and several staff members dead, the hotel destroyed, and his surviving family in complete ruin. The rest of the Foresters had scattered to the wind with whatever scraps of the estate they could scavenge, their bonds too weak to survive the tragedy and their name worth less than nothing in the places they'd called home. Lord Belleville was the only person of status who would have anything to do with David anymore, and even then, the circumstances were…extenuating.

Upon arrival at Belleville's door, David was brought to a handsome parlor, which was already set with sandwiches and sweetmeats on a tiered tray with coffee steaming from a silver spout. David felt immediately sick as he took up the familiar seat by the window, and though his stomach was grumbling from his meager breakfast, the smell of cold meat and coffee was nauseating. The footman poured a cup for him. He accepted it even though he did not want it. Took it black even though he hated it like that. He sipped at it in all its bitterest glory and smiled.

David waited, foot tapping on the fine silk rug. He let his eyes twist along the paths of vines and flowers that so plushily surrounded his shoes, his shoulders like stone and his belly like water. It didn't matter that he'd known it was coming: when the door opened again, he startled up straighter. He took as deep a breath as he could manage, then stood up with a smile.

"My lord," he said with a cheerful little bow. "Thanks so very much for agreeing to meet me today."

Belleville waved a hand. Though it was always hard to predict, he seemed to be in a pleasant enough mood this afternoon. "Please, sit back down, David," he said. "I'm sorry to have kept you waiting."

The footman set him up with his own cup and bowed out of the room.

David sat very still as Belleville took his time settling into his own place, running a hand over the chair cushion before he sat on it. The baron almost looked like a different person today than he had in his swirl of rage last night. His face—still disarmingly handsome halfway through his fifties—was set in pleasant neutrality, and he'd dressed impeccably in conservative gray with unexpected little pops of color: sapphire studs at cuffs and collar, a single orange stripe that twisted like a snake in the folds of an otherwise white cravat, a watch chain with alternating links of starkly different precious metals. His silver hair was swept back from his forehead so there was no missing the gleam of his ice-blue eyes as he stared a bit glassily over the beautiful, flowering view of the square that stretched out beneath the spotless window.

Lord Belleville indicated the tray of food, but did not touch it. "You're looking a bit pale. Have you eaten?"

"I'm quite alright, thank you," said David. "I take it you made your way home last night with no trouble?"

"Only the state of my shoes after winding my way back out of those alleys. Sometimes, I'm stunned anyone is willing to traverse them at all." He leaned in a bit toward his coffee cup, squinted slightly, then picked it up. "There's pleasanter paths to gin and cock, that's certain, and cheaper paths if unpleas-antness is your preference."

"Yes, isn't it fortunate that the Fox is much more than that." When Belleville did not acknowledge the assertion, David went on. "Anyway, there's no need for you to go back anytime soon. I've taken care of everything. The place is all cleaned up. When I leave here, I'll oversee the removal of the trunks. I'll keep it all in my house until we're ready to reopen, it's no trouble at all."

"About that."

Lord Belleville did not continue that thought, deciding it was the perfect time to slowly and carefully select a bite.

"Yes." David planted his feet firmly into the plush carpet and leaned forward. "About that. We know how this goes, don't we? They'll go in tonight, find nothing, make a mess and maybe nick a few things. I'll go back on Sunday with Mr. Bakshi and survey the damage. Perhaps Parker can check with your fellow at the station to make sure we're clear, and then next weekend—"

"David, look." He checked the filling of the sandwich by holding it very close to his face, then took an infuriatingly long time chewing. "We're not reopening next weekend."

Damn. That's what he'd suspected, but it was still disap-pointing to hear it aloud. "We need to give it a whole month again? Or longer?"

"Actually, I'm considering not reopening at all."

David fumbled his cup, sending a splash of black coffee onto the silk rug, drenching a perfectly rendered lily in soggy brown. "I—I'm so sorry."

Lord Belleville reached into his pocket and slipped a pair of silver spectacles onto his face for just long enough to survey the damage, then slid them to the top of his head and waved it off. "You've done worse to my rugs."

David took a deep breath before trying more successfully to get his cup to the table. The silence that followed was thick. David wasn't sure how to break it without making things worse.

"Eat something, David. You look terrible."

"No, thank you."

"I knew this would be difficult, so I had the cook fix those honey cakes you like." Belleville nodded at the top tier. "I know the sweets have been catching up with you the past couple of years, but in light of the situation, I think you can let pleasure win out over vanity for once, don't you?"

David couldn't work out what the right answer was, so he just took up a cake and nibbled at it without tasting it. "Why?"

Lord Belleville shook his head and pinched the bridge of his nose, like David's simple question was only the latest in a slew of incredibly stupid inquiries. "You know the club's numbers, David."

"Yes, I do," he said. "We do good business in the back and at the bar. We are consistently profitable."

"You really are a darling little thing sometimes," Belleville said, clucking his tongue as if dealing with a child. "Perhaps your circumstances have given you a distorted view of profitability, but given the level of risk we're taking, the Fox is simply not earning its keep."

"I can change that!" said David instantly. "Do you want me to take less pay?"

"It's not about a few shillings here or there. It's about risk and reward over time. To put it in terms a man like you will understand, the hand the Fox is holding simply isn't good enough to keep betting on the pittance in the middle of the table." He looked sharply sideways. "Does that make sense, David? What I'm saying?"

It didn't, actually, but he couldn't quite put his finger on what was missing. Risk and reward. Sure. He had no illusions there. At best, every room he rented was another count of conspiracy to commit sodomy. A prosecutor could argue that he kept a disorderly house, though he did not bring in nearly as much money as he would if he actually *did* keep one. He understood that he was not reaping the monetary rewards of the risk he took.

He also understood that this was mostly *his* problem. Belleville was well-protected. He was a baron for God's sake, and not a paltry one. Henry Belleville had a lucrative estate along with other, privately owned properties. Between his legal and illegal enterprises all over London, he had more money and power than David's whole family had tasted during the height of Hotel Silva's glory. There were layers between Belleville and his crimes. David himself was one of them. So, pittance or not, did it really matter—?

Belleville patted his knee and he jumped. "Do you need me to show you the sums?"

"No. My lord. Has something changed? I just don't see why we're having this conversation *now*. Seems a bit sudden, doesn't it?"

Lord Belleville's mouth grew tight. "Lady Belleville has had another flare. I admit, with my wife in pain like this, and no sign of improvement, the idea of dealing with raids on this silly little club feels like a dangerous waste of my time."

"Lady Belleville?" David had not expected that answer at all. He'd known the baroness was sickly, but couldn't recall that ever making much difference to Belleville's business life. Or his personal life. Or really trouble him much at all, aside from the resulting lack of an heir. "But she was doing so well."

"That's the nature of her condition." He sighed, staring blindly out over the square. "Last week I sent her back to my holdings early, you know, to see if the better air might help.

Eloise, her sister— Oh, she's expecting, did I tell you that? Eloise? Kills my poor lady to see that, over and over, you'd think Eloise would be a bit more sensitive—but anyway, she's sent word that it hasn't, so now my London season is going to be cut short as well. I won't be here to see it through the rest of the summer like I usually do, and with all these raids getting more and more frequent all over town... I don't know, David. It just occurred to me that it might be as good a time as any to be rid of the place."

The baron was waving his hand about like it was a bunch of arbitrary nothingness, but David saw the distressed edge behind Belleville's casual words and gestures. Nothing was ever simple and arbitrary with Belleville. Something else was going on. Something *complicated*.

"All over town?" David repeated quietly, carefully. "Have some of your other properties seen trouble lately, my lord?"

"My other properties are none of your business," said Belleville with snappish finality. But then he sighed. "But the Fox is, I suppose."

"Yes," David agreed. "It very much is."

"It's *your* responsibility, now that I really think about it," Belleville went on with an odd sort of emphasis, grabbing a honey cake of his own and holding it out almost like a toast to David's position. "*You're* the one overseeing the running of the place, after all. Renting the beds. Taking the money."

David glanced around the room, a strange, uncharacteristic paranoia creeping up his spine at words that sounded like they could have come out of a prosecutor's mouth in other circumstances. "Um. I suppose you could say that? Why—?"

"As such," Belleville went on, a little pensively, "I suppose it would make the most sense to get *your* perspective on the business end before doing anything drastic. We need to make changes, certainly, for your safety more than anyone else. I mean to say; if it goes bad with the Fox, it's you who will suffer most, don't you agree?"

"My lord, I—"

"Do you agree, David?"

There was a certain twist to the baron's mouth that David recognized as the one that came before an explosion that wouldn't do anyone any good. "Yes," he said, conceding. "I agree."

"Good." The twist softened. Belleville propped one of his ankles on the other knee, his bright stocking flashing in the sunlight as he jiggled the foot thoughtfully. "I just don't see how we'll have time for such an involved overhaul before I leave town. There's a lot of changes to make. You've really messed the place up, you know. Between the decor and the finances. And the *patrons*, my God, you're really scraping the bottom of the barrel for those, aren't you?" He chuckled cruelly as David expended every ounce of effort keeping his fists from clenching too obviously in his lap. "Any idea how we can coordinate under the circumstances?"

"Well." David swallowed a fresh wave of dread. Aside from the insults, there was an ease to Belleville's voice that indicated there was a right answer to this question, never mind the fact that he still hadn't provided David with enough context to know what it was. "Maybe you can explain in more useful detail what's bothering you, and we can come up with a plan from afar."

"And leave a paper trail?" Belleville scoffed. "Oh, David, surely you aren't *that* stupid."

That stung—it always did, even now that he no longer arranged his days around pleasing this unpredictable man—but he set the feeling aside with all the others. "You could leave it to your employees until you get a chance to return. I can work out the details with Mr. Parker."

"You and Parker? Heavens, no. The only thing worse than a paper trail would be hearing that my secretary and my proprietor died dueling each other in one of my properties."

To be fair, assuming that David and Mr. Parker would bother adhering to gentlemanly dueling protocols was actually rather generous.

"It's a shame," said Belleville slowly, tapping his chin, "that I can't just bring you along with me to the country."

So that was the answer. David's heart sank. It was logical, of course. If Belleville wanted more control of the club's workings and he was going to be in Hertfordshire, well, it made sense for David to be there too, particularly if the club was to stay closed in the meantime. Not much to keep him in London, as far as Belleville was concerned.

"Bring me along," David repeated, nodding reluctantly at the idea. He really couldn't bear to lose the Fox. If that meant following the baron to the country, then so be it. "Makes sense. When you aren't busy with Lady Belleville and other matters, we can collaborate."

Belleville sighed heavily. "It was my original idea when I understood our situation. But I admit to concerns."

"What concerns?"

"Bit suspicious, isn't it? You and I, appearing so friendly again after all these years and all the…" He looked David rather disparagingly up and down. "All the, ah, *unfortunate changes* in our circumstances."

"If anything, it's less suspicious than ever," David said, trying not to clench his teeth. "I'm your business partner. So long as no one knows what the business actually is, it's all aboveboard. Nothing to suspect."

"You've got it all twisted. Regardless of what we did when the doors were closed, our public acquaintance was *quaint*, back when you were inheriting a premier hotel. Everyone thought it was rather charming that I'd taken you under my wing. But now? Your father *burnt his own hotel to the ground*, David, something bad enough without all the damage it did to other people and properties. Your name itself raises a lot of eyebrows. Meanwhile, you're unmarried, nearly half my age, and you are the proprietor of a club so small we don't even have to worry about it being recognized. If we do not stick to our spheres of employer and employee, it will look very odd indeed, don't you think?"

"But we *would* be there as employer and employee," David said, voice coming out weaker than he'd have hoped.

"An employee with whom I cannot correspond from afar?"

He hated to admit it, but the baron had a point. He'd always been a suspicious character in Belleville's life, and Belleville was suspicious enough on his own. People might think they knew what it meant, if an heirless baron with no open mistress started dragging young bachelors of desperately low social standing back home with him as his "business companions." While he and Belleville had long since ceased to live out that assumed dynamic, suspicion of it might lead to questions about their current business partnership, which was, legally speaking, far more damning than the other.

Of all the things, he thought back to his conversation with Noah last night. The joke that had led to the kiss and all the rest. *You always wanted to get married.* Silly as it was, a wife was fantastic cover for a life of debauchery. People had trouble imagining that a proper man who proved his virility with a wife and children might also frequent places like the Fox, seeking the companionship of his own sex. The assumption was incredibly foolish, but after years of living the way that he did, David knew it was how most people thought about these things.

"What if," he said slowly, "I wasn't unmarried."

Belleville raised a brow, flashing one of those genuine smiles that forced David back to the early days, when his life was in shambles and Noah had left him alone, and that smidge of approval had been the only thing keeping him going.

"Not unmarried," Belleville repeated. "You mean *married*? You intend to somehow get married in the next week, just so you can come along with me and argue your case for the club?"

When he put it that way, it sounded mad, but David wasn't entirely convinced it was. Not considering what was at stake, anyway. "No one needs to see the parish register," he reasoned. "I could just bring a woman along, say she's my wife, diffuse the suspicion, and go our separate ways when we return to London."

"And why would I invite a *married* man of no social standing to my estate?"

"I'm not some bloke off the street," David insisted, frustrated with how much he cared to make this clear. "We were known as friends, before the..." After all this time, he still stumbled when he tried to speak of the fire that had ruined his future in an instant. "Just *before*. We were friends then. Say you heard I'd eloped and were filled with old sentiment. It will make you look generous and...and give your wife another woman to talk to while you're at it. One who isn't as painfully pregnant as her sister."

Belleville considered the proposition for a nerve-wracking beat. "You'd really do something that insane—"

"It's not insane," David interrupted before he could stop himself. "It's actually quite clever, and it might be nice if you would adm—"

"Something *that insane* for this stupid little molly club in the crustiest alley in Soho?"

"Yes," he snapped, boiling over with frustration. "Yes, I would. If you'll have me, and you'll actually take my proposals and opinions seriously while we're there, then I will do any number of *insane* things for my *stupid little molly club*."

David expected his outburst to be met with matching intensity, but actually, he wasn't sure he'd seen Belleville look so pleased with him in years.

"I'm glad to hear that, David," the baron said pleasantly. "Your loyalty to the place is…comforting. I'll take you up on this, give you a chance to get organized and make your case. It might be wise for both of us to be out of London for a bit anyway."

David paused. "What do you mean by—?"

"As for your wife." Belleville gave an unmistakable smirk. "Do you have a sweetheart, or do you need to hire one? Some of the girls at my other places could pass as princesses if they had to; certainly they can pull off being the wife of a pauper— er, *proprietor*, rather."

David skipped past the rudeness to the offer below it. He purposely tried to know as little as possible about Belleville's "other places," but back when the baron had thought him worthy of showing off, he'd tagged along to a brothel now and again that had been nearly as nice as the Hotel Silva itself. Hiring one of those girls for the role did make a certain amount of sense, but something about the offer made David uneasy. In fact, the whole thing was a little uneasy. It would be better if he could bring an ally of his own, rather than someone loyal to Belleville. There were obviously still facets of this plan to restructure that Belleville hadn't been honest about yet. A friend might prove good to have around.

The idea that came to him was very mad, and might not work, but he figured it was worth a try. One woman in particular came to mind as being adventurous enough to help him, if it meant saving a club that she loved as well as any of his more typical patrons.

"Maybe," he said. "But I'll be more convincing in the role if I can bring one of my own companions, I think. Obvious comfort and history will prove I didn't just pluck her out of nowhere. Much better cover, for both of us."

"Not the little daisy I encountered yesterday, I hope," Belleville chuckled. "Can't say she was exactly convincing."

It took David a moment to realize that Belleville was referring to having seen Noah getting into his makeup the night before. When he did, he lost his fight with the state of his fists, which clenched into tight, angry balls in an instant. It had been a long time since someone called Noah a rude name in his presence; with last night's dalliance still so fresh in his mind, he was quite consumed with the old itch to make a bully pay for his cruelty.

But this was a Mayfair mansion, not a schoolyard. Lord Belleville was not a boy with a bad attitude, but a wealthy, unscrupulous nobleman who owned David's house, held the keys to his livelihood, and had enough dirt to see him jailed. He couldn't break the baron's nose any more than he could still tell himself that the stairwell situation had been meaningless, schoolboy nonsense.

Some things, unfortunately, were not as straightforward now that he'd had a taste—or rather, a full, forced mouthful—of the real world's workings.

But it would be alright. Though he had to swallow his anger, sit pretty, and listen to Belleville prattle on about the club's bad decorations and poor monetary management, he carried a flicker of hope with him that lasted until he left the parlor. If he played his cards right, followed the baron's rules, and did not allow himself to become confused or distracted, he could still save the Fox.

If he could not escape the world's bitter workings himself,

the least he could do was keep offering shelter from it to the others. It wasn't much, perhaps, but it was something.

And "something" was everything to a man like David, who was not so far removed from having nothing at all.

As Mr. Shaw had so helpfully remembered, David usually felt the itch to come to The Ailing Hare after a meeting with Belleville, and tonight, he was glad to have chosen the place for more reasons than the usual. This crumbly public house full of rowdy men and disreputable barmaids had been the only place that would hire him in the aftermath of his family's fall, and was not only imbued with the resulting twisted nostalgia, but was objectively a great backdrop for illicit conversations, especially since none of the staff he'd worked with remained by this point.

For good reason, frankly.

There was a bit of ruffle through the rough mass of bodies as a conspicuous figure came in through the door. Noah usually tried to dress appropriately for every situation, but he'd never managed at the Hare. He simply did not possess the work-beaten corduroy or unkempt beard required to fit in with these blokes. His arrival in a pristine boater perched above long hair, smooth cheeks, and a dinner jacket made him stand out like a perfect rose in the middle of a thorn thicket. He looked through the glaring crowd with his usual air of desperation, so David stood and waved him over with a pint of ale that he followed like it was a lifesaving lighthouse on the edge of the world.

Noah inspected the splintery chair across from David before perching carefully on the very edge of it. A hint of his lilac-and-cigarette smell drifted across the table as he settled in, doing inconvenient things to David's mind. God, Noah was so perfectly clean and put together; how intoxicating to think this was the same person who'd made a wanton mess of himself with David in the stairwell just yesterday.

"God, David," he said, a little huffy as he leaned in across the table. "I cannot believe you are still dragging me here after all these years."

"And I—" David cleared his throat and his head, determined to be as normal as possible. He quickly pushed the pint over to Noah. "I can't believe you'll still follow me. You know what you're getting into, after all."

Noah grimaced his way through a gulp of ale, shuddering when he put it down. "Why don't they ever look at you like that? You're not exactly rough-and-tumble, either."

"Not today, but even the ones I've never met before can tell I've done my time. You, on the other hand…" David eyed Noah's jacket, which was more ostentatious than he usually risked at the Hare, sparing his best from the stink of sour ale and the stickiness of every surface. He'd clearly chosen it on purpose, though, because it wouldn't have been right for the showroom either, with those flashy buttons, slim cut, and silky…blue stripes.

Blue stripes? Every bit of last night seemed to have been engraved into David's mind, including that he'd expressed a preference for a similar *Prussian damask*. Surely Noah hadn't chosen the coat for David's sake.

Had he?

"So, really, David." Noah hung his hat off the back of his chair, tousling his hair a little self-consciously until it was back to just-so. "Why are we here?"

"Because, um." David shook himself a little. Clearly, these things were not for his benefit; since when did Noah need an excuse to look incredible…incredibly…*incredibly put together*? "Because it's a good place to talk," he blurted, "if you don't want to be overheard."

Noah froze. "Right," he whispered, taking another sip of ale that he obviously regretted quickly. "Talk. We should… We should probably talk, shouldn't we?"

David blinked. He'd meant they needed to talk about the Fox, but if Noah was actually willing to discuss the stairwell, he was all for it. He caught himself staring at Noah's hand wrapped around the pint glass, perfectly clean, but as strong and work-rough as any other in the pub. An unexpectedly impressive grip, honestly.

"David?"

"Um," David said. "Yes, Noah, we should certainly—"

"Unless you don't want to," Noah said in a rush. "Because maybe… Maybe there isn't much to say."

Disappointment dragged David's eyebrows down. "Isn't there?"

"Oh, probably not." Noah started twisting the glass, the heavy bottom of it scraping against the blocky table. "I apologize for making such a big deal out of my departure. It was a stressful evening, obviously. I suppose the shock made me act a bit silly."

"Silly," David repeated, the word feeling very hollow on his tongue.

"What else would you call it?" Noah gave a very false, self-effacing laugh. "I was being ridiculous."

David had thought about the reaction a lot, but the words *silly* and *ridiculous* had never crossed his mind. *Vulnerable*, perhaps, or *demanding*. *Out of proportion* or, alternatively and perhaps more honestly, *completely reasonable* given the circumstances.

"Silly," David said again. "So… In that case, do you think the whole thing was silly?"

"Of course it was," said Noah, almost like he was trying to convince himself as much as David. He glanced around, seeming satisfied with the other patrons' level of distraction as he lowered his voice a little. "A wank between friends. You've been running the Fox long enough to know it happens all the time. I'm just very relieved that you were able to stay practical when I lost my head a bit toward the end there. So. Thank you."

Practical. Sure.

Any regret David had about sending Noah home evaporated. He'd been right to give himself some time before listening to Noah so inevitably scour all emotion from the situation like an embarrassing stain. Just as he'd known would happen.

He considered admitting that this was the exact reason he'd rejected Noah's continued company last night, but damn if he didn't know this person too well to bother with *that*. And before he could figure out what else to say, one of the barmaids arrived to take their order, turning the conversation toward whether anyone in this whole damn place knew what meat (if any) was in tonight's "Special Pie."

"We'll take two, a plate of the oysters, and more beer while you're back there, love. Thank you so much," David said definitively, sending the wench on her way before Noah could start questioning the vegetables.

"So we have to finish the meal here?" Noah asked with a sigh. "Even if we're done talking?"

"But we're not done talking," said David. Noah looked distraught. All the pettiest fibers of David's being begged him to start unpacking every facet of their history here and now, but he took pity on his friend. "There's something else. I have an update on the Fox."

David explained his conversation with Lord Belleville. As he detailed the Fox's uncertain fate, Belleville's concerns about David's presence, and David's unique solution to the problem, much of the tension between them dissolved. Noah began to relax again, comfortable in a dynamic that had lasted the two of them half a lifetime. It was just the way he was; David knew better than to be disappointed.

In fact, as he let go of the idea that a moment of impulsive pleasure might have changed Noah's temperament, he could appreciate his friend's truth instead. He reacted with appropriate intensity to everything, mirroring David's despair, his hope, his determination in a way that was actually quite energizing.

And then David got to the part about the fake wife.

"Oh, Davy!" Noah slammed his pint down so hard it would have spilled if he hadn't already drunk most of it, completely back to normal at last. "You must let me do it!"

David laughed, shaking his head. "What? Are you insane?"

Though no one was paying them any mind (least of all their server), Noah lowered his voice to a desperate hiss. "Please, please, please?" He grabbed David's hand in both of his. "Oh, can you imagine? I can do it too. You know I can. Miss Penelope would make a far more convincing wife than Miss Liza over there."

He flicked his gaze toward one of the more grizzled barmaids. She wiggled her knobby fingers at the pair of them.

David gently shook off Noah's grip. "Noah. Darling. Remember when we talked about engaging in risky behaviors?"

"Yes."

"And how it's understandable to indulge these impulses up to a point?"

"Yes…"

"This is well past that point."

"Oh, stop it," said Noah, swatting at him. "It will be *fine*."

"If it's not, the failure would be catastrophic."

"But—"

"I'm not even going to entertain this."

"Davy—"

David put his glass down hard. "I said no."

Noah's eyes narrowed. He looked ready to argue some more, but then Miss Liza came over with their food and the fresh beers they'd need to wash it down with. A quick prod at the mysterious pie she left behind was enough to take the fight out of anyone; Noah sat back in his chair, defeated.

"Well, then, I suppose that's it for the Fox," he said, picking up an oyster that he'd clearly deemed suspicious. "You won't hire someone, and you've rejected the most eligible lady in all of London. With standards like those, I'm afraid you'll never settle down. You'll wind up a crumbling bluestocking like my sister."

"Oh, I never considered asking your sister," David mused. "Do you think she'd do it? We used to be friends, after all."

"Are you kidding? My sister hates you."

"Still?"

Noah gave him a dark look.

David rolled his eyes, trying not to let the sting settle too deep. "Never mind her, then."

"Any other ideas?"

"I have one," David admitted carefully. "It's very mad, but it's the best I've got."

"What is it?"

He swallowed a bitter sip of ale. It hurt going down, his throat constricted by the thought of what he was about to say. "I was thinking, perhaps, we ought to ask around at the Orchid and Pearl."

Noah's eyes widened. "You can't be serious."

"I might be."

"We can't go over there. Those girls will kill us, David. Some poor cleaning lady will find our bones in the basement a year from now, gnawed on."

"Charlie survived."

"Sort of. They spared his life, but now he's haunted."

"If the ghost I attract will pretend to be my wife for a week or two, I'll accept my fate." David took another nervous sip of ale, mind buzzing with doubt. "Assuming I can actually convince one of the sapphic girls to help me like this."

"What are you offering?"

"Well, his lordship's got a nice little castle near St. Albans," David reasoned. "Considering she'll have to stick with the other women and pretend she doesn't even know what sort of club the Fox is, it will be a jolly sort of holiday with no expenses."

Noah made a face. "Davy, you're asking a woman to take an enormous risk to her reputation. A 'holiday' might not be quite enough."

"At least one of them doesn't have a reputation to uphold, and has a personal interest in keeping the Fox open."

"Miss Jo?"

David nodded. Miss Jo—the "ghost" who'd befriended Charlie Price—was The Curious Fox's only officially female regular and a woman who was quite unconcerned with things like reputations. "Her husband prints erotica that she sells out of the back of Miles Montague's old bookshop, where she wears trousers in public and employs fallen girls. Not an awful lot at risk, is there?"

Noah suddenly looked scandalized. "Sure there is!"

"What?"

"The *bookshop*. Forget reputations. Miss Jo isn't some bored baroness. She's got a business to run. I can horrify you with jokes about coming along with you in drag, Davy, but I can't *actually* take a week away from work on short notice like that, and I don't even own the place. Jo's going to need more incentive than a holiday."

"Well, what do you suggest?"

A whole host of interesting expressions crossed Noah's features as he thought about it. David had always loved how expressive Noah's face was: big eyes, pink lips, perfect brows. He could have been an incredible actor, but the stage did not offer enough prestige to a person who'd been raised up to become a surgeon. Ah well. That was the rest of the world's loss. David felt lucky to have been able to witness him over the years, all the grins, the frowns, the curiosity, the intensity...

He ought to have kept his eyes open last night. He'd been so wrapped up in sensation that he'd forgotten to peek and see if Noah still made the same faces when he spent.

"A dinner jacket," Noah said suddenly.

David startled, mind snapping back to the present, where Noah was not spending, but did look incredibly mischievous. "A what?"

"Think about it." Noah leaned in conspiratorially over the table, lowering his voice and peeking around to make sure no one was listening in. "It's not so easy to march into a tailor shop or a dressmaker's and ask them to make you the wrong garments. It's all theater castoffs, altered pawn-shop finds, or whatever you can swap with friends. I'll go to great lengths for a passably fitted frock, you know. Jo's no better than the rest of us cross-dressing heathens, and yet her best suits are, well." He wobbled his hand. *So-so.* "If you want her to come with you, offer her a bespoke dinner jacket—"

"I'm not sure—"

"A *bespoke dinner jacket*, hand-stitched from the best fabrics, designed and fitted by the only current Harvey Cole tailor to have trained under Fiore Corsetti himself." He folded his hands on the table in front of him, looking wicked. "Trust me, *amore*. Joey won't be able to resist. And even if she surprises me, I guarantee you'll have another tribade waiting to take her place before you can snap your fingers."

David's jaw dropped as he realized what Noah was offering to do for him. "I can't ask that of you!" he said immediately. "You were just telling me you're so behind that you can't—"

"I'll make it work. I always do."

"Yes, *by wrecking yourself*, as we've discussed."

"Come on, Davy. I know how much the Fox means to you. Let me help you."

"No. Absolutely not."

"Then let me do it for the Fox," he snapped, loud enough to get a few eyes on him before he lowered his voice again. "I don't exactly want the club closed either, you know. So, if it will *actually kill you* to let me do this for you, then at the very least, stay out of the way and let me do it for my own damn self."

David sighed. "I can't talk you out of this, can I?"

"No, you can't." He lifted his pint, eyes flashing. "Are you in? Because I am."

Begrudging every drop of gratitude that swelled within him, David leaned in across the table with his own glass in hand, caught up in the excitement in Noah's eyes. A very sharp desire to close those last inches and kiss Noah again jolted across his mind, but he settled with clinking glasses and watching Noah's smooth-shaven throat as he swallowed.

Noah put his glass down heavily, his face a bit pink as he seemed to drag his own eyes up from somewhere to meet David's. "Lovely. Now, let's get out of this horrible place. I can't believe how long you worked here."

"Starting to remember why a life of crime seemed preferable?"

"Yes. I'd do the same, no question."

David smiled, but did not correct Noah's interpretation

of his career change, as if he'd simply gone from one sort of place to another with no degrading stops along the way. If Noah could not handle discussing their own simple history, the complicated truth about Lord Belleville might just send him off screaming.

They talked about little things as they finished their meal, tipped the staff extravagantly, and lifted their hats to Miss Liza on their way out the door.

Chapter Eight

Noah

A few years ago, the Fox's pianist admitted to knowing where a group of lively sapphists met for drinks and conversation. Tonight, since the early summer weather was pleasant, Noah and David walked from The Ailing Hare to the address that David had kept on a little card just in case.

It took them somewhere so drastically different from the entrance to The Curious Fox that Noah felt certain they had the wrong street. It wasn't a club, a teahouse, or anything remotely marked. It was a little town house, right in the middle of a perfectly normal residential street, populated by perfectly normal, residential people. The stone steps and black-painted door to Number 6 looked exactly the same as all the others.

"Are you certain this is the place?" Noah took the card from David and checked it over. "This doesn't look right."

David glanced behind him, up and down the street, then shrugged and pulled Noah along by the arm as they climbed the front steps. "I didn't realize they met in someone's home, but I suppose it makes sense. Not illegal for them, is it?"

"I'm not sure this is a good idea."

David grinned wickedly. "Scared of a few girls in suits?"

"You bet I am. Have you *met* Jo? I think the only reason she hasn't strangled me yet is because my skirts are too wide for her to reach my neck. I'm feeling utterly undefended without my crinoline."

"Oh, is that the point of a crinoline?"

Noah nodded. "It's a fortress."

David tapped the knocker a few times. After a moment, a woman peered out at them from the foyer. She looked as perfectly normal and residential as everything else, wearing a simple skirt and high-necked blouse, her brown hair in a tidy bun. She might have been around forty from the sparse lines on her plump face. She did not look pleased to see them. "Can I help you?"

David cleared his throat and politely removed his hat. "Good evening. I'm so sorry to call unannounced like this. My name is David Forester and this is my friend Mr. Clarke. I'm the proprietor of a gentlemen's club called The Curious Fox. You may have heard of it—"

She slammed the door in his face.

"Let's go," Noah whispered.

David knocked again. When no one came to the door, he continued hitting the knocker over and over and over until the woman reappeared.

"We're good friends of Miss Jo," David said before she could get another word in. "If she's here, I'm sure she'll vouch for us."

One terrifying eyebrow went up. "Miss Jo."

He reached into his coat pocket and took out a card. He elbowed Noah. Noah thought David had lost his mind, but gave in and handed one of his own over. David passed them to the woman. "Is she here? Let me talk to her. You won't regret it, I promise."

The one brow remained staunchly raised. "You want me to interrupt Miss Jo, pull her away from whatever she might be doing right now, in order to vouch for you?"

"If you'd be so kind."

Her face remained so still she might have been a painting. "Wait here," she said at last.

The door slammed again. The next time it opened, it revealed a different woman in a pinstripe suit and bowler hat. Miss Jo. David must have had more of her identity in the ledgers somewhere, but Noah knew her only as "Charlie's sapphic friend Miss Jo."

She leaned against the door frame, arms crossed and dark eyes disparaging.

"So," she said. "I hear there's a Miss Mary Ann Forester and a Miss Molly Clarke here to beg for my blessing to enter."

"On bended knee, if required," said David.

Jo rolled her eyes. "Spare me that. Just come in, will you. An hour, maximum."

Noah peeked around David's shoulder. "*Grazie*, Joey."

She led them through a splendid little foyer and into a prettily decorated drawing room. The walls were papered with white and cream stripes, the dark wood furniture all upholstered in powdery blues. Far from the Fox's rowdy atmosphere, this felt like they'd crashed someone's very exclusive dinner party, as a handful of sapphists in evening suits, sporting jackets, and frilly frocks eyed them suspiciously.

Jo sighed theatrically. "My apologies, everyone. I can't seem to keep them from following me home."

"You ought to quit hiding biscuits in your pockets, Joey, or they'll never stop," said a bright-eyed blonde at the card table, where she and her friends had the beginnings of an impressive card house between them.

"When will I learn? Anyway, they're awfully cute." She patted Noah's cheek. "Can we give them an hour? I swear I won't let them piss on the rug this time."

Noah turned to her. "Charlie *didn't*!"

"The fact that you believed that has just made my entire night." She cackled, then turned to the woman who'd answered the door. "Miss Withers, love, may I pour them something? They look so uncomfortable that it's making me uncomfortable."

Miss Withers looked like she was just fine with everyone's discomfort, but shrugged, sitting down at the piano with arms and legs crossed. "They're your guests, Miss Jo." As if to fill the awkward silence, she turned to the keys and began plucking out an aggressive sort of melody as a waistcoated woman hopped up to turn pages for her.

They sat side by side on a chaise in the corner of the room, a bit out of the way, and accepted glasses of chilled white wine from Jo, who had provided herself with her usual Irish whiskey. She settled across from them and leaned in, keeping her voice low as conversation picked back up elsewhere. "You can relax, but don't get silly, do you understand? It's nerve-wracking for some of us, having fellows in here."

"Fair enough," said David with a heavy nod that indicated more understanding than Noah might have expected. "I won't waste your time nor insult your hospitality by belaboring this. I'm in need of an extremely large favor, and I can't think of anywhere else I might be able to respectfully ask for it."

Jo leaned back in her chair, intrigued. "Go on."

"The Fox's owner wants to shut the place down. The only way I can talk him into reopening is if I go with him to his estate in Hertfordshire to plan. To do that, I need a woman to tag along and pretend to be my wife. I thought that if the reward was sufficient, you or one of your friends might be in a position to play the part without much negative consequence."

"Pretend to be your wife?" She considered that over a sip of whiskey, her face scrunched in confusion. "Why? I don't understand how that's connected."

"The Fox," David said carefully, "is owned by an anonymous nobleman. His wife suffers from a chronic condition that's flared up. He says he's too busy caring for her to 'bother' with the Fox."

"Does he usually do much for it?"

"No. He usually leaves me to my own devices unless there's a problem. Which there is, this weekend—"

"The raid." Jo nodded. "Charlie told me."

"Of course he did. Anyway, since we had to close down for a short time, he sees this as a good opportunity to cut it loose. I want to prove to him that we can reorganize things so they're safer and more profitable going forward, but he won't let—" He cleared his throat. "I can't work out how to continue the club on my own, but now he and his wife are going back to his estate, for her health. Obviously, we can't correspond from afar, or there would be a paper trail. He says I can come along to his country house, so we can plan, but I need to bring a wife along so it doesn't seem suspicious."

"What would be suspicious about it? Unless." She nodded with understanding. "You and the owner. Are you, you know, *suspicious*?"

Noah shook his head, but he noticed very quickly that David did *not*.

David smiled tightly under Noah's shocked glare. "I'm, ah, quite a bit younger than he is. Combined with the raids and everything, I suppose it just makes him nervous."

Jo seemed to accept that, but Noah took in all the little cracks of that brittle explanation. A hot swoop of—well, it couldn't be *jealousy*, that would be silly—but something equally as horrible nearly made Noah crush the cold wineglass in his hand. Fingers slipping on the condensation, he pulled it in front of his mouth instead. Jo would hear him, but he could at least feign discretion as he hissed through his teeth. "*David*."

"Yes?"

"Please tell me you are not *fucking* that horrible man."

David shook his head firmly. "No. Absolutely not."

Noah looked hard into his bright eyes. They were unblinking and tentatively honest, but he'd known this chap for too long to believe it for a second. It might be true, but it was not the whole truth. "We'll talk about this later."

With a massive sigh, David tried to get things back on track. "So, Jo. Does this sound like something you could do? For Charlie? For all of us?"

She narrowed her eyes, curious, but not quite convinced just yet. "What would the wife in question get out of this? You mentioned a reward?"

"Tell me, Jo. Have you and Noah ever discussed your outside lives?" David gave Noah's leg a proud pat as Jo shook her head. Noah tried to glare at him, but he was smiling so sweetly that it was hard to stay mad. "Beautiful, why don't you tell her what you do for a living?"

"I'm a tailor," he muttered, still a bit grumpy.

"And who employs you, Noah?" David nudged his leg again, doing an infuriatingly good job of forcing Noah to forgive him. "Don't forget to tell her that part."

She looked intrigued now, scooting forward to the edge of her seat. "Yes, Noah," she said. "Tell me."

He sighed, defeated. "I work for Harvey Cole."

The name of his illustrious employer always got an appreciative reaction, but the way Jo's eyes widened was almost comical. "Shut up."

Noah shrugged, not quite suppressing a smile.

"*You?*" said Jo. "What the devil are you always doing in frocks, then?"

"By the weekend, I find myself rather sick of suits."

"Sick of suits," Jo echoed, her voice a bit weak. "He's a *Har-*

vey Cole tailor and he's sick of bloody suits. Am I understanding this, then? One of us pretends to be your wife for a couple weeks at some fancy castle, chattering a bit with a doped-up noblewoman, and in exchange, she gets—"

"A custom dinner jacket designed and fitted by one of the most impressive workhands in the whole place," David finished for her, putting an arm around Noah's shoulder.

"Make it a three-piece, and I'm in."

A *three-piece*?

Before Noah could object or David could celebrate, the woman who'd been turning piano book pages suddenly sidled up and put her elbows on the back of Jo's chair. She had curly black hair, paint stains on her fingers, and a most winning smile. "Margot Levin," she said, not waiting for Jo to introduce her. "I'd like to put my bid in as well, if I might."

"Piss off," said Jo. "You don't even know what we're talking about."

She grinned right at Noah. No woman had ever looked at him so dreamily. "Doesn't matter. Whatever it is, I'd like to offer my services."

Once a third and then a fourth jumped in, Noah forgot to worry about how much harder a three-piece would be. There'd be no deadline anyway, and it was for *David*, who was busy being dangerously easy to care for as he leaned against Noah in giggles, clinking his wineglass. He returned the toast, letting their heads bump gently as well.

"Alright, everyone, alright." David held his hands out soothingly. "Unfortunately, I can only bring one, so let's talk it over. I'm sure we can figure out who will be most—"

"No, Davy—"

"*Suitable.*"

Noah collapsed across David's lap with a groan. Once they'd all gotten ahold of themselves, he turned from his side onto his back. David was grinning down at him. It was incredibly sweet. The victory, that is. The victory was so dizzyingly sweet he felt it all the way down to his toes as he looked up at the devious face of his lifelong coconspirator.

"Alright, you two." Jo nudged Noah's side with her foot. "Let him up, so he can go explain the situation to the others."

"How transparent can you be, Jo?" scolded Miss Levin. "You're just trying to get the tailor to yourself."

"So what if I am? Doesn't change the fact that you don't know the details, and you can't be in the running until you do, can you?"

Noah must have been getting tired, because the thought of being anywhere but right here was most unappealing. David smoothed his hair with another sweet smile, and Noah sat up just enough to let him out before flopping back down. The creamy upholstery was warm where David had been, and the comforting scent of him lingered as he went off to the card table, surrounded by his gaggle of new best friends. Noah watched him go, very content.

"So," said Jo, still lounging in her armchair as if confident she'd win this without effort. "A Cole & Co. tailor, eh? How'd you wind up there?"

Noah let his eyes rest on David and the others while he thought on an answer. "Didn't have much choice. I was supposed to go into medicine, you see." Jo looked satisfyingly horrified by the prospect. "If I did something else," he went on, "I had to do it very well to make up for it. Tailoring was a good compromise between technical and artistic. It involved, you know, *geometry* and *anatomy*—"

"And cutting and stitching?"

Noah never could keep from grimacing at that comparison, no matter how many times he heard it. "That too. My father liked that it was practical, but I had to lock in some status to convince him I was serious. I trained at the London tailoring school, then under a designer in Milan for a couple years as well."

"Milan?" Jo laughed. "You escaped all the way to Milan only to come back to this godforsaken little island? Are you mad?"

"My family was here," he said, the familiar words rising to his lips automatically, as he turned his attention back to where David was bantering with the sapphists, lighting up the whole room with a smile that had not always come quite so easily for him. "So, I came back, worked for a small shop until I could get Cole to take me on. Only as an associate at first, though. I was just changing out displays, keeping records, taking shipments. A wide variety of *nothing*. But I got noticed eventually, and taken on as a workhand."

"How did you manage that?"

"Well, it's fashion, isn't it? So first things first, *always* look the part." He finally sat up and straightened his silky blue lapels, wondering if David had liked the color of the jacket on him as well as the frock. "Then I started getting my writings and drawings in any design magazine that would have me. I dropped the right names and left my sketchbook lying strategically around the workshop so the other right names would see it. My favorite cutter finally noticed and took me on."

"Wow." Jo blinked at him a few times. "I am exhausted just listening to this. No wonder you've got nothing left to give your suitors at the club."

"You too?" Noah groaned. "Why is everyone on my arse about this all of a sudden?"

"It hit the gossip chain. No one can save you now." She sipped her whiskey with a naughty sort of smile. "Question, Clarke: do you actually turn them away because you're picky? Or is it more to do with Mr. Forester?"

Noah choked on his wine, thankfully getting it down rather than ruining Miss Withers's rug. "What would it have to do with Mr. Forester?"

"Well, I knew you were lovers, but the gossip has me wondering if it's something more exclusive than you've let on."

Noah was too shocked to speak for a second. "*Lovers?*" he said at last. "No. Absolutely not, we are not lovers. We're just friends."

"Just friends?" She turned to where David was still chatting up the others, all of them smiling, teasing each other, and probably telling him their entire life stories. "Are you quite sure? Because you've always seemed like—"

"How could I *possibly* be unsure about that?"

"Well, maybe it's for the best," Jo chuckled, lifting her whiskey to call Noah's attention to what was happening across the room. David was charming—not the pants, of course, but at least the bowler hats—off nearly everyone in the parlor, refilling their glasses, nodding along to their stories, shaking back that lock of toasty brown hair that always fell into his eyes. "He might be walking out of here with a real wife if he's not careful. See Cordelia, there?" She pointed to a frilly blonde. "She's not an entirely confirmed spinster, if you catch my meaning."

While Noah had joked about that notion yesterday, the idea now put that horrible feeling back in the pit of his stomach.

"A fake wife will do, I think," he said quickly.

Fortunately, David came back before Joey could say whatever thought she'd hidden behind that renewed grin of hers. Even more fortunately, the *unconfirmed* Miss Cordelia stayed at the card table while the more suitable Margot Levin came over on his arm.

"Well, Joey," said David with mock seriousness. "Miss Levin

has offered me a very handsome dowry and ten children. Think you can compete?"

Jo looked up. "If you bring me, I won't kill you. How's that for a dowry?"

"Significant." He leaned his hip lightly against the roll of the chaise, absently running a hand through Noah's hair. Jo smirked suggestively and Noah stuck out his tongue. The whole exchange was missed by David, who went on. "As much as I hate to play favorites, Miss Levin, loyalty demands that I offer the position to Jo first, if she'll have it."

"Yes!" Jo slammed her drink down and clapped her hands together. Then she leaned her head back far enough on the chair that she could see Miss Levin behind her. Jo grabbed the other woman's tie and pulled her in for a kiss on the cheek. "I'm sorry, mate, but all's fair in love and menswear."

"Oh, I knew it would go like this, anyway." Miss Levin rolled her eyes before resting them on Noah. "Mr. Clarke, I might still be interested in your services. When I've got the money, can I call on you for a discreet fitting, d'you think?"

Considering how behind he was at the workshop, agreeing to private commissions was madness. Oh, but wouldn't it be refreshing? He wouldn't have to worry about his professional image with Miss Levin, confined by nothing but imagination: fit, color, cut, fabric, all wide open to whatever would be the most fun.

Though it was a bad idea, Noah gave her his card, which she snatched up with a little grin before heading back to the piano to show it to Miss Withers. He should hope she never called on him, but he felt the complete opposite, eyeing her shape a bit as she went off, then Jo's. Now that it was official, his professional eye had flipped on, and he tried to imagine how he'd go about this. He'd never made a suit for a woman before. He'd made ladies' jackets and such for Emily a dozen times, but Emily was more boyishly shaped. He'd not really noticed before, but Jo was rather buxom and would require a different approach. Perhaps—

"Clarke, are you staring at my tits?"

"Yes." He looked up at Jo's eyes. "I assume you don't want a jacket that simply leaves them out in the cold, do you?"

She seemed to consider that. "Suppose not."

"Do you think I could get a couple cursory measurements?" he asked, mind awhirl with assignments and due dates, nervous to leave any scheduling to chance. "I'd like to wrap my head around the task a bit."

"Let's go into the parlor for it." She got up and started toward a staircase near the piano. "We should have a smoke while we're at it, yeah?"

That offer got Noah off the comfortable chaise so quickly that David laughed, giving him a scolding nudge that Noah returned as they followed Jo up to an intimate little parlor. A stale smoke smell lingered, very tempting to Noah as Jo got out her cigarette case and they all settled on the sofas, David and Noah next to each other. Small sofas. Not quite enough room to keep their knees from touching.

David accepted the case from Jo and took out one smoke each for himself and Noah. He struck a match. Without thinking about it much, Noah put the cigarette between his lips and leaned in for David to light his first. The match went out before David got a turn, so Noah beckoned him a little closer and lit it with the glowing tip of his own, the fragrant tobacco clouding around them, nearly as thick as the look Jo threw at them as she took the matches back.

Oh, bugger her. *Honestly.*

Fortunately, she made up for her silent accusations with quality tobacco, and Noah indulged in his horrid, fabric-ruining addiction amid pleasant conversation about nothing of much importance until Jo finally stubbed her ash into the tray.

"Alright, butterfly, you happen to keep tape on you at all times? I'm ready for my fitting."

"Certain things a lady must never leave home without." From his pocket, he pulled a spiral of measuring tape, his own cigarette case, and the box with his earrings, which got a laugh out of Jo. After one last, lingering drag, he positioned her standing in front of the fireplace and helped her out of her coat. "Something to write with?"

"In the desk."

"Got it," said David. He stood nearby with the pen poised. "Just shout them to me, beautiful. I'll be your apprentice."

He started by investigating the cut of Jo's own jacket. It seemed to have been made off-the-rack for a fellow and altered to fit. He could do her *much* better than something like this.

"Forgive me, Joey, but you'll have to lose the waistcoat. Thanks. Now arms out. Stand still. And don't punch me, please, I don't mean any disrespect."

It was the most compliant he'd ever seen her, moving and breathing however he asked as he got the numbers he wanted. Arms, shoulders, waist. The impressive chest measurement. He knelt down for the inseam and thighs.

"Careful!" She flinched. "Are you trying to wreck my bloody virtue with that thing?"

"Your *virtue*?" He grinned up at her, quickly getting through the sensitive part. "Still got that old thing, have you?"

"That's what my future husband thinks, anyway." Jo winked at David.

Once the measurements were done, Noah got the paper from David. He perched on the hearth and sketched a few notions while he still had her in front of him. The others settled back in on the sofas.

"So, David—I assume I can call you David now that we're married?" Jo asked.

"I suppose it's only natural."

"Thanks. So, David. Tell me about this mysterious Lord Owner. Who is he?"

Noah glanced up from his pen to see David tapping his foot anxiously on the rug.

"Out with it, hubby," said Jo.

David licked his lips, then said, faux-casual, "He's the Baron of Belleville. Lord Henry. It's a small estate in Hertford. You've probably not even heard of him."

Noah had not.

Jo, however, froze. "*Belleville*, did you say?"

The look on her face was a shocking change from the rest of their evening. The laughter, the humor, the curiosity were all gone. She looked quite pale, in fact.

"Y-yes," said David. "Is that... You've heard of him?"

Jo was looking at David like he was a stranger. She lowered her voice to an angry hiss. "You came into my place, uninvited, to trick an unwitting woman into keeping company with that...that... My God, he's owned the Fox this whole time? That's who my liquor money is lining the pockets of?"

"The bar's profits are mine to keep." David put his hands out and made his voice low and soothing, just like he would to calm an angry patron. "I waived your membership fee and you don't rent rooms, so the only pockets involved are mine and Warren's. I swear."

"Well, isn't that lovely." She stood up suddenly. Noah watched her, shocked, as she paced to the chessboard before turning back to look daggers at David. "How could you?"

"I—" David looked completely unfooted, his eyes wide. "I'm sorry. I didn't realize... I don't know what you've heard,

Joey, but he's not so bad. If he were, I wouldn't have asked. You can't possibly think I'd put you in danger."

"You don't know what I've heard?" She crossed her arms tight. "What have *you* heard, Mr. Forester? Tell me all about the lovely baron you work for. Where will you start, d'you think? With the fortune he owes Paul and me for printing his horrible little 'erotic tour guides' that he never bothered to pay for?"

"I didn't rea—" David stammered.

"What did I hear? Let's see. All kinds of gossip down on Holywell, you know." Jo and her husband's illicit print shop was located there, along with other creators and purveyors of pornographic content. "I hear all the good stuff. And the worse a man is, the more I hear. I heard he's so jealous that he poisons his wife, just a little here and there, keeping her out of society's eye."

"That's insane! She's ill, it's—"

"Or perhaps I heard about the boy they found last month down in one of our alleys, crown cracked, talkin' nonsense, but just lucid enough to cry about how angry his 'handler' would be that he'd got himself spoiled. A handler who treats all her charges like dirt, and reports directly to your baron. You know, I think her name starts with an F as well. Probably listed right next to you on the payroll."

"I don't know about any of that," said David quickly. "I just run the Fox, and I run it as ethically as I can. I don't know anything about anything else."

"Well, ain't that convenient?"

"I certainly didn't know he owed you… I'll talk to him. I will. About your situation, and about th-the poor boy. If his lordship knew the madam was acting like that, I'm sure—"

"You *cannot* be serious," Joey shouted over him, the usual whisper of Irish in her accent thickening as anger ate through her ability to hide it. "What's he care? And do *not* talk to him about me and Paul. We've counted the money lost, and good riddance. My God, I cannot believe you."

There was a switch inside of David, like the lever that turned a train from one track to the other. He ran along day in and day out, keeping everyone happy, making everyone like him, until something blocked that path completely. He'd often turn back at a blockage like that, but if the destination was important enough, the lever would flip. Sometimes, that was useful. Sometimes, it got bullies' noses broken and drunk fathers fought off. Sometimes, it got ill-intentioned patrons too scared to make trouble for his friends.

Other times, it was really best left alone.

"Davy," Noah whispered. "Let's just—"

David stood up sharply. His fists were clenched, his jaw was set, and his usual track was vanishing in the distance as he barreled breakneck along the other.

"And you're so much better than me, are you?" he snapped at Jo, suddenly all fire and sputtering acid. "You're pornographers, Joey, you and your husband both. You cannot stand there and act like some sort of saint while—"

"Why don't you ask one of our writers whether they'd be scared shitless to tell Paul they'd gotten hurt, eh?" Jo shouted back, stepping right into the altercation without a second thought, pointing furiously out the window like Belleville was looming in it right now. "What we do isn't comparable to that—"

"You go ahead and explain that to the rozzers when they come around for you. See if they can spot the difference—"

"Of course they can't. But *I* can. Are you honestly telling me you can't tell the difference between—?"

"I'm telling you that the Fox is *mine*!" He put his fist up to his chest, his face very red. "It's mine. He gave it to me, and I run it as I see fit." He started ticking things off on his fingers. "I do not keep renters. I look out for any sign that someone's been brought in against their will. I know all my people and I keep them safe night after night. If you don't like Belleville, fine. But *I've* looked out for you same as everyone else. You think it's incidental that in a room full of drunk men, no one ever bothers the only woman who possesses the parts? We don't all go the one way, sweetheart; plenty of mine aren't so opinionated as all that. You think I'm not running interference for you every time you come in? When you leave, do you think a doorman's not following you down the alley to make sure you get out of it unmolested?"

Jo stared, her mouth open as she blinked all that in. "My God," she said, incredulous. "You really are a paternalistic little shit aren't you?"

Such a negative response to the fact of his protection shocked David fully silent. Noah knew it wouldn't last long, and quickly jumped at the chance to get a foothold in this spiraling mess. He stepped between them, putting firm hands on David's upper arms. The muscles flinched under his grip, but Noah didn't let go, trying to look into his eyes. David didn't want to meet them, his gaze darting everywhere else, but Noah wasn't in the habit of giving up on him.

"*Amore,*" he whispered, coaxing. "Come on. This is *Joey.* Your friend. *My* friend." He glanced at her, where she stood still poised to attack. "She doesn't mean you any harm, David. No one does. We just want to know what's going on, so that we can help you."

David finally looked at him properly, his body unknotting, breath coming deeper, slower. He'd gone somewhere else for a moment there, but he was back now, the anger hissing out as he realized that the frustrations he was venting did not, perhaps, belong in this parlor.

"Yeah," he said quietly, barely more than a rumble in his chest. "Yeah. I'm so sorry, Jo. All this stuff has got my head twisted round. I couldn't bear it if you thought... He just owns it. I swear. I don't have anything to do with the rest of it. He tells me nothing. I'm nothing." He took a shuddering sort of breath. "I just run this stupid little place that he doesn't even care about. Once you take my lodgings into account, I suppose it really isn't making him very much money after all. He's right. I've failed miserably with it. He has no reason to give it back to me, none at all."

Jo began to relax a bit as well. Noah felt the enormity shrink down to something manageable.

"If there's no reason to bother," Jo said, "then why is he putting you through this runaround with the wives and the country houses? And if you typically run the show, then why are you putting up with it, screaming at *me* all the things it seems you should be screaming at *him*?" A strange look came over her face, half-amused, half-accusing. "Unless you're just as scared of him as everyone else."

Noah expected another outburst, but none came. David went very quiet, his lips pressed tightly together. He looked an awful lot like he had last night, when Belleville had him hard by the back of the neck.

A creeping feeling started up at the base of Noah's spine. He locked eyes with Jo, whose fury had slipped sideways into something closer to concern.

"David, what's going on?" He got no answer. David wouldn't even look at him. "I know you're in it deep, *amore*. I've known that. But, Davy, are you in over your head?"

David paused, then shook his head and forced a smile. He gently ran his thumb along Noah's cheekbone, a soft gesture that was clearly supposed to make him feel better, but only served to heighten Noah's fear. Ignoring what Jo might think of it, he captured David's hand on the way down. "Davy—"

"I'm not in over my head," David insisted, squeezing Noah's fingers before releasing them and turning to Jo. "I just want my club back. And I'll get it on my own. Please, forgive me, Joey. You're right. I shouldn't have asked that of you. Of anyone. Forget I ever mentioned it. And I'll just buy you the suit. If Noah will still do it, I'll still pay for it."

"Can you afford it with everything that's happening?" she said carefully. "He looks expensive."

"He is, but that's alright. It's been a long time since money was the problem."

"What's the problem?" Noah asked.

David pretended not to hear him. He gathered up the pages Noah had left on the hearth and tidied all the pillows up. He bowed his head politely as he approached the door. "Noah, I'll meet you outside. Joey, thank you for your hospitality. None of us deserve you, least of all me."

He left, closing the door quietly behind him.

Noah wetted his lips, meeting Jo's eye awkwardly in the aftermath. He could use another smoke, but he did not want to bother these poor ladies any further tonight. Something remained, though. "Joey. This Belleville—"

"He's a snake, Noah." Joey leaned in very seriously. "And I don't care if you're Forester's friend or his lover; if he matters to you at all, you'll make sure he watches his arse around that man, do you understand?"

Too shaken to speak, he nodded instead, drifting to the window to look out on the street below. David stood straight and tall near the stoop to Number 6, tipping his hat to someone as if determined not to look dodgy, in spite of all that fear and anger he'd carried out of the parlor with him.

"I'll look after him," he said quietly, the unnecessary softness of David's gesture sending a distinctive pang through his chest. He managed to tear his eyes away from the lovely form of his friend on the ground and turned back to Jo. "I'm not sure how, exactly, but I do know my house is safer than his. I'll start by making him come home with me tonight."

Chapter Nine

Noah was curled up on the plushest armchair in the Clarke family parlor, watching David and Emily deal the cards for another hand of rummy under the Christmas tree. He'd been invited to play, but opted to sit the game out with his sketch-book instead. He had work to do.

"You'll be working nonstop soon enough," Emily had chided. "It doesn't sound like Signor Corsetti plans to give you time to do much else when you get to Italy."

It was true, but the designs Noah was working on couldn't wait. After all, it wasn't every day David Forester came home with him for the holidays, looking absolutely perfect here in their family cottage. There was a happy ease to his posture that he never seemed to have at the London hotel where he lived. If Noah wanted his father to see how surely David belonged in their home when he made his case later, he would have to capture that sense of comfort just right.

So rather than playing, he peeked over the top of his sketch-book, trying not be noticed as he penciled the curve of David's shoulders, the fold of his sleeve where he'd rolled it to the elbow, the way his position altered the exact placement of his trouser buttons. Noah hid his burning face a little deeper in the book when he got to that, the glances going more furtive.

He'd gotten over the awkwardness of trouser design during his year at the London tailoring school, but apparently, that didn't apply to someone whose trousers he'd unbuttoned so regularly. Still, it would be *highly* unprofessional to gloss over such details. He gave every part of David's clothing its due attention, glancing up now and then to check his accuracy until he looked up to find David staring back.

Noah's pencil froze and his hand clenched in preparation to slam the book shut. He'd hate for anyone to see what he was working on. Not because there was anything *wrong* with it, of course; he just didn't like to let anyone see his unfinished work. And this suit design for David was still very much unfinished.

"Sure you don't want to join in, Noah?" David held up the deck with a pleasant look on his face. "You've been awfully quiet."

Emily glanced between the two of them. "Be careful what you wish for, Davy," she warned. "You must know by now what a terrible loser he is."

"Oh, I do." David's eye twinkled a bit, stark competition for the glittering tinsel on the tree above him. "But he tends to do quite well when he plays me, so I don't worry about it much."

Emily gasped and threw a gambling chip at his chest, where it bounced off the folds of his neckcloth. "You let him win?"

"Well, I didn't say *that*—"

Light footsteps and a slim shadow from the entryway cut them all off. David sprung a bit awkwardly to his feet, sending a scatter of pine needles to the ground as Noah's father—Dr. Phillip Clarke—came into the drawing room looking a little disheveled but in generally good spirits.

He waved one of his small, steady hands in David's direction. "Back down, back down, David. Don't let me interrupt your game." He turned to Noah. "So sorry to leave you waiting, my boy, but I really did have to get that letter off in all possible haste in case the snowstorm makes good on its threats this afternoon."

"No trouble, Papa." Noah closed his sketchbook and tucked it nervously under his arm as he stood, watching from the corner of his eye as David settled back in that impeccable place across from Emily. "So, we can talk now?"

"Of course, of course."

He waved Noah along, past the shelves of books and potted plants that lined the parlor, along the well-lit halls and stairs of the house, up to his study. Noah felt oddly gangly as he followed; the year in London had sent him home, not *tall*, but quite a bit tall*er* than his compact father, putting him at a disorienting angle that he still wasn't used to. Once they arrived at the study, Papa indicated one of the chairs and closed the door. Noah sat in the familiar room, perfumed so nostalgically with the furniture's leather tang, the musk of a hundred medical books, and the soft green of more ivies and ferns in a dizzying assortment of pots.

Papa sat across from him, somehow having procured one of the balls of brightly colored clay he liked to fiddle with. He said it kept his hands strong, which, for a surgeon, was of the utmost importance.

Watching him made Noah flex his own hands a bit, hoping Papa might notice that they'd grown strong and skillful as well. He wished he could say it, call attention to it himself— *I've been working my arse off and I've gotten very good at my new trade*—but speaking it would only lead to admonishment for vanity. Good things had to be *noticed*, and so far, it seemed that Noah's skill would not be noticed until the day he ensured it could not be missed.

"So, what's on your mind, Noah?" Papa leaned back in the chair, kneading the clay and smiling a little wistfully. "Not here to tell me you've changed your mind about Milan, I hope?"

Noah always longed to call him out when he did this, pretending he was all in for his son's sartorial ambitions. He hoped quite the opposite, and they both knew it.

"Not today," Noah said, playing along. He had some reservations about the years away, admittedly, but he would not be discussing those with his father. Not directly, at least. "I was actually hoping to speak to you about Emily."

"Emily?" Papa scrunched his face up, confounded. "What about her?"

"We're eighteen, now, you know. If we were in London, it would certainly be time for her to enter society and—"

Papa held a hand up, a warning look on his face. "But we are *not* in London, are we? Nor are we participants in the sort of society that keeps careful track of your sister's age."

"And thank goodness for that!" Noah said quickly, backtracking a bit before he gave the wrong idea. "In fact, that's exactly why I wanted to talk to you. I've had a surge of inspiration regarding the issue."

"What issue?"

"Emily's marriage prospects."

Papa crossed his arms tight over his chest. He glared like all his gravest suspicions about Noah's life in the London fashion world had come true at last.

"Emily has expressed no desire to marry," Papa said coldly. "She has, however, expressed interest in learning the family profession, which I fully support. We've been discussing her options for medical college, which will be difficult enough as it is. Potentially impossible if she were married."

That was certainly the end of the conversation. Clearly, there was nothing else to be said about it. And yet, as Noah thought back to what he'd just left, to the sight of David so happy and *here*... Anxieties that had been plaguing him since his acceptance by Corsetti reached a nasty pitch in his belly. It had been surprisingly simple to abandon his position as Papa's protégé, moving from Surrey to London, knowing he had a friend in that new city and a family back home who would still be there for him—begrudging though it was sometimes.

He did not quite have the same assurances now, leaving London for Milan. What if Noah came back from Italy to find David had run off with some ballet dancer like David's brother just did? What if he never had occasion to sit under the Clarke family Christmas tree again? Or to share Noah's room, sneaking from the cot they'd set up for him into Noah's bed for a much simpler indulgence of appetites than they'd had to arrange in school...

Not that they'd do that last one, he realized, horrified that he'd even had such a ridiculous thought. That schoolboy *interestingness* was just to keep them busy until they got married, after all, and if David married Emily, then obviously neither of them would *ever* consider—

"Noah, are you alright?"

"Yes!" He sat up straighter, as tall and official as he could make himself, smoothing the folds of his jacket, compulsively checking to see if Papa noticed how impeccable he'd made the drape. "Though I must insist that you hear me out regarding a potential match. She ought to be given the option, you know, if I happen to have found one."

"And who is this match?"

"David Forester."

Papa's eyes went wide. "David Forester?" he repeated. Then he pointed to the door, toward the rest of the house. "*That* David Forester?"

"Didn't you see them?" Noah gave a tight smile that was hopefully more convincing than it felt. "They're a beautiful couple. They clearly enjoy each other's company very much. And David is handsome and thoughtful and courteous and well-connected and…and *handsome*, and—"

"Noah, I appreciate your enthusiasm, I really do." Papa shook his head and squished the clay between his fingers again. "But absolutely not."

"Papa, if you'd only listen—"

"I like David well enough. He is welcome in our home anytime. But frankly, I think that lad has brought enough *London society* to my doorstep already. He himself is clearly growing into a good man, but he comes from a shallow, undereducated corner of our culture, and—based on how he flinches like he might get cuffed if he steps out of line—his family strikes me as disturbingly ungentle. I worry enough about *your* proximity to that world. His household will not be a suitable environment for Emily, I'm afraid."

It was reasonable. Oh, God, it was so terribly reasonable, and yet Noah felt like his very heart was on fire with…with something. With anger. It was certainly anger. Rage, even.

"You can't judge him by his family," he snapped. "It's not fair."

"Fair?" Papa put his clay down, putting his elbows on his knees and leaning in so that Noah could not miss the gravity of his tone. "Is it fair for you to treat your sister like a doll you can dress up and marry off just because you and your flashy friend from London have decided you want to be brothers?"

"That's… That's not it!"

"No." The word was briefly sharp, but then it softened. His whole demeanor softened. He leaned back, took the clay up again, and sighed heavily. "No, I suppose it's not, is it?"

The words had some terribly vague and disconcerting truth woven through them, like embroidery pulled so tight the fabric scrunched and threads began to snap. Noah could not meet his father's eye. He could not sit here, was standing up and throwing the door open before he could stop himself, blinking tears out of his eyes as he stormed through the halls with his stupid sketchbook feeling heavy as a paving stone under his arm.

He slammed it on a table just outside the parlor, opening it up to the ideas he'd had, an elaborate wedding dress for Emily, a few options of suits and haberdashery for David that would coordinate to make for as lovely a pair as any in the whole damn world. He found each of those pages, including the one he'd just spent another hour on, and he ripped them all out, leaving scraggly edges behind as he crumpled them up. He strode into the parlor, which boasted the nearest, hottest fire in the house.

As he watched it all curl to nothing in the crackling flames, he felt someone come up behind him. David. He knew it was David by the weight of his footsteps and the particular, familiar heat of him as he put his hands on Noah's arms. He wanted to lean back, to have David hold him tight until he could breathe right again. But he couldn't think of a good reason for a pair of friends to touch each other like that, so he stayed upright and unheld as he bit back more tears.

"Where's Emily?" Noah asked once he'd gotten control of his voice.

"She went to see about some tea." David rubbed at the tight knots in Noah's shoulders, an automatic and gentle gesture that made Noah feel even worse. "What was all that?"

The sketches were mostly ash now with a weak, doomed glow here and there. "Nothing," Noah whispered. "Just a very silly idea."

The feeling of David's hands working at his shoulders made him want to cry again, so he shook him off and went over to the stretch of carpet under the tree where the card game had been spread. He sat crisscross and picked the deck up.

"It's just going to be difficult," Noah said quickly, cutting and shuffling the cards. "Milan is feeling very far away right now."

Staring at the arcs of slapping cards as he shuffled the deck again and again, Noah didn't have to see whatever crossed David's face in the silence that followed.

"That makes sense," David said at last. "If I had a home like this, family like yours, I'd be questioning the idea of leaving it all too. In fact, I'm sort of shocked you chose London over this in the first place—"

"I love London," Noah said, much too harshly. He glanced up from the cards at last, to see David looking stunned. "It's London I don't want to leave. My family will always be here, but... *London*..."

"Um." David faltered. "Where exactly do you think London is going to go while you're gone?"

"Not *London* London!" Noah snapped, half the cards spilling out of his hands to the floor as he fumbled a shuffle. He had no idea what he was trying to say. None at all. He was blathering like an absolute idiot, plagued by a mad desire to beg David to go elope with Emily, or to come to Italy with him, to do something, *anything* to prove their friendship mattered as much to him as it did to Noah. "It's just, things might not be the same, when I get back. It's a big city. It changes, you know, changes all the time."

"You could stay." David rather carefully knelt down across from Noah, scooping up the cards he'd dropped and corralling them back into the stack. "There are brilliant tailors much closer to London. *In* London, I mean. If you love it, you can stay."

As if Noah hadn't tried that first. As if he hadn't been up

and down Savile Row already, laughed off as an eccentric's whelp from nowhere who'd splattered *feminine* and *un-English* designs all over his sketchbook, a tight thread through their insults not unlike the one his father had just yanked on in the study. Not that anyone—not Papa, not David, not *anyone*— would ever hear that that was the reason he'd started putting in applications in Paris and Milan instead, where his work had gotten much better reception.

Noah shook his head. "I just wish I could bring it with me."

"Noah—"

But he stopped at the sound of Emily coming down the hallway. There was nothing else to say, anyway. Talk couldn't save him from whatever this feeling was any more than it could catch his father's attention.

So he just shuffled and dealt out for three.

"Let's set some house rules and play for a bit, shall we?" he said, forcing some pep into his voice. It must not have been terribly convincing, because David and Emily met each other's eyes for a moment, making some silent, pitying pact to pretend he wasn't about to set those rules solidly in his own favor.

They were right. He was a dreadfully sore loser, and he felt the most recent loss acutely. But he could at least win a few hands here, if he arranged things right. There were worse ways to ease his misery, he supposed, than cheating at cards now and then.

Chapter Ten

David

London's West End, June 1885

David considered easing his misery by trying to put his fist through the side of the Orchid and Pearl Society building. The destruction that such a surface would throw back at him was sort of appealing at the moment. He decided against it, however; it would be very rude to bring negative attention to Miss Withers by being a madman in front of the neighbors. So, he stood properly under a streetlamp while he waited, hating himself in the politest manner he could manage as he lifted his hat to the occasional passerby.

The door finally opened. Noah stepped out onto the stoop and so lightly down the stairs that he might as well have been floating. The sight of him gave an instant jolt of relief, and David felt like a puppy watching and waiting for his acknowledgment. Closer up, the look on his face beneath the brim of his boater stopped David's tail from wagging and sent it right between his legs.

"I'm so sorry," David whispered. "Does she hate me?"

"No, *amore*. It's alright." Noah put a hand on his back and started them walking back the way they'd come. They turned onto the larger thoroughfare, where more frequent streetlamps cut through the full darkness that had finally fallen, lighting up swaths of pedestrians dodging around clopping and clanging traffic. The two of them were irrelevant on the busier road, a pair of nobodies talking about nothing, going nowhere.

Going the opposite direction from David's neighborhood. "Where are you taking me?" he asked, slowing his steps and moving to the side so that others could pass them while they worked out their destination.

Noah didn't seem interested in slowing down. He took David's arm and whisked him back into the flow of pedestrians. "I'm taking you home with me."

"But Emily—"

"Oh, she'll hate it," Noah agreed with a grim nod. "But I'm going to do it anyway."

Though he wasn't keen to upset Emily, David couldn't help but be happy with Noah's decision. He'd always loved going to Noah's, whether that meant his current set of rooms near Piccadilly, or the quaint suburban cottage he'd grown up in. When they were younger, David had treasured every second he spent with the Clarkes; not just Noah, but his father and sister too, all three of them interesting, radical, and brilliant. They were so entirely different from the Foresters—and indeed, so different from everyone—that David sometimes still had trouble believing they existed.

The excitement he always used to feel when he got to have supper with the Clarkes or stay with them on holiday, however, was long gone. Oh, they'd been supportive and kind when The Silva burned down. They were *Unitarians*, after all. David still wasn't entirely sure he knew what a Unitarian was, but it seemed to mean that destitution, scandal, and social disparity did not alarm them like it had alarmed everyone else in David's life. Even being a sodomite was acceptable in their circle nowadays, so long as one avoided vulgar terms in favor of something scholarly and polite like "Uranian." No, it was his position at the Fox that had lost him all respect with Noah's family. David didn't blame them. As they turned onto Noah's street, he simply counted himself lucky that he would only have to survive Emily's disapproval tonight. Dr. Clarke would not be here to lift any eyebrows or purse any lips at the sight of him.

They went up to Noah's rooms, where he unlocked the door, then knocked gently before opening it a crack. "It's me!" he said before opening it the rest of the way. "Don't kill me, please."

"Kill you?" David whispered.

Noah rolled his eyes exasperatedly as if to say *sisters.*

It was a two-storied set of modern but very cramped and narrow rooms with its own woodstove and a couple of street-facing windows hung with fluttering, summer-weight curtains. The sitting room walls were covered in strange paintings and gilded maps, the furniture all made from dramatic black-painted wood and sumptuous, earthy fabrics. Every surface seemed to be covered in either pillows, candles, or stacks of art and design magazines, many of which published Noah's own articles and illustrations. There were rolls of fabric in the umbrella stand, hand-carved figures all over the mantel, and the air smelled of wood shavings and cardamom.

Emily was kneeling on a pillow at the coffee table, dressed in the height of homebound rationality in a simply patterned robe over what appeared to be a woolen union suit. She was older than the last time he'd seen her, the curves of her face and angles of her petite frame all a bit softer, while her waves of mousy hair had been tamed into a hard, tight knot on the top of her head. She was whittling away at one of the little wooden figures she'd carved as a hobby for as long as David could remember, arts and crafts occupying the spare hours of her life, instead of exploding into every crevice like they had for Noah.

She was clearly absorbed in the task, but managed to say, "Evening, Noey."

"Ems, I've brought a guest."

She looked up at last. Her eyes grew cold when they fell on David and she gripped her carving knife alarmingly tight. "Mr. Forester," she said. "How lovely to see you."

"Doctor Clarke." David took off his hat and gave her a little bow. "A pleasure as always. I hope you're well?"

"I was until just a few seconds ago, thank you for asking."

The sound of scraping wood filled the room, slow and awkward.

David tried not to take that too personally as Noah rolled his eyes. "If I make us tea, will you want some?"

"I think not." She watched Noah check the kettle for water and light the stove. "Should I take this into my room?"

"No. We'll be in mine. You can just pretend we're not here. Sorry to have disturbed you; we won't bother you again." He sighed and brought David upstairs to his bedroom. "Make yourself comfortable. I'll be right back."

Noah lit some candles and left, his footsteps and a few words to his sister audible as he went back downstairs.

Because of Emily's feelings about David's profession, he had not been in Noah's home since she came to London last fall, and had not expected to until she left next month. She'd left her mark on the rest of the flat, but Noah's bedroom was still very much his own: trim and tidy in every way that mattered, but with a certain frantic cluttering in the passionate corners. The little table by the window was covered with sketches, pencils, and an assortment of drippy beeswax candles. Rings of fabric swatches sprawled on the bureau. There were *two* wardrobes, one of them bulging slightly behind a lace-trimmed silk dressing gown that hung from the front handle. The bed was a comfortable size, the headboard carved with dragons and draped with swaths of red fabric, the bedding brocaded and dramatic with a haphazard and impractical stack of pillows.

The awkwardness with Emily being what it was, he still had his hat and coat with him. He tossed them on a velvet bench at the end of the bed, then settled himself into a chair covered in an unlikely flowered paisley. It was not especially comfortable, but he melted into it as best he could. It had been an awful day, hadn't it? But it all felt rather far away from this cozy, bohemian little nook that smelled like the lilacs of his best mate's perfume...

The sound of cups clinking woke him up. He opened his bleary eyes to find Noah grinning at him from the end of his bed, teacup in hand, legs crisscross.

"You really did get comfortable, didn't you," said Noah.

David sat up straighter. "Damn, I didn't realize how tired I was."

"Rough night without me?"

"Yes, actually."

Noah sipped his tea smugly. *"Ti sta bene."* Serves you right. "Do you want something to eat?"

David realized that a teapot, the fixings, and a simple little supper had appeared on the table, all the sketches tucked away somewhere.

"You didn't have to," he said automatically.

Noah raised his eyebrow. "Not hungry?"

As he settled into this little haven, he realized that he was indeed hungry. If he tried to claim otherwise, his stomach would give him away soon enough. He begrudgingly poured some tea.

They were quiet for a bit, focused on the quaint assortment of pantry foods Noah had spread out for them. Some of the habits he'd acquired in Milan could be a bit much, but he'd learned the art of snacking nearly as impressively as he'd learned tailoring, regularly traipsing down Clerkenwell to stock up on all his Italian culinary vices. Thick slices of fluffy bread, spicy sausages, sheep's cheese, odd little green olives, fruit preserves, and peppers, all served with aggressively perfect English-style tea. David tried not to dig in too eagerly, but he caught an amused little look on Noah's face now and then that said he was not very successful.

"Feeling better?" Noah asked as he poured the last of the tea into his own cup.

David nodded. "Look. About Jo—"

"I told you I'm not ready to talk about it," he said. "I don't think you are, either. We'll both get miserable, and we'll probably argue. Perhaps tomorrow we can try to make sense of it all, but I don't want that tonight."

Something about the words made the sound of rattling pearls flash through David's mind. "What?" He cleared his throat. "What do you want tonight?"

Noah went a bit stunned for a second. Then he unstuck, finished off his tea, and escaped into his best Miss Penelope, a hand on his chest, lashes fluttering. "Well, darling, I'd most prefer a normal Saturday night. All prettied up and padding my bosom with winnings." He put on one of those innocently girlish looks he gave the unsuspecting as he swept all their money off the card table.

David laughed, relieved to be doing so after the day he'd had. "I think I could use a bit of Penny myself. I know we all shall miss her during this hiatus."

"You've got my frocks, but I suppose I could sneak something from Emily."

"I do not think I want to stretch your sister's hospitality quite that far."

"*Fine,*" Noah huffed, flopping backward onto the bed, where he was caught by his many pillows.

Quite unbidden, an image lit up David's imagination. Noah right there, right where he was lounging on his bed, in tousled shirtsleeves and one of those floofy underskirts, just the very start of his makeup painted on like it had been last night. Done up only halfway to Penelope.

Or perhaps undone halfway from her.

"You alright?" Noah asked.

David shook the notion off. "Of course."

Noah moved over and patted the space beside him. "Come here."

He hesitated, but the spot made for him looked too inviting to resist. He lay down on his back. There was just enough room for both of them to lie shoulder to shoulder. He sighed and settled into the plush pillows and the warm companion beside him.

It seemed he'd hardly closed his eyes when he felt Noah's fingers on his waistcoat buttons.

"Hey," he mumbled, brushing the ticklish sensation off. It was darker than it had been, the scent of smoking candlewicks and peppermint toothpaste curling up in his nose. "What do you think you're doing?"

Noah propped himself up on an elbow and fought his way back to his task, his smile very sly in the dim light of one remaining candle. "You can't sleep in my bed full-dressed in the clothes you wore to The Ailing Hare, *amore.*"

"Fair point." David closed his eyes and let Noah handle the rest of his waistcoat.

When he finished, Noah said, "Are you making me do the rest too, then?"

David shrugged. "I'm accustomed to a valet."

He expected to get shoved off the bed for that one, but Noah did quite the opposite, sliding his hand up to untie David's cravat more slowly and carefully than any valet would. Once it was loose enough, he went for the collar pin beneath. David startled a bit at the caress of Noah's fingers as they brushed his throat.

"What's the matter?" Noah whispered.

"I was just kidding." Forcing a chuckle, David stood up and started getting his cuffs, tie, and collar off himself. "You don't have to be my valet."

Noah surprised him again by watching, eyes glinting in the candlelight. As David finished with the trimmings and put them on the vanity, he noticed that Noah was already under the covers. At some point he must have put on a nightshirt that was so delicate it was really more of a nightgown. He'd tidied up after their supper and tied the top half of his hair out of his face with a bit of black ribbon. The effect was so stunning that he wondered whether Noah had set the scene for his benefit.

But that was ridiculous. David started on the buttons of his shirtsleeves, determined not to lose his head. "How long was I sleeping for?"

"An hour at most. You were snoring a bit. It was darling, I hated to wake you, but the linens come first."

"Naturally."

"Do you want to wash up?" He put his head back on one of his less-decorative pillows. Most of the beaded ones had found their way to the floor already, in a deliberate sort of stack by the nightstand. "I put warm water in the washbowl, but I can heat some more up if it's cooled too much. Use whatever you need; what's mine is yours. And don't worry about working out what actually *is* mine; the line gets blurry quickly when

Emily's around, so just lock the door on her side and she'll never be any the wiser."

David stared at him, suddenly so grateful that it felt like a knife in his gut. "Thank you," he said quietly. "My God, Noah, thank you so much."

"For what?"

"All of this. I don't deserve it after what I put you and Jo through."

Noah's confusion crinkled into obvious offense. "Stop being ridiculous."

David's throat tightened and his voice threatened to break on him. "I showed up at someone's house uninvited, made a truly offensive request, threw a tantrum, and then asked... asked for this."

Noah sat up a little, leaning on his elbow again. "Asked for what? Some company? A meal, a bed, and a warm basin?"

"It's too much. Considering—"

"Considering that a man you're clearly terrified of is threatening to take your club away?" Noah let out a low, sarcastic whistle. "Wow. A crime against humanity, that is. Anyone who lets a trifle like that whip him up has certainly lost all right to his basic necessities."

"Noah—"

But Noah wasn't listening and David didn't know what he was going to say anyway, so he broke off as Noah swung his feet to the floor and into the slippers he'd left by the bed. He whisked past David and into the water closet that adjoined the two upstairs rooms.

"What are you doing?" David asked, following him.

"Checking the water." The candlelight stretched just far enough that he could see Noah take his hand out of the washbowl on the stand and shake it. A few cool drops dampened David's sleeve.

"I'm sure it's fine," said David.

"Yeah, that's what you'd say even if it were a bloody block of ice." Noah tried to nudge him out of the doorway. "I'm going to put the kettle on. I'll be right back."

"I don't need—"

Noah steered him out of the way and up against the wash-room wall. David gasped and started to ask *what the devil*, but then Noah put a finger to David's lips. They were close, nearly as close as they'd been in the stairwell.

Noah leaned in even farther, whispering against the finger trapped between them: "Will you please, *please*, let me do something for you without making a fuss for once?"

The unexpected roughness and sudden proximity sent a sharp spike of desire through David's belly. For a strange, suspended moment, he imagined that Noah might spin him around, grab one of the jars of pastes and potions that lined the shelves, and fuck him like this impeccable private wash-room were no better than a Hyde Park cottage, a collision of beauty and vulgarity that got David's heart racing the second it crossed his mind.

"Well?" Noah hissed. "Will you?"

Pinned, aroused, and utterly dumbfounded, David just nodded.

Without another word, Noah left, his nightgown swirling with agitation at his ankles. David did not move. His heart thundered and his cock swelled a bit stupidly in his trousers, but the rest of him stayed stock-still until Noah came back with a candle and a kettle. He put the candle down, poured water that steamed up the mirror above the basin, and swirled it with his hand like a mother testing her infant's bath. Satis-fied, he dipped a cloth in, squeezed it out, and handed it to David with a bar of soap.

"Wash up, *amore*."

David took it in a trance. "For you?"

Noah paused for so long that David was sure he'd misread everything and spoiled fifteen years of friendship forever. But then Noah stepped closer. With a careful hand, he cupped David's face. He licked his own lips and bit the bottom one in a way that made David instantly desperate for the same treatment. Then, with the sort of deep breath one takes before a mad dive of unknown depths, he traced two fingers lightly over David's lips until he'd coaxed out a trembling sigh, then pushed them into his mouth.

David moaned and sucked on them before he even knew what he was doing, gasping as the wet fingers slid down his lower lip, his scruffy chin, the hollow of his throat.

The searing touch made him realize something that should have been obvious. Through their history, he'd seen many sides of Noah. He knew horny Noah, and bored Noah, and scared Noah. He also knew flirty Noah, playful Noah, and Miss-Penelope-Primrose-Noah.

But he had never met the Noah who shoved his fingers in men's mouths, then looked up through his eyelashes in a manner that meant one thing only, purring in a voice so blatant it would hold up in court, "If that's the motivation you need, then yes. Do it for me."

Wow. Alright. He wasn't sure he deserved such an introduction on this night of all nights, but this version of Noah seemed awfully hard to argue with. The apparition was so enthralling that David could only wait and hope that those fingers were headed where he thought they were. His stomach turned sensuous flips as Noah skimmed the hair that peeked out the top of his collar, swirling down button after button until David was flexing his hips, bracing for the touch that he wanted like he couldn't remember ever wanting anything.

But Noah stopped short of the mark and leaned in the doorway, like he intended to watch, to drink David in with his big gray eyes and then… Then he didn't know what, exactly.

Every nerve taut with tension, David finished unbuttoning his shirtsleeves. He expected a scold or a click of the tongue when he slid the suspenders off his shoulders and let the shirt fall to the tiled floor, but Noah said nothing. He just watched, biting his bottom lip again as David carefully started on the buttons of his trousers, fumbling around a ferocious cockstand.

"You're so pretty," Noah whispered as the trousers fell too. In the tiny space, David could hear how his breathing had gone heavy, his gaze shamelessly transfixed on the tent David's excitement had made of his linen drawers. "I miss doing this."

"Doing what?" David asked.

"Watching you take your clothes off, of course." Noah smiled the most beautiful smile as the words sank in and nearly gave David's younger self a heart attack. "Don't act so shocked. You knew I was doing it. You liked it." A playful accusation. He took one finger and trailed it lightly along David's jutting cock, the whisper of pleasure releasing the pent-up growl in David's chest. "And you like it even more now. So. Go on."

Noah hadn't been talking about getting him hot water, had he? *Let me do something for you for once.* Noah was not good at putting words to feelings, but maybe if David had ever taken a moment to let Noah put *actions* to them, he'd have seen a different message.

Very gently, Noah tugged at the drawstring, then helped David step out of the last scraps of his clothing. A slow smile spread over his pretty face. David put up nothing resembling a fuss as Noah steered him to the washstand, kissing his shoulders from behind as David finally dipped his hands in the bowl of warm, wonderful water and scrubbed his face, wetted his hair, lathered the soap. Through the thin layer of sleepy white silk, Noah pushed up against David's back as they floated

through the task, fingers tweaking soapy nipples, tongue sliding over stray water drops, stealing the cloth and using it to
touch every intimate crevice of his body in a way that David
had never even thought to hope for back when all they knew
how to do was tug and devour.

As Noah reached around to stroke him with a slippery hand,
finding his own gentle friction temptingly close to where it
was really wanted, David glanced at the mirror above the
washstand. He didn't care for mirrors. He half-expected to
be jolted right out of the moment, but tonight he recognized
the man he saw in the glass. Undressed, unstyled, with fuzzy
torso and long limbs that were undoubtedly his. Noah's chin
on his shoulder looked as real as it felt as he nuzzled the curve
of David's jaw with his eyes closed, oblivious to the ribbon
slipping from his hair or the utterly wanton set of his features.
That was them. It was really them: *here, together, now.*

Washed, rinsed, and dried at last, Noah kissed the nape
of David's neck, long hair tickling the damp skin. "To bed,
Davy."

To bed. To bed with Noah. *With Noah.* Not a cupboard.
Not a bush. A fucking *bed*, a big fancy one with pillows and
nice linens and an entire night stretching out ahead of them.
He grabbed Noah by the hand. It was hard to say who yanked
whom, but next thing he knew, they'd toppled each other to
the mattress, both laughing and shushing each other when the
dragon headboard banged against the wall.

David pinned Noah to the bed. He felt so incredible under the
flimsy silk that a sort of wildness destroyed any lingering hesitation David might have had. He ran his hands roughly down
the warm lines of Noah's torso, lining up to slide their pricks
together through the smooth fabric, kissing down Noah's neck
until David could press his lips to the pearly button at the hollow of his throat.

With teeth and tongue, he got the little button undone, then licked the skin beneath it, which made Noah gasp and arch his back. It would be humiliating to admit how much time he'd spent perfecting maneuvers like that, but Noah's response made the time seem incredibly well-spent.

He moved to the wrist buttons, taking his time to nibble and soothe what turned out to be a surprisingly sensitive spot. Noah lifted his hips and whimpered incoherently until David finally hiked the nightgown up and over Noah's head, the two of them burrowing under the covers to kiss and caress and grind into the wetness that had dripped between them.

"Oh, God," Noah moaned, his mouth pressing against the curve of David's neck and his nails dragging down his back. "God, Davy, please."

The sweet plea tingled all the way down his spine. Davy? No one ever called him that in bed. He looked down incredulously at Noah, who smiled with that old mischief and playfully licked David's bottom lip.

A dam broke. Something David had not realized he was still holding back released all at once, the fire in his body suddenly spreading to his brain. Thoughts of sensual skills and deliberate teasing went out the window, replaced with the frantic motion of tongues and hands and hips and skin. Oh *God*, how had it not fucking *killed* him to look at this incredible person day after day, year after year, and not taste every inch he could reach? He moved down a smooth throat, a lightly haired chest, pausing to lap up the drops of spend they'd both left on Noah's navel, the salty trail leading him exactly where he most longed to be.

"Fuck, Davy!"

Noah bucked up uncontrollably as David took him in his mouth all once. He hadn't meant to, would have liked to linger and tease, but he couldn't resist. Noah's cock was swollen near to bursting, harder than David could remember him ever being before.

David was positively feral with the fact that he'd made Noah want him like this. He picked up the pace, understanding now why Noah was so picky. Noah could be selfish and status-driven at times, but there was nothing selfish in the way he received pleasure. As he received, he gave David back everything he'd ever wanted. Writhing, moaning, telling David he was *good, so good, so perfect*, stroking his face, petting his hair, saying *Davy Davy Davy…*

"Davy, I'm…"

The unfinished warning was unnecessary; David knew good and well it was about to happen and he was damn near desperate for it. Noah twisted tight hands in his hair, lifted his hips, and flooded David's mouth.

David was so wrapped up that by the time he'd swallowed every drop he could get, he was humping at the mattress like the poor thing was his mistress. He was about a second from spending like that, but then Noah sat up and grabbed his arms. With surprising and thrilling roughness, he pinned David on his back. He kissed him deep and filthy, like he was trying to taste himself on David's tongue.

"What do you want, Davy?" he whispered. "Tell me. Do you want me to suck you?"

The answer to that seemed painfully obvious. David wished he could summon words as thrilling as Noah was probably angling for, but speech was more than he could manage with his body strung tight and his heart on the verge of explosion. He moaned something vaguely like *please*, and thank God Noah was well-primed to meet him in the world of actions instead, starting under the blankets and rephrasing the question with his eyebrows raised in a silent *This?*

David nodded desperately, watching Noah's head move

down. Kisses on his stomach asked again and again, *This? This?* And David kept nodding until Noah finally kissed the very tip of his cock, and David finally found one word:

"*Yes*," he gasped. "Yes, yes, yes…"

He repeated it over and over, along with other words, probably; he wasn't quite sure, because he ceased to exist outside the feeling of Noah's rough hands digging into his tense thighs, a wet mouth on his prick and his balls and crease of his arse, a wild curiosity leaving no inch of him unexplored until, with a loving moan, Noah took him in deep, humming and bobbing, clutching David's hand where it had tangled in his hair.

David banged the back of his head against the dragon-carved headboard, his awareness going white-hot. He bit his knuckles to keep from shouting as his own crisis ripped through like it hoped to kill him now so he could die happy.

Truly spent in every sense, they collapsed against each other amid the jumble of pillows. David was sweat-slicked and shivering. Noah pulled the blankets up over both of them.

They touched foreheads and clasped hands. Panting and speechless, David stared at Noah's face, overcome with a sweetness that he couldn't seem to find the words for, either.

After a moment, Noah pulled David's fingers to his lips and kissed them lingeringly.

"Goodnight, Davy." There was a desperate edge to his whisper. "I… God, I just. What I'm trying to say, is…"

"I know, beautiful." He snuggled in, warm with body heat and pure understanding, and softly kissed the top of Noah's head. "I love you too."

Chapter Eleven

Noah

When Noah awoke the next morning, it was still real. They were both stark naked, lying in his own bed in his own home and they'd been sober and everything.

Bloody hell.

David was sleeping. Hints of daylight creeping through the edges of the curtains lit up the bits of gold and bronze in his hair like some god really had combed him through with precious metals.

Noah got up quietly and slipped into a pair of silk trousers and his lace-trimmed dressing gown, definitely *not* staring at David. He never smoked in his home, already plagued by the hypocrisy of a smoking tailor, but today, he went into the bathroom and allowed himself exactly two forbidden puffs of a cigarette. He disposed of the evidence, sprayed some perfume, and brushed his teeth, as if that would actually undo his lapse.

Another peek at the vision in his bedroom. Still there. David, still there, sleeping, too beautiful to be believed. David, in his bed. Not just in a friendly way, but *in his bed* in the most *in bed* way possible.

He caught himself biting his lip as he thought back on what they'd done.

Oh, it had been *good*.

He felt sick. Sick and excited, like he'd already had one too many goes on a carousel, but was itching for one more spin. He'd felt like this the first time he went properly to bed with someone too. Far from home in a *trattoria* that he stupidly called a *pub* and couldn't pronounce the proper name of either way, he accepted too much Campari from a stranger he could barely speak to and woke the next morning with the sense that he'd partaken in either a miracle or his own death sentence. He felt the same way as he watched David's chest rise and fall under the blankets. He felt foreign and lost and absolutely thrilled.

But what sense did that make? This was his room, his bed, his best friend. He'd done nothing new, nor drunk anything more interesting than English tea. He knew just who he was, what it was, what it meant. His lover was a Londoner whose name he knew better than any other on the planet. He was home, home, home, but for some bizarre reason, he wanted to shake Davy awake and tell him what had happened like it had happened with someone else.

But that was even more insane than the letters he'd scribbled to David about his lovers in Milan. He hadn't sent those, and he didn't wake David up now. He should let his friend sleep. He'd been so tired last night, and Noah had kept him...up. Best to let him be.

Noah went down to the kitchen. Emily was at the little table, dressed in comfortable skirts with her hair hidden in a cotton cap. She was reading the paper and drinking black coffee, like she did every Sunday.

Her eyes flicked up for just a moment when he came in, then back down to her paper. "You're up awfully early," she said. "Planning to come with me today?"

Noah blinked more haze out of his eyes. "Where are you going?"

"Papa and some of the other Meadrow Chapel folks are coming into town for one of those transcendental talks, remember? You're invited along, of course; I know Papa and the rest would love to see you."

"I don't think I'm up to it."

"That's unsurprising." She sipped her coffee, eyes never leaving her paper. "Something tells me you didn't get much sleep last night."

Shit.

"Emily, please."

"Please what?" Exasperated, she put her paper down and looked at him wearily. "What am I going to do? Tattle on you? I should hope we're a bit beyond that."

Noah threw himself into the chair across from her. "I'm sorry." He rested his forehead in his hands. The entire cosmos had collapsed down to him and David last night. He had certainly not behaved like his *sister* was a room away. "I'm so, so sorry."

The chair scraped as she stood up. A rough hand tousled his hair and a moment later, a steaming cup of coffee appeared on the table beside him.

"Thank you," he muttered.

"Noey?"

"Yes?"

"Is that how it is between the two of you?"

Noah peered up at her through the curtain of his sleep-mussed hair. She looked much less irritated than he'd expected. He shook his head and took up his coffee. "No. Not really."

"I didn't think so." She sat back down across from him. "Why now?"

He shrugged. "To bother you, I suppose."

"Noah."

"I don't know." He rolled his eyes to the ceiling. "This is mortifying. Please kill me for real this time."

"Too easy. You have to live with it."

"I didn't plan it, I promise. It just happened."

"Just *happened*? You're very lucky you're not a girl. You wouldn't last a week."

He shot her a severe glare. "I make a lovely girl, ask anyone."

"Speaking of, make yourself useful and put my hair in order before I leave, will you? For some reason I had to spend a significant portion of the evening with a pillow over my head and now it's a knotty mess."

He took the ribbing and went to get her combs and pins from the tiny second room that he used as a study when he had no guests. Let her tease him and boss him around a bit; he deserved worse, and most in his position would get worse than they deserved. While he was upstairs, he peeked in on David, who was still sleeping but had turned so his bare shoulders and upper back were facing the door. There were some little red lines across his skin. Scratch marks.

Good God.

He shut the door on that. David had possessed those *exact* same shoulders last week. They were nothing to get silly over now. In fact, they'd probably even been scratched up by someone, what did he know? If last night was the norm for him, he was probably well-scratched at all times and for good reason.

Emily catching them was mostly Noah's own fault; he was not quiet, and since he'd never been stupid enough to fuck in that bed, he hadn't realized the headboard would bump against the wall like that until it was far too late. Still, David shared the blame. Who took their clothes off like that? Who could actually get buttons undone with their *teeth*? Was that even *possible*? And what on earth had he been doing with his mouth? Did he have three tongues Noah didn't know about? No one could be expected to behave themselves under the influence of such ministrations.

He was nearly overwhelmed by the desire to get back in bed, but he couldn't. He needed to do his sister's hair, after all. He needed to do anything, really, aside from stand here and obsess over whatever insanity was happening between him and David. Silk trousers did not hide such obsessions particularly well, after all. He tied his dressing gown more firmly around his waist.

Once he finally fetched Emily's things, he went back to her and got started on the snarls. She continued with her paper as he took up a piece of her long hair and started untangling it from the bottom with a jade comb that looked terribly dull compared with a certain pair of eyes…

In his distraction, he hit a nasty snag.

"Careful there!" Emily swatted at him. "Noey, I have a question."

He put the comb down and used his fingers and a little pomade to loosen the knot. "Is it going to humiliate me further?"

"Probably."

He got the comb back up and smoothed the section before moving to the next. "Out with it, then."

There was something of a sigh in her voice. "I still can't see a good reason for you to be associating with Mr. Forester—"

"Will you—"

"Let me finish." She turned her head just enough that he could see the side of her rather serious expression. "Friends with so little in common usually drift apart, don't they? Yet, you're just as attached to him as you've ever been. You won't hear a word against him, even though there's enough words to say that if you said them in court, they'd lock him right up. So… I'm not sure why it never occurred to me before, but are you in love with him? Is that what this has been about all along?"

Noah became very careful with the comb. He would not

want to hit a snag now. She might read into it. *He* might read into it.

He knew the answer to this. He loved David, of course. But *in love*? The answer was *no*. Obviously.

But he could not seem to say that. He continued not saying it until Emily sighed.

"You poor thing," she said. "Have you really been pining after him all this time?"

"I didn't say that." He started on her braid with tingling fingers. "I haven't said anything."

"You've said enough."

"Stop it." He finished the braid, spiraled it into a knot on the top of her head, and took up the pins. "This is very complicated, alright?"

She sat quiet for another moment. Then she laughed. "I suppose it's very good that Papa didn't let you marry me off to him, then."

Noah froze. Dear lord, he hadn't thought about *that* debacle in years.

"God, Ems." He secured a pin slowly, distracted. "Papa told you about that, did he?"

"He wanted to see if I was in on it."

"Why didn't you mention it?"

She grew a bit thoughtful. "I don't know, exactly. There was just something so strange about it. I thought it was best if we just pretended it never happened."

He took that in, going silent as he thought back on the bitterness he'd felt at that loss, a melodramatic, end-of-the-world feeling that had not matched the situation at all.

Unless…

"Noey?"

He startled and looked down to see that he'd frozen with a pin half-situated, the rest of them having somehow made their way between his lips. He quickly settled the loose one, then began securing the rest, hands flitting about the task erratically.

Oh God.

He *had* been pining after David back then, hadn't he? No one sat around burning things and crying because their sister couldn't marry their friend. Noah hadn't realized he was pining, of course, because how was he supposed to know that was even possible? They were hardly the first pair of friends to get cozy in a boarding school broom cupboard, after all, and he'd not understood that *love* was possible until later. He hadn't known what he wanted from David, just knew that he wanted *something* from him, something vague, something big, something that had driven him to the only outlet that made any sense...

A gentle hand on his wrist brought him screeching back to the dining table. Emily turned around and looked at him. He wasn't quite sure what she saw on his face, but it must have been terrible, because she stood up quickly and pulled him into a tight, pitying embrace.

"You poor thing," she said again. "I can't believe I never saw it. No wonder. My heavens, no wonder you follow him to these wretched places. You'll follow him anywhere, won't you?"

A little creak on the landing startled him before he could look that question in the face. It was David, coming down the stairs dressed in yesterday's rumpled evening clothes, his gleaming hair tousled and his tie draped loose over his shoulders. He leaned in the parlor doorway, a little smile on his scruffy face.

Noah clutched the front of his dressing gown, hoping it would keep his suddenly panicked heart inside where it belonged.

"Good morning," said David. "I apologize for taking the liberty of such a lie-in. You could have woken me."

Noah stared at him, and he saw it. He saw what Jo saw. What Emily saw. What his own father had seen, a decade ago. That thread he had not understood. That he'd never taken back out to examine, even after he'd acquired the knowledge to grasp it. He hadn't wanted to know what it was, because if he did...

If he did, he'd have to face how terribly he'd mucked it up.

"Mr. Forester," said Emily in a solemn greeting. "No apologies necessary. Your presence was not missed."

"That's quite a relief, Doctor Clarke."

"Breakfast?" said Emily. "There's some eggs and toast on the stove. Coffee as well."

"Far too generous. I can't tell you how much I appreciate your hospitality. Noah, have you eaten?"

Noah gaped dumbly at his friend's question. Eaten? Who could eat at a time like this? Didn't David realize what was happening?

"Noah?"

He managed to sort of shake his head, and the others returned to their chilly politeness, wandering into the kitchen to fix plates while Noah started to feel like he could not breathe. He went to the window and opened it farther. It didn't help. He needed to smoke. He needed to do something with his hands. Oh damn, he was already worrying at the lace on his wrist without noticing, spoiling it.

When they returned, Noah felt them looking at him, but could not bring himself to acknowledge it. He sat down at the plate they set for him. He ate without tasting as they snipped back and forth, his eyes darting to David and back down again, over and over until he was dizzy. He could tell that David thought something was wrong. It was there in the way he narrowed his eyes. Noah tried to smile, to ease the concern, but he probably just made it worse.

He sort of heard a brisk knock at the door. Emily stood. "That'll be Papa's coachman."

She left the table to get her hat and parasol, then returned to kiss Noah's cheek and say her farewells.

"At least come see Papa later, while he's in town," she said. "You know we'll all be at Bradigan's taking coffee for ages after the meeting's through. Will you?"

"M-maybe," Noah stammered. "Send my regards, in any case."

She gave him a meaningful, pity-laden pout before she left.

Once the door was closed behind her, neither Noah nor David said anything for a torturously long time. When they did, they started in at the same time:

"Noah, about last night—"

"Jo thinks we're lovers."

David stopped short as Noah's words lingered more thickly in the air. Noah's face burned. He got up, chair scraping, and wandered distractedly to the warm stove. There was still enough coffee in the pot for each of them to have half a cup. Coffee was terrible on this side of the channel, and Emily's was the worst of it, always gritty and weak. He pushed the slightly less-terrible portion across the table to David and took his own to stand in front of the bookcase.

"Jo?" David cleared his throat, confused. "Jo thinks we're lovers?"

"Yes."

Noah took a long, tortured drink of the sludge in his cup. He could feel David's eyes piercing holes into his back.

"And that's what you want to discuss this morning." David's voice was even for now, but incredibly, unsustainably tight. "You want to talk about Jo. And how *she* thinks we're lovers."

Oh God. He was angry. And not due to some panicky flare of temper, either; he had every right to be angry. Especially when Noah's incredibly unhelpful mouth went ahead with the words: "Yes. And apparently, Emily does too."

Noah knew the posture David would be sitting in, his knees at angles with elbows digging into them, rubbing his eyes with the heels of his hands. He peeked over his shoulder to check. Indeed, Noah's mind had done him up just right.

"Emily." David laughed at the ground. "Emily and Jo think we're lovers. Isn't that fascinating?"

"I think—"

"So, what did you tell them, Noah?" David turned, leaning an elbow on the back of his chair, flashing the dark smile of a man at the end of his patience. "Did you tell them we're just friends who get a bit *silly* sometimes? That we just flirt and kiss and *fuck* when we're somehow drunk on one toddy or some tea and olives?"

Noah turned fully around, tucking the edges of the dressing gown across his chest, but no matter how tightly he crossed his arms, they couldn't shield him from the pain in David's voice. "I'm sorry I got carried away last night, David," he whispered, suddenly wretched with regret. "If I'd known it would hurt you like this, I wouldn't have—"

"Why do you do always do that?"

Noah's fingers froze on the lace. The look of pained curiosity on David's face made his heart pound beneath them, threatening escape. "Do what?"

"Act like it would be the end of the world for both of us if you had feelings for me."

Noah's first impulse was to shout that it *would* be the end of the world. That spoiling so vital a friendship with the messiness of spoken feelings was obviously apocalyptic. It was entirely irrational, yet he felt it so strongly that he couldn't come up with a more reasoned response before David cut him off with an eye-rolling, cynical sort of laugh.

"You know what?" David said. "I don't have it in me to push this issue with you today, I really don't. You win."

"I…win?"

"You got carried away," said David in an empty echo. "You didn't mean anything by it. It was sweet, it was silly, it was all in good fun. Fine. I'm not going to drive myself crazy trying to beat that hand. Why bother?"

He put his head back into his hands, going very quiet. His silence threatened to crumble something in Noah, some vital support beam that he might not be able to live without. He went over and started to stroke David's hair, but David jolted suddenly upright and out of his chair so fast that his hair dusted Noah's nose on the way up.

"I have to go," David said, tugging at his rumpled clothes. "I have to call on the staff to let them know what's going on with the club."

Noah watched in stunned silence as he vanished upstairs, coming back with his hat and coat and heading for the door. "Now? You're leaving now?" Noah said, voice rising in panic. He didn't know what to do; David had never done this before, going cold, threatening to leave. "David, please. You can't—"

"You're not the only one with a job to rush off to, you know." David popped the hat onto his head. "I've got half a dozen staff to call on and more than sixty club members to think about today. They need me. You, on the other hand, are obviously unaffected by getting *carried away* last night, so I might as well focus my attentions where they're needed."

"Wait!" He grabbed David by the arm and pulled him back so they were facing each other. Noah had to fix this, do whatever was necessary to prevent a separation that felt frighteningly final. "Are you really just going leave? Just like that?"

"Yes." David shook him off, and Noah stepped back holding the lace at his own throat closed as his mind raced through disturbingly few options. If he couldn't get David to stay...

"Fine," he said. "Then give me a minute to get ready, will you? I'll come along."

David's fingers paused on his coat buttons, lapsing into an incredulous, uncomfortable silence. "You're not invited, Noah," he said at last, the harsh edge in his voice nearly crumbling Noah's resolve.

But he breathed through his reluctance and said, "That's alright. I won't get in your way. Just give me a minute, as I said."

David narrowed his eyes, like he couldn't possibly believe that Noah was being serious. Finally, he sighed and hung up his hat and coat on the rack they'd never made it to yesterday. "Bloody hell, I wish I could stay mad at you for more than thirty seconds."

"What are you doing?" said Noah.

"Getting comfortable, I guess." David sat back down in the chair. "I've never seen you get ready in *a minute* before, and I doubt you're going to start now."

Noah couldn't seem to move. "So. I can come along when you leave?"

"Do I have a choice in the matter?"

"No."

David gave an impressively thorough shrug. "Well, then."

The lace along Noah's collarbone was growing soft with the agitation he was putting it through. "David, we should, um. I think we should talk."

"Should we?" David's voice was still snappish and his face was skeptical. "I admit, I didn't think you'd ever say that."

"I'm a bit shocked myself."

"Will you be able to say anything else, do you think?" His skepticism softened to a reluctant smile. "Or was that the limit?"

Noah shook his head, feeling a thread slip out of place between his fingers. "I'm not sure yet."

He expected David to push him, to challenge him, to demand he put all his thoughts and feelings on display for inspection immediately. Instead, he stood up, chair scraping, and crossed the room to gather Noah up into a warm, solid embrace. Noah closed his eyes and melted into it, breathing him in. The hint of Noah's soaps still clung to the skin of his neck, but after a fuck, a sleep, and a return to yesterday's clothes, that unmistakable, earthy something that was *David* stood out stronger.

"Where do you want to start, Noah?" David said gently. "I know this is hard for you. So where do we start? You pick."

How was he supposed to do that? Noah started everything by understanding the rules. The dress codes, the proportion charts, the winning conditions. He didn't always follow them, but if you didn't know what they were, you couldn't make them your own. That's what Signor Corsetti had told him, as he absorbed the mathematics of aesthetics into his marrow; easy enough, considering his father had drilled the rules of nature and science into his head for years by then.

The only rule he and David had ever had was to stick together. And yet... They'd broken that one once, hadn't they? When Noah left England. When David made no move to follow.

That chill started back up at the base of Noah's spine as a suspicion took shape in the recesses of his understanding.

"David," he said carefully, knowing that it was a strange place to start, but suddenly certain that if they tried anything else, the whole structure of the conversation would lack the most basic integrity. "Davy, who is Lord Belleville to you? Really?"

David's chest expanded with a very deep, very bracing

breath. He clutched Noah tighter, kissing his forehead with a soft reverence that meant whatever he was about to say next felt to him like a dreadful gamble.

"We were lovers," he said, in a straightforward way that his tight body language put the lie to. "Well. That's how I saw it, anyway. It eventually became very clear that we were not on the same page about that. To him, I was more of a consort. A mistress. A pet," he added in a cynical mutter.

Noah nodded against David's chest, the real question, the one he was really asking, building up and threatening to burst the seams. "When?"

David paused. And then he said it:

"When you were in Italy."

Noah knew he should look up. That he should meet David's eyes for this. But he couldn't. In fact, more than anything, he wanted to vanish into this warmth that had been his security blanket for half his life. He held David's lapels, pressing mouth and nose against the scratchy hollow beneath his jaw, worried, for the first time in a very long time, that this might not be there for him anymore once this conversation was over.

At last, Noah took a step back. David looked surprisingly stoic; Noah, on the other hand, was certain he looked just as messy and chaotic as he felt right now.

"Davy, will you tell me what happened? While I was gone?"

"I don't know. When I'm done, will you tell me what last night really meant to you?"

"Yes," Noah said, desperate to agree to anything David asked for. Based on the way David pursed his lips, he'd heard how the word had come too quickly to mean much.

"I'm going to hold you to it," he warned. "No cheating."

"No cheating," Noah agreed. "I promise."

"It's a long story," David admitted, returning to the table. He picked up his coffee cup, but once it got too close to his nose, he seemed to think better of sipping it and put it back. "It should give you plenty of time to decide what you want to say. And when you do say it, Noah, whatever it is, I want you to know that I will believe you. I will hear your words, believe them, and never, ever ask you again. One chance. All in. Do you agree?"

Noah was not so quick to answer this time. The idea still scared him, but if he rejected this deal, he'd only manage what he'd been trying to avoid in the first place: losing David for good.

"Yes," he said, once he'd swallowed the lump in his throat and could mean it fully. "I agree."

David held out his hand. A hand that, in the past two days alone, had fixed him drinks, stroked his face, gotten him off, and held him steady. Noah took it. He shook it. Then he pulled it to his lips and kissed it.

"That's binding," he whispered. "But you first."

David leaned against the little blackwood table that creaked under the weight of him. He toyed with the handle of the coffee cup. "Things weren't ideal for me, when you left. My father was deep in the bottle and the debts were piling up. My brother had run away, my sister eloped, my mother essentially stuck her fingers in her ears when I tried talking sense into her. It was all crumbling under my feet and no one would help me—or even just *let* me—do anything to stop it. And once you were gone, I was faced with the fact that it was never getting better. There was no magical apprenticeship on the Continent for me. No sensible family and radical congregation holding a net out in case I slipped.

"I needed a way to survive when it inevitably fell apart. So, I got the maître to let me work as a waiter at some of the big events when no one was paying attention. I kept squirreling away little bits of money here and there, praying it would be enough. And then I met Lord Belleville. At one of the events. He didn't know I was anyone remotely important, and so he was… Well, an intelligent person would have called it *obscenely rude*. I simply considered it *forward* and *complimentary*. It occurred to me that I might have stumbled upon a golden opportunity."

He gave one of those naughty smiles he pulled out for the sake of a good pun. It was weak. Noah's mouth had gone dry and he could not bring himself to return it.

"You see where this is going, don't you?" said David. "His wife has always been sickly. When she left early, I slipped him the number of an unoccupied room and met him there. I was such a cocky shit, thought I was so clever and pretty for getting the attention of someone like him. Once he got there, though, I found that fooling around with you and a few frisky debutantes had not prepared me for the situation. When he was through with me, I was fit for Bedlam, sobbing and telling him everything, absolutely everything. Who I was. All my family's troubles. All the…" He paused, meaningfully, but seemed to decide against following whatever had occurred to him. "Just everything. He was actually quite kind. He listened, or at least he pretended to, and then said all the right things. I was *beautiful*, I was *underappreciated*, I was *unjustly abandoned*. I was very impressed by that last one. *Unjustly abandoned*. I fell in love with him right then, just for that. He said he'd take care of me, and at that time, I was genuinely powerless to resist those words."

Noah picked at the lace on the edge of his dressing gown again, letting it blatantly unravel as he became more uncomfortable than he could remember ever feeling in David's presence.

David went on as if he had not just turned Noah's belly into a boiling, bubbling froth of guilt. "At first, it was exhilarating. I'd warm his bed and accompany him to his clubs, which were all either rich and luxurious or excitingly scandalous. Meanwhile, he gave me money and gifts and the feeling that I was worth something to someone. But then things changed. I'm still a little fuzzy on how it happened, or when, but at some point, the arrangement became sort of nasty. He was very good to me in some ways, but in others… Well, in any case, the, uh, the fire happened."

That's how David always put it. Though the truth had plastered the papers until everyone knew it, David only ever referred to the disaster of his father's death as "the fire."

He went on. "I was so stupid that I thought Belleville might actually help me, house me, *save* me like he said he would, but no. When I got difficult and couldn't keep up with his standards for me, he dropped me."

"You didn't say anything," said Noah, his head spinning. How could he not know something so vital about the man he called his best friend? "I understand why you never put it in a letter, but I started for home as soon as I heard about the fire. We talked eventually. Why did you leave all that out?"

David shrugged again. "I was half-relieved anyway, and fully prepared to pretend it never happened. But a few years later, I got fed up with my situation at The Ailing Hare. I went back to see if he might have some proper work for me, something in one of his clubs."

"Which he did," Noah said slowly. "Because he'd just opened the Fox."

"Yes. He gave me the barkeep position and I let him put me up in the town house. We sort of struck things back up for the first year, but it wasn't formal and by that point, we had both become a bit volatile. I got a little nervous about where it might be headed, with our tempers what they were."

Noah didn't like the sound of that. David had a habit of

using equivocating language when he spoke of his violent father, too, always taking at least half the blame even when he deserved none of it.

He seemed to sense that Noah wanted to call him out, so he continued in a rush. "So, when the proprietor position opened up, I suggested he give it to me and we go on as strictly business partners. He agreed. Technically, we're not involved anymore. But he still houses me, and… It's just very, *very* complicated."

Noah pulled his dressing gown tighter once more, like the flimsy fabric could possibly protect him from the harsh reality of the circumstances he'd left David in, not because he needed to, or even really wanted to, but to ease his own panicky need to be noticed.

David smiled very sadly at the ground, pushing the hair out of his eyes. It was not a charming gesture right now. Merely an attempt at clarity as he glanced up at Noah like he was peering at an eclipse.

"There you go," he said. "That should make it easy for you to make your move. Now that you know how pathetic I've been, mooning after you, degrading myself for Belleville, it should be easy enough for you to just tell me once and for all that—"

"I love you, David." He'd said those words plenty of times before, but not like this, so solid and certain that they bounced off all the plush, painted surfaces of his parlor. Far from frightening, the admission was actually freeing, more affection than he'd let himself feel before blossoming to life as he watched that stupid hair flop right back into David's eyes.

"No," David said, shaking his head. "No, you don't. You can't possibly—"

"You said you would believe me." Noah stepped in, arms crossed so tight it was painful but eyes open and insistent as they locked onto David's. "Those were the rules you agreed to. If you go back on it now, it's cheating."

Now that David had what he wanted, he didn't seem to know what to do with it. He grabbed the coffee again, and actually sipped it this time, though his regret was immediate and obvious.

"I think she brews it in the hopes of making more patients for herself," Noah said. David smiled a bit, but it had a confused, young look to it. Noah came over and saved him from the cup, setting it back on the table with the dishes. He wanted desperately to touch David, but wasn't sure he knew how anymore. "I never meant to abandon you, *amore*."

"I know. I figured that out, eventually."

"You felt like I did, though," he went on. "At the time."

David nodded reluctantly. He looked exhausted, like this conversation had cost him more than Noah could ever understand. Noah hated to demand anything more of him right now, but there was still something, a notion that sat on his tongue and refused to be swallowed.

"David," he whispered. "Did you know you loved me then? Or were you as clueless as I was?"

"I didn't agree to tell you that."

"It was implied."

"Not really."

"David."

David looked into his eyes, and then away. His voice came like tiptoes on gravel, rough and almost too quiet to hear:

"Yes. Noah, I've known that I love you for a very long time."

A frightful combination of joy and pain flooded Noah's chest. "But David, if you loved me, and you were so terribly unhappy with your family, why didn't you just come with me?"

David froze so fast and so completely that it was a wonder

that ice crystals didn't form right on his beard. "What did you say?"

"You heard me."

"Come with you? To Milan?"

"No, to the moon. God, David."

David still looked very frosty. "If you're joking, I want you to know I don't think it's funny."

"Why would I be joking?"

"Because you didn't invite me to Milan!"

"Well, of course I didn't. You were needed at home. It would have been insulting, given the circumstances. You'd have been furious."

But David was shaking his head before Noah was even finished. "No. No, I'd have gone in a second. I wouldn't have run off on my own, but if *you'd* asked me, if I thought you wanted me with you, I'd have dropped everything."

Noah stared at him, likely looking every bit the fool he was. "You must have known I would have brought you along if you'd asked. Or if you'd shown up on my doorstep. We were writing letters constantly; you knew where I was. If it was bad like that, why didn't you get on a boat and follow me?"

"Follow you?"

"That's what I'd have done." Emily's words ghosted across his mind. *You'll follow him anywhere.* "If you didn't invite me, and I wanted to go, you wouldn't have been able to stop me. When you didn't ask, and you didn't follow, I assumed that meant you weren't interested."

David put his fingers over his own lips, muffling his voice like he hardly dared put the words out. "Noah. Did you want me to come with you?"

"Of course I did!" Noah blurted. "Maybe I didn't know what to call it, but David, I was panicking so much about leaving that I tried to get my father to make Emily marry you, to guarantee you'd still be here when I got back."

"You did *what*?" David gasped with such honest shock that Noah was more embarrassed than ever to have done it. He ducked his head sheepishly.

"If it makes you feel any better, he said no."

Miraculously, David laughed. Noah wasn't sure whether to join him or burst into tears.

"Oh God. Oh Davy, how did we make such a dreadful mistake?"

"Perhaps if we met at a better school, we'd have been a bit smarter. If you'll indulge me in an understatement, Deer River wasn't exactly Eton."

He started laughing *and* crying at that, giggles bubbling out of his throat while David gently wiped the tears off his cheeks. He sniffed.

David smiled and pulled him in for the warmest, sweetest kiss of his life. Goodness, kissing was difficult with trembling lips, wasn't it? Once a salty tear snuck in, Noah leaned back to wipe his eyes again.

"I wish you'd said something." He took a deep, gulping breath, struggling for stability in his voice. "I wish *I'd* said something. I just don't think I knew what to say. I was so confused, I didn't understand how important..."

He pushed a damp strand of hair off Noah's cheek. "Shh. I know, beautiful. I know."

"We're obviously fools, but it's not too late, is it?" Noah hadn't realized quite how set he'd been on a positive response until he watched David's face fall through the floor. "Davy?"

"I..." Looking a bit grim, he threaded his fingers through Noah's hair, above his ear, holding on tight. "I suppose that will depend on what happens next with the Fox."

With an invasive sort of jolt, Noah realized something they

both must have known in their cores last night: the police had likely been in the club while they were tangled up here in bed. Touching everything. Snooping around. Probably knocking things over and roughing things up. There'd be broken glass somewhere, and filth tracked into the bedrooms. If they'd missed anything, any indicator of David's identity or anything incriminating enough to open an investigation on Belleville, things could get ugly very fast.

"David, I'm going to ask you one more time," said Noah. "Are you in over your head? With the Fox? Or Belleville?"

David licked his lips, thinking. "Even if I am, I know how to swim these waters. I just need to get down there today. I'm meeting Warren to survey the damage. And then…" His face grew grim. "Then I suppose I'm letting his lordship outfit me with a lovely wife while he holds the damn club over my head for a week or two."

The notion sent a violent shiver up Noah's spine that sat him up straight. "No."

"Noah—"

"Absolutely not." He stood up, all his weeping chased off abruptly by the threat. "David. You are not going. Not with him."

He didn't like the look that crossed David's face. Not at all. Calming and closed off; the sort of look you gave someone you weren't going to bother arguing with. He stood up. Noah shook him off as he tried to run soothing hands over his arms.

"You're not going," Noah said again.

"I'm doing what I have to do to keep the Fox open."

"Let it close," said Noah on a wild breath of fear. "Forget it. It's not worth it."

"Maybe not to you."

"Not to you, either." He faltered a bit as he watched David's face close down even further, every muscle accounted for, completely blank. Still, he pressed on, sure he could use their love for each other to cut through David's love of the club. "We don't have to make the same mistakes again."

Wrong move. David turned away, pretending Noah had said nothing at all as he started to stack the breakfast things.

"Davy. You never, ever have to be desperate when you have me. You know that, don't you? Never. I'm doing very well for myself; nothing you ask would be the slightest burden."

The flowered china clinked around his words, floorboards creaking as David started toward the kitchen.

"Consider this your official invitation. You're invited. David!" Noah stayed right on his heels the whole way, standing too close as David scraped scraps and loaded the basin of water Emily had left. "Davy, listen to me. Have supper here every day if you need to. Sleep in my bed. Drink all my tea. Smoke all my cigarettes. Whatever you need. If it's mine, it's yours. I'm yours."

David's eyes flicked subtly to him as he took in those words, as if trying to ascertain the truth of them without Noah noticing. But Noah did notice, and he finally stopped trying to keep his whole heart held tight in the silk of his dressing gown, spreading his hands and letting it slip and relax to reveal his throat, his heart, the bald truth that David Forester had come out of nowhere to break his tormenter's nose and lay claim to a part of his soul that would apparently never grow out of it.

No wonder it never worked with anyone else. No wonder he eventually got so fed up with every lover he'd ever had. No wonder he didn't care who left his card table with the words *tease* and *cheat* on their lips. What did it matter? They weren't David. When push came to shove, he simply couldn't bear such an offensive flaw in their characters.

David had his own flaws, though. He looked at the ground

and went back to the dining room. "Do you want my coffee?" He held it up. "I don't drink it black."

Noah snatched the mug, and the other one too, before David could get to it. He put them on the far side of the table and stepped in close enough that David couldn't escape this time. His body felt strangely light, like the necessity of keeping his hands off David's waist, their bodies a respectable distance apart, had been a heavy set of chains he hadn't noticed he was wrapped up in until they fell. David's arm twitched in the direction of the table, but there would be no more of that. Noah grabbed his wrist, and on a surge of inspiration, pulled David's hand right between his legs.

David's eyes widened, he looked down, and then he threw his head back and laughed.

"Have I got your attention?" said Noah.

A little squeeze, then he trailed his hand up to cup Noah's face. His expression grew warmer in spite of himself. "I suppose so."

"I'm yours, David," he said again, a whisper against the soft space just beneath his ear. "I won't put words in your mouth; I won't say you're mine. But I know for a fact you aren't his. If the Fox is keeping you stuck with him—"

"It's more complicated than that."

"Are you sure? Because it seems rather simple to me—"

"It's not."

"But—"

"*Noah.*" David's voice hardened, not with the flash of his temper, but with something measured and much harder to argue with. "None of this has ever, or will ever, be simple. I need you to understand that. Alright? I need *someone* to understand that. If you mean what you're saying, then please, *please*, take me at my word on this."

Defeated, Noah pressed his cheek to the curve of David's jaw.

"But anyway," David went on, stroking his hair, "it may not be simple, but I can handle it. Things have been fine the past few years, they really have. Belleville is bored with me. I'm not nineteen anymore, after all, and only getting less nineteen every day. If I can prove the Fox is worth its keep, he'll leave me alone again to run it and everything will be fine."

"You don't know that."

"Well, I'll know either way soon enough, won't I?" He gently pulled back, stepping away. "Beautiful, I have to go."

"Can I—?"

"No."

Noah crossed his arms. "I hope you have a very good plan to stop me."

David opened his mouth but said nothing, because he was in possession of no such thing.

"I'm coming with you," Noah said, leaving no room in his tone for argument. "We'll see about the rest of the staff, and then—" Something occurred to him, something that stopped his planning short. He tried to shake the odd notion off, but he found he couldn't.

"Noah?"

I didn't have a sensible family and radical congregation holding a net out for me.

That shouldn't have been true. The Clarkes—Noah included—should have offered meaningful help long before he got involved with the baron. And quite frankly, his father and sister should still be willing to help him *now*. Far from telling Noah that he should abandon David *again*, they ought to be asking what they could do for the man who had done nothing but love and protect Noah for half their lives...

And then it all became painfully clear.

They blamed David.

Not because of the club; that was just a convenient excuse to let their resentments fly. They blamed him for all of it. Noah's choice of profession. His move to London. His "gentlemanly vanity" and who knew what else.

"We'll get dinner before you meet up with Warren," Noah said at last. "We'll go to the coffeehouse. They've got a lovely kitchen, you know. And their coffee itself is far more drinkable than my sister's."

David went still aside from one eyebrow drifting upward. "With your family?"

"They'll be thrilled to have you."

"That is demonstrably untrue."

"Well." Noah hesitated. Yesterday, he'd have ignored the impulsive tug to slip his hands around David's waist and draw him in tight. Today, though, he gave it free rein, and when all David's sharp, frozen edges softened in his arms, he wondered how he'd lived without that feeling for so long. "They'll be thrilled to have *me*," he said. "And if they want me, they'll have to figure out how to accept you as well. I've had enough of their disapproval. You have done nothing to warrant their mistreatment."

David gave a cynical snort of laughter. "You can't possibly—"

He grabbed David's face and kissed him so hard on the mouth that his words were instantly forced into the shape of a surprised grunt. Noah pulled back and looked him even harder in the eyes. God, those gorgeous eyes. Forget outshining a jade comb; they were enough to embarrass an emerald.

"You've done *nothing*," he whispered, "to warrant *anyone's* mistreatment, David. And I will not hear a word to the contrary. Not even from you."

David's muscles started to stiffen again, the sentiment threatening to become too heavy for either of them. Noah lightened it by swatting David on the bottom, then started for the

staircase to get dressed. When he realized David wasn't following, he turned around.

"No more waiting for invitations, Davy," he insisted. "If
you want to come along and watch me dress, then come along
and watch me dress."

David hesitated. He glanced at the door. Back up at Noah.

Then he smiled through that lock of hair and grabbed hold
of the banister.

Chapter Twelve

David

Oh, it was mad. It really was. David belonged in an intellectual coffeehouse even less than he belonged in a ballroom these days. His knowledge of politics began and ended with what was required to avoid arrest in work and pleasure, and to top it off, he didn't particularly care for coffee, no matter the skill of the person who'd brewed it.

But right now? Noah could invite him back to a boarding school mathematics class and he'd take up a slate with no argument whatsoever.

The visit wouldn't last long anyway. The world Noah had been born into was very hostile to David's sort. *Certainly* they thought he should have gotten help rather than fines from the Crown after the fire. *Of course* they believed he and Noah ought to live and love in freedom. But it was temperance, education, and transcendental prayer that would see these causes through, while David's *lascivious, frivolous lifestyle* would only set the whole country back worse than ever. The way they saw it, David was personally responsible for the degradation of society itself.

So, it wouldn't be a long visit, probably. But it was very sweet of Noah to try. And try he did, putting himself together to be as unthreatening to *the cause* as possible. He bypassed the bright fabrics and tidy silhouettes in his wardrobe in favor of soft breeches, a somber earth-toned jacket, a drooping bow tie, and a truly ridiculous floppy hat that David hadn't realized he owned.

"Wow," David said when Noah stood finished before him. "You look ready to discuss whatever nonsense Parliament's gotten up to this week."

Noah adjusted the angle of his hat. "In *excruciating* detail."

From his spot on the edge of the neatly made bed, David made note of his own clothes, which were very rumpled from an evening of wear and a night heaped on the floor. "Can we head back to mine so I can spruce up a bit before we go? I'd like to look respectable if I'm going to be foolish enough to approach your father."

"Fair enough." Noah smiled and moved closer until he was standing between David's knees, fussing at the wrinkles in his jacket. "Though even like this, you don't look *quite* as debauched as he believes you to be."

"Really?" With an impressed frown, David whipped the tie off his own neck and passed it around the back of Noah's legs to pull him in closer. "Exactly how debauched does he think I am?"

"Maximally."

A little thrill raced through David when he caught the gleam in Noah's eyes.

He'd dreaded this day for years: the day Noah found out that he'd played mistress to a bawdy-house-owning baron while Noah was off across the channel becoming a respectable tradesman. That Noah could still look at him with such obvious affection—and *admit* to feeling it—was like some dizzyingly lovely dream.

"Maximally debauched. I think I like the sound of that," he mused. With the tie still wrapped around his hands, he grabbed Noah by the hips and nuzzled at the lacing of his silly breeches. "But I don't look the part, you say." He lowered his chin and raised his eyes, stroking his thumbs along the divots of Noah's doeskin-covered hip bones. "Want to fix that for me?"

They got going a bit later than was prudent, perhaps, though the staff members they called on didn't care how debauched either of them looked, so long as they came bearing the good news that no one had been arrested yet. They handled those calls first, then went to David's so he could change for their much-less-advisable meeting with Noah's family.

Last night's fear of his home had faded somewhat this morning, everything made lighter and brighter by Noah's insistent presence. Even his valet's terse disposition seemed less intolerable, though Noah teased David for his "devotion to the Greek ideal" the second the front door closed behind them.

"I hope you got references on that chap," he giggled, face flushed. "He is *much* too handsome to be a valet. I don't believe it. Smells like an entrapper to me."

David rolled his eyes. "Oh? And what does an entrapper smell like?"

"Cheap cologne and blond hair, I'd imagine."

"You're just jealous that such a pretty thing is in charge of my wardrobe."

Noah didn't say anything for a moment. When David looked over at him, he'd gone a little pink.

"Perhaps I am." He shrugged. "A bit."

David grinned like an idiot and all but floated the rest of the way to Bradigan and Son's Coffee House.

In his floppy hat and breeches, Noah made his way between the place's spindly tables and overwrought artwork looking for all the world like he belonged right here and nowhere else. After a little over-caffeinated chatter with a server who knew him by name and peered at David curiously, Noah led David along a narrow hallway and up a creaky, treacherous set of stairs. Hearty voices and the sounds of clinking cups drifted down to them.

David's stomach turned flips as he imagined Phillip Clarke up there, talking medicine and politics with a pack of his fellow teetotaling geniuses. "Noah, are you sure this is a good idea?"

"A good idea?" Noah laughed and put a hand on his back as they found the landing. "Not at all."

"It's not too late, you know."

"You're right. It's not too late." They paused in front of the cracked doorway that led to the parlor. Noah leaned in and kissed his cheek. "But it *is* long overdue."

Before David could call him out for deliberate misinterpretation, Noah pushed the door open.

The upstairs parlor was much like the downstairs, but with more open windows allowing light and air to take some of the weight off of the heavy decor and overstuffed bookshelves. A couple dozen simply dressed men and women carried on with coffee and conversation, sparing curious looks when they spotted Noah's arrival with what must have seemed a very gaudy newcomer. David had tried to be appropriate, but just as Noah couldn't fit in at The Ailing Hare, David did not possess the garb of a rational dissenter.

"Noah, you *came*?"

Emily approached them and took her brother's hands incredulously for a moment before glancing at David with an unmistakable cringe. "And you brought Mr. Forester."

David took his hat off in greeting, Emily's obvious apprehension burrowing into his own belly. Her feelings for him aside, he was obviously out of place in this parlor, a potential embarrassment even under the best of circumstances.

When she was through looking him over (clearly finding him wanting, but not enough to say anything about it), David followed her gaze as it drifted to a couple sitting under the far window, deep in what looked like a jolly sort of debate. One of them, with his light beard, slim build, and upturned nose, was a man David had not seen in five years but would recognize anywhere—Dr. Phillip Clarke. The other was a woman around the doctor's own age, with a freckly, light brown face and a voice that carried across the room on an unabashed French accent.

"Who's that?" David whispered to Noah, watching the doctor and the woman converse. They were so wrapped up in one another that Dr. Clarke didn't seem to have even noticed his own son's appearance.

Emily glared like his question had been a precursor to some rakish intentions for the old woman. "That's Papa's friend Madame Rochelle Baptiste. A highly talented map artist, a very respectable and well-traveled woman."

Her tone dared David to say something dreadful, though what exactly she thought he would disparage in a pleasant-enough stranger, he wasn't sure. All he knew was that her assumption of ill-will stung. She'd known him better than that before everything went to hell.

Noah sensed the tension and returned his possessive hand to David's upper arm. "She made that one of the Mediterranean next to my bookcase. The one with the gold leaf."

"Brilliant," said David, thinking back on the piece with admiration and letting the ruffly thrill of romantic gossip distract him from Emily's defensive posture. "Noah, why didn't you tell me your father had taken a paramour?"

The impropriety of voicing the obvious was almost too much for Emily, but she stuffed it down at a look from Noah.

"I didn't tell you, because he still hasn't told *us*," Noah said.

Both twins watched the pair with disconcertingly similar looks of annoyance on their faces. "They're *dear old friends*, you see."

"Ah." David nodded heavily. "Relatable, that is."

"Isn't it?" Noah laughed and nudged David's shoulder in a feminine, flirty way that would be nothing at the Fox, but was worth a sidelong glance pretty much anywhere else. "Shall we greet them, *amore*?"

Emily chewed on her lip anxiously. "Noah, I think I understand why you're doing this, but just make sure you behave yourselves, will you?"

"Oh, we always do, don't we, David?" Noah said with a little wink.

David gave the sidelong glance himself as Noah led him away from Emily, toward Dr. Clarke's corner. "Awfully bold."

"Not really." Noah shrugged, casually drifting far enough away from the center of the room to allow them a few hurried whispers. "I've known some of these folks since I was up to their knees. There's as many tiresome opinions on my 'Uranian temperament' as there are people in this room, but none of them want to cause me trouble."

"I suppose, but Emily—"

"*Emily* heard us last night," Noah whispered out of the corner of his mouth as he waved to a couple over near the bookcase. "If there's anyone here I cannot shock any further, it's her."

David withered at the notion. "Did she now?"

"Oh. She did now."

"Are you certain she understood what she was hearing?" David muttered, watching Emily carry on very seriously about something with a stooped and grim sort of gentleman. "This is Emily we're talking about. The spinster to end all spinsters."

Noah chuckled, but also shook his head. "She means well. They both do." He nodded to where his father and Mme. Baptiste finally seemed to have noticed their approach. "That's why I'd like to give them a chance to bring their actions into alignment with their intentions."

In a few determined strides, he closed the distance and David rather suddenly found himself face-to-face with Dr. Phillip Clarke.

He was slighter and fairer even than his children, almost wispy now that age was starting to have its way with him. Still, when he stood up to greet them, his movements were uncannily sturdy in spite of his stature. He embraced Noah heartily with a genuine, crinkle-eyed smile and an exclamation of surprise and pleasure at his presence.

And then he turned to David.

David felt no older than sixteen under the glare of his appraisal. Oh, he had admired Dr. Clarke so very much; the contrast to his own father was so striking as to be surreal. He was intelligent and respectable, and though the death of his wife during the birth of his twins had left him a little mad, it was a gentle madness that David would have taken over drunken rages any day.

The disappointment that the doctor now held for him was suddenly more painful than gin on a splinter.

Once the *old friends* had been given proper introductions that David hardly noticed through his creeping sense of dread, he stared at Dr. Clarke, wondering how it was possible to feel so small from so many inches above someone.

"Mr. Forester," Dr. Clarke said in a tense but pleasant-enough voice. "It has been a very long time. You're looking well."

"Thank you," said David, applying the image of a friendly smile to his face. "I could say the same about you. It's… My goodness, Dr. Clarke, it's a delight to see you again. Truly. I admit, I thought I never would."

The words were out before he could stop them, earnest and frankly pathetic enough that Mme. Baptiste struggled to purse her lips over an obvious smile.

"I could use some more coffee, I think," she said, standing and smoothing a lacier, more structured gown than most of her "rational" counterparts in the room were wearing. She pressed kisses to Dr. Clarke's cheeks and swept off with her cup, quickly joining another conversation away from what she'd clearly realized was an awkward enough reunion.

Dr. Clarke watched her go, then pulled a third chair into the nook.

"Well. Sit down," he said, settling stiffly into his own seat. "Would you, ah, care for a cup—?"

"We've got our own pot coming." Noah sat on the edge of one of the seats, gesturing for David to do the same.

Dr. Clarke smiled. "*L'Italia?*"

"*Certo.*" Whatever he said next was in Italian, but David gathered that it was something along the lines of *The English can't roast a bean to save their souls.* It made Dr. Clarke laugh.

"You always do have your opinions," he said with his gaze drifting briefly to David. When he was caught at it, he added, "So, Mr. Forester. Tell me, ah, how have you been? It's been so long, I confess, I'm not sure where to begin."

David's mouth went so dry that he was tempted to see if the lukewarm, black coffee in the middle of the low table might provide enough hydration to let him speak. "It's, um. In general, things have been going along well enough, I'd say."

Dr. Clarke nodded into the awkward silence.

David cleared his throat. He wanted to ask about Mme. Baptiste—he was a shameless glutton for that sort of thing— but since the doctor was being coy about it with even his own children, the pry probably wouldn't be well-received.

His mind raced with other conversational options that would suit Dr. Clarke better.

"How are the cavies?" he said brightly. Pets, he'd found, were the safest of subjects, and Dr. Clarke had a collection of guinea pigs standing a most unintimidating watch over his garden. "I had a particular fondness for baby Darwin. How many do you have scurrying around these days?"

A miniscule but unmistakable smile twitched the edge of the doctor's whiskers. "You haven't changed a bit, have you?"

"I don't know what you mean."

Dr. Clarke looked like he doubted that. "I've seven in the herd at the moment," he said, just a bit begrudging. "Though Darwin was rechristened Elizabeth Blackwell once she and Pasteur's whelps came along."

David nodded knowingly. "It happens."

Another silence, cruel and crushing. Even worse than the doctor's disapproval was knowing how disappointed Noah would be if this reconciliation went poorly. Though he'd prefer to take the hint, tip his hat, and spare them all the awkwardness, he tried again. For Noah's sake.

"It must have been a difficult year for you," he said as pleasantly as possible. "With Emily in the city instead of—"

Dr. Clarke put a hand out. "Dav—*Mr. Forester*—I appreciate your attempts to soften this. I do. But it is not working, and I would prefer we simply got to whatever it is the two of you wanted to speak with me about." He turned his gaze to Noah. "Or the one of you. I have a feeling I can guess the instigator."

"Me?" Noah put a shocked hand his chest. "When have I ever instigated anything?"

David and Dr. Clarke reconnected for a moment, as they shared in a meaningful look.

"We're here, Papa," said Noah firmly, "because it's the first

Sunday of the month. I wanted to see you while you were in town. And as for David, I simply invited him along."

"What's the reason for such an invitation today?" Dr. Clarke said. "Why not invite him last month? Or wait until next month?"

Noah smiled and batted his lashes in a way that made David brace himself for whatever was about to come out of his wicked mouth.

"Well," he said carefully, "because we eloped this morning, you see."

Eloped? He'd expected Noah to say something shocking, but this one surprised David in the best possible way. He had to bite his lip to keep from laughing—or, more accurately, giving free rein to the lovesick giggle that threatened to escape his throat. *We eloped.* Fuck. If Noah had managed to pull out some excuse for David to kiss him here and now, he'd have done it.

Dr. Clarke, on the other hand, looked more tired than surprised. He took a very deep breath and a very long drink of coffee.

"Eloped. I see," he said, doling out a sigh. "Care to elaborate on that a bit?"

"He's jesting, of course," David reassured him quickly.

"Obviously," said Dr. Clarke as confidently as any man who'd never helped a friend pull one over on the parson. "But he's said it for a reason. Go on, Noah."

Noah sat back in his chair with his legs crossed tight and his fingers worrying at his waistcoat, staring at the coffee fixings at the center of their little circle. Around them, the other Unitarians chattered on, spoons clinking in cups, coffee pouring from spouts, ideas swirling in a mass upon the early summer air coming through the windows. His determination seemed to be faltering.

David nudged his foot under the table to catch his eye, shaking his head subtly when he did. Noah had done more than enough, bringing him here and making that absurd declaration to his father. He'd never felt as loved as he did right now, and didn't need or expect anything else.

Though he tried to communicate that silently, the implication had the opposite effect. Noah sat up straighter, narrowed his eyes like he did at the card table, and said something that surprised David nearly as much as it seemed to surprise the doctor:

"It's not David's fault I didn't go into practice with you, Papa, and I'm sick of pretending your trouble with him is based in anything else."

Chapter Thirteen

Noah

The first words fell heavily, crashing like stones into a pond that had been still too long. While the chilly splash of them stunned Papa and David, they spurred Noah on with a thrill and a shiver.

"It's not his fault I moved to London," he threw out next, getting a little giddy as their eyes widened and jaws dropped. But he wasn't done; now that he'd started talking, he found he had a whole bucket of weighty things to churn the water with, and he couldn't bear the thought of leaving it upright a second longer. "It's not even his fault that I go to *those places*, though he is likely the reason I've never been arrested, and as such, you should probably thank him rather than vilifying him for his part in all that. Treating him poorly is not fair. It's not right. It's not even *productive*. And honestly, I am so sick of it I could scream."

"What?" Papa looked so bewildered that it was nearly comical. "Noah, this has nothing to do with—"

"Yes, it does." This one was a veritable boulder that left no room for argument, but did catch the attention of a few of the others. He resigned himself to a lower voice, but he wasn't done. "Do you really think you can sit there and tell me you think it's *David* who's chosen the wrong profession? His work

is none of your business. But mine is. And you and Emily may think you can spare my feelings by convincing yourselves it's David who disappointed you, but I can see right through it. And you need to see it too. Now. Because David is..."

Oh God, how he wished he could stand up in the middle of the table and declare that David was and always had been the love of his life. Now that he'd admitted it to himself and to David, he wanted to make everyone in here, from his well-meaning father to the least of their acquaintances, shut up and deal with the absolute reality of him. There was no coming back from the miraculous realization of what he and David meant to each other. He wanted to do something equally mad in the outside world, something as honest and wild as the love bubbling inside him.

But while the rules of the world were more relaxed than usual here, to flout them might sharpen the more ambivalent opinions in the room into unpleasant ones. He could poke the rules, and challenge them, but he didn't have the power to shatter and reshape them. If he tried, he would succeed only in looking, as David did, like a threat to everyone's uncertain peace on the margins.

"David is," he said again, with slow intensity that would bleed just past the edges of the appropriate framework without breaking it, "my *best friend*. He will remain my *best friend* for as long as he wishes, no matter what either of us has taken as our profession."

Beside him, David looked no less shocked than Papa, a soft, incredulous sort of surprise. His hands were clenched in his lap, like he was struggling to resist touching Noah. Noah loved him madly for being brave enough to be here, to sit through this, to be—as always—the one who inspired Noah and watched his back as he strove for these scraps of authenticity in his life.

A little further past the edge, about as far as Noah dared, he brought his hand to the back of David's neck, tracing the line of his hair, a gesture that everyone knew meant *mine* even if no one would be able to prove it. David shivered reflexively under the touch, suppressing it enough that it wasn't visible, but not quite enough to hide it from Noah's fingers.

"You don't have to like it," Noah said, growing quieter as the last of the pebbles made their less dramatic way into the mellowing water. "But if you want me to do things like come to the coffeehouse and visit more often once Emily goes home, then you do have to accept it. If I've learned anything from the people in this room, it's that the search for truth is paramount. And this, as I think you already know, has always been the truth of us."

As Papa looked between the two of them, a twinge of regret tickled Noah's ribs. He hoped he hadn't been too harsh. Papa wasn't perfect, but he was loving. In the spectrum of English fathers, most settled a little closer to David's than to his own. Now that the fervor was cooling, he wondered what right he had to complain about something so insignificant, when the things that mattered most had always—

"You're right, Noah."

Papa's voice was so quiet and polite that one might think Noah had made an observation about the weather. He was nodding pensively, even grimly, staring around as if just notic-ing rain clouds he'd ignored to his own detriment all morning.

"I am?" Noah said.

Papa turned to David. "Forgive me, Mr. Forester—"

"*David*," David said in a rush, leaning forward onto his knees in childlike eagerness. "You can… That is, if you please. Sir."

Noah's heart swelled so happily he feared it might burst. Apparently, he wasn't the only one who'd nursed a desire to see David welcomed by his family. It confirmed what Noah had always known deep down: that they'd belonged to each other since that very first walk around the duck pond.

"Hmm." Papa considered that. He didn't seem quite convinced, but didn't reject the offer, either. "Well. *David*." He took a moment to look bemusedly between the grins that had lit up both their faces at his acceptance. "And, Noah. This isn't really the place to delve deeply into all of this." He waved a steady hand toward the center of the room. Aside from Emily, who was unsuccessfully pretending not to eavesdrop, the rest had found more interesting topics of discussion once volume wasn't drawing their attention. That, however, could quickly change. "That said, I am very open to continuing this conversation. Soon. Perhaps the two of you would like to get out of the city for a spell? Rest your weary lungs and tell me more about what this, ah, *elopement* means to you?"

Noah stilled and quieted. He ran a hand through his hair in a destructive way he rarely indulged in, gnawing his lip and trying to figure out what on earth Papa might like him to say to all that.

Eventually, David, relentlessly likable bloke that he was, saved him from the silence. He smiled out from behind the flop of his hair and said, "That would be lovely, though to be quite honest, we're not exactly solid on what it means ourselves. I'm sure you understand how that can be."

Papa smiled, nodded, and—of all things—turned a little pink beneath his pale skin as he glanced at a particular lace-clad Frenchwoman across the room.

Their coffee and sandwiches arrived before Noah had really found his footing in a wild success that seemed to have been won far too easily. Papa should be furious. Or disappointed. Or embarrassed. Something sensible, in any case. But instead, he was letting David fix him a fresh cup of Italian dark roast as they talked about the ducks and guinea pigs in the family garden back in Surrey.

"I am so looking forward to it, Dr. Clarke," David gushed, filling Noah's cup before heaping sugar and cream into his own. "Is that little pond back there still as beautiful as ever?"

"As ever," Papa assured him, lifting the coffee to his mouth and luckily not catching the way David nudged Noah's foot under the table again, because ponds with thickets of lilacs and summertime cattails had always been a preference of theirs over a broom cupboard. Papa went on, oblivious. "Now, don't let my blathering stop you from enjoying your dinner. Don't mind me. Eat up."

And so they did, though the "blathering" did continue through it, because Papa seemed as unburdened by the outburst as Noah was. And David too. Eventually, Mme. Baptiste joined them, she and David both so utterly charming that others from the congregation kept sidling over, hinting for introductions and drawing them all into conversation.

Even Emily, though still tense, came by at some point with the excuse of "Seeing that Mr. Forester has been treated with respect by everyone, and not made to feel lesser for his lack of intellectual pursuits."

Noah grinned up at his sister, impressed by the unflinching reliability of her temperament. On the surface, such a scolding remark might imply continued enmity. Papa gave her a warning look, but Noah didn't mind. He saw it for what it was. The concession managed to scold, perhaps, but it was a concession nonetheless.

David was right. A little honest talk, apparently, had been just what Noah needed to get what he'd wanted all along.

Chapter Fourteen

David

When it was time to go, the farewells were protracted, but they eventually escaped onto the stoop of the coffeehouse. While David still felt bright and cozy from the afternoon's meeting, the weather hadn't kept up very well. The morning's sun had given way to thickening air and thicker clouds. Rain seemed imminent. Noah peered suspiciously at the sky, so goddamned beautiful that David couldn't take it.

He grabbed Noah by the sleeve and dragged him into the narrow alley. He backed up against the side of the coffeehouse himself, instead of pinning Noah (and thus his clothes) to sooty brick. After checking that no one was looking on but a mangy cat near the bins, he stole a quick, dirty kiss in broad daylight.

"Noah," he panted. "Th—"

Noah cut him off with another kiss. Fierce. Even reckless, considering the hour.

"Noah," David chuckled, pulling back with some difficulty. Noah tried his damnedest to drag David back by the neck with his teeth before David finally got a little distance by flattening himself against the wall. "We promised your sister we'd behave."

"Oh, bugger her."

David jerked to the side as Noah went for his neck again. "That would certainly *not* be in the spirit of behaving."

"Then bugger me, why don't you?" Noah grabbed him by the hips, and he was properly caught this time, falling into another kiss, wet, open-mouthed, unjustifiable in every way. "Thank you, David."

David pulled back again, glancing at the alley's mouth before opening his own and realizing he didn't know what to say. "Huh?"

"Thank you for doing this for me," Noah said, panting, stroking David's face, pawing at his chest. "Coming along today. I've needed to do that for a long time now. Assuming I can ever spare a few days for a visit..." His fingers twitched against David's necktie, as if anxious about the prospect of idleness. "In any case, the conversation's been started. So, thank you. I think it went alright, don't you?"

David was struck silent. Noah was thanking *him*? After risking the very fabric of his family for the sake of their treatment of David? It was absolutely backward. "Um. Alright? Yes, I suppose it did."

Noah did that lovely thing he'd always done, where he smiled and nodded right along with David's clueless stammering like it was some brilliant insight. Then he grasped David's lapels and pulled him in for another kiss, which David reluctantly dodged, stepping sideways and out of Noah's grasp before they leaned any further into unreasonably risky territory.

"Why don't we take this to The Curious Fox?" David suggested, a bit winded as the sight of Noah's crooked jacket and reddened lips made the club seem awfully far away. The old-fashioned leather lacings on the breeches were a particularly unique sort of temptation, as he imagined undoing them with his teeth. "Once I'm done with Warren maybe we can get one of the rooms to ourselves for once."

"A room does sound lovely." Noah tugged at his own sleeve a bit, clearly conflicted. "But I had hoped that after seeing you have support from my family, you wouldn't be so eager to head back to the club."

"Where else would I go?" David asked.

"Home with me." Noah shrugged a little and glanced at the ground. "I've got to get through one of my backlogged accounts tonight before Rosenby's fitting next week. You could keep me company."

"Not exactly useful of me, compared to cleaning up the club."

"You don't have to be useful all the time," said Noah. "Though I could put you to work on the buttons, if you insisted."

The offer of a slow, domestic evening in with Noah was almost cloyingly sweet. As a man with quite a taste for sweets, David was even more tempted by that than by the lacings.

Belleville would never find you there.

The realization struck him all at once. David had kept Noah's name and address out of the club ledgers, using a fake this whole time to protect his best friend's identity. If David simply walked away from the place instead of catering to Lord Belleville's whims—which might amount to nothing anyway—he would not be found at Noah's. Or, if things really went sideways, at the Clarke family cottage. That's what Noah was saying.

He'd be safe there.

Protected there.

The thought felt wonderful for just a second, before his better reasoning caught up with him. David was the *protector*. Not the *protected*. That was his lot in life, and it was no meager one. It had started with Noah, but had expanded too far from there to walk away now. He had too many others relying on him, and frankly, he liked it that way.

But maybe there was a compromise.

"I have to go today," David said reluctantly. "The club is my life's work, Noah. I can't abandon it, and everyone in it, without a fight."

Work-obsessed himself and obviously still sensitive to the idea of abandonment after their conversation this morning, Noah's face twisted with guilt-ridden understanding. "No," he said quietly to the cobbles. "I suppose you can't."

"But perhaps," said David, "I don't have to bring that fight all the way to Hertfordshire."

Noah crossed his arms very tight, like he hardly dared believe it. "You're not going to go with the baron?"

"Not until I've exhausted my other options," David said. "Which I very much haven't. Once I see how bad the raid was, I'd like to put together a proper proposal, with numbers, projections, designs, all that. Something he can't argue with if he'd ever had any intention of hearing me out."

"Yes!" Noah grinned. "Yes, David, that's perfectly reasonable. If he can't hear you out in London, why would he hear you out anywhere else?"

"Exactly. There's just one problem. It's got to get done before he leaves on Wednesday."

Noah's grin faded. "That's quite a tight turnaround."

"Indeed."

"In that case…" Noah groaned and stomped just a bit with his boot, a characteristic petulance that made David smile. "In that case, I ought to make headway on this account while you're with Warren. Annabelle helps me catch up sometimes; I'll see if she's available today, so I can keep up the pace. Otherwise, I might not be able to help you with the proposal."

"I don't need help—"

Noah grabbed his face and shut him up quite effectively.

Turned out that refusing your best friend's help was much trickier when his tongue was in your mouth.

As they went their separate ways, the weather finally gave way to a wet and misty rain, a fitting accompaniment to shuffling across town to investigate whatever damage the police had done to the club last night.

David padded through grimy puddles, wishing his umbrella could spare him from the thick air. Before turning the last corner in the alleys that led to the club, he heard voices coming from the direction of the entrance. The first was familiar, though he could not place it or distinguish the words.

The second was Warren:

"We're *closed*. No one comes in, not for any reason." The first spoke again, quietly, until he was interrupted by Warren's vehement, "I said, *bugger off*."

The first man's words were perfectly audible this time: a slew of cruel insults that made the gray of the alley seem to go red around the edges.

David rushed the last turn to find the usually deserted doorway blocked by three soggy people: Warren, leaning against the door with his arms crossed and his eyebrow up, a lean and wealthy-looking stranger, and Belleville's secretary, the red-faced Mr. Parker.

This couldn't be good.

Warren met his eye, then gestured toward him for the benefit of the uncouth visitors. "Take your sniveling up with him, would you? You want *exceptions*, they'll come from him. Not me." He added his own spit to the alley's filth. "You won't get nothing from me."

The secretary stepped in, putting an angry finger in Warren's face. "See here, you litt—"

David dropped his umbrella and replaced it harshly with

Parker's thick wrist. He put himself between the two of them. "Can I help you, Mr. Parker?"

Parker blinked up at him, mouth still twisted in disgust. He tried to shake off David's fierce grip, looking a bit alarmed when he couldn't. David released him, and he rubbed angrily at the white finger marks that had appeared on his skin. "What the devil is going on here, Forester?" he growled.

"I'm not to let anyone in off-hours, remember? I was given no exceptions. Mr. Bakshi is simply trying to do his job." He turned just enough to see Warren giving an unapologetic sneer from beneath David's rescued umbrella. David turned back to the others. "What are you doing here, anyway, Mr. Parker? You shouldn't be here."

Parker stepped back and straightened his hat. "I'm here to show the property to this extremely interested investor who would have every reason not to be interested anymore after having been sworn and spat at by this—"

David took back the ground Parker had given, stepping in toe-to-toe. "If you insult Mr. Bakshi again, you will regret it." When Parker only gaped up at him like a dying snapper, David went on. "Try again. Politely, this time. Why are you here?"

The third man finally spoke, lifting his hat and smiling rather awkwardly. "Forgive me, Mr. Forester, did he say? We're simply here so that Mr. Parker can show me the property."

He handed David a card, and suddenly it was he who'd been wrenched out of the sea and into a harsh reality.

"An *investor*?" he gasped. Parker had said the word a moment ago, but it did not take hold until he looked at the card. "But wait just a moment. The property isn't for sale."

The investor looked politely perplexed. Parker shook his head firmly. "No, no, it is," he assured, glaring sideways at David before turning back with as pleasant a smile as he was capable of. "He just must not have mentioned it to Mr. Forester yet."

"And, ah, who is this Mr. Forester?"

Parker waved a dismissive hand. "The former proprietor of the place."

"Splendid," said the investor, his smile surreal as the word *former* ripped a gash through David's chest. "Perhaps he could answer questions for me, if it's not too much trouble."

"What? No. I just spoke with him about the property yesterday!" David spluttered. "He said he wasn't selling for another few weeks, if at all. We were going to…"

Trailing off, David watched Parker pull a key out of his pocket. A key to the Fox. A key to David's club, which he could only have gotten one of two places and it certainly hadn't been from Warren.

Stunned, David was shunted to the side as Parker unlocked the door and held it open for the investor. Under his breath, Parker whispered, "Sorry, Forester, but no one's holding out a lot of hope that your brilliant plans will save the place. Do try not to take it personally, *poppet*." He feigned an effeminate tear and followed the investor into the Fox.

David's stomach churned with confusion and dread. All his determination to handle this professionally drifted away like steam off a horse's flank.

Warren came up next to him, holding the umbrella over both their heads. The barkeep had a way of looking concerned that made it seem like he was about to burst out laughing, and sometimes, he did just that. Now, though, he just said, "I take it we're not reopening next weekend?"

"Suppose not." David stood for an uncertain moment, listening to the patter of raindrops hitting the umbrella. Beside him, Warren drew breath to speak, but before he could, David turned and yanked on the doorknob, heart pounding in his ears. "I'm going in. You should go home."

Warren laughed at him, closed and shook out the umbrella, and followed on David's heels into the club.

It was only a few moments before Warren seemed to regret his decision. Neither Parker nor the investor was currently in the parlor, but neither was much of anything else. When he saw the state of his bar with nothing behind it, the alcoves stripped of their curtains and pillows, the smell of incense muddied by lye and vinegar, Warren stopped in the middle of the parlor. He clapped a hand to his mouth and said in a muffled, shaky voice, "Fuck, Forester. You bloody *didn't*." He went over to the bar, touching the empty shelves like he couldn't believe it was really all gone. "This does not look like a club that's reopening to me, mate. Fucking hell, you didn't tell me it was this bad—"

"I'm sorry," David said. "I didn't have a choice."

Warren threw a glare over his shoulder. "I can think of a few options."

The sound of voices from behind the back door interrupted them. Hackles up, David turned toward Parker and the investor as they came back out into the parlor.

"So, you can see, sir, the possibilities are…" Parker drifted off as he spotted David and Warren. "Mr. Forester."

David crossed his arms. "Hello. I came to see if I could offer any assistance or information. Seeing as I, unlike you, spend most of my life here."

Parker looked nervous, but the investor looked rather pleased. There was a set to his smile that reminded David of his dull valet, one of those perfectly English fellows who did not express emotions more interesting than *graciousness* or *polite perplexity*. "Thank you, Mr. Forester," he said with a friendly nod. "If it's not too much trouble, I was hoping to see the rooms."

"You didn't show him the rooms?" David asked.

"They're locked," Parker said as coldly as he could get away with in present company.

"I did very much like the parlor upstairs," the investor said.

David nodded enthusiastically. "Oh yes, plenty of room for activities up there."

"I was surprised there's no billiards table."

"There was."

"What happened to it?"

"It broke." David shrugged off the investor's questioning stare and took out his key ring. "Shall we?"

He went back to the door they'd just come through and held it open for them. The gas bulbs cast their dim glow over the dark hallway. "My apologies about the locks. It's a rowdy neighborhood, so his lordship insisted I secure everything to the utmost while it was unoccupied."

"Understood," said the investor. "I think that was wise. Goodness, I'm old enough to remember when Soho was still very fashionable. Hopefully getting a few respectable places up and running in the area will help to clean things back up."

David still didn't know exactly what this was about, but it didn't bode well at all. Hiding his queasiness, he began unlocking the doors one by one.

Parker's glare was thicker than the gaslight. "Why doesn't my key work? The one he gave me?"

"He must have given you the old one," David said smoothly. "I had to have the locks changed a few months back."

"I can take that one from you, if you'd be so kind," said Parker as the investor wandered into one of the barren bedrooms. "You and your barkeep can clear out, and I'll lock up behind me."

David tucked the keys back into his pocket. "Not a chance."

"You could stop making things difficult," Parker hissed while the investor was distracted by one of the fireplaces.

"Difficult? I'm helping."

"You changed those locks without telling him."

David put a wounded hand to his chest. "I would never."

The investor came back out into the hall. David and Parker put on pleasant expressions and made all the appropriate noises at his enthusiasm until he went into the next. Then the smiles dropped.

"Tell me what's going on," David said under his breath. "I need to know what this is about right now. Last I heard, he wanted to plan some massive overhaul with me. Since when is he selling?"

"That's not mine to divulge, I'm afraid."

"Oh, and since when you do have integrity?"

"Me? Look, Forester, I was tending to Lord Belleville's business matters while he was still bending you over the beds in your family's doomed hotel. Forgive me if I prioritize the sale of his building over smoothing things over with one of his discarded whores. I don't even understand how you got him to go along with this Fox madness in the first place, but I'm relieved to see you heading back into your place. Or, you know, wherever he decides to put you, going forward." Parker looked David up and down with cruel eyes. "I wouldn't assume he wants to keep you around to watch these grays spread."

He reached out like he intended to touch David's certainly not-graying hair. David grabbed his hand tight, ignoring the pain it caused in the half-healed cut on his palm so he could inflict something comparable on this—

If not for the investor sticking his happy head back into the hallway to report his satisfaction with another room, David might have broken Parker's wandering fingers. Instead, he dropped it and plastered a friendly face over the unbearable insults and terrifying implications.

"So it's over, then," he said in a lower voice to Parker, as the investor went out ahead of them into the parlor to engage a reluctant Warren in conversation. With the investor's back turned, David caught Warren's eye, nodding and gesturing, hoping that he got the message to distract the old man. "It's to be sold, and there's nothing I can do about it."

"That's not quite what I said, Forester." Parker leaned against the back door with his hands in his pockets, watching the investor examine the bar. "He wants to keep all the balls in the air. Though I've advised him against it, your balls are a pair he'd like to maintain a hold on. He wants you waiting in the wings in case he doesn't get a good enough offer."

"What if I don't want to *wait in the bloody wings*?"

"Then I suppose I'll be taking those keys after all." Parker held out his stubby hand. "The ledgers too."

The ledgers?

"What's to be done with the ledgers if the club closes?" David tried to keep the panic out of his voice. The club ledgers were a bizarre artifact, to be certain. Very dangerous to have all the patrons' names and habits recorded, but it was the existence of the record that kept anyone from turning to informing or blackmail in times of desperation. Some of the most regretful moments of his life were when he'd had to use those records to threaten a patron, but that regret was nothing compared with what he might have felt if he'd not had them handy. "Parker. You have to tell me that at least."

"If it closes, we'll burn them," Parker said, still watching the investor to ensure he was distracted enough to miss their muttering. "If it doesn't, we'll pass them along to your replacement. Refusing to go with Lord Belleville will amount to a resignation, after all, but don't worry. We'll replace you easily enough. If, of course, this old codger can't bring the cash his lordship is hoping for."

No. *Hell* no. Those ledgers could cause disaster in the wrong hands. The club patrons had trusted David to protect them. Not Lord Belleville. Not Tom Parker. Not whatever younger, prettier proprietor he was eventually replaced with. They'd trusted *David*.

"My good sirs."

The investor's bland voice startled him so badly he outright jumped, an embarrassing reaction that made Parker sneer unpleasantly.

"Seen enough?" Parker said to the old gentleman.

"Indeed! Thank you very much, I shall be in touch."

David forced another smile as they got themselves ready to go, any final, foolish notions of controlling this situation through the force of his own will dissolving like sugar in the bottom of a cocktail. Perhaps that's how it worked in fashion. In coffeehouses. In functioning families. It was not, however, how the rules worked under the oppressive combination of nobility and illegality. Particularly not for a whore with a ring of keys and a sense of power as inflated and unconvincing as Miss Penelope's bosom.

When it was just him and Warren again, David sat on the bar, right where he'd been when Noah dumped blazing gin on his injury. He put his head in his hands. That was just two nights ago, wasn't it?

"Look what I found!"

The singsong voice brought him out of his head. Warren brandished a dusty bottle of bright yellow liquor with an ostentatious label. He was clearly still upset, but had returned to his habit of covering it with cynical humor. Humming in unconvincing merriment, he cut through the wax and got the cork out. The sharp alcohol-and-lemon scent poured forth and tightened the knot in David's stomach.

"You missed a spot, mate. This was in one of the bottom cupboards." Warren poured the syrupy limoncello into champagne glasses, far more of the stuff than anyone should drink at one time. He handed one to David, who tried not to grimace. "Didn't Charlie and Miles bring this back from Italy for you? Back in, what, September?" He lifted his own glass to his lips, but paused. "Wait, were you saving it for something?"

David shook his head and waved him on. "No. I just forgot it was back there. Drink up."

They clinked glasses, and David took a tiny sip of the stuff. He didn't think it was quite as good as Noah had claimed it would be, but then, Noah liked his cocktails to be about half-lemon. He closed his eyes. "Warren?"

"What is it?"

He shouldn't say it. He really ought to keep it to himself. But gossip was gossip even if it was his own, and he could think of no better way to soothe his anxiety right now.

"I bedded Noah last night," he said. "And this morning. Friday, too, depending on how you define bedding."

When he peeked, he saw that Warren's cynicism had been replaced with shining and wicked amusement. "Yes! That's the best news I've heard all day by far." Warren toasted and tossed back the rest of the thick liqueur, making a face as he choked it down. "Let's see. That means Annabelle owes me two shillings. One from Charlie."

"What?" said David, stunned as he watched Warren cackle into his cup. "What are you talking about?"

"We knew the two of you couldn't keep your hands off each other forever," Warren explained in a straightforward way that made David feel he'd lost his marbles. "They thought you'd hold out through the end of the year, but I knew better. Because, you see, they just think you're suffering from attraction, while I know good and well you've been fully in love for ages."

"Excuse me?" David was bewildered, but admittedly a bit pleased to hear Warren's assessment of the situation, now that he and Noah were settling into something solid. "How exactly did you know?"

"Unlike Charlie and Annabelle, *I* saw what you did to that actor. You know. The *April Fourth Actor.*"

A prickle of irritation coasted through David on a wave of limoncello. "Georgie Winters. What exactly did I do to him?"

"What's he drink, usually? Georgie?"

David hesitated. He knew where this was headed. "Gimlet with a cherry."

"Is that what he got that night? After he and Noah finished with their room?"

"How am I supposed to remember—?"

"Oh, stop it. You always remember that sort of thing."

David brought the glass to his pursed lips. "We'd run out of cherries. It happens."

"Very brief shortage. I had no trouble finding some to get Annabelle a smash later in the evening."

"I must have misplaced them."

"Right, right. Probably put 'em right back by this lemon stuff, which came from the place you've held a grudge against since Noah fell in love with it. You can pretend otherwise, but I know the truth, Forester: you're a petty little bitch, and can hold a grudge against anything from a horny actor to an entire European nation."

"I don't know what you're talking about."

"Honestly, I think the whole thing is fantastic. Assuming all this shutting-down business isn't secretly because Lord Moneyballs is in trouble, and you don't end up put in prison or tossed into the Thames in the next few weeks, then I'm thrilled for both of you."

David glared at the sudden return of Warren's barely shrouded pessimism. "You are relentlessly comforting, you know that?"

"Good. Now, comfort me a bit." Looking a little tipsy already, Warren wandered over and leaned his elbows on the bar next to David, the topaz twinkling in his ear as he looked up. His rough edge didn't vanish, but it did soften, likely without his permission. "Forester, I need this job. There's nothing else like it."

David nodded solemnly. Warren's neighbor was able to keep an eye on his mother the nights he worked, but most of the week, he had to stick very close to their home. Mrs. Bakshi's fainting spells were unpredictable and severe, so she could not be left alone for long stretches. His unique position at this unique establishment (along with, perhaps, a uniquely indulgent supervisor), while still illegal, kept him from having to resort to more desperate means of survival.

"What am I going to do?" Warren scrubbed his hands through his dark hair, anxiety hardening his shoulders. "I've got a plan for the worst, you know. If I wound up in jail, the neighbors would take Mum in till I got out. Figured a raid or an informer would do me in eventually, but I never planned to just get *sacked*. It's almost a shame there wasn't a raid. Might have gone easier in the long run."

Horrified that Warren would wish jail on himself, David drew breath to tell him off, but then paused as the full meaning of the words sank in.

"No raid?" he repeated. "How do you know?"

Warren gave him a sideways look, then gestured to the parlor. "Either that or they sent only the most *orderly* of the orderly daughters to tear the place up. Wiped their feet on the mat and everything."

David got down off the bar and stared around the parlor with increasing dread. Clean floors. Undisturbed lamps. Every chair and table just as he'd left it. The bedrooms, when he'd gone in with the investor, had been as boring and spotless as he'd left them, every rug and drawer in place...

"Oh," he said. "Oh, *shit*."

"That's one way to put it."

"He lied." David walked incredulously into the middle of the tidy parlor. "There was no raid. He lied to me, so I'd clean the place up for him before the investor got here."

"Sounds about right."

"*Fuck.*" David clenched his hands open and shut, pacing over the impeccable floors, trying to chase out the urge to punch a wall or kick a chair. "That fucking arsehole. How can he do this to me? After all this time, after everything... Why is he doing this?"

"Because he can, mate," said Warren, pouring more syrup. "Because he's rich and titled, and you're not. Simple enough."

"It's not simple!" David snapped. Fortunately, Warren was a steady sort of bloke who knew David very well, so he didn't flinch. "It's not. Everyone is always trying to make it out as so simple. *Gosh, David, either give him his way or tell him no. Do what he says or don't. Stay or go.* Well, it's not like that. It's never been like that. I don't know what to do, Warren. I can't do as he says, but I can't get out, either. I'm trapped."

Warren came closer, put his hands on the sides of David's shoulders in a hard, bracing way that helped bring something slightly solid back into David's body.

"What's Noah think?" Warren said softly.

David took a steadying breath. "He thinks I should let the Fox go and hide out with him or his family until whatever this is blows over."

Warren tried to keep his face impassive. To his credit, most people would have missed the way his lips parted for just a split second, eyes flashing for an instant of absolute panic. He shook it off quickly, forcing a smile, patting David's back before stepping away a bit.

"If that's what you need to do," he said, not quite meeting David's eye, "then I certainly won't try to stop you."

"Warren—"

"No." He crossed his arms and shook his head firmly, digging his toe into the rug beneath them. "You've been saving everyone else every night for years. If you can't keep it up any longer, Forester, no one will blame you. Well. I won't, anyway." He rolled his eyes and chuckled. "Some of the twats you keep letting in might, but anyone who matters will understand. You've done your time. A place like this ain't forever. We know that."

The lies, the schemes, and the stress were more than David could process. But what he *could* handle was that look on Warren's face. Warren's worries. Warren's needs. Those were right there, obvious and…fixable. Yes. David could fix this. What choice did he have? Sure, with Noah's support and things righted with the Clarkes, David himself might scrape through the club's closing. And Noah, precious Noah, had long since outgrown the need for David's protection. He didn't need this place. Not really.

But there wasn't another soul in London who cared about the fate of Warren and the rest, all his patrons along with an assortment of their family members like Mrs. Bakshi who—mostly unknowingly—relied on David's careful management to keep their lives from going up in smoke. If he did not do all he could to talk Belleville out of this sale, who would ever give any of these people a second thought?

"Don't do anything drastic," he said, facing Warren across the bar. The distress he found in those usually scorching eyes fortified his resolve into something enormous and unmovable. "Neither your mum nor anyone else will be better off with you in prison, do you understand?"

"Forester—"

"I will fix this," he insisted. "I will talk the baron out of this. In the meantime, I will continue to compensate you."

"You're barking."

"I am not." David had long ago learned how to hide money where those in charge of him could not find it. It was nothing compared with what he might have inherited under other circumstances, but it was far from a pittance. "I will manage. Meanwhile, take care of your mum, take care of yourself, and leave the rest of this mess to me."

Chapter Fifteen

Noah

"You *slut*! I knew I shouldn't have made that bet; this was bound to happen the second I left the two of you alone."

"Slut?" Noah flicked a button toward Annabelle that vanished into the folds of her skirt. He shook his head as he carefully put the next stitch into the shell of a half-finished waistcoat. "Seems like mere hours ago that everyone and their sister was calling me frigid."

Annabelle gave him a look. "Times change."

She took up the little shears and snipped a thread of her own. She held a different waistcoat from the same order up in front of her, checking the placement of a gleaming black button. Though no one admitted it, all Noah's colleagues called on independent seamstresses to some extent. As an odd girl given to an odd life filled with odd jobs, Annabelle was happy to help Noah out of the occasional tight spot, providing company and skill while commanding a wage that certainly didn't leave him feeling like he'd taken advantage of anyone.

So, since he was a nervous wreck about David going to the Fox on his own and because the workshop locked its obsessed heathens out on Sundays, he'd taken his work to the kitchen table in the cramped, homey set of rooms that Annabelle shared with Bertie, a gentle giant of a fellow that David had set her up with. The place had a private entrance and was situated above a small theater where the two of them worked building sets, mending costumes, hanging lanterns, and keeping troublesome drunks on the right side of the doorway during shows. The tinkle of a piano, the voices of performers, and the roar of rowdy audiences rattled up through the floorboards almost every evening, but it afforded enough privacy and excuses for the pair to live their lives without too much trouble.

Tonight, they worked on waistcoats accompanied by the clatter and shout of last month's *Hamlet* set being torn down in preparation for next week's comedy rehearsals. The table was covered in all the swaths, spools, and notions that Noah had brought along from home, studded here and there with the components of Annabelle's prized blue-patterned tea set.

Apparently content with the placement of the button, Annabelle set the waistcoat aside to refill their cups with tea, sugar, and the brandy she'd put in the cream pourer, because, *"Milk spoils so fast in the summer, why bother?"*

"So," she said over the rim of her cup. She paused so long that Noah had no choice but to look up from his stitching. Like Noah, she had strict modes of attire for different circumstances, though they both relaxed a bit when it was just the two of them in for the evening. Noah hadn't bothered to change from breeches to proper evening clothes, pinning the front of his hair up in a mess of a knot he'd never wear in public; Annabelle looked comfy in an unstructured tea gown, a blonde braid dipping just past her shoulder. "Come on, sweetheart, you can't just drop that without a few more details. Everyone knows he's been mooning over you for ages."

"Oh, stop it." Noah swatted at her skirts, trying not to look too pleased that David had liked him enough for others to notice.

"Does he know his way around?" she asked with a knowing nod. "He strikes me as the sort who really knows his way around."

Noah smiled into his stitching. "You could say that."

"Tell. Me. Everything."

"Why?" He took a swig from his teacup, nearly choking when he discovered how heavy-handed someone had been with the summertime cream. "So you can report it back to everyone else?"

"In my defense, with the rumors of your frigidity and Forester's weepy little Hyde Park jaunts, the two of you could only benefit from a bit of publicity."

"Oh, leave him be. Who doesn't take a jaunt now and then?"

"Probably you." She looked him up and down. "You frigid slut."

Noah leaned his head on the back of the armchair. "There's no winning, is there?"

"Not in my house," she said with a grin. "Now quit playing hard to get. I can tell you're dying to confess it all. So tell me. *Does he know his way around?*"

Noah's face burned a little as he pulled another stitch. "Annie, I would be a liar if I said he was anything less than *un dio dell'amore.*"

Annabelle shrieked, Noah laughed, and then it was all buttons and brandy and talk of love and sex as the soggy sky out the open window settled into to a cool, rainy dusk. David was Noah's best and oldest friend, but was no longer his only friend. Gushing like this to Annabelle brought all these new developments out of the timeless, private world of *David-and-Noah* and made them real.

It was surprising to find that this reality continued to exist once it was spoken. That what they'd done together these past few days, how they'd loved each other all these years, could extend beyond a broom cupboard or even a bedroom. It could make Annabelle grin and tease and speculate. It could prove to his father that he was confident in the life he'd chosen for himself. It was so bright and shiny, so interesting and unique that as he spoke about it, the plain wool of this blasted waistcoat started looking duller and duller in his aching hands.

During a little lull in the conversation, he held the thing up. It was coming together, by now, the basic structure taking shape.

Annabelle must have caught something of his feelings for it on his face, because she shook her head and said, "Hideous."

Noah couldn't seem to muster any indignance. "It's on-trend and well-made."

"Yes," Annabelle agreed. "Simply hideous."

"He's paying out the arse for these things. A gray, a brown, and a black each for himself and his two sons."

"You don't even see the money, though, do you?" Annabelle asked. "You're salaried."

"There's a small commission tacked on, from Mr. Covington."

"If I had your level of training and reputation, I'd work for myself. I'd never bother with this sort of thing," said Annabelle, shaking her head and finishing another button. "Working yourself to death on *gray, brown, and black waistcoats*, for God's sake. I understand why you have to start that way, but at this point, don't you think it's time you started reaping the benefits of all that effort? I bet you could do half the work, make the work more fun, and bring in nearly as much money if you struck out on your own. They do not pay you *that* well, considering what they're charging for this stuff."

"My own name will never rival Harvey Cole," said Noah. "Never."

"You baffle me sometimes, sweetheart." She patted his hand

and gently took the waistcoat from him, replacing it with his cup. "Are you a name? Or are you a tailor?"

Noah rolled his eyes toward the window, watching as the drizzle picked up to a full-bodied rain. "Oh, what do you know about it?"

"About choosing work that lets you live a bit more happily?" Annabelle stamped her foot on the wooden floor once as if to indicate the clanking, clattering theater below. "I know literally everything there is to know; where would you like me to start?"

Her words struck a particular nerve that might normally spur him to argument, but after all that had happened the past few days, he felt softer than usual. He was able to sit with the feeling instead.

Are you a name, or a tailor?

"Annie," he said slowly. "Theoretically, if I were to—"

He broke off as a squeak from the outside stair caught their attention. Someone knocked, the soft, unthreatening knock one used when everybody one knew was afraid of law enforcement. It coalesced into the pattern they used at the Fox.

"It's me!" came a low voice from the other side. "It's Forester. Open up."

Another blue patterned cup was procured. No one bothered pretending that David might want real milk or even any tea in it.

"I had to talk to you," said David, his wild eyes fixed on Noah as Annabelle half-forced him to sit at the table. He looked dreadful. Soggy and sooty, in desperate need of fresh clothes and a few hours of sleep.

Noah sat in the other chair, pulling up close. "Davy, you're soaked."

"Bit of a walk, all around. I went back to your place first."

A drop of rainwater dripped down his face. He wiped it, shivering. "Forgot you said you'd be here. Emily reminded me where you'd gone."

"You went from Bradigan's, to the Fox, to my place, and now *here*? In the rain?"

Noah felt Annabelle squeeze his shoulder. "I'll go find him something dry to put on."

As she left for the bedroom, David went on in a rush. "I should have waited until tomorrow to talk to you, I guess. But I couldn't stand the thought. I never would have slept if I'd tried. I would have just been up all night thinking about it."

"What's happening?"

"There was no raid." That sounded like good news, but based on David's hurried, panicked air, it must not have been. "No raid. It was a lie. He wanted me to get rid of all the decorations so he could show the place to an investor. He's going to sell it if I can't talk him out of it as soon as possible."

"David—"

"I absolutely have to go with him to his holdings. Wednesday. If I don't go, he'll consider it my resignation, and either sell the place or replace me. Time is of the essence and there's no other way, but I know I can talk him out of this, as long as I get a chance. I *know* it."

Noah stared. "How far along is this sale?"

"Not very far. The investor was just looking the place over with Parker when I arrived—"

"Shut that mouth until you're dry, Forester," Annabelle snapped from the bedroom doorway, returning with her arms full of clothes and blankets. "You will not catch your damned death in my sitting room, I swear to God."

They got him peeled out of his dripping suit and changed into Bertie's enormous blue jumper, a pair of Annie's trousers, and a pair of thick wool socks. Noah revived the small woodstove in the corner, and they sat David down before it with a blanket around his shoulders and the brandy poured near to spilling from his teacup.

"Not a word from you until you've drunk half of that," said Annabelle.

Noah winced. He'd heard only the beginning, but suspected that David's ability to discuss the Fox would not benefit from intoxication. "A few sips, *amore*. Until your teeth stop chattering."

David looked a little better than he had when he came in, but there remained a tightness in his body and a wild edge to the green of his eyes. Still, he managed to lift one side of his mouth. "You going to tell me those *microorganisms* of yours cause colds, as well?"

"That's not exactly…" Noah shook his head. This was really not worth getting into at the moment. "Yes, David. They do."

David raised his overfull cup and said, very exhausted, "To the health benefits, then."

Noah spent the quiet moment that followed in a nervous chill of his own. No raid. An investor. Lies upon lies. And David… In spite of the fact that he knew he had Noah, knew he had something like family to see him through this, David was *still* babbling nonsense about following this arsehole to some remote estate to convince him of something that was obviously long since decided.

The calm silence did not last as long as Noah needed to get his thoughts in order. With some of the pink leaving David's cheeks and the smell of brandy swirling around him, he looked over at Noah again, all that wild determination—which was obviously just fear and despair that he'd never name as such—still there on his face.

"So. I want to preface this with the fact that I know it sounds mental. But if I want to save the Fox—"

"Davy!" Noah snapped. "There's no saving the Fox. How do you not understand this? *He lied to you.*"

The intensity of his voice had Annabelle gesturing to the door. *Shall I?* When Noah nodded, she gathered herself up. "I'm going to see about the breakdown downstairs, I think," she said. "Take your time with the one up here." She kissed David on top of his head and Noah on the corner of his mouth, put on her shoes, and went down to the theater.

Once they were alone, David looked at Noah with maddening calmness.

"Have you even spoken to the baron since finding this out?" Noah asked.

"No, but it doesn't matter. Parker says he still wants to bring me along as a backup in case the offer is no good."

"What if that's not true? What if it's another lie, or there's more to it than he's saying?"

David blinked at the stove a few times, taking another shaky drink from his teacup. "Then I'll have to deal with it when I get there. If I want even the slightest chance of getting the club back, I have to show him I can play nice."

"You cannot play nice with someone who treats you like—"

"I have to play *especially* nice with someone like him," he whispered, voice quiet but so sharp that it cut through Noah's outburst like a knife. "We are not talking about a Cole & Co. cutter, Noah. We're not even talking about someone like Fiore Whateverthefuck—"

"—Fiore *Corsetti*—"

"—who seemed harsh to you, but only because you don't even know what harsh looks like until you're at the whims of a noble peer of England. I have to play along with him, or not only will I lose my chance to save you lot from wandering the West End for places who botch their raids and sell their servers, but he might end up deciding that I'm not worth keeping around at all." Those words fell heavily, like they'd surprised even David himself. He went on very quietly. "And in *my* industry, Noah, that's not just a bad reference and a few weeks' missed pay."

Noah squatted down next to David's chair, loving him so much in this moment that he suddenly thought he'd do monstrous things to let David Forester live out the rest of his life in perfect peace. "David, you need to cut ties. Now. If you are genuinely worried for yourself, then burn all the ledgers and come stay with me until it blows over."

"But the club—"

"Is just a club, Davy. It's a wonderful club, and everyone adores it, and adores you, but it isn't worth proving to this terrible man that you will *play nice* whenever he snaps his fingers."

"It is not just a club." That calmness finally gave way, not quite breaking, but bending dangerously. David's temper was clearly trying to peek out over his sense of defeat.

That was good, maybe. Anger was appropriate here. So Noah went on poking at it, hoping it might bring David to grips with what was a genuinely infuriating reality.

"Are you still expected to find a wife for cover, then?" he challenged. "By *Wednesday*?"

David squeezed his eyes shut. "If I am, Belleville will provide her."

"Put one of his allies right on your arm. Brilliant, David. Really. Accept more favors from this arsehole; what could go wrong?"

"For the sake of sixty members who've entrusted me with their lives?" He finally opened his fiery eyes, lifting his cup while he was at it, as if toasting Annabelle and all the rest even as he'd rather smash the thing against the wall. "I suppose I'll take the risk. Hasn't killed me yet."

"Dear *God*, David," Noah said, nearly shouting this time, like volume had been the problem all along. *"It is just a club."*

"Maybe it is," David admitted at last, matching his intensity. "But you need it."

"No," said Noah, forceful and unblinking. *"You've* decided that we need it, because you think that if we don't need your protection, then we don't need *you."*

Speaking harsh truth had won the day with his father, but as he watched David's face go blank, all that potentially useful fury hissing out like air from a balloon, he realized that it had been a devastatingly bad move to make with David.

David stared into his cup, then took down enough brandy in one go to make Annabelle proud.

"I don't want to talk about this anymore," he muttered.

"I *do* need you, David," Noah stuttered, scrambling to put a patch over his misstep. "I always have. I always will. The others too. But it's not because of the Fox. It's not what you *do* for us, Davy. You don't have to be useful. You don't have to protect anyone. It's just *you*. You are—"

"I said *I don't want to talk about it anymore.*"

Perhaps if they were regular lovers, or regular friends, Noah would keep trying to reason with him. But reason had nothing to do with this. He watched David put the teacup on the ground with a shaking hand, even now tenderly protecting Annabelle's favorite china from the danger of his own impulses. And Noah finally understood what David had said to him earlier. *It's not simple.* None of this was simple. Not because the circumstances were complex. They weren't, really: Belleville was a cruel, wealthy prat who found someone raised to be pushed around, then preyed on his vulnerability and protective nature to keep the upper hand in everything from an affair to an illegal business venture.

It wasn't simple, because everything that had happened to

David, from his father to the fire to this monstrous nobleman, had left something broken within him. There was a pile of smoking rubble in his head that was protecting—not Noah, not the others—but something in David himself, something too precious to leave vulnerable, even if its defense choked and burned the rest of him in the process.

While words were David's preference, Noah suddenly feared that if he spoke ones harsh enough to get through the wreckage to the parts it was protecting, he'd do more harm than good.

But there were other options.

Stick together.

Words weren't going to cut it, no matter how honest or heartfelt they were. It was Noah's way that was needed this time. Action. And not just any action. The one he'd failed to take when it mattered most, the thing he'd been too ambitious and self-absorbed to notice the need for.

Bullies were not confined to the schoolyard, after all, and no one should be left to face them alone.

Noah left off harsh words in favor of a soft touch on the shoulder, taking cues from how David had handled their difficult conversation this morning. David startled a bit at first, but eventually relaxed into the touch enough that Noah felt alright giving an even gentler kiss.

David seemed surprised by the sudden switch to sweetness, even more so when Noah pulled back, pushed the damp hair out of his eyes, and said, "I'm going to ask Emily to go with you as your wife. So you have an ally in the house, someone smart who can keep an eye on things and get word back to me if anything unexpected happens."

"What?"

"Please don't argue," Noah said quietly.

David's brows collapsed with concern. "Would she really do that?"

"Yes." Noah swallowed hard, glancing toward the doorway. He'd have to talk to Annabelle. He only knew how to play this game by his own rules; the real, immutable rules of the outside world were different. "Yes, she will do it. I don't know how long she will be able to do it for, but it should be long enough to appease the sensibilities of anyone wondering about you and Belleville's relationship."

Noah watched the wheels turning behind David's eyes. "Assuming she would go along with that, why would I ever let her?"

"Why wouldn't you?" Noah said, trying to keep the challenge in his voice to a minimum. "Unless, of course, you think Jo is right about the baron being dangerous. If that's the case, though, I have to wonder: why are you still willing to go yourself, particularly with no one along to watch your arse?"

David, at least, had the decency to avert his eyes. "Ask her, then, if you want," he sighed. "She won't do it anyway, so it hardly matters, does it?"

Noah put his teacup on the table and then took both of David's hands. He kissed each of them and then pulled them to his chest. His heart was pounding. He wondered what David might think of that, or if he'd even notice.

"I think you'll be surprised, *amore*," he whispered, "to learn what everyone is willing to do to protect you, if you let them."

When David left, Noah went down to the theater to collect Annabelle. He spoke with her at length about how he might handle the details to make his own doom less likely, during the time he would spend as Mrs. Emily Forester. His build and complexion would buy him a few days, Annabelle figured, but more than that would carry untenable risk. A country estate wasn't London, after all, where Annabelle herself could blend in alongside performers, foreigners, and eccentrics amid the sort of privacy that only came in populated places. There would be more oversight in a noble household than either of them had ever lived under before. She gave suggestions for excusing himself from the intrusion of the ladies' maids, special makeup to spare him from more shaves than his skin could tolerate, and explanations for his form that would not save him if discovered, but might buy him just enough time to start running.

It was not, altogether, an especially encouraging conversation.

Next morning, before he went to the workshop to figure out how on earth he might manage to skip work for a few days, he wrote out a message to David:

My dearest Mr. Forester,
She will do it, but my rational sister has no formal clothing suitable for a baron's country estate. She might not even have a proper corset for all I know. Please send along Miss Penelope's things as soon as possible so that I can make the necessary alterations on a couple of evening dresses.
I am forever, your most dearly devoted,
Noah Clarke

He stared at his letter, the paper looking very stark against his kitchen table. For a brief moment, he considered crumpling it back up and forgetting the whole thing. But in the end, Emily was right.

He really would follow David anywhere.

Chapter Sixteen

The Ailing Hare, April 1878

Cleaning the tables was about as useless as it was unnoticed in a place like this, but it had become David's habit in the early evenings. It offered the distraction of chatter with the factory hands as they settled in after work, and, more importantly, gave him an excuse to stay out of the kitchen. Hopefully, the day would come when he could witness the lighting of a stove without all the walls seeming to close in, but that day had not arrived just yet.

Table cleaning, on the other hand, was a task that suited him well enough, particularly as the pub filled with noise and the comforting presence of people asking him to fetch beers or capture the attention of a server.

As he was working at a particularly cementlike streak of what was hopefully potatoes on one of the back tables, the door creaked open. He didn't look up until he heard a whistle from one of the customers. Probably one of the painted girls, then. Bit early, but still he threw the cloth over his shoulder and turned to go escort her in. It was best that the Hare's patrons witness someone looking out for these women, someone who might not take kindly if they came down from one of the rooms looking anything but well-paid.

He started for the door, but once he saw who the new visitor was, he froze, completely rooted to the spot. He'd not seen that face in nearly two years, years that had passed like a decade in a war zone. He blinked rapidly, certain he'd lost his mind at last.

But his mind, even in its very weakest state, could never have reinvented Noah Clarke so beautifully. No wonder there'd been a whistle—he was dressed to call all manner of sinful attention to himself, artfully feathered in a purple plush jacket and bright red neckcloth, tall leather boots, and hair he'd grown out until it nearly reached his shoulders.

"You lost, little lady?" one of the customers snickered. Noah picked at the lacy trim on his lapel, looking like he certainly was lost, thank-you-very-much, and was about to turn around and walk right out.

David darted around the tables to get to him before it was too late. He'd not gone out of his way to make sure Noah could find him, but now that he was here, the thought of him leaving was intolerable. When Noah reached for the handle, David barked out, "Mr. Clarke, wait!"

He turned back, caught David's eye, and then every bit of decorum they'd ever learned flew right out the grimy window as they ran into an embrace so tight and long-needed that the whistling started back up. For a second, David didn't give a fuck, too amazed that he was actually holding Noah Clarke in his arms again to care about anything else.

But he came to his senses eventually; it would do neither of them any good to draw more attention to themselves in this crowd. He pulled back reluctantly for a more respectable handshake.

Noah looked at him with red, wet eyes. There was an undeniable distress on his face as he looked David over, and David remembered that he probably looked as different as Noah did, though in the opposite direction. Aside from the opulent

set of evening clothes from Henry—or rather, *Lord Belleville*,
now—that he'd been wearing at the time of the fire and had
already pawned, the rest of his wardrobe had been burned up
and replaced with cheap corduroys and plain flannels. He'd
let his face grow scruffy to avoid being recognized, helped
along in that task by his lean new diet of whatever was left in
the kitchen at the end of the night.

"David, what on earth are you doing here?"

"How did you find me?" David asked, not certain Noah's
question merited a response.

"Asked around." Noah's face furrowed and his voice went
tight and quiet with barely contained fury, almost screechingly
posh and pretentious amid the factory hands and sticky tables.
"Asked around *everywhere*. I heard what happened, you know.
From my *father*. Who heard it from *the papers*. Why the devil
did you stop writing me? I was worried sick. I—"

David grabbed his arm gently, glancing at the patrons behind him, some of whom were watching the reunion with
interest. "Not here," he muttered, checking to make sure the
proprietor was safely tucked back in the kitchen out of sight
before pulling Noah toward the rickety staircase. "Let's talk
upstairs."

A few catcalls followed them up, drowning out the creaking.

"Why are they doing that?" Noah asked when they reached
the landing.

David cracked a little smile in spite of himself. "Because
you look like a prostitute, mate."

"Oh." He'd expected Noah to take offense, but he looked
oddly flattered. "Do I really, *amore*?"

"*Amore*?" David shook his head as he opened the door to
the tiny room he called his own, turning to hide the blush
that might give away how intrigued and charmed he was

by Noah's beautiful attire and acceptance of its implications this side of the Channel. "You should know that if you start throwing your Italian around like the whores and the actors do, you'll be furthering the likeness, so be warned."

"*Bona*," Noah quipped, and for a moment—a brief, smiling moment—things felt almost normal between them. But that was before Noah saw the state of David's room, peering hesitantly into a space hardly bigger than a closet with nothing in it but a cot, a simple table with a washbowl, and a trunk of the few things David had to his name right now.

"Come on," David coaxed, pushing through his embarrassment. Once the door was shut, he pulled Noah in for another squeeze. He smelled like home and something heavily floral, his velvet coat the softest thing David had touched in months. The utter, unexpected comfort of Noah's arms around him proved a grave threat to the brittle structures that had kept him upright since the fire. He felt like his bones would turn to dust when they parted, and he let go quickly, as if to prove to himself that it wasn't true. He did stay standing. Incredibly, he stayed dry-eyed too, though Noah was wiping his own cheeks with his lacy cuffs.

"I'm really glad you're here," David said.

"You could have made it a little easier," said Noah in a shaky voice. "I had no idea where you were, David. None. And I never would have looked here if I hadn't gotten very lucky with who I asked. I was starting to think I might never see you again."

I could have made it easier? Well, that's simple enough for you to say, out there getting a nice tan and stitching plush jackets while I was left on my own to serve champagne in my own hotel until—

"I'm sorry," David said, cutting the flow of ridiculous resentments. He'd dwelled in those enough already over the past two years, and they seemed particularly uncharitable now. His mind felt like a sieve for dates, but some part of him knew that for Noah to be here today, he'd have had to drop everything and hop right on the first train out of Milan. It wasn't the same as being together the whole time, but it was something significant. "I didn't know how to tell you. It was like... Like if I told you, it would be real."

And he'd been right. He felt the structures he'd built within him cracking already. He sat on his hard, squeaky cot, hoping to strain them less, staring at his shoes until Noah joined him.

He glanced up then. God, Noah was stunning like this, wasn't he? Not just the clothes, but the obvious health, the evidence of sunshine and hearty food and work that he loved. He wanted to grab him by those plush lapels and start kissing like they used to, pull him over so all that goodness Noah had cultivated could hold David down on the cot and become part of him.

Could he do that? He didn't know. As frightening and confusing a lover as Lord Belleville had been, David had at least come away from his bed and clubs with one good thing to show for it: a better understanding of why Noah's departure had devastated him so badly. Not only he could love and desire a person of any sex, but the love and desire he'd felt for Noah at school had been precious and irreplaceable. Had Noah learned anything similar in their time apart? He didn't know how to ask. A question like that could destroy what little was left of the only true friendship he'd ever known.

"When are you going back to Italy?" David asked instead.

Noah looked at him like he was crazy. "I'm not."

"What?"

"I'm not going back." He crossed his arms, a distinct look of disappointment crossing his features before he could quash it. "It was close enough to the end of my time anyway. Signor Corsetti has written all the appropriate letters and certificates

for me. Now that I've found you, I'm going to take my portfolio to the Savile Row shops and make my name in London."

"You didn't have to come back," David said, quiet and so
full of guilt one might think he'd begged for this outcome,
rather than avoiding it.

"The decision to stay is more complicated, so don't go feeling responsible for that," Noah said a bit falteringly, like he
wasn't sure what he'd said was true. "But, David, of course I
had to come back."

"Why?"

"Because…" Noah looked at him, and through all the fin-
ery and flowing hair was that same person he'd loved forever,
who'd saved his life and broken his heart, and then come back
to hopefully—please, dear God—hopefully he would say it. He
had to have felt it, didn't he? Maybe not as strongly as David
did, but some tiny portion of it?

Noah bit his bottom lip and reached out for a second, heading for David's cheek. David closed his eyes, ready for the gentle touch that would wreck every hard structure he'd built to
tide himself over, replacing it with that sweet softness they'd
found under the lilac bushes.

But the touch didn't come. He opened his eyes to see that
Noah had stopped with his hand a solid foot from David's
face. He smiled and patted David's leg instead.

"Because you're my dearest friend in the world, David," he
said, his voice sticking, and shaking, and his eyes everywhere
but David's. "My absolute dearest."

And so the hard structures did not fold, but something else
did. Something David decided quickly was needless, small,
not load-bearing. He could live without the sort of love he'd
hoped for, content with a dear friend who would cross coun-
tries, risk opportunities, and scour London to show up in
velvet to a place like this. That, surely, was treasure enough.

"And you're mine," David whispered, putting a hand on Noah's leg too, so their arms crossed for a moment. Noah retracted his first, and David reluctantly took the hint. "How's the return to Britain treating you?"

Noah gave him a very sideways look. "You want to talk about *that*? When your—"

"I want to talk about literally anything but my own circumstances," said David as lightly as humanly possible, and therefore still a bit on the heavy side. "So. How's it treating you?"

Noah glanced around the damp, drafty space and the yellowed window like it was a prison cell. "Bit of an adjustment, honestly," he said in a tone that matched the look. "There are certainly aspects of the European way of life that suit me better." He fiddled with the red cloth around his neck and David remembered with a jolt deep in his stomach something he'd heard from a Roman fellow working at one of Belleville's brothels, something about what a tie that color could signify in parts of Italy.

So he *had* learned something interesting about himself in Milan. David could have been jealous, but it would be better to turn that hot, sickening feeling into something else. Protectiveness. David's inclinations had gotten him into that terrible situation with the baron; he determined that such a thing would never, ever happen to Noah Clarke. Not on his watch. He wanted to say something to that effect, to make sure Noah knew that David would do anything necessary to take care of that precious part of him...even if David was not, as he'd briefly hoped, the object of his affections.

"Meet anyone, ah, *interesting* over there?" David nudged Noah's shoulder with his own. Noah suppressed a reluctant smile and nudged back.

"Maybe I did," he said slyly. "But I doubt you want to hear about all that, after everything."

Everything. David couldn't tell what Noah meant by that. Was he referring to David's lost family and future? *Everything* that had happened after Noah left?

Or did he mean the other everything?

He supposed it wasn't worth pushing the issue. His answer was the same either way.

"Noah, after everything, there is no topic in the world more interesting to me than someone else's romantic exploits." He tugged on Noah's sleeve to suggest they lie down together. Not with Noah on top of him, like he'd have preferred, but side by side. Still warm. Still here. Still more than good enough. "So let's hear it, before someone makes me get back to scraping up potatoes."

Chapter Seventeen

Noah

London's West End, June 1885

As the time of the ill-advised departure grew near, a thick dread seemed to settle on the very surface of Noah's skin, as sticky and unpleasant as whatever coated the tables at The Ailing Hare.

On Monday, David made it worse by asking to discuss the details with Emily before they left. He wanted to ensure they could play the role of husband and wife convincingly and with compatible stories. That was a reasonable demand, one that Emily—once she heard what Noah planned to do—reasonably rejected with a colorful series of curses that Noah was surprised she even kept in her proper and practical head. And so Noah told David she was too busy wrapping things up with her mentor to spare even an hour.

Though Noah genuinely could not spare an hour with a week away from the workshop on the horizon, he did it anyway, escaping for an unusual lunch break to meet with David and go over everything "in Emily's stead." He comforted himself with the knowledge that, when this rather inevitably resulted in his ruin, he would not have to worry about his dull, neglected Harvey Cole accounts again anyway.

He'd rather hoped, as they settled in for a discussion and a hurried meal, that David might have come to his senses. But no. Quite the contrary, in fact. Poor David had been to see Belleville in the meantime, who'd filled him with even more misplaced hope that the club could be saved and well-placed fear that something untoward might occur should David call this off.

Noah hadn't seen his friend in a state like this since his grief-stricken days working at The Ailing Hare. His eyes were wild, his speech hurried and stumbling, the smiles crossing his face compulsive and tight. It might have been heartbreaking, had David himself not been the very thing holding Noah's heart together. This protector needed protecting now, and Noah took the role on with surprising ease. He saw to it that his friend was fed, that their plans were solid, and that a story was concocted that would excuse "Emily's brother" escorting her to the station instead of her "husband," so that David didn't try to pick her up at home and spoil everything.

When they finished, David invited Noah back to his house for a proper farewell. But no. The meal had gone on too long as it was, and he had to get back to the workshop as soon as possible; he had Rosenby's second fitting in less than an hour. An embrace would have to suffice. It was tight enough for a side-eye or two. Not quite enough for anyone to comment.

Until Noah was walking back along Savile Row alone and felt someone fall into step beside him.

His cutter's other workhand, Cecil Martin, touched the brim of his own hat. "Clarke."

"Martin."

"Looks like you've got quite a close companion, eh?" he said carefully. "Who was that bloke?"

Noah kept walking past the decked-out windows of the

other tailor shops on the Row, not looking at Mr. Martin even as he kept perfect pace.

"Mr.—"

"You know who he was, Martin," Noah snapped. "I'm in a bit of a rush, so please don't waste my time with stupid questions."

"You ought to be more careful with things like that," Martin said.

Was that a threat? Noah glanced sideways at last. Martin's face was pinched with a sort of incredulous worry. Not a threat. A genuine warning.

"It's none of your business," said Noah, refusing to let a little concern soften his feelings for a rival. "You'll be better off if I'm out of the way anyway, won't you?"

Martin laughed. "I don't think like that, but I suppose it's good to know you do."

"Yes," said Noah. "Perhaps it's you who ought to be more careful."

They walked on. The shop displays were filled with the sturdy fabrics and sporting cuts that the visiting nobles would need when the Season ended and they—like Belleville—left the city for their country estates. The offerings they passed were ostentatious and parrotlike. Harvey Cole did not put displays in the windows. Unlike these places, he did not need to. The name was sufficient. The details—and the tailors themselves—insignificant.

"Mr. Clarke. Are you well?"

Noah squeezed his eyes shut, wishing Martin would stop talking. He was forcing Noah to think about that thing he'd been trying to ignore out of existence: that if, by some miracle, he and David came out of this intact, he would have more on his plate at the workshop than he could possibly catch up on.

He slowed, then stopped entirely, propping himself on the

sill of a competitor. He felt absolutely sick, but he couldn't lie to himself any longer.

"Mr. Martin," he said, throat sticking a bit. "I've had second thoughts about the Rosenby account. It was unsporting of me to take it. You should do his fitting, when we get back. I apologize."

Martin stopped beside him, staring through the window at the display. "Oh, don't worry about it. Honestly. I know you enjoy the eccentric ones. Have at it, if you like; I'll have more opportunities later anyway."

"But—"

"I have a question, Clarke. Do you really intend to stay with Cole & Co. until you look like Mr. Covington?"

Noah pretended to blush. "Why, Mr. Martin, I'm flattered you think I could ever procure such a luxurious mustache." They both chuckled, and it was strangely nice to do that. When they'd finished, Noah put a hand up. "In all seriousness, though. Assuming nothing goes…*amiss*…then of course I do. Cole & Co. is top-tier. Anything else would be a step down."

Mr. Martin nodded, glancing at the display behind him. "You've really never considered starting your own enterprise?"

Are you a name, or a tailor?

"I don't know," Noah said. "Have you?"

"Absolutely," said Mr. Martin. "I came to Cole to become the best I can be, but honestly, even if you gave me half your accounts, I don't think I'm going to rise much higher than I have."

Noah was shocked. "But…they say you're…"

Mr. Martin raised his eyebrows. "A *true savant*?"

"Yes!"

"Perhaps," he admitted with a modest shrug. "But it's a *Corsetti-trained cutthroat* like you who goes far at a place like that. Only a handful of us will go on to be cutters and designers, and even if I did, it's years off. Years of stupid games like the ones we're playing, assembling my superiors' ideas day in and day out, worrying arthritis will set in before I get a chance to really make anything of my own.

"So, anyway. I figure I'll give it a bit longer, really make sure my skills are up to snuff. Then I'm going see about getting my own storefront off the Row, or at least start taking commissions out of my flat. I have a friend who's doing well with that, you know. Just him, his home workstation, and a couple seamstresses, and I'll tell you what, he made three jackets for Oscar Wilde's American tour." He held up the appropriate number of envious fingers. "Not the czar of Russia, of course, but I'll take it, and you might too, if you were being honest with yourself."

He glanced pointedly at Noah's own jacket, embroidered with foliage and cut in the modern Italian style. Even it was very modest in comparison with what he dreamed up and sketched out in his free time. Which—since Noah had a habit of flashing his sketches around like a damn peacock—Martin knew well enough.

"But that's just me," Mr. Martin said. "Which is why, if you want Rosenby, you should take him. You're better suited to Cole's culture, I think, than I am. Though…" He looked appraisingly over Noah's jacket. "If you ever found you wanted to move sideways, rather than up and up, I'd certainly not say no to a collaboration. You scare me a little, but you're damn good at what you do."

That was a lot more than he'd bargained for, and he wasn't sure what to think about any of it yet. All he knew was that he still wanted that Rosenby order.

And he couldn't take it.

"I appreciate all of this, Mr. Martin. More than you know." He licked his lips, trying to prepare the way for words he very much did not want to say. "But I had no business taking Rosenby. Not just because it was unfair, but because I was already behind. And now I have to leave the city tomorrow. I don't know how I'm going to manage my current accounts, much less anything else."

"Is there anything I could help you with?"

Noah leaned back a bit as if he'd been insulted. A biting reply sprawled out on his tongue, but he stopped it from rolling out.

"Let's walk on." He nodded in the direction of the shop and they started off. "You'll be late for Rosenby's fitting. We can discuss whether you really want to help me once you've got your own accounts sorted."

Once his work things were settled for the coming week—helped by the bewildering generosity of Cecil Martin—all Noah still needed was a brother to borrow as an escort for the morning, along with someone more skilled than Emily to help him into his corset and skirts. He knew quite a few mad chaps who might be willing to help, but only one who possessed the correct balance of madness, trustworthiness, and proximity to the station to be of any use.

Which was how he found himself having his trunk brought across Piccadilly first thing in the morning, to a cozily sized but well-decorated set of rooms where his old chum Charlie Price now lived with an erotic novelist named Miles, working as an accountant and mostly managing to stay out of trouble.

Perhaps he was missing trouble, because his brown eyes sparkled when Noah dragged a trunkful of it into his bedroom and opened it up with a pathetic sigh. "Help me. I've really gotten myself into something this time."

Charlie grinned at the pile of petticoats while Noah clung to his arm. He stroked Noah's hair and kissed his temple.

"Cheer up, butterfly. We'll make you a respectable little wifey in no time."

"Not as respectable as you." Noah traced a finger along Charlie's absurdly starched collar. Noah only saw Charlie at the club or occasionally the theater, and had never seen him dressed all in conservative gray like this, not a single jeweled ring or peacock feather in sight. "Are you very sure this won't make you late to the bank?"

"I'm sure it will, and thank God for that." He rolled his eyes, his dark hair distinctly not flopping into them, totally slicked and ready for polite society. He jerked a thumb in the direction of the doorway, lowering his voice as Miles's heavy footsteps fell elsewhere in the flat. "Do you have any idea how responsible he's made me? It's sickening. I'm on time nearly every single morning."

Noah felt a smile creeping past all his nerves. He touched an ominous metal loop that someone had drilled into the bedpost. "Is that because you're afraid to lose him, or afraid *of* him?"

Charlie grinned like a madman and blushed like a maiden as he helped Noah out of his jacket. "Now, that's the question, isn't it?"

Noah started switching out of vest and drawers for a chemise and knickers while Charlie hung his clothes up. When it was time, Charlie picked up the corset and indicated for Noah to turn around. Together, they got it in place along with a set of inserts, and Noah held his breath while Charlie started lacing him up.

"Anyway, butterfly," said Charlie, "are you certain that this whole…thing…is a good id—?"

"Tighter."

Charlie paused. "Really?"

"Yes… No, not like that. *Tighter.* Really give it a good pull."

"I don't want to hurt you."

Noah turned to give a serious look over his shoulder, but was interrupted when the bedroom door creaked open. Miles stepped in, his broad shoulders and wild hair making him seem to take up quite a lot of the doorway.

He adjusted the specs on his nose, gaping at Noah in his knickers. "You aren't going out in public like that, are you?"

Noah gasped, modestly covering himself with scandalized hands. "Well, I had intended to put my *frock* on, you wicked man."

After looking between the two of them a few more times, his dark brows drawn together, Miles finally came over behind Noah and took the lacings from Charlie's hands. He fiddled with them for a moment, then gave a series of sharp tugs that squeezed the breath right out of Noah's chest. He handed the lacings back, then went to the bedside table. He picked up a book and returned to the door. "I think I'd like to know nothing else about the situation at all, if that's alright."

"*Perfetta*," Noah said, voice tight as he adjusted to the pressure around his ribs. "*Grazie, bello. Ciao.*"

Miles closed the door quietly behind him.

"That *is* tight," said Charlie, eyeing the lacings. "How do you breathe in that thing?"

Noah adjusted his bosom helpers. "Sparingly."

They finished getting him dressed, powdered, and pinned to perfection. Noah looked himself over in the looking glass with a critical eye, popping open his parasol over his shoulder and inspecting all the angles he could manage. He didn't love what he saw. He was not as good with the paint as Annabelle, never having had occasion to blend in before and opting instead for hearts and swirls and butterfly wings. He was not pretty or interesting like this, but he supposed that was for the best. Burgundy and cream had been a good choice, at least, bringing a bit of color to his cheeks. With long sleeves, gloves, and a high, lacy neck, anything associated with masculinity was well-concealed. He turned and looked over his shoulder, inspecting the fall of the bustle.

"What do you think?" he said to Charlie, once he'd gotten a good look at himself.

"You're stunning." Charlie came up behind him. Noah put up a gloved hand to keep him from kissing his cheek and mussing the powder. "Without all the extra glitter and hearts and whatnot, I honestly don't think anyone but Forester is even going to look twice. And him only because he's going to like what he sees."

Charlie winked in the mirror, but the words made Noah uncomfortable. He watched his own mouth twist a little, as Charlie's eyes took on a suspicious narrowing.

"Noah, I know we're all worried about Forester," Charlie said carefully. "But are you absolutely sure about this?"

"Unfortunately, yes. I am."

Charlie put his hands on Noah's shoulders and leaned in, kissing the air an inch from his forehead. "Any finishing touches, then? I feel like something's missing."

It was. He took a little box out of the pocket of his jacket. He opened it and handed the string of pearls to Charlie before turning around to have them clasped around his neck. Though chilly, they burned against Noah's skin, like they'd been forever imbued with the heat of the stairwell, the essence of David's body, the caress of his mouth. He prayed there would be a chance for more moments like that, but if not, at least they hadn't gone to their graves pretending their love for each other was silly.

"Thank you, *amore*." He turned back to Charlie. "Would you please ask Miles to help with the trunk?"

Noah watched Charlie leave the room, calling across his cozy flat casually-as-you-please for the nice fellow he got to spend his evenings with.

Chapter Eighteen

David

"Can I show you to your compartment, sir?"

"Not just yet, dear boy, I'm—"

Mr. Parker cut David off, speaking loudly and clapping him on the back. "He's still waiting on his new little wife, you see. Left home without her. Can you imagine making such a mistake?"

David shook Mr. Parker's hand off as roughly as he dared in the middle of a bustling platform.

The young attendant glanced up at the hands of the clock that loomed over Kings Cross. He nodded solemnly, not commenting on just how little time said wife had left before the express train departed, and not needing to; Mr. Parker handled commentary quite well enough, after all.

The grimy bastard had come along to see Belleville off, and while he was not leaving London, his presence had proved very useful when his lordship needed to punish David for daring to arrive separate from his new bride. Belleville's gray brows had drifted upward as he finished a final cigarette before he boarded. *"I'm certainly not going to wait around for her brother to escort her, David. I'm going to get settled. Parker, I'll leave the assessment of David's wife up to you."*

And so, David had spent the past quarter hour standing

dumbly on the platform, staring at the clock face and trying not to hear any of Parker's nasty quips. The air was thick and muggy, filled with soot and the hundred separate hair oils in the swarm of humanity milling about the station. The buzz of chatter was not enough to keep the bark of every too-loud attendant and blare of every train whistle from making David jump.

At last, he thought he spotted Emily through the throng, though it was a version of her he'd never thought to see. Lacy and corseted, nipped and tied to perfection under a dainty little parasol. It certainly looked like Emily—and he was fairly certain he'd seen that red-and-white frock before—though as soon as he started for her, he paused. Who was that man with her? It certainly wasn't Noah. Too tall, too broad, too darkly complexioned, with a smile so big he could see it shine from halfway across the platform.

Oh.

Oh, fuck.

It was *Charlie*.

A heavy hand on his shoulder startled him so badly that Mr. Parker quite nearly got the punch in the face he deserved.

"That her, then?" he said, watching as Charlie raised a hand in greeting and ushered Emily along as he pushed her trunk, clearly forgetting that he ought to stay out of sight. "A bit plain, but still too pretty for you. No one will believe it."

"Would you kindly piss off, now?" David said through his teeth. "She's made it. She's suitable. I will take it from here."

"And miss meeting the lovely little bird? Never."

"If you think I would even consider introducing you to a respectable woman like her, you are absolutely mad." Before Parker could say anything else, he strode swiftly to meet his friends before they could get too close to the secretary. He needed to find out why Charlie was here, whether Noah had simply been unable to get away from the workshop, or if there was some other, more insidious reason…

"David!" said Charlie brightly, closing the space between them and abandoning Emily's trunk to shake his hand and embrace him. "Or should I say, *brother*."

"What the devil are you—?"

He paused as Emily came up behind Charlie, still half-shaded by her parasol. For just a second, his perception wobbled around the edges. Charlie was of average height for an Englishman, while Emily was quite small even for a woman. Seeing them beside each other, everything was suddenly all wrong, him too short, her too tall…

She was too tall.

That was not Emily.

He stared into those intense, familiar eyes and froze completely.

That was not Emily.

Not-Emily—Noah—licked his lips guiltily. He looked nervously frayed around the edges of his impeccable costume. "Good morning, darling," he said in a quiet alto, very unlike the brash voice he used for Miss Penelope. "I apologize for being a bit late. Father and Mother did go *on* with their farewells."

David gaped at him, speechless. He could feel Parker approaching from behind, but he could think of nothing to stop this impossible collision.

Charlie touched his arm, glancing suspiciously at Parker before turning his charm back on. "Don't blame her, David," he said, clearly trying to be overheard as he kept himself in character. "It's the rest of our fault. That said, giving her back to us for a bit really has smoothed things out with Pop. The whole family is wishing you a lovely honeymoon."

Parker settled beside him with hands in his pockets, skeptically appraising Noah like he was a racehorse. It was worse than vulgar. "No need to play the game with me, old boy," he smirked at Charlie. "I know everything that goes on with his lordship, this little charade included. I know perfectly well that no girl so fine as this ever agreed to marry David Forester."

Charlie's grin faltered. "I… Oh."

"You one of Forester's little clubmates, then? Called in for a favor?" he chuckled. "Or is he blackmailing you for the use of your poor sister?"

All traces of grins—and color—slipped from Charlie's face. He touched his hat, taking the opportunity to let it shadow his face a bit further. "I think I ought to go."

Noah patted his arm. "Farewell, brother. Do remember that you owe me the world after this."

Charlie seemed to force himself to nod, then turned on his heel and went swiftly away from the platform.

"You've sure got him scared," Parker mused, turning his smarmy face to David. "*Did* you blackmail him for the use of his sister? I was half-kidding."

"Could we please move on from such dreadful topics?" David growled. "There is a lady present."

Parker made a little noise that showed he very much doubted the lady-ness of his present company. That would have been maddening if it were really Emily, and in that case, he might have said more. Now, however, David didn't mind if Parker doubted that the person before him was a lady, so long as he believed she was a *woman*.

The shrill blast of a whistle cut right through David's skull. He glanced at the clock. Before he could even decide what to do next, another figure had appeared beside him. Mr. Shaw, his valet, bowed politely to Noah. Dullness had its uses; Shaw had had no problem absorbing and sticking to the story of David's wedding, simply taking in his instructions, and now following them to the letter with no fuss. David was really growing to appreciate the fellow, in spite of himself.

"Mrs. Forester," Shaw said pleasantly. "Lovely to see you again. Shall I bring your things up to the attendants? It seems our departure is near at hand."

Noah smiled sweetly at the valet, the twitch of his lips showing that he was also sort of laughing at the way Shaw's blond hair and blue eyes gleamed too beautifully in the sun. "Oh, please do," he said in that same high, quiet voice. "I should hate to keep everyone waiting any longer than I already have."

As Shaw collected the luggage cart, David wondered at the extent of Noah's composure. He himself felt like he was about to crack right down the middle.

"David," Noah whispered, eyeing Mr. Parker. "Would you care to introduce this gentleman?"

He knew it was just a basic nudge toward the manners he'd abandoned, but the idea filled him with disgust. "I think not, darling," he said as lightly as he could, extending his arm so Noah could take it. "Mr. Parker is a far cry from a gentleman. You're better off without his acquaintance."

Parker's face reddened spectacularly, the swaggering gone out of him and replaced with mirrored loathing. "I think I'll go have a word with his lordship, then." He looked the pair of them up and down with a cruel glint in his eye. "Make sure he hasn't come to his senses about bringing along his whore and…oh dear. What do you call the wife of a boy whore, anyway? I'm afraid I don't know."

"Hmm," said Noah, a high-pitched and dismissive little sound. His look of disapproval made all of Parker's sneers seem cordial in comparison. "I think you call her nothing. That's the whole point of skipping introductions, isn't it?"

Parker stalked off. David watched him go until he felt Noah elbow him in the ribs.

"Davy," he whispered, still keeping his voice false in case they were overheard. "I'm sorry."

David couldn't even tell if he was angry with Noah. All he knew was that he wished none of this was happening. "You were never planning to send her, were you?" he managed. "Why did you lie?"

"You wouldn't have let me come."

"You *shouldn't* have come." They started walking back toward their car, arm in arm like a real husband and wife. Noah was a touch tall, a touch broad in the shoulders, but anything on him that was outside the agreed-upon parameters of femininity was covered. To question what he might have under all those petticoats would be obscene. What everyone saw as they crossed the platform was a lucky man with a well-dressed woman clinging to him.

Somehow, through—or maybe because of—the immense stress of this morning, the notion that he was the only one who knew what this really was shot a sort of desperate thrill through him. Fortunately, the loud whistles and voices kept him from getting too obviously excited, but somewhere under all his terror, there was a dark sort of stirring at the thought of Noah doing this for him. In public. Where everyone could see them.

But he could not think that way. Noah could not play his wife, oddly enticing though it was. Noah had to go *home*. Now.

He stopped a few yards short of their destination, turning to take Noah's hand and look him hard in the eye.

"This is stupid," he whispered. "It's too dangerous. It was bad enough just with Emily, but Noah, if you're caught like this…"

Noah put a finger to his lips. "Then we'll be caught together."

David shook his head. "I don't want to be caught together. If I'm going to be caught at something, I'll do it on my own."

"No, you won't." Noah shrugged and squeezed his hand. "I told you before, Davy. I'll follow you anywhere. You're not doing any of this on your own. We stick together."

"But *why*?"

"Because I love you." Noah looked over his shoulder, a little nervous. But they were inconspicuous for once, just another pair of lovers on the platform. He leaned in and pressed a warm kiss to David's cheek. "Alright? You got me to say it once, and now I'll say it again. I'll scream it, if you like, tell the whole damn platform. *I've always loved you.* I can't stop loving you, no matter what you get yourself into." Noah turned red and smiled a little sheepishly. "I think I've forgotten how to live without you, *amore*. So I suppose I have to just carry on with you. Whatever that looks like. And today... Well, I think it looks alright, don't you?"

He looked down and twirled around, indicating his dress. He looked alright, yes. More than alright; he looked incredible. David loved seeing him done up like this, always had. He wasn't sure why, but he knew better than anyone that desire could be deliciously confounding.

So yes. Noah looked alright.

But nothing else did.

It must have shown on his face, because Noah's expression fell. "Davy?"

"What about...what about your deadlines?" David asked wildly, scrabbling for anything that might bring him to his senses. "You can't spare the time. You told me that yourself."

"I asked for help," Noah said. "Believe it or not, it didn't kill me."

David swallowed thickly, feeling like he was taking half the station's soot right down his throat. "Noah. You have to go home."

Much to his surprise, Noah smiled. That mischievous, devious, charming thing that had graced nearly every worthwhile moment of David's life. "You're going to call me dreadfully sentimental, Davy. But home is wherever you happen to be. So, forgive me, but I'll stay right where I am."

The whistle blew and the conductor shouted out for final boarding.

Noah took his hand. "Let's go."

David held tight, but did not let himself be pulled in the direction of the train. Noah meant it, didn't he? He loved David. He would not leave David's side again, no matter where it led him. To the stress of the schoolyard. To the sticky tables of The Ailing Hare. To their precious little corner of London's underworld. To Belleville's castle, to prison, to the bottom of a lake with bricks tied to their ankles if things went that way.

Wherever it was, if David was there, Noah was coming with.

"Davy?"

With someone as precious as Noah Clarke on his heels, David really needed to be more careful about where he wound up, didn't he?

"David, we're going to miss the train."

If that meant he never wound up at the Fox again, well… He hated to let everyone down, but perhaps, if he was honest with himself, Noah was right. Protecting the others had always been a proxy for the much more difficult task of daring to protect himself.

But *this*—following Belleville's confusing whims, isolating himself from friends, ignoring every instinct within him that said this was all wrong—this wasn't going to protect anyone in the long run. It felt satisfying now, but it wouldn't solve the root problem. It was a false sort of safety. Cool water on a splinter that should have been cleansed with gin.

"*Amore*, we really must—"

"Noah, can I stay with you for a while?"

Noah cocked his head to the side, confused. "Stay with me? What do you mean?"

"I…" David could hardly drag the words out, but he forced them to cooperate. He glanced at the train, where Lord Belleville and Parker were waiting for him. "I admit that I still don't really know why he's insisting on bringing me along. It's a bit strange, isn't it? His whole invitation? With the sale and the investor and Parker and everything, I just have an awful feeling that there's more to it than he's mentioned."

Noah nodded slowly. "What do you need, David?" he whispered, his painted lips shaping the barely audible question.

"I need somewhere to stay." He closed his eyes and suddenly he did not have to force the words; they poured out of their own accord. "Somewhere he can't find me. I'm in over my head, Noah, I am. I really am. I've made a terrible, terrible mistake and I need you to help me before it's too late."

Without any hesitation, Noah nodded again, firmer. He stroked David's face softly, right in the middle of everything. "Of course I will, Davy."

"I know Emily's already staying with you. I know it will be too much and she won't like it, but I—"

"Hush." Noah smiled, gentle, quiet. "She'll like you much better if we leave now. Trust me."

Now that he'd initiated it, he could think of nothing else but getting away. His body filled with the itchy desire to start running for the exit. He looked around wildly, finally spotting Shaw as he rushed back. David gave Noah's hand one last squeeze, then ran up to the valet.

"Mr. Shaw, I'm so sorry," he said in a rush. "We're not

going. We're staying in London. Is it too late to get our trunks back out of the train?"

Shaw looked calmly behind him, watching the attendants as they ushered in the final stragglers. "I may be able to manage. Let me—"

"No." David shook his head at himself. "Never mind. That's ridiculous, there's no need for you to put yourself out doing such ridiculous things. Please, just alert the baggage men, would you? See about having them hold it, and we can collect it when the train returns to London."

"If you're certain, sir."

"Absolutely. And one more thing," he added. "I regret to say that there is a very good chance I will not be returning to the town house except to gather the last of my things. When it comes to light that I've not boarded the train…"

Most unexpectedly, Shaw raised his gloved hand. "Say no more, Mr. Forester. Truly. And I think that, indeed, it might be best if you did not return to the house even once. I shall see to it that your things are taken care of. Where shall I have them sent? No need to write it down, I can remember."

David glanced back at Noah. "Same place you sent Miss Penelope's trunk."

"Anything else?"

"Yes," David went on in a rush, peeking toward the train doors, lowering his voice. "In the safe. There's a stack of ledgers. I need you to—"

"Oh dear, Mr. Forester. I hope you didn't need those ratty old books." Shaw's voice pitched to some semblance of concern, though his face remained bland as ever.

David blinked. "What do you mean?"

"Goodness me, they looked so terribly outdated and useless that I'm afraid I took them for a pile of garbage." Shaw gave a token attempt at looking regretful. "I couldn't imagine why you were allowing such things to take up space in your safe, so I took the liberty of removing them and seeing to it they were put to appropriate use in the fireplace before you rather foolishly left London for whatever the devil all the rest of this is." He sighed innocently. "I do hope you won't miss them."

He burned the ledgers?

What on earth was David supposed to make of that? He stared at the chap, half-tempted to believe his bullshit excuse, because the alternative was realizing that his rather ho-hum valet was actually extremely sharp—much sharper than David himself—as well as proactive and loyal and a bit sneaky to boot.

"You understand things," David said carefully, watching the expressionless portrait of a face. "You understand them even better than I do, don't you?"

At last, after all these months, Shaw finally smiled, revealing a surprising set of lopsided dimples. "I'm afraid I have no idea what you mean, sir," he said simply. "I am simply very relieved to hear you will be staying in London after all."

David found himself smiling back. He wanted suddenly to crush the odd little bugger in a tight hug. He doubted that would be well-received, however, so he settled for a handshake. With one last innocent, dimply grin, Shaw went off to see what could be done about the luggage.

Noah approached and slipped his pretty arm through David's.

"*Dimples?*" he whispered appreciatively. "Davy, you are a dog."

A bubble of laughter escaped David before he could stop it. "Look, I've told you before, he came well-recommended and—"

In the moment just before the car door shut, Mr. Parker

returned to the platform. He strode right over to them as the whistle trilled and the heavy forward chug of the train began.

"What in blazes are you still doing out here?" he barked, face as red as ever. "You useless little prat, his lordship is going to pitch a fit."

"Oh, so you told him Emily was suitable, then?" said David. "I simply assumed you were going to have him call it off, so I didn't bother asking her to board. Thought it might be insulting."

Parker's face twisted with disgust. "God, Forester. Sometimes you are so full of absolute shit that I can hardly believe—"

With calm, incredible subtlety, Noah released David's arm, stepped forward, and proceeded to shut Parker's mouth by punching him so hard in the stomach that whatever other hatred he'd been about to spew came out as no more than a gasp.

David felt his mouth open in unbecoming shock he could not hope to hide. Parker had gone redder than ever as he struggled to catch his breath. What he'd do with it once he'd gotten it was unclear—no one seemed to have noticed the disturbance in light of the train's noisy departure, and no fellow in his right mind would call attention to having been successfully assaulted by such a harmless-looking creature.

Noah handed David his parasol so he might adjust his gloves, looking down at the hunched secretary.

"I'm sorry I didn't go for the nose, Davy," he said in that same sweet voice. "The dress, you know. I'd never get a bloodstain out of the cream." He took back his parasol and bloomed it open. "You were right. I ought to have gone with the Prussian damask."

David sprung for a quality hansom, one that would afford some privacy from the driver. In spite of the nice weather, he closed the curtains against the sun's intrusion as well. Once the horses started trotting along, he pulled Noah close and kissed him in a manner that not even a proper husband and wife ought to display in public.

Noah breathed in sharply, momentarily stunned, but then he let that breath out as a low, quiet moan and dropped what remained of his ladylike facade.

A coach, however, was far from ideal for this sort of thing. Bumping along the street, stopping and starting with the rhythms of traffic, it wasn't long before they'd had too many near misses with cracked teeth and trimmed tongues to feel comfortable continuing. He moved his mouth to Noah's neck, lace tickling his chin as he tried to lose himself in the feel of impressively smooth and fragrant skin, the chalky taste of makeup clinging to his lips. He dipped his tongue under Noah's high collar, loving how it made him sigh and tip his head back on the stuffed seat, letting David unpin the little gold brooch that held it together so he could press open-mouthed kisses to his bared throat.

They'd eventually need to discuss what had happened at the station, but for now, all David wanted to do was bask in their escape like it was seaside sunshine. As the coach rumbled on, he ran his hands over Noah's face, his shoulders, the bumps of lacing along his spine. He squeezed the fake bosom until Noah laughed him to his senses, then dragged his hand down to Noah's lap, groping around until he found a veritable tent pole under all the skirts and Noah's laughter collapsed into a satisfyingly wanton groan.

"You know," he said on a choked whisper. "When we get back to mine, Emily won't be there. We'll have the place to ourselves."

"God, yes," David growled, biting his neck. "And when we do, I'll do anything you want. Everything you want."

Noah opened his eyes. They were slightly devilish. "I have

a better idea." He started trailing a finger up one of the lines on David's thigh again, tempting David to request that all his trousers be replaced with pinstripes for good and all. "How about I please you exactly how *you* like it?"

David froze, leaning back to get a good look at Noah's face. He could not recall anyone ever saying anything like that to him before.

"Noah," he said, feeling his face burn bright. "I'm not sure I'd even know where to start."

Noah smiled, but he didn't laugh. Just touched David's cheek very softly with his silky, gloved hand and said, "You can start wherever you want, *amore*. We'll figure the rest out as we go."

David closed his eyes with a rush of gratitude, nuzzling greedily against Noah's hand and whispering his lips against the warm silk. "These might be involved, in that case."

Suddenly, Noah gasped. He sat bolt upright and snatched his hand back to clutch at his own chest.

"What it is?" said David, alarmed.

"Oh bollocks!" he said, pressing a horrified hand to his mouth. "The doorman! I can't go home like *this*!"

David couldn't help it. It was too absurd to do anything but laugh. "Where are your clothes?"

"Charlie and Miles's place. I'd bet Miles is still at home."

"That's the safest bet you've ever made."

Noah slid open the divider and instructed the driver to change destinations. Then he closed it up and collapsed back against David. He undid the first few buttons of his dress, reaching in and taking his cigarette case out from the stuffing. He put one in his mouth, and then offered the case to David.

"We really shouldn't," David whispered, looking pointedly in the direction of the coachman. "This is a nice coach."

"You weren't saying that when you were pawing at me a

minute ago." He placed a vogue between David's lips and lit them both.

When the coachman unsurprisingly kicked them out a block from Piccadilly, Noah held David's hand as they ran off down the street together, looking like a married couple while they giggled like troublesome boys.

Chapter Nineteen

Noah

They made it back looking mostly respectable for the door-man, though there'd been no way to avoid hauling the frock back with them. When they tried to leave it until later, Miles looked like Noah had suggested they leave a murdered body or a cart of stolen diamonds in his wardrobe for a day or two.

"Can you believe," said Noah as he hung the thing up, "that Charlie claims he used to be *more* paranoid?"

David did not answer. He'd lain down on Noah's bed as soon as they'd gotten in. Noah turned to find him staring up at the ceiling with an arm slung over his head. He looked just right there, in his shirtsleeves and undone waistcoat. It was very hard to believe they were here, comfortably sequestered in Noah's room, rather than speeding along to whatever horrors had awaited them in the country.

Noah's work ethic had him antsy at the thought of repose at this hour—if they were staying in town, he really ought to hightail it back to the workshop—but if David could do it, then so could he. He lay down on the bed, nice and close, letting the familiar smell of him chase out any thought he might have of catching up on work. He traced imaginary lines on David's satiny green waistcoat until David closed his eyes and took a deep, shuddering sort of breath.

"Alright, *amore*?"

He patted Noah's hand. "I'm alright."

Noah glanced at the bedroom door. He'd shut it, in case Emily came home early. And things were locked downstairs. Yet, he wondered… "Davy, you aren't worried he's going to send Parker looking for you, are you?"

"I have absolutely no way of knowing what he's going to do, Noah," he admitted. "All I know is that he won't go looking for me over here."

"Are you sure? My name and address are in the club ledgers."

To his surprise, David chuckled, taking Noah's hand and examining his fingers like they were some fascinating work of art. "First of all." He kissed the first finger, soft and sweet. "Little Hyacinthus has mistaken the ledgers for a pile of garbage and destroyed them."

"*What?*"

"I've rather changed my mind about him, I think." He went for the next finger, darting his tongue out like it might help him memorize the prints. "Second of all, your information wasn't in them anyway. I used another name for you. There has never been record of you visiting The Curious Fox."

"David!" Noah squirmed as the glorious feeling of being specially singled out mixed with the sensation of David's increasingly obscene attention to his fingertips. "What name do you use? Please tell me it's lovely."

"Oh, it doesn't matter."

"Yes, it does!" Noah arched his back as David pulled his pinkie in entirely and sucked on it. "What is it?"

David smiled darkly. He released Noah's hand, gave it one more peck, then clutched it to his heart. "Robbie Snyder, bank clerk and graduate of the Deer River School for Boys. And won't he be surprised if anyone ever goes looking for his crooked nose on a sodomy charge?"

It took Noah a moment to put together whom David was talking about. When he realized it was the lad whose nose he'd broken on Noah's behalf some million years ago, he gasped and hit him with one of the pillows. "David, you didn't!"

"What can I say?" David threw that pillow to the ground and pinned Noah to the rest of them, heavy and playful. "Warren is right. I'm a petty little bitch."

"Oh, are you now?" Overcome with a surge of adoration too strong to put off, he rolled and pushed until he was on top, kissing David between his eyes. Oh, he was beautiful and he felt so incredible, all warm and broad, his body a perfectly solid mosaic of hard and soft underneath him. Noah moved the kiss to his mouth this time, slow and deep until he felt David's excitement swelling beside his own. "In that case, tell me, Davy. Do you want to be my petty little bitch tonight?"

David stared up at him, his lips parted with something like guilt, all red and wet and too kissable to be allowed. "M-maybe. If you're interested in going that way."

Interested? Noah purred and flexed his hips to show just how interested he was. "You should have asked me for it last time," he scolded. "I had a feeling, you know. I'm not oblivious."

"I was worried you'd say no."

He put his elbows on the bed above David's shoulders, leaning in so their noses nearly touched. "David, you must remember what we learned in those liberation pamphlets my father gave me a while back."

"Those pamphlets managed to make all my favorite sins sound about as exciting as banking reforms. I remember nothing from them."

"Well, they made sweeping assertions that my disposition was automatically passive."

"Ah." David chuckled and blushed. "So, of course, you have to prove them wrong."

"It's my moral duty, David."

"Well. If it's for the sake of your morality…" He slipped warm hands into the back of Noah's trousers. "Will you do something for me?"

"I love to do things for you, Davy."

David licked his lips. In spite of the daylight creeping through the curtains, his pupils were wide and jet-black. "Put one of those petticoats back on. And your gloves. Some jewelry."

Noah's breath caught deliciously at the notion. "I can put the whole thing back on, Davy. It's not that much trouble."

"No. Just a few bits." He turned red, very red, a red that Noah had thought impossible for him now. "You're always so put together. It's lovely, but I like seeing you sort of undone."

Undone? A sweet shiver ran down Noah's spine and went straight to his groin. It wasn't easy to pry himself off David to return to the wardrobe, but the reward would be worth it. He gave his cock a stroke on the way, to tide himself over a bit. "Cover your eyes," he panted as he wrenched open the wardrobe.

He started gathering up some of his things. Drag wasn't exactly a fetish for Noah, but David's enthusiasm for this aspect had his heart pounding and his overeager fingers slipping on his buttons. As he changed, he bit his lips to quiet their demand for kisses while he let his clothes fall irresponsibly to the floor, his cock so sensitive that the soft rasp of the petticoat was nearly unbearable…

"Like that, do you?" came a low murmur from the bed.

Noah closed his eyes and tried not to move too much, lest the fabric be ruined instead of David. "Quit peeking."

"Sorry. It's fun to be the one watching for once."

Noah opened his eyes. Fun indeed. While his back had been turned, David had managed to become a debauched dream, torso bared to the waist, trousers undone with his hand inside them as he brazenly pleasured himself. Noah was mesmerized by the sight of his slow strokes.

"Don't mind me, beautiful," he said. "You just get your-self dressed."

His expression was a bit testing, but, of course, Noah didn't actually care if his eyes were open or closed, so long as David was getting what he wanted.

Not that Noah was playing the martyr, here. *Frigid slut* that he was, he hadn't done this outside his own head in a while, and the promise of the sensations that awaited him in that bed had him trembling and tripping all over himself, struggling to get his gloves on, only to realize that he could not latch the pearls once they were settled.

"Let me." David sat up and made space. Noah sat on the edge of the bed, gripping the counterpane as David nudged his hair out of the way and clasped the pearls so they dangled like little balls of ice against Noah's neck.

It was an absurd little getup. He would never let anyone else see him like this; he didn't really even want to look in the mirror. But that did not matter now, because David liked it, and so Noah did too. He sat perfectly still as his best mate ran reverent hands all up and down his back, making him shiver as he pressed light, fluttery kisses in spots he shouldn't have been able to find so easily. Noah wanted to turn around and positively maul him, but David seemed to be settling in for now, his knees on either side of Noah's hips, his kisses growing messy, his shaft like an iron rod between them. Noah thought he might lose his mind if it went on like this, and then David reached around and gripped him through the petticoat, and he did lose his mind a bit, thrusting up into his hand and making a sound he did not recognize.

Nothing had ever felt this good. Nothing. As David stroked and kissed him, picking up the pace and tonguing the pearls where they rested at the crook of his neck, an incredible release started peaking over the horizon. He wanted it now, but managed to resist, stopping David's hand and finally turning around to give him a deep kiss.

Then he stumbled to his vanity for the jar of cold cream.

David shucked off the rest of his clothes and lay back on the pillows with his knees bent and legs spread. *God.* Noah *pounced*, overcome with a lust too powerful to resist any longer. He shoved one of the pillows under David's hips, not caring which one it was or what might happen to it. Somehow, he managed to get the jar open, taking off his glove and scooping with two fingers.

Noah leaned in so his lips touched the center of David's ear. "Tell me how much you need me, *amore.*"

"I do." He put his arms around Noah, pulling him close, kissing him like their mouths had been made to be one wonderful cavern of closeness. "I need you. Now."

Unable to wait another second, Noah slid his hand, slick and messy, under David's balls to the scorching heat he was hunting. He met very little resistance as he got one and then two fingers into David, moving around until he got just the right angle.

He watched as David's head tipped back, mouth open, lost in the pleasure Noah gave him. He had never, ever been more wonderful, more lovable, more perfect. They could do this. They could protect each other, and make each other laugh, and make each other come. It was what they'd always done, and it was what they should keep on doing for the rest of their lives.

There were details—so many and so harsh—but they'd work those out in time, on the scaffolding they'd built together.

David's squirming neediness was catching. They'd waited long enough. Noah lifted the petticoat while David watched in fascination, slicking himself up very carefully, trying not to burst. Then he adjusted the folds of cotton and lace, settled his hips between David's legs, and looked right in those gorgeous eyes.

"What do you want, Davy?" he said, voice rough with the effort of remaining just at the threshold of a bliss he'd waited too long for already. "Tell me. Say it. God, I want to hear you say it."

David licked his lips. "Fuck me, Noah."

"How?"

"Hard. Rough." He grabbed Noah by the hair and pulled his head down to whisper in his ear. "Do it like I belong to you."

"Do you?"

"Yes." He arched up and pushed down, groaning, insistent, ready. "I'm absolutely yours."

Letting a deep breath out in a long, lovely sigh, Noah pushed slowly into David, every delicious inch wrapping him up in pure pleasure. *Oh, fuck.* He did it again. Again. A little faster. A little harder, trying to pace himself, to keep Davy comfortable even as his entire being seemed to pulse and sparkle...

David grabbed him by the arse, his hands filled with fabric and flesh. He pulled hard, growled low. "Like you mean it, beautiful."

A floaty smile crossed Noah's face. "Is that a challenge, *amore?*"

David yanked on him again, coaxing him deeper. "If that's what it takes."

Nothing resembling resistance remained in Noah's body. He kissed David with a lifetime of passion and allowed himself to fuck the daylights out of his very best friend until David was utterly undone, ruining that damned petticoat with more spend than seemed possible. He dragged Noah explosively over the edge with him into whatever gorgeous, terrifying, and gloriously inevitable future had waited so patiently to receive a pair of lovesick, overworked rogues like them.

It would have been lovely to lie in each other's arms the rest of the day, night, next day, and so forth. But though they both fell asleep in sticky exhaustion, a nightmare woke David after a short rest, and they decided that dinner would be better than trying to remain outside of time any longer than they already had. They splurged on a swanky little French place that David liked, where they ate and drank too much and couldn't seem to stop smiling. They were not half-discreet enough in the way they leaned across the table to whisper and brush hands and taste each other's food, but there was no helping it. Something had changed at Kings Cross, and neither of them had learned to resist the pull of it yet.

They returned to Noah's to find that Mr. Shaw had left a valise of clothing and important personal items with the doorman for David. The rest would "be along as soon as possible."

"I hope you don't mind," David said, once they were back in the parlor. "I don't have much to move, really. Nearly everything but my clothes belong to...you know."

They were sitting together on the sofa. Noah pulled David's head to his shoulder and kissed the top of it. "There's space."

David chuckled. "Not in your wardrobe."

"We'll figure it out."

At last, warm and fed, they gave in to the inevitable discussion of circumstance. David lay down with his head in Noah's lap and rambled on for a bit, about what happened at the station, about his various relationships with Belleville, about the Fox and how painful it was to let it go. They talked about worries and then eased them, going in circles of potential disasters and all the reasons they would not actually happen, yet what they would do if they did. But, of course, they wouldn't, because...

It left Noah uneasy. But this was their lot, it seemed, and they'd make the best of it. They'd kept each other alive and free this long; they'd manage this time too, even if it led them to conversations that neither of them really wanted to have.

"David?"

"Yes, love?"

Noah stroked his hair, soft from washing and sporting one charming little gray that he hadn't noticed before and resolved to never mention. "If it does go bad, promise me you won't stay here to see it through."

David blinked up at him. "Leave England, you mean?"

"Yes," Noah said. "If it starts to look like you have to go, then you *have to go*. Promise me."

"God, I hope it doesn't come to that." David sighed and pulled Noah's hand to his mouth. "I couldn't bear being separated from you like that again. After all this."

"I didn't mean alone!" Noah said quickly. "If you had to go, I—I suppose I'd go along."

"You'd do that?" David looked very skeptically upward. "You'd leave your family? Your job? You would walk away from the *Harvey Cole showroom* just because I'd gotten myself into trouble?"

Noah sighed sadly and slid his fingers through David's hair again. "I'm not in love with Harvey Cole, David. Or Fiore Corsetti. And certainly not Ambrose Covington and his mustache. I'm in love with you. Where would you want to go? Greece?"

"Wouldn't you prefer Sicily?"

Noah chuckled. "Well of course I would. It's not the same as Italy, but at least most people speak the language. But you wouldn't prefer it. You've made no bones about your feelings for *la bel paese*."

"Is that Italian for the old boot?"

"My point exactly."

David smiled against the back of Noah's hand. "I was just jealous of her, Noah. I suppose this is as good a time as any to forgive her affair with you at last."

"We'll make it a three-way this time," Noah promised.

"If we have to."

"Which I'm sure we won't."

David kissed the tips of Noah's fingers like they'd been his own. "*Perfecta.*"

"*Per-fett-a.*"

"Is that so?" David widened his eyes. "Since when are you the expert in Italian, eh?"

Noah put his hand over David's face and kept it there even as David laughed and licked his palm.

The sound of the key in the lock startled them silent. Emily was home. As she came in the room, the two of them scrambled to stand up, to put space between them even though it probably didn't matter. With her medicine bag in one hand and her parasol in the other, she stared at them, eyes flicking back and forth.

Then she dropped her things, ran across the room, and flung her arms around David's neck.

David looked stunned, awkwardly patting her back. "Doctor Clarke, I—"

"Oh, *Davy*," she said in a shaky voice, his name slipping out of her mouth for the first time in years. "I was so scared the two of you were actually going to go through with it. Thank you for bringing him home. Thank you, thank you, thank you."

"Ems," said Noah, "David is going to have to stay with me for a while. I know it might feel a bit overcrowded, so I'm not sure if you—"

She gathered him up into her embrace, hugging them both and assuring them that they'd work it out somehow. She stepped back to wipe her eyes. "Apologies," she said with a sniffly laugh. "Goodness, Noah, I don't think I've ever been so happy to see you and Davy together in my entire life."

"Not a high bar," said Noah. "But I suppose I'll take it."

Chapter Twenty

David

The next few weeks could not rightly be called a honeymoon. In fact, while it was delicious to at last share a home with Noah, things were inevitably strained. Lovely as it was to end the day in Noah's bed, David was not sleeping well at all, usually banishing himself to the parlor halfway through the night so his tossing and turning did not disrupt Noah's rest. Shaw brought the rest of his things, necessitating that Noah pack some of his own up to make room for this third person in a home built for one. And when Noah went back to work on Monday, David was left with the daunting task of staying out of the rooms until the housemaid was finished, feeling guilty over how he'd increased her load while looking over his shoulder everywhere he went.

It wore on Noah too. There was a frazzled edge to him as they all tried to work out the rhythm. He took to asking calm little questions like, "How's Hyacinthus getting on?" or "Still keeping up with Warren's lost wages?" To test the waters of the potential disasters that might be on their way, as time went on without a word about Belleville or the Fox. David could tell he was stressed, but he'd returned to the habit of not talking about it directly. Noah preferred to drown fears, rather than dwell in them, so when he was not working his fingers

bloody, he insisted on nice meals, a constant stream of cigarettes, and increasingly complicated card games that had David
and Emily bonding over the confusing loss of the gambling
chips, biscuits, and buttons they played with in the evenings.

David hated that he'd brought such uncertainty and discomfort along with him. Danger too, if Belleville ever did
figure out where he was and found that he cared. More than
once, he considered running off and unburdening Noah. But
he stayed, and every night the burn of guilt was eased when
Noah stacked all the pillows on the ground to make space
for him on the mattress. No matter what else had happened,
no matter how awkward things had been in the household
or how badly they'd slept the night before, Noah still gathered him up triumphantly, like David was the biggest, richest
pot in the universe, scooped from the center of the table and
right into his arms.

"I cannot believe you're putting up with all this," David
said one night, very late, the words landing along with a kiss
on the top of Noah's head.

Noah settled in tighter. "Trust me, anyone but you would
be out on his arse."

"Would you rather I was out on my arse?"

"Of course not. I'd rather you were on *my* arse, quite honestly. I think it's my turn, don't you?"

So he stayed. And the rhythm grew easier. Itchy with un-
employment, David started doing a bit of the housekeeping,
which ingratiated him with the maid. It wasn't much longer
before he was friends with the doorman, who thought David
would be well-suited to a position like his. David wasn't sure
about the silent stretches such work might require, but he decided to follow up with one of the fellow's suggested building
managers anyway, just to see.

He brought the idea up at supper one unseasonably chilly

Friday evening. It was a jolly sort of night, the air coming fresh and crisp through the window and mixing with the warmth of the fire. Emily was nearing the end of her time with the London doctor, and had taken one of her last opportunities to bring back mushroom pies and fine bread from the bakery across from his practice. The comfortable weather and good food had Noah's rooms feeling more spacious.

They opened one of Noah's stashed Chiantis and discussed all their futures. Speculation about how Emily's apprenticeship would improve her father's practice led to Noah wondering aloud whether he should consider Cecil Martin's proposal to forgo the status of Cole & Co. to make a more joyful, if less prestigious, career for himself. With such big, ponderous questions on the table, it felt silly asking about his ability to be a *doorman* of all things, but Noah insisted he contribute, so David mentioned it and the twins took it as seriously as their own more illustrious affairs. *Of course* he'd be a delightful doorman, they concluded, and more than capable of handling trouble-makers, but would he *like it*? That was the question. They discussed other possible careers too, all of them respectable and even noble. The fact that both Noah and Emily thought he could succeed at so many things warmed him more than the wine or the fire.

"You two," he said at last, blushing and splashing the last of the bottle into Noah's glass. "You're being ridiculous. No one is going to let me *manage* anything. I don't have the references to manage the smallest pub, let alone another hotel."

"You don't need references when you have charm," said Noah, a skilled tradesman with no idea what went on in the world of hospitality and service. "Just smile and show your dimples. They'll give you whatever you want."

"I don't have dimples. And I am telling you for the last time, he *had* reference—"

There was a knock on the door, hard and insistent.

"Were you expecting someone?" Noah asked Emily. She shook her head.

The mirth dissipated. Noah put down his glass and steeled himself. He started to get up, but David beat him to it, putting a hand on his shoulder.

"I'll get it," David said quietly.

"I'm sure it's nothing," Noah said.

"Still."

He started for the door, then went back. He gave a grateful glance to Emily for being such a radical darling, then kissed Noah quickly on the mouth. When he pulled back, Noah's eyes had gone to saucers.

"What's that for?" he asked.

"Just in case."

David took a breath and turned to the door. If this was it, the beginning of the end of him, at least he'd spent his last weeks of freedom here, with Noah. He'd treasure these awkward weeks for the rest of his life.

When he finally got up the guts to turn the handle, what he found on the other side was too shocking to be believed. What had he expected? Belleville and Parker, maybe, cold and ready to drag him back to his proper fate? A stranger with a pistol, sent to silence him for his disloyalty? A street officer with a bat and a pair of handcuffs with his name engraved?

The two men at the door were officers, but not the normal sort. They had long coats and nice gloves. Detectives.

And not just any detectives.

David knew these detectives.

One was old and polite-looking, with a face David had never expected to see again. The other was young, a little too young, a little too blond, a little too lovely to be a coincidence.

David's legs threatened to give out. He gripped the door frame as his whole world went cold.

The two familiar men both looked at him with something that might have been pity.

"Good evening, Mr. Forester," said the detective who'd posed as an elderly investor, that rainy afternoon with Parker and Warren. "I regret that we were not properly introduced last time. My name is Detective Inspector Barrows. And this is my partner—"

"Detective Inspector Shaw," said David weakly, staring at the young man who had served him tea and helped him dress every morning for months.

The dimples appeared. "Can we come in, Mr. Forester? There's something we need to discuss."

Emily did not need telling twice that she ought to go upstairs, close the door, and hear nothing. Noah, on the other hand, wouldn't budge.

"This is my house," he said. "Anything you have to say to Mr. Forester in my house can be said to me too."

"Noah—"

"It's alright, Mr. Forester," said Inspector Shaw. "There's no harm."

"Are you sure?" David snapped.

"Quite."

They all sat in the parlor before a fire that desperately needed tending. But, of course, David did not dare touch a poker in the presence of law enforcement. He didn't dare speak, either. All he could do was sit, and stare, and agree with Noah that perhaps references really *were* useless after all.

"We apologize for disrupting your supper," said Inspector Barrows, sounding surprisingly sincere. "It's just that there's not much time before the papers get hold of the situation. Inspector Shaw insisted that we see you before you found out that way."

"Am I under arrest?" David whispered.

Barrows cocked his head to the side, politely perplexed. "What would you be arrested for?"

David blinked a few times, his throat completely stuck. He could see Noah's hand balled up at his side, clearly wanting to comfort him as they sat stock-still beside each other. Whatever this was, it was nice not to be facing it alone. Assuming he did not end the encounter dragged out by his bound wrists, he'd have to thank Noah for staying by his side like this.

Shaw leaned his elbows on his knees, an unfamiliarly casual posture that had him looking like a boy playing dress-up as a detective. How old was he, really? Older than he looked, that was certain.

"It's difficult to know where to start," he said, blue eyes drifting toward the ceiling. "I've worked for you long enough to know you're a fellow of admirable sentiment, Mr. Forester, and—"

"Will you out with it?" said David, his voice a low rumble.

"Your former employer, the Baron of Belleville, is... Well, he was found dead this morning."

The words hung on the air, not quite able to make it all the way to David.

"That's impossible," David said, so stupidly that the detectives both chuckled and Noah finally gave in to the impulse to put a hand on his shoulder.

"Like it or not, it's possible for any one of us at any time," said Inspector Barrows pleasantly. "And when one is caught— as Lord Belleville has been—to be leading a rather extravagant ring of every sort of questionable activity imaginable, it often speeds up that timeline quite a bit."

David stared, completely numb, as Shaw put two fingers to his own temple behind Barrows's back in a grim pantomime.

"You've been spying on us," David whispered, horrified. He could not seem to take in the rest of it, but he was finally able to latch on to *that* at least. "This whole time."

"Us?" Shaw raised an eyebrow very high, almost in warning. "Not you, personally, of course. We've known about Belleville's activities for years, and decided that the best way to catch him at his crimes was to creep in through his *legitimate* enterprises. As I suspected, playing valet to one of his *proper* proprietors was the perfect way to gather more information. We don't blame you for keeping what little you knew to yourself—informing could have been exceedingly dangerous, particularly if you didn't provide enough evidence to get him convicted."

"Seeing as The Curious Fox seemed respectable enough when I visited," said Inspector Barrows carefully, "I was happy to grant Shaw's request for your immunity, especially since your willingness to socialize with your staff gave him several useful leads that ultimately led to the baron's charges."

There was no way in hell that these two believed the Fox had been respectable. If they had managed to uncover enough dirt to make Belleville... David shuddered, trying not to picture the claim of his death in detail. In any case, every man in this room certainly knew the truth of The Curious Fox, whether or not there had been feathers in the flower vases when Barrows visited as an investor. David glanced at Noah. His friend's face had never been so stonelike, his jaw set uncomfortably tight. It felt like they were all suspended in a bubble of denial that could pop with any sudden movement.

Dead?

David genuinely could not believe it. Could not believe any of this. It had to be a trap. They were trying to get him to admit to something, to play nice until he'd twisted himself up for them, maybe even with Noah along for the ride.

"I think I need to speak to a solicitor," he said.

"If you wish." Barrows shrugged. "But as I say, Mr. Forester, you are not the only innocent party tangled up in all this. That is why we've moved slowly and carefully through this case; Lord Belleville's strategy was to make sure his right hand never quite knew what the left was doing. A very complicated web. If we followed the wrong path—to you, for instance—charges could have been dismissed, or the wrong men could have wound up in prison, or he could have simply gotten away with everything and made us look ridiculous if we ever brought it up again. This has been a years-long process, involving some more disturbing offenses than I think you realize. I daresay, if it was you we wanted, we'd have gotten you a long time ago."

The bubble nearly popped as Barrows smirked. It was an impolite and cynical expression that looked odd on his bland face.

"I know this is shocking, Mr. Forester," said Shaw kindly. "And it may grow more shocking yet. Mr. Parker has been arrested, as have several others you know. You may worry, as things progress, that you will be next, but I had *plenty* of opportunity to observe your activities and never did find significant evidence of wrongdoing. Unless, of course, there's anything you'd like to add to the record."

He raised his brows and took out a pad of paper. As Noah laughed nervously, David realized that Shaw was joking, a dry sense of humor that he'd hidden so long that it was hard to recognize now.

"N-no thank you, Inspector," David whispered, feeling disconnected from his own words as he tried to believe this was happening. "So he's really... He's *dead*?"

"Most sincerely." Out of his case, Barrows pulled a copy of a record that he passed to David. David could not seem to read it, it was sort of blurry...

"Davy, breathe."

He felt Noah's hand on his arm and realized it was blurry because his hand was shaking so badly. He passed the page to Noah, who pointed out the most relevant words on the certificate: the name, the date, the cause...

It was too clear to avoid. The knowledge froze David so completely that he started to feel like a pair of eyes peering from a mess of sharp, brittle crystals. Noah tried to get him to take the paper back, but he couldn't seem to move an inch. The paper went back to Barrows instead.

"I confess a disappointment that we never got him into custody," Barrows said as he snapped his case shut. "Though he was likely to hang, so perhaps it will be better for his wife that the inevitable was not public and prolonged."

Hang? David turned his eyes to Shaw, who nodded grimly. Perhaps there *were* details that David had not been privy to, crimes he was truly ignorant of. His voice somehow managed to form a rasping version of, "Did he kill someone, then?"

"As I say," said Shaw carefully, "no one blames you for not coming forward with what little you knew."

Beside him, he felt Noah sag against him a bit.

Perhaps to keep himself from dwelling in the dark fates that might have awaited them at Belleville's estate, he latched onto something else Barrows had said. "What will happen to his wife? She's ill."

"With no heir, the barony dissolves with his death," said Shaw. "She will have whatever assets can be had, given the circumstances, and shall go into the care of her sister's family. I daresay, she seems in shockingly good spirits. I think she shall be alright in the long run."

I bet she will be, David thought, remembering the appalling accusation Jo had made that the baron was poisoning her. Had it been true? He wanted to ask, but when he opened his mouth, nothing came out. Much to his surprise, Shaw got up and with a word of help from Noah, brought David's wineglass over from the table and handed it to him with a little bow, like he was still David's servant. He sipped it automatically, though he couldn't taste it.

"Now," said Shaw as he sat back down. "There's one last matter to discuss before we leave you to your evening."

"The Fox," David whispered.

"The Fox," Inspector Barrow agreed. He took out another paper. "I've the deed to the place here. The sale of the building allowed me access to some of the final bits of information we needed to catch Belleville at last. So, shortly after his departure from London, I completed the sale with Mr. Parker. It was a complicated bit of trickery, but I will keep things simple by saying that the property would normally go straight to the Crown. Given the bizarre nature of this case, however, we were bestowed permission to allow the former proprietor a chance to purchase the building at a discount. Plenty of upstanding fellows are going to lose their positions as a result of this case. We would like to do what we can to minimize the collateral damage to Belleville's innocent pawns."

"You want to sell the building to David?" said Noah incredulously. "Because he's an…innocent pawn?"

Barrows held the deed up with a look of caution. "Under one condition."

"What's that?" muttered David.

"You tell us everything you know about Tom Parker," said Barrows. "While our case is strong, I should hate to see that dreadful man walk free. Will you talk?"

"About him?" said David with a bark of uncomfortable,

almost painful laughter. "Inspector, if it's Parker you want, I'll bloody *sing*."

"But not tonight," said Noah protectively. "Surely, you don't mean to have him do that tonight."

"Of course not," said Shaw. "The two of you and the lady upstairs ought to rest after such a shock. We shall be in touch regarding Mr. Forester's testimony and the transfer of the property. We simply wanted to be sure no one panicked and did something drastic when they saw the papers."

Barrows stood too, and headed for the door. As Shaw followed, David shot up and grabbed him by the sleeve. Shaw turned, hanging back with David as Noah showed Barrows out.

"Yes, Mr. Forester?"

"Why?" David begged. "Why are you doing this for me? You know I don't deserve it. You know it better than anyone."

Shaw glanced at the doorway to make sure Barrows was out of earshot. He crossed his arms and bit his lip for a moment.

"An assignment like this," he said, slow and quiet. "I've had them before. I possess the correct countenance, you know."

David nodded. He sure did know that.

Shaw went on. "This was by far the most elaborate of them. Playing valet to one of Belleville's men for months at a time. I knew it was necessary, but I cannot say I was looking forward to it." He paused, and David—slow as ever with this sort of thing—realized that the odd expression was something very close to admiration. "I was ready for half a year of hell. Imagine my shock when I suffered nothing but a few over-eager attempts at small talk. You've done no harm, to me or to anyone else. It would be a poor way to repay you, following a desperate man's silly little crimes to conviction, when Belleville and the others have done so much worse. I couldn't bring myself to do it."

David absorbed that, putting the tips of his fingers to his temples as if that would make it easier. "And the ledgers?"

"Ash in the hearth. Every page. I'm confident you know your people well enough to find them again eventually."

"You can't do that!" David hissed. "You can't do any of this!"

"Seems I did. I even used a contact of mine to suggest that Belleville get all the club's decorations taken down before Barrows's visit, so that we could say with 'all certainty' that you were innocent."

"That was your idea?"

"Yes. You nearly negated it by marching right into his country house trap." The scolding expression on his face made him look like a lad playing dress-up again. "He knew we were closing in, and had no intention of planning some grand reopening with you. He just wanted to have someone else nearby to diffuse the blame, should things get sticky. Which, obviously, they did. I meant it when I said I'm glad that you and…" He glanced toward the doorway, where Noah had gone with Barrows. "I'm glad that you and yours had the sense to stay home."

He touched the brim of his hat. "I do hope you'll keep yourself out of trouble. You won't get any from me personally, but the Fox has not seen the last of it, especially if you continue the way you have been."

"Do you have suggestions, then? For the reopening?"

He laughed, a charming sound. "Well, I suggest you don't encourage illegal behavior on your premises. But if you can't manage that, then at least be smart about it."

One last flash of those dimples that the detective must have confiscated right off the face of an expensive rent boy, then Shaw followed after Barrows into the hall.

Noah came back, locking every bolt behind them. With

eyes that looked like they might never blink again, he rushed to David and grabbed his arms. He was saying something, something comforting, but David couldn't hear it. It was all too much. He could only be grateful that Noah was right there to ease him down as his knees finally gave out and they could sit together on the ground while horror and grief and relief and gratitude combined in an explosive sort of mess that he would hate for anyone else in the world to witness.

All the while, Noah, his Noah, held him and stroked his hair and whispered something over and over. His voice was low and gentle, and eventually David had enough sense to hear the words: "It's alright, Davy. It's alright. I'm here. I've got you. It's all going to be alright."

Repeated enough, David not only heard it, but started to believe it. It *would* be alright. It was not alright today. Not at all. Not even a little bit. But eventually, someday, it would be.

And Noah would be right here with him when it was.

His best mate.

His lover.

Following him into something lovely, for once. What it would be, exactly, David did not know, but after all they'd seen each other through, they deserved nothing less than lovely.

Chapter Twenty-One

Noah

As promised by the detectives, the story hit the papers first thing in the morning. On the way into work, Noah bought one and skimmed it standing on the street corner. Once he absorbed the details of Belleville's crimes, the extent of his cruelty, his sudden and disturbing demise, Noah crumpled it up and got to the workshop as quickly as he could.

"I need two weeks off, starting today," he told Mr. Covington, right in the middle of the bustling rows of tables. Several other tailors lifted their eyes from their work, listening in with very little subtlety. "I didn't end up taking the days I requested in June," he went on, firm and reasonable. "I need them now."

Mr. Covington's mustache twitched with irritation. "For what?"

"A family emergency."

"Mr. Clarke," he said, almost too slowly to tolerate. "You're still behind from—"

"It doesn't matter," Noah interrupted. "Mr. Chapman can survive in his old wool trousers for another few days."

A few whispers and a blatant chuckle hissed through the workshop. Here he was, a darling of Cole & Co., one of the most promising and well-regarded tailors here. For him of all people to stand up and break their protocols open like this was to make an absolute spectacle of himself.

Mr. Covington's eyebrows got involved as he took in the hiss of chatter around them, making for a total of three snowy crescent moons tasked with portraying his astonishment.

"Mr. Clarke, what—?"

"I can complete the most urgent pieces from home. But I cannot come in or do anything extraneous for two weeks. That's..." Noah knew better than to say *that's the rules*, but he tried to get it across in his eyes. "That's how it has to be."

Mr. Covington stared him down, but there was no way to twist even that mustache into enough disapproval to convince Noah to leave David to suffer through the early days of this mess alone.

"One week," said Mr. Covington.

"Two," said Noah.

"I am not certain we will have need of your talents two weeks from now, Mr. Clarke." There was a grim warning in Covington's voice. The others were listening. Watching. Seeing what they, too, might be able to get away with. Covington seemed more aware of them than he was of Noah standing before him. "Impressive though those talents are, they are not irreplaceable. I must assume that you are under a lot of stress, to be acting so terribly out of character. I can forgive this brief lapse of sense, and I can honor the days that were agreed to prior, but I cannot hold your place at this workshop for two weeks. Surely you know that."

Of all the things, Noah was struck with a memory of Milan. It was the morning before the news would finally reach him that David's life had been shredded to a fate that one gossip rag had called worse than death. Noah had spent that morning with his heart pounding from the amount of espresso required to keep his energy up, sobbing over a crooked seam, getting yelled at by Signor Corsetti, and finally cutting himself so badly on the shears that he'd had to call it a day embarrassingly early.

It was unfortunate but forgivable that he'd not been there for David during those early days; he'd known he was leaving David in unpleasant circumstances, though he hadn't predicted anything as dreadful as the fire. But if he was going to leave his best friend all alone in hell for weeks at a time, he could have at least been spending those days doing something beautiful, artistic, enriching.

He would not make the same mistake again. Playing by made-up rules that weren't his own, for the sake of some stupid name that didn't even belong to him.

He touched his hat. "I suppose, in that case—"

"You'll take the week," Covington interrupted.

"What? No, no." He shook his head and smiled, strangely at peace. "In that case, I'll be sure to collect my things on the way out today, so as not to bother you for them later. Harvey Cole may not need me in two weeks, but at that time, I guarantee any one of your competitors will be more than happy to have me." He shrugged. "Unless, of course, I decide to simply rely on my own na—" He cut off, correcting himself. "Unless I decide to rely on my own artistry and business acumen in the future. I suppose we'll see. I wish you the best, Mr. Covington. Truly."

There was a smug satisfaction to the look on Mr. Covington's face. The old cutter didn't want to lose Noah, not really. His talent *was* irreplaceable. They both knew it.

And they both knew, as the others let out sighs and grumbles and returned to their work having watched yet another of their number burn out, that there was really nothing either of them could do about it.

"Best wishes to you as well, Mr. Clarke," he sighed. "And my regards, of course, to your family."

He was permitted to bring no patterns and no sketches that had been made for Cole & Co. clients, but he did get to gather up his own supplies in a box, helped in the task by his unexpected new ally, Cecil Martin.

"You really keep me on my toes, Clarke," Martin admitted. "I'll miss you around this place."

"No, you won't." Adjusting the box to sit on his hip, Noah used his other hand to take the card case out of his pocket. He nodded for Martin to take one. "You're going to call on me in two weeks' time. I've got two clients lined up already."

Martin looked over Noah's calling card with a slow smile spreading over his face. "Are they interesting?"

Noah thought of Miss Jo and Margot Levin.

"Oh, yes," Noah said. "I predict some extraordinarily interesting clients for us in the future."

Over the past few years, all Noah's visits back to his childhood home in the village of Farncombe were soured by the sense that every minute spent enjoying the quaint markets, the pretty hills, the comforting presence of his father and sister was a minute he could have used to keep ahead of his projects. He couldn't even enjoy a few hours in the garden without keeping his hands busy with whatever he'd brought along, as if to prove that he too had a real occupation that required him to be as available as a doctor.

But not this time. Noah had turned all his ongoing projects over to Mr. Covington and Cecil Martin. He had no reason to bring along so much as a single needle. All he brought was a trunk of his favorite clothing (pearls and all), the most esoteric of his art magazines, and the comforting presence of a tape measure and a fine pack of cigarettes.

And, of course, David, who was formally invited along. He followed without hesitation, but did take a few drops of poppy on the train so he could doze with his head on Noah's shoulder instead of jumping at every whistle the whole way to Surrey.

The house, as always, was clean and bright, filled with books, fascinating instruments, and potted plants. Late July had turned the back garden into its usual haven of greenery and wildlife, from the family of newly hatched ducklings testing out the tiny pond to Papa's collection of cavies, scurrying about their enclosure like furry potatoes on legs.

It was lovely to be home, though the first few days out of the city were inevitably odd. David slept a lot, as if he'd been waiting a decade for a spot safe enough to close his eyes. Meanwhile, Noah talked to his father and to Emily—who had returned for good a few days before him—more than he could remember talking to them in his entire life. Whether they were pacing the garden, walking to the markets in the center of town, or sitting up late with cups of coffee in front of the kitchen fire, the talks covered everything from congregational gossip and medical innovations, to tears and apologies and truly heartfelt corrections to some crucial missteps and miscommunications. The conversations were overdue, perhaps. But not too late.

It restored something in Noah that he hadn't realized he had allowed to wither. As for David, it would obviously take him more than this to get back on his feet—or, perhaps more accurately, to find some solid footing for the first time in his life—but even a few days of rest did both of them a lot of good.

The Tuesday (Or was it still Monday? How beautiful that it did not matter.) of the second week away, while Papa and Emily were out on house calls, Noah and David strolled the garden with their collars loose and shirtsleeves rolled up against a July sunshine that danced off the lavender threads in Noah's waistcoat and the bronzy streaks in David's hair. With hedges trimmed high and a household staff that was small, loyal, and busy with their own tasks, they were able to walk close and hold hands as real lovers.

When at last they sat nestled side by side on a grassy patch beside the pond, uncovered by darkness or the occlusion of a thick shrub, Noah put his head on David's shoulder, breathing in a distinct combination of scents—David and grass and still, cool water—that had been relegated to dreams for longer than he cared to think about.

"I wish we could stay here forever," he whispered suddenly, the words out before he considered whether they were even true. They weren't. They were as temporal as the fluff on the line of ducklings floating past them. Noah loved the city, the full-grown plumage it required, and the space to spread his wings. If he'd wanted to swim around Farncombe on his father's tail feathers, treating people's chest colds, he'd had every opportunity.

Still, David kissed his head lingeringly, letting the words be what they were, before whispering one that surprised Noah:

"Penelope."

Noah looked up into David's eyes, which seemed to soak up the sunlight and the color of the grass, so lovely that to call them emerald was too trite. They were surely diamonds in disguise. Diamonds in *drag*.

"Yes, *amore?*"

David shook his head. "No. No, I just realized it means duck. In Greek."

"You told me that." Noah's face burned. He'd gone so long without being caught for this, that he'd stopped preparing himself for it. "Back at school. You started joining me on my walks, you know. Around the pond. You mentioned it once, during your, um—"

"My notoriously short-lived Greek phase?" David laughed, but it faded. Not unhappily, but sweetly. Thoughtfully. "Why did you pick that?"

Noah rolled his eyes, certain he was bright red by now. "Isn't it obvious, Davy?"

It was. The thrill on David's face showed that well enough. But he still shook his head. "No," he said. "I need to hear you say it."

Noah hooked his fingers into the edge of David's waistcoat, reveling in the pulse of his heartbeat.

"I chose Penelope," he said slowly, luxuriating in the way David watched his mouth form each syllable, "because I fell in love with you surrounded by a ballroom's worth of flirting ducks."

He leaned in at the same time David put a hand behind his neck to pull him closer. The kiss was slow and sundrenched.

"That," David finally whispered against his grinning lips, "is certainly one way to describe the overgrown pond where we met to wank each other off."

"Hush!" Noah scolded, batting at David's chest as he tried to choke down a deeper laugh than he might have hoped for. "Oh, God. You really are terrible."

"Terribly—"

"Stop it!"

"—in love with you."

David toppled Noah to the grass and kissed him again before he could complain. Noah softened into it, twining his arms around David's neck and opening his mouth to the welcome attentions of David's tongue.

"Is the staff likely to catch us like this?" David asked after a while, the words sprinkled between kisses pressed to the side of Noah's neck.

"No." Noah loosened David's neckcloth, his itchy fingers

finding something useful to do with a bit of fabric at last. "You can't see the pond from the house."

"Can we pretend that maybe they could?"

"You're wicked," said Noah, even more heat shooting through his belly upon hearing David say what he wanted with such certainty. God, he loved this man. More than anything. More than should have been possible.

And at last, for the first time ever, that fact did not hurt in the least.

He ran his hand down David's chest, stopping to tease the top button of his trousers. "Will it get you harder if we do?"

David thrust against his hand. Seemed it already had.

"In that case," Noah whispered, glancing toward the house. "There is *one* window in the drawing room that has a narrow view. I don't see why they'd go in there, but you never know..."

Epilogue

London's West End, September 1885
Grand Reopening!

To put such a sign up in the dingy alley would be stupid beyond measure, but as David stared at the door to the club—
his club, now, in every way that mattered—he couldn't help
but wish otherwise. Getting this place back up and running
had been an ordeal, from dealing with detectives to scraping
together the money to accepting the loss of the decorations he
hadn't been able to rescue from Belleville's old town house.

He wanted to celebrate this win as lavishly as possible, and
a brightly painted reopening banner seemed like the least of
all possible celebrations.

"You *could*, though," Noah said on a breath of cigarette
smoke, slipping his arm through David's and surveying the
doorway like he was about to start measuring its seams. "They
haven't managed to make *signs* illegal yet, have they?"

His voice held a bitter edge that he and most of their friends
had been falling into a lot since mid-August, when someone
in Parliament used the genuinely horrible crimes of Belleville
and others like him as leverage to criminalize basically any
sort of fun that a couple of gents might get up to together.
The new law was so vague, the evidence permitted for it so
terribly undefined, that it made Miss Penelope's card games
look very fair and winnable by comparison.

The whole situation nearly scared David off opening the club back up at all. But while he hadn't quite worked out what he would be able to allow in the long run, he had until the end of the year to figure that out. In the meantime, his devotion to the safety of his friends and patrons still held too much meaning for him to give up on them entirely.

So for them and—he could now admit it—for himself, he set loose the word-of-mouth announcement that he was opening the parlor back up for drinks, companionship and commiseration. Hopefully for more, eventually, when he understood the new rules they were playing by. But he'd learned over this past summer by Noah's side, that a little stability and familiarity went a long way when the world around you was harsh. He could share some of that stable feeling with the others, at the very least.

He slipped a hand around Noah's shoulders, letting thoughts of that solid foundation bring his excitement back. There was no returning to the way things were, both for better and for worse. So, it was not going to be a normal night, perhaps, but it would be a jolly one. He kissed Noah's head, breathing in the scents of tobacco and lilac, and was just about to unlock the door, when a sound of voices and something scraping caught both their attention.

"Pull your weight, you dandy fool, or I swear to God—"

"You're going too fast, Joey. These shoes slip on—"

A third voice, pitched high with a performer's clarity: "Would you two shut up? You're going to get half of Berwick down here after us with all this fussing."

David and Noah shared a look, which broke into a smile, before they followed the voices to find quite an ensemble in one of the narrower alleyways. Charlie Price and Miss Jo Smith were squabbling at each other from either end of a cumbersome trunk. Beside them was Annabelle in trousers and jacket with her blond hair tied in an old-fashioned tail, with the hulking form of Bertie beside her carrying another, smaller trunk all on his own. Behind all of them was Warren with what appeared to be a few boxes of baked goods and, in a shadowy hat and high collar so discreet as to be suspicious, Miles, whom David hadn't expected to ever leave his house again in light of the new law.

"What the devil are you doing?" David called down the alley on a cusp of a laugh, making everyone glance up guiltily from their burdens. He went to take Charlie's end of the trunk. It was *heavy*. "What is all this?"

"We heard you lost the decorations," Charlie said, trying to pretend he wasn't panting as he fixed the fall of his Italian-cut jacket, one David recognized—along with Jo's—as having been made by Noah and Cecil Martin's new tailoring service. "I had a few art pieces to spare, ones I thought might fit the atmosphere but that Miles has been glaring at relentlessly for the past month. Figured they'd get more appreciation here."

"A few…" David struggled to take all that in. "What?"

"I managed to nick all sorts of things from the prop room," Annabelle went on, pulling a large purple feather out from the folds of her coat and running it under Noah's nose as the two of them fell into step. "The Season's pretty much done, and it's all brainy tragedies coming up in the fall. By the time anyone might notice, we'll have scrounged so many new trinkets it won't matter anyway."

"She found bells," Bertie muttered, the bass of his voice at odds as he jingled the trunk in his arms. "For the curtains. We'll get 'em sewn soon as we can."

David was glad for the heavy trunk in his hands. It kept him from staring too stupidly at them as a swell of love and gratitude muted him until they were nearly at the door. As he and Jo put the trunk down so he could unlock the bolt, he caught Noah's eye.

"Did you know about this?" David asked.

"You think we told *him*?" Jo rolled her eyes under the brim of her bowler hat. "Of course we didn't. He'd have spoiled the surprise in a second."

Noah shrugged languorously, smoke trailing along from the cigarette still clutched in his fingers. "Listen to these monsters," he said, voice drifting halfway to Penelope. "Criticizing a lady for always being honest with her husband."

While the words and the smoldering look that came with them made David blush, Annabelle gasped and pretended (with disconcerting credibility) to stab Noah through the heart with her feather.

"What's that for?" Noah asked, feigning deep offense.

"Club. Rules." Annabelle looked between David and Noah as scoldingly as a schoolmarm. "Or have we all forgotten how Forester made me and Bertie participate in that humiliatingly over-the-top wedding…*thing* before we could indulge in formal titles in his nosy, meddling, matchmaking presence?"

Each of these last words was accompanied by a tickle from the feather that left David himself hardly stifling a sneeze.

"Well, Annie," he said once he'd stopped scratching his nose, "what do you suggest we do about it?"

"Molly house wedding," she hissed while behind her Bertie shook the jingling box and the others cackled. "What else?"

Grinning and blushing such that his entire face and neck burned something dreadful, he finally got the door open. The parlor wasn't in terrible shape, considering what he'd had to work with. He'd gotten to keep the furniture and most of the lamps and vases, along with the chandelier and the drapes on the ceiling. He and Warren had restocked the bar more modestly than it had been, but certainly well enough to get everyone good and drunk, even if it wasn't on their preferred cocktails.

But when Charlie and Jo dragged the big trunk to the center of the room and Warren threw it open to reveal gaudy, opulent treasures that ranged from paintings to feathers to fabrics, he had a sense that the new place was going to be better off than he'd even dared to dream. Not the same. Never quite the same. But lovely nonetheless.

Annabelle set about pinning pieces of tulle to David's and Noah's heads ("I make no assumptions about which is which with you two.") while Warren went about stacking some biscuits and sticky buns on the bar into what might have been intended to look like a cake.

"Now, let's stay practical, here," said Jo, arranging David and Noah to stand next to each other in the frame of one of the alcoves. "Everything's a bit strange at the moment. Certainly no time for anything as *indulgently protracted* as Mr. Forester generally subjects his poor couples to."

"Boo!" said Annabelle from her new place on the bar, stealing sticky buns as Warren tried to swat her away.

Jo held up a solemn, gloved hand. "There are all sorts of circumstances that lead to hasty elopements. So. Let us all dream up the most devilish one we can for these two love birds, and get 'em hitched quicker than the coppers can possibly catch."

As she and the others went on loudly with the game—cheering, popping corks from gin bottles, taking turns at imitating the worst vicars imaginable—David stood with Noah, smiling like he couldn't remember ever smiling in his life.

"They're all bonkers," Noah muttered out of the turned-up corner of his pretty mouth, the words floating through the matching layers of tulle that threatened to fall from their heads.

"Sure are," David whispered back. "I do love them."

"Me too." Noah leaned in close, warm and forever familiar in his place right at David's side. "Love you best, though."

"Same," said David, nuzzling at his ear. The stud in it was modest, but defiantly present. "Bit unfair. No one else ever stood half a chance."

Noah shivered happily. "Kiss me, Davy."

"I can't yet. They're still doing vows…" He nodded to where Charlie had inexplicably started in on a dirty limerick while Jo tried to fold a bit of paper into his collar so he'd look like a priest. "…Or whatever the devil *that's* supposed to be."

"Oh, come on." He nudged David with the side of his hip and tipped his chin so he could look up through lashes and veil in a way that set David's heart pounding harder than ever. "Who sets the rules in this place, anyway?"

"Oh. Fair point." David looked around. At his friends. His club. His lover and best friend. "I suppose it *is* time I started acting like I own the place, isn't it?"

David threaded his fingers through Noah's hair, cupping the side of his head gently and leaning in so they could crush their smiling lips together. It was hilariously inappropriate, he thought, that the kiss was accompanied by scandalized accusations that the pair of them—who'd managed to pine and pretend away their love for half their lives—were getting *terribly* ahead of themselves on the consummation all of a sudden.

★ ★ ★ ★ ★

Acknowledgments

They say sophomore novels are the hardest, but with the support of so many incredible people, I can happily report that I have made it through that milestone!

Thank you to Michael Rauh for loving this story from the first messy draft; your enthusiasm kept me going when I thought it was broken beyond repair. To my brilliant editor, Alissa Davis: I was not expecting the suggestions you had for this one, but they were really spot-on and made all the difference! Working with you on this book has been an awesome experience. And, of course, a thank-you to my agent, Laura Zats: everything feels so much calmer and more manageable knowing you're there to help with whatever the publishing process throws my way.

To Kerri, Katixa, Stephanie, and the rest of the amazing team at Carina: I so appreciate everything you do behind the scenes! Thank you so much for all the hard work you put in making these books happen.

Many thanks to my beta readers: Perry Lloyd, Meg Mardell, Marin McGinnis. Your feedback and ideas were so incredibly helpful! And a special shout-out to Bridget Kraynik, who read it and promptly texted me the first Lucky Lovers "fanfic": you basically made my life with that.

*Is their real-life love story doomed to be a tragedy,
or can they rewrite the ending?*

Keep reading for an excerpt from
The Gentleman's Book of Vices
by Jess Everlee

Chapter One

Charlie

London's West End. October 1883

The front parlor of The Curious Fox had gotten awfully crowded over the past hour. It was fortunate that Charlie Price's lungs were permanently coated with a slick of cigarette smoke and perfume already; the air around some of the tables was nearly as thick as the fog was outside. In here, however, the choking mist was tinted pink by the vibrant glass lamp-shades, while flashes of crystal glasses and well-dressed gentle-men drifted through it like drunken ghosts. Charlie thought the dreadful weather would have kept everyone home in their beds, but then again, their own beds did not allow for quite the same company as the beds that lay beyond the Fox's parlor.

Charlie had arrived early enough to claim his favorite of the alcoves across from the gleaming, dark wood bar. With the curtains drawn back, he watched the crowd comfortably from his flowery chaise, a glass of gin in one hand, the other settled disinterestedly around the shoulders of the newcomer who had somehow become the newest timid barnacle to at-tach itself to him.

The newcomer ran his inexperienced fingers lightly along the checkered wool over Charlie's thigh. He kept glancing over, more nervous than lustful, and when Charlie finally glanced back, the chap looked downright terrified. Not just new to the Fox, then: he was likely new to the whole business of it. Charlie wanted to say something encouraging, but he'd forgotten the chap's name, and... Damn, he was not drunk enough for this, was he? Charlie took a pull of bitter gin, the rings on his fingers clinking against the crystal.

As he scanned the parlor—from the tinkling piano in the back, past the crowded bar, and over the tables of cards and conversation—he caught movement near the front entrance. More? Really? Were there even this many men in the whole of London who were trustworthy enough to gain access to a club like this?

Trying not to squirm under the tickling attentions of his companion, he watched the patron hand a dripping overcoat and umbrella to the doorman. Perhaps he could manage an upgrade, if the newly arrived patron was more interesting than this one.

However, while the visitor was dressed like a man and came so indecently unescorted into a gentlemen's club as if that were her birthright, he realized with a happy little rush that it was not a man at all.

It was Miss Jo.

Charlie sat up straight, his heart leaping to his throat as he watched his friend work her way through the smoke toward his corner. He hadn't even realized what a dull night it had been until she came along and saved it. He adored her always, but particularly tonight. Because tonight, she held a folded paper in her gloved hand.

Without a doubt, it was the one Charlie had been waiting for.

He glanced sideways at his awkward companion. In light of Miss Jo's arrival, he was no longer even passingly interested in educating this chap in the finer points of pleasure. But there were other lessons Charlie could teach him.

For instance: men you picked up in places like this were terrible.

He pressed a hearty kiss to the side of the fellow's head and then disentangled himself, waving his newly freed hand. *Shoo, shoo.*

"Wh-what?" the chap stammered. "Did I do something wrong?"

Charlie's eyes hardly strayed from the clutched paper in Miss Jo's hand. He gestured to the bar, to the smoke, to the various other sofas and alcoves. "Go on, lad."

"Lad?" The fellow was at least ten years older than Charlie.

"I said what I said. Now go on, *lad*. I'm busy, but there's plenty of other nonsense to get up to, so go get up to it. Over there somewhere."

"But—"

"It's been a pleasure, my boy. Godspeed."

Poor man. Charlie felt bad for him, slinking off to sit alone at the bar. He was a handsome thing, but he had that sadness about him that was as depressing as it was hard to escape on a Friday night at the Fox. It was when all the tragic ones came in.

Charlie watched affectionately as Jo darted around a particularly raucous table of fellows and other fine folks who positively dripped silk skirts and strings of pearls. Noah Clarke—another of Charlie's friends—was among them, done up in extravagant drag. His character, the lovely Miss Penelope Primrose, spent her Friday evenings hustling admirers out of their money in nearly every card game imaginable.

When Miss Penelope spotted Jo, she gathered her in and pressed a powdered face to Jo's bosom. The two of them talked a bit, going on so long that Charlie nearly gave up and went to pry Jo away before she got sucked into whatever game was going on. But Jo finally kissed Penelope's gloved hand and continued along the path to Charlie's corner.

She sat heavily beside him and took his drink right from his hand.

"Get your own." Charlie tried to take it back, but she downed the rest of the gin and tonic in a single gulp. He was left with an empty glass. "Don't let Penelope drive you to drink, Jo. There's nothing she'd love more in this life than to know it was she who caused your downfall."

"It's you who's driving me, by making me come in here." She straightened her pin-striped lapels and smoothed her tie. "I don't have to come into this rouge-soaked hellhole. I do it for you."

Charlie put his head on her shoulder. "Lucky me, then."

"Who's that man you sent off?"

"Oh, I don't know."

"Poor chap," Jo said. "There was no need to banish him if you were having fun. I'm not going to be here very long. I only came to give you this." She brandished the paper between two kid-gloved fingers. Charlie reached out, but she tugged it back. "Ah, ah," she said. "I went to a lot of bother for this. A lot of snooping in places where snooping gets good little girls into barrels of trouble."

"Well, thank God you went instead of me," said Charlie. "Anyone looking at us knows which is the good little girl."

"I do hate you."

"I know. That's why I'm going to buy your drinks all night."

"All year."

He tried to snatch the paper again, but she switched hands with the deftness of a stage magician.

"Oh, come off it," he said.

"Six months." Her dark eyebrows danced up toward her

bowler hat. She had the most devious eyes in England, set into a heart-shaped face with smirking lips. "Minimum."

"I have no money, Jo, and you drink like a man twice your size. What am I going to buy it with?"

"The money Daddy is going to slip you once your vows are final. That's why you're leaving us for a wife and twenty brats, ain't it? So you can afford to buy my drinks?"

"I'm not *leaving* exactly—"

"Six months."

"Three."

With a languid motion, Jo held the folded page over the candelabra on the table beside them. As the edges grew toasty and brown, Charlie's stomach knotted. They looked each other hard in the eye.

"If it was that hard to get it," Charlie said, "then there's no way you'll burn it."

"Don't try me, princess; I have no use for this thing."

The corner of the page caught, a thin line of fire dancing along the edge, adding a whiff of burning paper to the tobacco and incense already swirling in the air.

"Fine! Six months!" With a huff, Charlie snatched the page out of Jo's hand and blew out the flame.

Miss Jo wasted no time snapping her fingers at a young man who did not even work here, demanding a glass of top-shelf whiskey so commandingly that he nearly sprinted to the bar in terror. She kicked her shoes up over Charlie's lap and settled into the chaise. Though she complained about The Curious Fox—*so* much less *civilized* than the Sapphists' little place—she certainly knew how to get cozy here.

"Go on, then." She crossed her arms over the front of her three-piece. "Open it up. It's by far the best wedding present you're going to get, and if you wait too long, you'll have to share it with wifey. I have a feeling Alma won't be interested."

Charlie eyed the smoldering paper, suddenly nervous to see what was within. Why was he nervous? All he'd see was a name, perhaps an address or place of employment. The whole thing was a silly little fancy anyway, a last whim before all his scandalous souvenirs went into his safe deposit box until the end of time. If he was going to have to hide his most precious possessions from a wife, he at least wanted the satisfaction of knowing he'd squirreled away something special.

"Are you sure this is him?" He clutched the still-folded page to his chest. "He's well hidden, you know, and for good reason."

"If you don't open it, I'm going to set it on fire again, and you along with it."

Chastised at last, Charlie opened the paper and read, in Jo's scrawl of a hand, the address of a Fleet Street bookshop, and below it a name:

Miles Montague.

He allowed his lips to mouth the name. Miles. Miles Montague. A very normal-sounding name, yet somehow striking. "Better than his pen name," he said.

"How can you say that?" Jo laughed and took her drink from the onetime serving lad, who ran off before things could become more confusing. "*Reginald Cox* is a brilliant name. I'd take it myself, if he hadn't already claimed it."

Carefully, Charlie knocked the ash off the paper and into the cigar tray. He tucked the little treasure in his coat pocket. "How did you find him? Not to brag, but when it comes to uncovering the identities of notorious pornographers, you know I'm the leading expert."

"Yes, a rare and valuable skill you have there."

"I assumed you were kidding when you said you could find him," he went on. "If I couldn't, I assumed no one could. What'd you do? Who'd you talk to?"

She sipped her drink luxuriously, staring at the gauzy ceiling as if unsure how much to divulge. The silence was cut through with the sounds of piano music, laughter, and something decidedly off-rhythm coming from one of the private rooms. "Well," she began slowly, "first, I drew a circle in chalk out in the chicken coop. I killed one of the birds—the worst of the birds, don't worry, real bitch—and with the blood and my pentagram—"

"I'm serious, Joey." Charlie nudged her with his elbow. "I'm really grateful, so I just—"

Jo took his hand and kissed the tops of his knuckles with her rough, unpainted lips. "If you're really grateful, Charlie, just let it go. I have a connection. It's that simple."

"Is it?" He raised an eyebrow.

She raised hers back. "That's exactly what I want to leave you wondering. I have an air of mystery to maintain. Don't take that from me, or I'll never do anything nice for you again."

"Alright, mate. I suppose I'll just continue to imagine you breaking into safes, sprinting away from pornographic print-house goons, leaving maidens fainting in your wake."

"Thank you kindly."

They stayed a little longer, eyeing the crowd and gossiping. There was always gossip to be had at The Curious Fox, after all. Miss Penelope and her companions were constantly up to something amusing. Behind the bar, Warren Bakshi—the impossibly handsome barkeep—had memorized everyone's drink orders and flirted so mercilessly that his tips bordered on payment for immoral services. Meanwhile, the proprietor Mr. Forester set himself up with a ledger near the piano to oversee the renting of back rooms, a post he would keep until Warren inevitably abandoned the bar to take up with his latest best customer. Forester was the best for gossip, since it was his job to know who was taking whom to do what, and the states of rooms when they were done.

"Warren's at it again." Jo pointed with her drink to where the barkeep was peeking over his own shoulder as he escorted a friend toward the back rooms. "And there's Mr. Forester, turning his back and pretending not to see. He's too nice."

"To Warren anyway. Anyone else tried to sneak into the back without paying, I'm pretty sure none of us would ever forget the sound of their screams."

"Too nice to you as well," Jo accused.

Charlie wished he could bury his burning face into the safety of yet another unpaid-for drink, but Jo had not ordered him one. "Let's, perhaps, choose a different subject."

"Alright. Who's that Warren is with, anyway?"

"That fellow?" Charlie watched the pair vanish through the door. "Oh, he's been here once or twice."

"Have you taken him for a test run?"

"You make it sound like I'm familiar with every last new-comer."

"You are, aren't you?" she asked.

"Well, *yes*," he admitted.

Jo looked a bit too judging. "I'm surprised they even come back after being subjected to you. You've been a right prick to them all, ever since—"

"*Anyway.* Warren's chap," Charlie interrupted. "He's alright, depending on what exactly you want him for."

He stared Jo down, daring her to turn the conversation back.

She shook her head, defeated. "Fine, I'll bite. What do you mean?"

"You'd never guess to look at him, but he's hung like a damned horse. Never seen anything like it."

"Isn't that good?" Jo asked.

"To a point. Warren seems to like him, though, bless his heart and his arse. He never does know when to quit."

Jo stood and stretched, then downed the rest of her drink. "Well, on that lovely note, I think that's it for me tonight. The Beast comes home from his latest expedition tomorrow, and I need to turn into a lady by morning."

She leaned down and kissed Charlie on the cheek. As she pulled back, he squeezed her hand. "Thanks again," he said. "You really are heaven-sent. Or hell-sent. Don't tell me which."

"Do you want me to come with you? When you go to meet Mr. Montague?"

Charlie thought about it. "No. All I want is for him to sign the book. I should go alone; I'd hate to scare him."

"Yet, I'd hate for anything to happen to you if he's scared anyway. Like you said, he's got good reason to be anonymous. He may not take kindly to being called on and identified."

"I'll be alright." He smiled to put her at ease. "You know me. No foolish chances. If I catch the barest whiff of danger, I'll make my escape, autograph be damned. I promise."

"It's a stupid thing to do, you know," she scolded. "It's just a signature, on a book you're planning to hide in a deposit box and never look at again."

Charlie sucked in a deep breath and swirled the boozy ice melt Jo had left at the bottom of his glass. "I'm sure I'll look at it again eventually."

"You know what I mean."

He wasn't enjoying this turn in the conversation. The line of her mouth had grown a bit serious. "You're not about to start *looking after me* again, are you?"

"Charlie—"

"Because I don't need it. The wedding is eight weeks out, and it's going to be lovely. So what if I have to tuck some of my more incriminating things away? All the better. It's the secrets that make it so delicious, isn't it?"

"Is it, though?" Jo asked.

"And I'm going to have a secret autograph from Reginald Cox. That should be more than enough to keep me from looking like that bloke over there." He gestured to where his rejected companion chatted morosely with Mr. Forester, who'd taken up Warren's spot behind the bar.

Jo smacked his arm. "It better be. If you get married and then start moping about like that, I'll break your damn jaw."

"That's very reassuring."

"And anyway, are you entirely sure Alma still wants to marry you? After all this time, you haven't managed to scare her off?"

"Quite the contrary." He sighed. "She's picked out her dress, and we're tasting cakes and wines for the wedding this week. All is going perfectly smoothly, and she's happy as can be."

"She must be mental."

"Don't insult Alma," he said seriously. "I'm the mental one."

Jo looked at him. She was doing it again. She was fretting about him. "Charlie... Look, I would just hate to see you—"

"Don't you have to go?"

"Charlie—"

"Please tell The Beast that I said hello, and reiterate my offer to have his babies if he grows tired of your refusal."

"Of course, I'll tell him word for word." She placed her bowler at an angle above the dark bun at the nape of her neck. "Good night, Charlie, you sodding idiot."

She mussed Penelope's hair on her way to the door, earning a most heartwarming scream and swat. But both were smiling as Penelope turned back to the card game and Jo retrieved her shape-obscuring coat from the rack and went out into the chilly night.

Miss Penelope turned her otherworldly stare on Charlie and beckoned him over. Charlie obliged, leaning in so that Penelope could stage-whisper in his ear, "Your girlfriend is a menace."

"Oh, Penny." Charlie cupped her face. Up close, he could see that she'd painted intricate butterfly wings around the corners of her catlike eyes. "You really mustn't talk about yourself that way."

The others at the table hooted happily, but then the lot of them were back to their cards, their cigars, their hennish chatter. They were every Englishman's very worst idea of mollies. Charlie loved them to hell and back.

"Sit down, *amore*." She patted her petticoat-padded lap. "You look a bit lost. Play with us."

"I'm fine. And I don't gamble anyway, which you well know."

She looked over her cards. "That's why I want to get you at the table. I'll have you cleaned out in ten minutes."

Instead, he went to the bar. If he was going to sacrifice his money to the ladies, he was going to decide what the losings were spent on.

"Charlie." Mr. Forester nodded a friendly greeting. He leaned his elbows on the bar, his closed ledger tucked safely beneath them. "Haven't managed to have a word with you all night. I've wanted to tell you, you look—" He laughed warmly. "Well, let's just say, I'm impressed. I can count on you to be on the cutting edge."

Charlie straightened a wrinkle in his indigo neckcloth. His trousers were checkered in a matching hue, and, really, it was a fine little getup. He was pleased to have it noticed. "Thanks, Mr. Forester. You're looking awfully fine yourself."

Forester looked amusingly doubtful. "You don't have to be

nice, Charlie. It's been a very hectic night. I look something, I'm sure, but I don't think *fine* is the word you want."

"Oh, come off it."

"You been keeping busy?" Forester asked.

"Not as busy as Warren, but I've kept my hands occupied."

David Forester was a tall, lanky fellow with floppy hair the color of burned toffee and a close-trimmed beard. Though he couldn't have been any older than Charlie's thirty-three, he'd clearly seen a lot over his years at this place. He glanced down the bar at the sad fellow, then leaned in farther to whisper, "Are you looking for something in particular, Charlie? There's a few other new fellows tonight. If it's not working with that one, I could introduce you to Mr. Brady's friend. Sharp wit and money to burn. I think you might—"

Charlie held up a hand. "Much as I appreciate it, Miss Matchmaker, I'd most like to be introduced to another gin and tonic. And throw in a round for the girls while you're at it."

Forester gave Charlie a sideways sort of look, then glanced over at the card table. "You're feeling awfully generous tonight. I assume this is going on *the tab*?"

"Don't make it sound like that. There's money in my future, so a little more debt in my present isn't going to harm anything. You'll be paid in full in the blink of an eye."

The skeptical look remained unchanged. "If you say so, Charlie."

Charlie sat back on a stool as Forester busied himself with glasses, bottles, and what looked like quite a lot of extra ice in Charlie's drink. He felt eyes on him and peered around. The sad fellow was looking over from his own barstool, but quickly looked away when he was caught at it. Feeling sorry for him, Charlie went over and ran a hand from the fellow's feathery brown hair and down his shoulder. Bloodshot eyes turned back up to him.

"I apologize for my manners," Charlie said. "If you can forgive me, I'll pick back up where we left off."

The man really should have said no. Charlie did not deserve a second chance. But once Charlie had gotten his drink and started back to his nook, the man followed. They sat together. Charlie pulled him in close before he could change his mind, drew the curtain and finally got around to testing out the newcomer properly. Jo was right. He liked newcomers. They were too skittish to demand much of him, and since he never took up with any more than once, it was quite a sustainable arrangement and his friends did so love to hear his exaggerated retellings of the most interesting ones.

It would go on like this for the next few weeks, until he found himself with Alma waiting at home for him each night. He did not know what he'd do then. The future seemed alarmingly blank just now.

Well. Not the whole future. There was still a bright spot. As Jo's discovery crinkled in his pocket, he was glad to know he had one thing to look forward to.

Miles Montague. The name itself nearly made him shiver. Charlie could always rely on the white-hot imaginings of his favorite smut author to get himself going under nearly any circumstances. Though the newcomer's hands were stiff on Charlie's chest and his kisses were awkward, Charlie could find the pleasure in anyone.

Just so long as his mind remained a thousand miles deep in Montague's fictional filth.

Don't miss The Gentleman's Book of Vices *by Jess Everlee, available now wherever ebooks are sold.*

www.CarinaPress.com

Copyright © 2022 by Jess Everlee